MICHAELLA NEAL

# Ignited

*Eyes of Fire Series: Book One*

*For those who love the wonder of fantasy,*
*but long for stories filled with light.*
*For the ones drawn to fire—not to be scorched,*
*but to be guided.*
*May you always choose the flame that leads,*
*not the darkness that deceives.*

# Content Warning

This book contains depictions of ritual sacrifice, as well as references to violence, religious persecution, and implied sexual assault. While not described in graphic detail, these themes may be upsetting to some readers.

Please take care while reading.

# Chapter 1

This time, I would leave.

*Drip, drip.*

This would be the moment I dishonor my family, piss on my own title, and spit on the nauseating traditions that have chained me for so long. The heir. The girl meant to one day kneel at the altar and lead others into this madness.

That's what they saw. Not me.

My fingers tapped rapidly on the black linen of my dress, an insistent war drum demanding attention. The sheer veil brushed lightly against the rounded tip of my nose, a haunting whisper I couldn't ignore. Each deep breath pushed against the oppressive fabric, defying my mind's frantic pleas to stay calm.

I would storm out.

I would run from this cursed temple and never look back.

I couldn't kneel here through this nightmare again.

Not this time…

This time was not like the others. The others had been bearable—barely.

But now, my stomach churned with such violent force that I thought I might expel my last meal right onto the *sacred* floors. Acid surged in my throat, burning with defiance, but

1

I swallowed it back, forcing the bitterness to stay where it belonged.

*Drip, drip.*

That sound only made it worse. I knew what trickled onto the burning coals of the ashen stone pit. The deep, red liquid oozed onto the black glowing pit and evaporated into the atmosphere surrounding us. My eyes trailed the smoke as it loomed from left to right. Rising higher and higher. Sweat had begun to pool at the base of my neck, causing my tight coils to shrink due to its moisture.

Dozens of people sat, frozen stiff in awe. This event was holy. This event was sacred. I shook my head, dispelling the dizziness, trying to think of anything but these moments.

*Drip, drip. Tssss...*

The remnants of the blood danced around our heads, spinning and twirling like sinister shackles binding everyone here. I looked up at the solitary light piercing the oppressive darkness of the sanctuary. The skylight hovered directly above the altar, casting direct beams of light onto it. My gaze followed the light beams down until they rested on the glowing coals below.

Death.

Death, suffering, and depravity.

I could almost laugh if the circumstances weren't so grim. But the pride in this room was a palpable, disgusting presence. It was a dark beast with eyes that glowed bright like the scepters held before me. I turned my head slightly, looking at the royal court surrounding me. All dressed in black garments, they were glamorized by the beast. Thick, armored, and impenetrable, it cloaked every soul hideously.

They all believed this was okay...

*Drip, drip, drip, drip, Tssss...*

The beast delighted in the smell. The smoke. The incense.

I gagged again, squeezing my eyes shut tight as if the avoidance of the sight before me would restrict my other senses. Exhaling again, I opened my eyes.

Catching the reflective skin of the gold-faced gods that stood before me. The golden pillars towered at least twenty feet high above us. Their bodies were molded to a perfect figure, but their heads held the faces of beautiful beasts.

This ritual was the sweetest gift we could sacrifice to the gods. The gods required our sacrifice to act on our behalf, to bless the land of Naedorn. To bless our country, Anima. This offering was the sweetest to Vitaeus, Goddess of Life and Death.

*Vitaeus* would be pleased.

I scoffed beneath the veil.

My parents, wearing long black robes of fine linen, stood atop the dais between the two priests. One recited incantations in the ancient.

Words I've spent many mornings trying to learn.

Words spoken before the Great Liberation that only few knew or could afford to study. I could decipher only a few words as his loud voice rang out over the crowd.

*Death.*

*Sacrifice.*

*Child.*

*Atone.*

My eyes left the priest who held the ancient book and recited the aged words to the other who wore robes of deep red like blood. The only colored garments in the room. I shouldn't have looked at him again, not after what he'd just

3

done. I shouldn't have allowed my eyes to find him. But, there he was, standing there and at his side, the dagger that pierced the offering.

I swallowed hard, sweat prickling my brow. I shook my head slowly under the sheer black veil. From the corner of my eye I saw my sister turn. Her eyes lightly fluttered under her own veil as she eyed me suspiciously. She grabbed my hand from under the stone bench where we knelt and squeezed.

I couldn't stay here; I couldn't take any more of this—my senses were disobeying me. The smell… the smell was the most unbearable. Metallic and coppery.

*Drip, drip, Tsss.*

I inhaled too deeply and too quickly. Taking a full draft of the smoke-filled room around me. But it wasn't just the smoke from the coals I inhaled now.

Nausea crashed into the back of my throat. I rushed to my feet. My mother, who stood on the other side of the dais, whipped her head towards me. I didn't need lights or a room clear of smoke to know that anger burned on her face from under her black veil.

Everything stopped: the priest, the servants, the appointed guest who joined the ceremony. Even time seemed to stop. I stood in the front of the room in the middle of my siblings, who remained kneeling before the dais. I turned, meeting the eyes of the bewildered nobility, watching me.

"Kae'Dinah, kneel back down," my older brother whispered. He reached for the black dress that pooled around my feet. I backed away, taking a step towards the aisle.

*Drip, drip, Tsss.*

I flinched at the insistent sound and stepped back towards

4

the doors again. Voices hissed in judgmental whispers around me. I turned, avoiding the audience's gaze, only to find the dark, empty aisle directly behind me—my exit.

"Kneel now!" My brother frantically whispered, reaching for me. I backed away from his touch yet again.

*Drip, drip, Tssss.*

*Drip, drip, Tssss.*

I gagged, my hand rushing to cover my mouth. My chest burned tight with anger, disgust, and sickness. My mother still stared at me. A small candle in her hands now illuminated the fury that shone through her eyes. My stomach gurgled a warning. My eyes flickered from my mother to the stunned priest and then... the offering displayed before the room.

His face was pale, too still. Not the stillness of sleep, but the kind that never ends...

But I knew better. I knew he wasn't.

The memory of his mother's screams echoed in my ears, raw and unending. I had seen her collapse to the ground, begging the gods, begging anyone who would listen, to release her son. Her anguish had spilled out like blood from an open wound, her cries piercing the air and embedding themselves into my soul.

I stepped back again, away from the altar, my chest tightening with every movement. The Goddess of Life and Death had demanded an exchange today, her faithful messengers had told us so. I could still see the woman's bloodied knees dragging across the cobblestones of Floos as she fought for him, her son. Guards had shoved her away, indifferent to her pleas, her desperation. She had begged for him, borne him, loved him.

5

*Drip. Tssss.*

*Drip. Tssss.*

The sound of his blood meeting the stone filled the silent chamber. My lungs clawed for air, heaving as though they had hands of their own, reaching and grasping for something pure to breathe in. But the air here was thick, tainted, heavy with the coppery stench of his blood.

My hands began to tremble. I needed to leave. I needed to escape this.

I glanced down the aisle again, my heart pounding with indecision. If I ran, I would dishonor the gods, disgrace my family, perhaps even doom us all. But how could anyone sit here, silent and complicit, as his life was taken before our eyes?

*This isn't right.*

I inhaled sharply, the metallic scent burning my throat, and then—I ran.

Gasps rippled through the room as I sprinted for the exit, the sound of my footsteps reverberating off the walls.

"Kae'Dinah!" The king's voice roared behind me, but I didn't stop.

I burst through the heavy doors and collapsed, emptying the contents of my stomach onto the stone floor.

The foyer was littered with servants and footmen, their hushed conversations dying as I stumbled into their view. I could feel their eyes on me, but my body heaved again, wracked by the weight of what I had just witnessed.

"Your Highness, breathe."

A cool hand gathered my hair, pulling it back from my face and removing my veil in one smooth motion. Another hand rested lightly on my neck, its soothing touch a stark contrast

6

to the turmoil raging within me.

They had killed a boy. We had killed a boy. A precious gift. For what?

I spat the last remnants of this morning's breakfast onto the gleaming white floors of the temple before staggering upright, propping one hand against the cold stone wall for support.

"Paxium, help us," the familiar voice whispered.

I turned to see Kelta, who'd been with me since I was a child—more shadow than servant—held my veil like it mattered. Her face was pale, fear flickering in her wide eyes. She was calling Paxium, the God of Peace, but no peace came.

Not for me, at least.

The heavy doors of the sacrificial chamber flung open, slamming into the walls behind them with unnatural force. It seemed like the opposite of peace was what searched for me now. The queen's piercing gaze found me instantly, flames of fury dancing in her eyes. She strode toward us, her heels clicking like thunder against the temple floor.

She stopped short, her eyes sweeping from the mess I had made on the floor to my face.

"Paxium, help us indeed," I whispered bitterly, bracing myself for her wrath.

*Fire and ice.*

That's what it felt like when her hand struck my cheek, the sound ringing in the silent foyer. My head snapped to the side, and before I could recover, her hand was on me again, this time wrapping around my neck.

"You forget who you are and who I am," she hissed. She slammed me against the wall, her grip tightening as I gasped for air.

"You filthy, irreverent little brat," she snarled through clenched teeth.

Tears burned in my eyes, my fists balled at my sides, but I didn't fight back. I couldn't—not against her. My vision blurred as her grip remained unrelenting, the room spinning as I coughed weakly, choking on the air I couldn't reach.

"Your Majesty," Kelta's voice broke the tension, soft but urgent. She kept her head bowed, her hands trembling as she fidgeted. "Many people are watching."

The queen's fury simmered beneath the surface as she released me, her grip loosening just enough for me to gasp for air. A desperate cough came from my throat as I tried to regain my composure, while she straightened herself with the precision of a seasoned performer. Her gaze flitted about, catching the glances of curious temple-goers.

She smiled—a cold, calculated curve of her lips. Regal. Perfect. Unyielding. "Compose yourself," she snapped, her tone cutting.

I flinched as her hand moved toward me, but she ignored the reaction, smoothing my dress with practiced ease. A practiced ease I'd worn since childhood. Forced affection, stunts for the public. I feared her every time. She didn't care about my fear, only about maintaining the pristine image of our family. Perfection was her armor, and I was nothing more than a tarnished reflection.

Her grip on my elbow was relentless as she propelled me forward, her strides quick and forceful toward the waiting carriages. The weight of her anger radiated through her fingertips, searing into my skin.

Outside the temple, familiar faces of my guard greeted me—Captain Corin Nagel and Captain Jahiel Wilt, both standing at attention near the carriages. Captain Wilt's dark eyes flicked over me, a shadow of concern softening his otherwise stoic demeanor. I caught his subtle furrow of brow, the only sign of disapproval he'd dare show under my mother's scrutiny.

"Take her home!" my mother, their queen, barked at the men and Kelta, her voice slicing through the tense air. "She doesn't leave her rooms. Do you understand? If people ask, say she couldn't control the illness. Don't you dare let them know she's a coward. "

Captain Wilt remained by the carriage door, his expression unreadable except to me. I'd learned his mannerisms over the years, the tension in his jaw betraying his controlled calm. He hesitated, his gaze trailing over me from head to toe, assessing, making sure I was okay.

"Open the doors!" my mother snapped again, and the venom in her voice broke his hesitation.

With a sharp movement, Captain Wilt swung the carriage door open. His grip on the handle tightened, his knuckles pale. I could see it—the storm brewing beneath his carefully maintained exterior. He was holding himself back for my sake.

My mother shoved me into the carriage with no regard for my footing. My elbow slammed into the wooden bench, sending a sharp sting up my arm. Kelta rushed to gather my skirts, her hands trembling as she tucked the fabric into the cramped space.

"What were you thinking?" my mother hissed, her voice low enough to avoid being overheard. Her glare could pierce stone, but her sharpness wavered when she glanced toward Captain Wilt. He lingered near the carriage, his dark eyes narrowing ever so slightly, watching her every move.

"Why are you still standing there like a fool?" she questioned him.

The captain looked at her, "My apologies, Your Majesty." He nodded, then moved to help the others ready the horses.

She gazed piercingly back at me. "Do you even understand what you've done? Our most sacred rituals—and you humiliate us all by running out like a spoiled child! Vitaeus should have struck you halfway down the aisle for such disgrace."

Her words cut deep, each one a lash against my already fragile composure. I love my mother with the exact amount of love I was taught to give her. I want to obey her... most days. But this—this couldn't be what the gods truly asked of us.

Moments like this have become monuments in my mind. Pillars of reason for why my heart can no longer agree with her. With any of them. With all our so-called practices.

And it makes me wonder, again and again—how could I be the only one in that room who felt it? Who felt the ache. The loss.

I held her gaze, searching for even a flicker of compassion. But there was none. Only disdain—and the wounded pride of a queen who valued her image more than anything her daughter felt inside.

"Go home and bathe," she said, her tone cooling to a dangerous calm. "The rest of us will celebrate here without you." Her final words twisted like a blade in my chest. "Such a disappointment."

"Mother, I—"

The door slammed shut, silencing me. The scent of

jasmine, her signature fragrance, clung to the air like a ghost. A few moments passed, then the carriage jolted forward, and the lump in my throat tightened.

A brisk, familiar triple knock sounded from the outside of the carriage. My heart skipped. "Are you okay, Princess?" Captain Wilt's deep voice was muffled but steady, a lifeline in a suffocating dust storm.

I pressed a hand over my mouth, suppressing the sob that threatened to escape. Swallowing hard, I returned the same rhythmic knock against the carriage wall.

That was one of our silent, practiced responses. We only used it with each other when words were not an option.

Moments later, I heard the murmur of Captain Wilt issuing commands to Captain Nagel, his voice calm but firm. The carriage began its journey south toward the palace.

As I sat in the dim carriage, I smoothed the creases in my gown, willing myself to be composed. Outside, I knew Wilt rode close, his presence a quiet reminder that even in moments of isolation, I was not entirely alone.

# Chapter 2

The light of the full moon spilled across my face, unrelenting despite my attempts to find peace. I couldn't sleep. I couldn't eat. The only thing I could do was lie here, trapped between waiting for my family to return and the faint hope that sleep might finally claim me. I tossed again in my oversized bed, turning away from the light streaming through the windows.

I had spent hours in the bath, scrubbing myself until my brown skin glowed with angry red undertones, desperate to rid my body of the smell—the choking smoke that seemed to cling to my soul like second skin. Twice, I submerged beneath the steaming water, trying to cleanse the stench from my hair. But even now, my loose, damp curls clung to my back, soaking the sheets and pillows around me.

And still, I could hear it.

*The dripping.*

*The sizzling.*

I could still see his face—so still, so pale. He was sleeping. I had to keep telling myself he was just asleep.

I grabbed the pillow beside me and shoved it into my face, letting out a scream of my own. It wasn't like hers—the mother's. It could never be. Her wails had pierced the air like shattering glass—sharp, and impossible to forget.

As much as I tried to silence it—push it down, push it away—the same question kept echoing through my mind.

How could the gods take something so precious?

How could they steal a life that had barely even begun?

The boy was only a month old.

But I wasn't supposed to ask that.

We weren't allowed to ask that.

The gods' ways were said to be above us—too *holy* to be questioned, too ancient to be understood.

But why?

Why was I the only one who ever felt like they *needed* to be questioned?

Because if obedience meant killing the innocent, then what kind of god was I meant to serve?

I rolled onto my side, clutching my stomach as that familiar ache twisted inside me—grief, yes, but something else too.

A deep, aching doubt.

Of all my studies, all the lessons and rituals forced upon me, I had never been able to make peace with the sacrifices. Especially the ones offered to Vitaeus. Hers were the worst. So violent. So foul. So final.

And yet no one else ever flinched.

No one cried out when a child was taken—except the mother.

No one wept for the lost but me.

There had to be another way.

I inhaled deeply, the scent of clean linens mingling faintly with the memory of burning flesh. My stomach turned, and I flung the covers aside. My bare feet landed on the cool stone floor, and I leapt over scattered books and parchment—fragments of studies, half-formed thoughts, desperate questions no one dared to answer—to reach the vanity across the room.

My fingers fumbled for a strip of leather as I hastily pulled my black curls into a loose bun.

I leaned on the vanity, bracing myself with trembling hands. My reflection stared back at me—hollow, weary, familiar and foreign all at once. The cream-colored night tunic and shorts hung loosely on my frame, as if even my clothes had begun to retreat from me.

Then there they were.

The eyes.

Bright gold.

The color of fire. The color of the gods.

Eyes like no one else's.

They called them a blessing—proof that the gods had touched me before I ever took my first breath. The people adored me for them. Worshiped me, even. I had golden eyes, just like the gods themselves. It made them believe I was divine. Destined.

It made my mother smile through gritted teeth.

She would never admit it, but I saw the way her gaze lingered too long when the priestesses praised me. I heard the cold edge in her voice when others marveled.

They saw it as glory.

She hated them.

I... I no longer knew what to make of them.

I rubbed my eyes with the heels of my palms, willing myself to feel something—anything but this restless, numbing fatigue. It wasn't the kind of tiredness sleep could cure. My mind was unraveling, drowning in the images that returned each time I closed my eyes: the boy's face, the mother's torment, the blood.

And the way they still expected me to smile.

For three days, I had dreaded the moment it would happen. And it did—right in front of all of us. I stood beside my family, watched as the guards tore the woman's child from her arms, and did nothing. None of us did.

But it was her screams that stayed with me—wrapped around my throat each night like a curse. I woke once, shouting her name, sure she had clawed her way into my dreams just to ask me why I hadn't stopped it.

Vitaeus demanded human blood. And in the past three years, babies had become a rare blessing in Anima. Infertility was the plague in our land.

Every new child had become a miracle—and a target.

The rituals never changed.

My mother made the decree.

My father said nothing.

I hated how he bowed to her. How he let her voice carry through the hall like law—unchallenged, final. I hated how he stood there. Wordless. Spineless. Letting her rule as if the crown were hers alone.

She wasn't Queen by divine right. He was King.

So why did he act like her shadow?

That was the part that tore at me the most. He had never seemed so weak before. I knew his heart—had seen the kindness behind his sternness, the restraint in his strength. He wasn't cruel.

He used to be stronger than this. I remember that.

At least—I thought I did.

There had to be another way. There *has* to be.

Tears burned behind my eyes, unbidden and unwelcome. I swiped at them with the back of my hand, more angry than sorrowful. I was tired of crying. Tired of pretending faith made this any easier to swallow.

"Ganosi," I said—out loud, though it felt like a curse more than a prayer. "Goddess of Wisdom and Knowledge, hear me."

I stared at my reflection, voice trembling. The words slipped out the way they always had—soft, rehearsed, in-herited. A ritual carved into the bones of my childhood.

But there was no faith left in them. Only muscle memory.

And doubt.

So much doubt.

"Was this truly the best you could do?" I whispered. "Wisdom, and *this* was the answer? A baby boy?"

My voice cracked, sharp with disbelief. "What kind of wisdom demands the blood of the innocent? What kind of gods build peace on the backs of screaming mothers?"

No answer.

There never was.

Not when I begged for rain. Not when I pleaded for the fever to pass.

Not when I asked—*begged*—for the boy to be spared.

Especially not then.

I swallowed hard, blinking back the heat behind my eyes.

A sob slipped through anyway, and I lowered my head, watching as the tears hit the vanity below like drops of guilt.

Like drops of… *blood.*

I gasped, stepping back from the mirror until I pressed into the corner of my room. Sliding down the wall, I cradled

16

my face in my hands, tears spilling between my fingers. The sobs came hard, punctuated by flashes of the pale, lifeless child. His face flickered in my mind, colliding with the sound of his mother's broken cries. The two torments alternated, their agonizing chorus hammering in my ears.

The thought that the death of an innocent child could restore our country churned violently within me. It didn't add up. We'd given our best livestock, our finest harvests, and now the rarest gift of all—a healthy baby boy. And where were the gods? Where were their messengers? Where was the relief?

I lifted my gaze, staring again at my reflection from the floor. The dark purple mixed with my own brown on my cheek, still vivid from the queen's slap, glared back at me in the dim moonlight. My throat tightened as the memory clawed its way to the forefront of my mind.

My mother had struck me.

Again.

The one who raised me and taught me how to be royal. The one who once smiled at me. She'd changed; something within her had changed. My mother, the queen, now valued the gods above all else, even her own children at times.

To me, life was sacred.

To her, life was obedience.

Obedience without love for life becomes cruelty. So, how do we all survive this? How do we prosper in a system that demands so much blood?

It had to be more than this.

I knew I couldn't raise my tongue against her, but I couldn't remain silent anymore. Not about what I questioned. Not about what no longer made sense.

So I let my actions carry my word.

Three sharp knocks at the door interrupted my spiraling thoughts. They were soft, yet urgent. I wiped my face with the edge of my tunic, clearing away the tears.

"Who is it?" I rasped.

"Kelta," came the familiar voice.

I rose and opened the door, my legs heavy beneath me. Kelta stood there, her gaze lingering on my tear-streaked face.

"Oh, Kae'Dinah," she whispered, stepping inside and wrapping me in her arms. Her embrace was warm, grounding. Kelta was smaller than I was, but she had always felt larger, like a sturdy pillar I could lean on. Her family had served mine for generations, their loyalty as unyielding as the stone walls of this palace. And because of her longevity and proximity, she was one of the few friends I had.

I buried my face in her shoulder. "This isn't fair," I choked out, anger rising alongside the grief. "How could they take a life so young? So rare?"

Kelta pulled back, her hands gripping my shoulders. Her firm gaze startled me.

"Do not ever question Vitaeus!" she snapped, her voice sharp but trembling. "Sanyitum and Ceresius both agreed this was the only way. The only way women can conceive again. The only way life will be restored to us."

"What if they're not listening?" I whispered. "What if it doesn't work? What if we've wasted that child's life for nothing?"

Her hand flew up, pressing a trembling finger to my lips.

"Your Highness," she hissed, lowering her voice, "Vitaeus hears us. Even now. Silence those fearful thoughts."

18

Her hands moved to cradle my face, cool against the fever burning beneath my skin. She flinched at the heat.

"Are you well, Kae'Dinah?" she asked softly. "Have you eaten?"

I shook my head, eyes squeezed shut. How could I eat when the stench of burning still clung to my memory?

"I won't eat," I said, my voice brittle.

Kelta said nothing at first. She stepped back, wrapping herself in composure like a cloak. Adjusted her apron. Straightened her posture. Her silence was a closing door.

And just like that, the room felt colder.

She could pretend this was normal. Acceptable. *Holy.*

So could the priests. So could the guards.

So could my mother.

And worst of all—

So could my father.

I sat in the quiet after she left, jaw clenched so tightly I thought something might crack.

Maybe it already had.

I stared at the flame flickering in the corner lamp, watching it dance like nothing had happened.

Like no child had screamed.

And I wondered—truly wondered—how everyone else could still worship gods who demanded so much blood.

I used to believe they were listening.

Now I wonder if they ever deserved our prayers in the first place.

# Chapter 3

I t had been more than a day since the sacrifice.

The second day of silence pressed against my skin like a second layer. I had barely moved.

They'd brought me food—fruit, broth, a warm loaf split in two—but I only picked at it. Nothing tasted like anything. Nothing mattered enough to finish.

I ate only enough to keep the ache in my stomach from becoming sharp. Just enough to make them think I was still here, still functioning.

But I wasn't. Not really.

I craned my neck further into the corridor and saw no one. The stillness of the early morning lingered; the sun rose over the bay, painting the air golden. Stepping further into the shared space, I grabbed my bed coat from the back of our chair when I heard the soft rhythm of breathing.

Oh, there was someone.

Megorna.

She was curled up on the chaise in the corner, her hair loose, her nightclothes wrinkled from sleep. One arm dangled over the side, a book open on her chest, fingers brushing the floor. No sign of ceremony or mourning. No trace of the ritual's horror on her face—just peaceful, dreamless sleep.

She must've fallen asleep while reading; I hadn't heard her in here at all. I hadn't heard anything.

I stood there, watching her breathe, a strange tightness creeping into my chest. How could she sleep so easily? How could any of them?

I turned away before bitterness could build.

Crossing the room quietly, I reached the main door and twisted the handle slowly, careful not to wake her.

But when I opened it, I was met by a pair of dark brown eyes.

Captain Wilt.

His gaze flicked down, then back up—a quick scan for injuries, for blood, for signs I was still myself. Tension sat in his shoulders like armor. His jaw was tight.

I leaned against the door frame, arms folded. "I'm safe," I muttered.

He gave a short nod, but didn't smile. "Didn't look like it the other day."

I sighed, jaw clenched. "Well. Now you know."

He didn't move. Just grabbed the wooden stool beside the door and sank onto it, bracing his elbows on his knees.

"You're alive," he said.

*Wrong words.*

I flinched, and his eyes darted to mine—instantly regretting it.

"I didn't mean—"

"Yes, I *am* alive," I cut in, voice flat. "Shame I can't say the same for the boy they burned."

Silence cracked between us.

"I wasn't trying to be cruel."

"Then don't be careless."

He nodded once. Took it. Didn't fight.

"I didn't mean to say it like that."

"Doesn't matter how you said it," I muttered. "It's still true."

A long silence passed between us. Then I asked, "Why are you here?"

"Why are *you* sneaking out?" he replied, dropping his voice.

"I'm not sneaking. I just needed air." I crossed my arms tighter. "My room started feeling like a cage. Or a tomb."

His eyes flicked up to mine. "So you waited until now to... sneak out?"

"I didn't want to be followed or questioned by the night's watch."

"Then you should've known better than to open your door with me standing guard."

That almost earned a smile from me. Almost.

"You're not usually posted here this early."

"I'm not."

I studied his face. "So again—why are you here?"

He didn't answer right away. His uniform was still crisp, but his collar was uneven. His jaw was dusted with scruff, and there were faint creases under his eyes—nothing dramatic. Just quiet proof, he hadn't slept.

"I don't trust the rotation," he said finally. "So I volunteered to stay over."

I blinked. "You don't trust the other captains?"

"I don't trust the Queen not to order one of them to remove you in the middle of the night."

The air between us shifted. My throat tightened.

"She wouldn't do that."

He met my gaze. "She's never looked that angry before,

Kae'Dinah."

My breath caught. Memory surged—the Queen's hand wrapped around my throat, the air stolen from my lungs. I fidgeted with the sigil ring on my finger, refusing to let my mind go any further.

I looked away. "Have you even slept?"

"Enough."

"Not a real answer."

"Neither was yours," he said, quietly.

I sighed. "What exactly are you here for, Captain?"

His head tilted. "You locked yourself away for thirty-six hours and said nothing. I'm here to make sure you're not slipping through cracks no one else sees."

I stared at him. "So it *is* about checking the box. I'm alive, you can carry on."

He frowned. "That what you think I'm doing?"

"I don't know what anyone's doing," I snapped. "I don't even know what *I'm* doing."

He went still. Then—softer—"You're allowed to be angry, Kae."

"I *am* angry," I whispered. "But you don't have to concern yourself with that. Right?"

He reached for my hand but stopped short, his fingers barely grazing mine before pulling back. "Everything you do concerns me, Princess."

The way he said it—low, careful, like a secret—lit something beneath my ribs. Heat bloomed in my cheeks, uninvited.

I needed it to stop. He always did this. Said too much. Said it too softly.

"I'm fine," I said flatly, stepping away. "You don't need to—"

"Because the Queen put her hands on you—"

"I said I'm *fine*." The words snapped out too sharp. I looked away. "It's not the first time."

His jaw tightened. "It's the first time she looked like she wanted to kill you. Your neck's still red. I didn't know if she'd come back."

I swallowed hard, my chest twisting. "That doesn't mean you should run yourself into the ground or ignore your body's demands for sleep. That's why there are *rotations*."

He leaned forward, eyes fixed on the ground. "I ignore my body's demands around you more often than you realize."

I blinked. "What?"

His voice dropped. "If it's between sleep and making sure you're safe, I'll choose you every time."

There it was again—that *too much* tone. The one that lived between duty and something deeper.

He rose and walked to the sideboard, uncorked a water skin, and drank. The water spilled slightly along his jaw. I hated how I noticed.

He wiped his mouth with the back of his hand. "Water?"

"No." My voice was tight. I didn't meet his eyes.

Silence settled between us, brittle with everything unsaid.

"So," I murmured, "if the Queen demanded to enter my room… would the others let her in?"

"Yes."

I turned toward him. "Would you?"

"No."

"Why not?"

His gaze met mine. Steady. "You know why."

"But she's your Queen." I pushed the line. I needed to know it would hold.

"And you're my Princess."

The air thickened between us.

I looked away, my heart pounding. I didn't know what scared me more—that he meant it… or that I wanted him to.

That I wanted someone to choose me.

Even if it could never be him.

"Jahiel," I whispered, barely audible. "We can't…"

The words hovered, fragile as ash.

"I know," he said. Quiet. Certain. Heavy with everything he'd buried long before now.

Footsteps rounded the corner—the soft rumble of wooden carts and maids' chatter coming closer.

I shut my eyes and leaned my head against the door frame, bracing.

"I'll sleep tonight," he murmured. "Promise."

I nodded, still facing away. "Speak to Kelta. The healers may have something to help."

"Yes, Princess."

The title rang like armor sliding into place. His voice pulled back behind protocol.

I felt it. I *always* felt it when he retreated.

One last look passed between us. Then I slipped back inside before the moment could stretch too thin—or be seen by the wrong eyes.

The door clicked shut behind me, sealing him out.

I leaned against the wood, forehead pressed to the grain. My chest felt tight—not with longing, but frustration.

He was my friend. That was all I wanted him to be.

And I wished he'd stop making it so hard to forget that.

# Stance

*Milo, two years before...*

"Stop leaning forward like that. You're going to get yourself killed," I snapped, rising from the bench to stride toward her.

"I'm not doing it on purpose, Milo. My feet just... do that," she muttered.

"Then your feet will get you skewered," I hissed, nudging them into position with mine. "Shift your weight properly or your opponent will shift it for you."

She scoffed and rolled her eyes.

"Don't roll your eyes at me just because I'm right—and you're being corrected."

She hated being corrected. It was a matter of pride. She read so much, studied so hard, armed herself with knowledge so she wouldn't have to be. She was brilliant—especially in history and strategy. Smarter than any of the boys in our war councils, including me. The heir.

I didn't mind her brilliance.

Father did.

He praised her for being herself, sure. But he pushed me

harder each time she outshone me. Late nights, endless scrolls, volumes of military journals—none of it ever stuck.

I stepped in to fix her shoulders. Her golden eyes scanned my face. Eyes no one else in our family had.

The nobles said they were a blessing from Lunauctius, god of the sun and moon. But I always thought they were a gift from Ganosi, goddess of wisdom, or more compelling, Cassidam, goddess of war. They dazzled—but like bait. They lured you in, softened you just enough before she struck. It's probably why she understood the art of war so well. The execution? We were still working on that.

"Did you sleep last night?" she asked, catching the fatigue in mine.

I couldn't lie to her. She couldn't lie to me. I'd known her her whole life—she'd known me all but two years of mine. There was trust there. Real trust. In a palace full of secrets, we had almost none between us.

Except this.

The pressure. The quiet shame of not being the best.

"No," I said, adjusting her stance again.

"Why?"

I took the wooden blade from her, repositioning her fingers around the hilt.

"Balance your weight evenly," I said. "If a skilled opponent sees your weakness, they'll use it."

"Why, Milo?" she asked again, louder this time—more demanding.

I sighed, letting go of the breath I'd been holding and dropped my head, stepping back from her.

"Milo?" Her voice softened. Like a hand—gentle, reassuring. A kind of comfort I'd only ever found in her. Never from our mother. Never from our father.

Our parents were strength and pride, nothing else. No softness. No space for weakness.

But Kae'dinah was warm.

She was unlike anything else here.

She taught me how to see people the way our parents never had. She loved with a maternal tenderness I didn't even recognize at first—but once I did, I clung to it. I protected it. Because the world would see that softness as weakness. And they'd try to extinguish it.

"I've been staying up late," I finally admitted, lifting my eyes to hers. Her curls were twisted into a messy bun, high and out of her face—just like I taught her.

"I've been studying."

"Studying what, Milo? You're brilliant,"—she brushed her hand across my shoulder, a half-laugh in her voice.

"Not as brilliant as expected," I muttered, turning away and walking back to the bench beside the sparring mat. I slumped into it, leaning against the wall.

"What else do they expect from you, King?" she teased. "To walk around with a head stuffed full of every war account known to man?"

She paused, then smirked. "Well… you've definitely got the enlarged head part down."

I cracked a smile. Of course there were jokes.

"I think you got the enlarged part," I mocked, pitching my voice high and dramatic.

"I mean your head is massive," she laughed—a sound golden, like her eyes.

"Enough," I chuckled, the sound slipping easily between us.

The laughter faded into quiet. Not heavy. Just still.

She nudged my shoulder gently. Her way of telling me to go on. To finish what I started.

"I'm not as brilliant as you," I said quietly.

Her gaze flicked to mine.

I looked away.

Her expression was layered with too many things—confusion, hurt, uncertainty. I almost stopped there. But it was our truth. All of it.

"My little sister… a young woman… top of our class," I said. "The nobility was already in an uproar just because you were there—because you weren't tucked away in the temples. But you weren't just present, Kae'Dinah. You were better than everyone. Including me."

I paused.

"I was proud. I really was. Until…"

"Until what, brother?" she asked. Her voice was distant now, eyes on the floor.

"Until Father scolded me for it. He yelled at me, Kae'Dinah. Said I should be ashamed—ashamed—that you were excelling while I wasn't. Told me an heir to his throne masters everything. And that I'd better master the classroom before he leaves this world."

She was quiet for a moment. Then she lifted her wooden blade and pointed it at my chest.

She didn't say anything at first. Just crossed the mat and dropped down beside me on the bench.

"I'll help you study," she said after a moment, her voice even. "But in exchange… I want more hand-to-hand lessons. Real ones. Not just you shouting corrections from across the room."

I looked over at her. She met my eyes—serious, steady.

"We'll trade," she added. "You feed me dates, I'll feed you facts."

A grin tugged at the corner of my mouth. "Fine. But if you mess up mid-swing, I'm not going easy on you."

She smirked. "If I mess up, it's probably because you've pronounced a generals name incorrectly."

I chuckled under my breath, shaking my head.

So we made a plan.

Mornings filled with sparring and shouted dates. Movements paired with names of fallen general's and battles we swore we'd never forget. A rhythm of blades and memory. Of blood and brilliance.

Recite and strike.

Learn and survive.

We could do both.

Our blades clashed, echoing through the stone walls of the training room. Her voice didn't waver as she recited the terms of the Treaty of Falemar while I blocked her strike and corrected her grip.

She was fierce.

She was fire wrapped in flesh.

And I—

I would never let anyone extinguish her.

Not while I lived.

Not even when I am king.

# Chapter 5

The large wooden doors of our private dining hall swung open with a deep groan, cutting through the quiet. The murmur of conversation among the two seated at the table abruptly ceased, leaving the stale remnants of their words hovering in the air.

I lifted my gaze from the cold, black stone floors. The long emerald velvet curtains, heavy and imposing, framed the rectangular room. They cascaded from the ceiling, pooling into lush puddles of green on the floor. These curtains embraced each window, and in front of every panel stood pedestals holding arrangements of white roses. Beyond the windows, the sun was just revealing its full face over the bay. Across the shimmering water lay the bustling heart of Anima's capital, Floos—our city. Our people. They must be stirring now, beginning their day.

My throat tightened as my eyes burned with unshed tears. I was terrified. I was scared of the consequences that awaited me. I had avoided them yesterday, but I couldn't anymore. But I was also still mourning. Mourning the senseless death of that baby boy. Somewhere in the awakening hum of the city, a still mother mourned with me.

A deep voice cut through the silence, pulling me back into

the room. I straightened my shoulders, lifting my chin into the posture my mother had drilled into me since childhood.

*A princess holds her head high. Her spine straight. Always.*

Even now, I hated how she never left my memory.

The mahogany dining table stretched down the center of the room, gleaming and dressed in gold-trimmed plates. Five emerald napkins rested at the place settings, each one wrapped neatly around a single white rose.

Two sets of eyes landed on me. Worried. Watching.

No one spoke.

"Come sit, little sister," Milo finally said, his voice tired, commanding, and still warm. "You'll sit beside me this morning."

His sharp eyes flicked to our sister, whose face had already begun to twist into a frown.

Prince Santu Milo Ickree, Fifth of His Name. The heir to the Anima throne. The oldest of us. Raised to rule, carved into a king before he ever had a choice. But despite the burden of his birthright, Milo had always protected me. He loved fiercely and without apology.

As I crossed the room toward him, he reached out and pulled me into a gentle, one-armed embrace. I let my head rest briefly against his chest, catching the faint scent of rosemary clinging to his tunic. It brought a flicker of warmth. But only a flicker.

I lowered myself into the empty chair beside him, pretending not to feel the weight of what I'd done—the ritual I'd walked away from, the line I wasn't supposed to cross.

But Milo didn't care about lines. He just wanted me close.

He couldn't publicly defy Mother, not outright. But this was his way. Quiet, unspoken loyalty.

He caught me watching him and raised an eyebrow. I smirked. The tension eased, barely.

"Mother isn't going to be pleased with that, Milo," Megorna said, stifling a yawn behind her hand. Her voice was clipped, sharp around the edges. She eyed the seating arrangement, fingers fussing over the tiniest misalignment like they were crimes against the crown.

I rolled my eyes. Of course.

Meg never defied orders. She never misstepped, never misspoke. Perfection clung to her like perfume—deliberate and suffocating. She didn't invite trouble because she didn't leave room for it.

She was everything I wasn't. And somehow, we made that work.

Princess Megorna Bryn Ickree, the youngest of our royal bloodline. The gods' golden child, destined to be someone's perfect queen—if not this kingdom's, then one like it. Her dark hair was woven into an intricate crown braid, her cream gown pressed and spotless, her wrists heavy with jewels. A picture of refinement.

And then there was me.

My frame was stronger, taller. Only a few inches shorter than Milo, and built like someone who didn't hide from sparring matches. My hips were full, my arms lean from work—not decoration. My hair, thick and wild, spilled down my back in waves that refused to be tamed.

Today, I wore a dark linen gown, the color just a shade deeper than my own terracotta skin. The bodice clung to my frame unapologetically. There was nothing subtle about me.

Meg and I were summer and winter.

And yet—we shared the same blood.

"She wants her daughters on one side of the table, and Milo on the other," Megorna murmured, tracing the golden edge of her plate. "That's how it's always been."

"Maybe she won't notice," Milo said, rubbing his temples with two fingers. The gesture was familiar—his default when dealing with Meg… or Mother.

We both knew she'd notice.

Milo just didn't care.

"She'll notice," I muttered, slipping out of his embrace.

I circled the table in silence, my gown sweeping across the polished black floors. I lowered myself into my usual seat—left of Father, directly across from Milo.

"She always notices," Meg added, her tone quieter now. "Especially when it's about you, Kae'Dinah."

She wasn't wrong. And she knew it.

She didn't say it with malice.

Just truth.

She smoothed the skirt of her dress, exhaling through her nose like she, too, was bracing for something.

I sat upright. Still. Calm.

Mourning didn't belong at this table.

Not today.

Not in front of them.

"I know," I sighed, plucking the white rose nestled in the folds of the napkin before me. I twirled it slowly between my fingers, its delicate petals soft against my skin.

From my side, Megorna narrowed her eyes. Disapproval—plain and immediate.

The mixture of anger and fear still simmered beneath my skin, a sickness I couldn't shake. But when I glanced across the table at my siblings, I saw it mirrored in them.

They were afraid.

For me.

And that—I couldn't allow.

So I made a choice. If I couldn't feel lightness, I could at least offer it to them.

Even if it was just for a moment.

Even if I had to fake it.

I glanced sideways at Megorna and smiled—small, crooked, intentional. I gave the rose another spin between my fingers. Something inside me bloomed with it.

Desperation for joy. Or distraction.

"Is there a problem, Meg?" I asked, raising a brow, my tone laced with quiet mischief.

"Yes," she hissed, arms crossing tightly. "Leave the place settings alone. At least until Mother and Father arrive."

"Break a rule, Meg," Milo chimed in, plucking the rose from his own napkin. He leaned forward and grabbed the others nearest him, grinning as he collected them like trophies.

I couldn't help it—I laughed. I stood abruptly, striding to claim the one tucked into Mother's setting before anyone could stop me.

Meg's eyes snapped to mine. A silent challenge passed between us.

We lunged at the same time.

She reached to rescue. I reached to steal.

My fingers landed first. I plucked it triumphantly, holding it in the air like a prize.

"Thank you," I said with a playful bow.

Milo shook his head, grinning as he turned to Megorna. "Now you're the only one who looks like she doesn't belong."

Her eyes narrowed, flicking between us in annoyance—then, slowly, defiantly, she reached for her flower and tucked it behind her ear. A smirk tugged at her lips.

She did it.

"Unbelievable," Milo muttered. "Such a rebel."

Megorna stuck her tongue out at him, a rare spark of playfulness glinting in her sleepy eyes.

Then—

The doors burst open.

We all flinched.

Meg's hand shot to her ear, yanking the rose free and shoving it beneath her thigh. My heart stopped.

But it was only the servants, wheeling in trays of food.

A collective exhale rippled through the room.

I sank back into my chair, tension sliding from my shoulders. For one breath, I'd believed it was her. And from the looks on my siblings' faces, they had too.

Milo broke the silence with a bark of laughter.

"What is *wrong* with you?" I asked, half-gasping, half-scolding.

He just laughed harder. "I can't be the only one who saw how fast Meg hid her rose."

He wasn't. We all had.

Even perfect Meg was afraid.

Megorna's cheeks flushed as she pulled the flower from under her leg and placed it neatly back on her plate. I smirked and tucked mine gently back into the napkin.

"Maybe that's enough fooling around for one day," I said, casting her a pointed look.

She nodded once. The playfulness was gone.

I stood and returned the two roses I'd taken. Milo sighed,

rising to return the ones he'd gathered as well. One by one, the room's brief lightness dimmed.

We sat again in silence.

Because no matter how much we joked, no matter how hard we tried to bend the moment into something bearable, we all knew the truth:

We couldn't afford to truly defy her.

Not with the mother we had.

Not even the ones she favored.

She would have order.

Always.

And I had disrupted it in an unthinkable way.

I'd always been the one to challenge her—bend her expectations, break them if I could. Her attempts to mold me never worked. It was like the shape she tried to force onto me had been made for someone else. It fit her. It fit Megorna. But on me, it cracked.

The mother Anima praised as dutiful and devoted wasn't just our Queen. She was our enforcer. The hand of discipline in this family. The architect of obedience.

Queen Breetun Vete Ickree wasn't merely consort to the King of Anima—she was a force. Born into Aartier's royal line, she had been sent to marry our father and seal a union between nations. We had known the gods—respected them, honored their names. But *she* had trained as a high priestess before her marriage, and our customs were too soft for her tastes.

She brought their ways with her. And slowly, she reshaped Anima. Its people. Its culture. Its fate.

She named herself High Priestess and was declared the nation's spiritual anchor. With the gods behind her, she promised prosperity, fertility, favor. And for a time, she delivered.

But her power came at a price.

Even Father—with all his might and presence—stood in her shadow. He'd never admit it, still parading the title of King like it meant something. But we knew the truth. Everyone did.

When things flourished, her name was whispered in reverence.

When they failed, the people blamed him.

Until seven years ago, when the gods went silent.

And suddenly, both monarchs bore the weight.

I'll never forget those early weeks.

Sacrifices piled high. Prayers, songs, wails—spilled across the city like wine, soaking the streets in desperation. But the gods gave nothing in return. No visions. No whispers.

Crops wilted. Livestock sickened.

Then came the stillbirths.

Then... nothing.

Month after month, the silence grew louder. The people wept louder. The courtyard outside the palace filled daily with mourners, messengers, the desperate and the devout.

And I remember—because that's when she changed.

She came back from a ritual one night, her dress still wet with some offering I didn't want to name, and looked at me like I was something broken. Something *ruining* everything.

The warmth in her eyes died that night.

She never turned on Milo. Never on Meg. Only me.

At first, it was quiet. A colder tone. A withheld smile.

Then it bled into silence. Then scorn.

It wasn't until a year later—when the glances became grabs,

and the bruises started appearing—that Megorna and Milo noticed.

I looked around the table now and saw them—tense, paralyzed, scarred in different ways. They were afraid. But they shouldn't have been.

I was the one who had sinned.

I was the one who had walked out of the sacred ritual.

I was the one who had embarrassed the High Priestess of Anima in front of gods and mortals alike.

A sigh escaped my lips—the only part of me bold enough to run.

*Only Ganosi would know how she'll handle me today.*

The goddess of wisdom. I didn't know why her name even came to mind. It spilled from my thoughts like habit. If Ganosi truly cared, wouldn't she have intervened by now? Or maybe cruelty *was* wisdom, and I was just too slow to understand it.

Before I could spiral further, the muffled sound of raised voices echoed from the corridor.

Our parents. Arguing.

The words were hard to make out, but the tension carried clearly, sharp and heavy.

I gripped the edge of my wooden chair, bracing.

Under the table, Megorna's hand slipped across the space between us, palm-up on my thigh. I startled, then grasped it tightly.

We were not like me and Milo. Meg and I had always loved each other, but warily—like two dancers on opposite sides of a line. She played by the rules. I kicked dirt over them. That was where our bond frayed.

But in this moment, her hand in mine, there was no line.

Only shared fear.

The double doors burst open.

Father entered first. His boots struck the marble with practiced power, but today there was no performance—only fury. His brow was set, jaw clenched so tightly it looked painful.

He didn't look at us. Didn't pause, until he noticed me. But only for a moment, then he walked to the head of the table and sat without a word.

And we waited.

My mother entered next, her emerald gown sweeping the floor, the golden chain at her hips gleaming under the light. Her sharp brown eyes burned as they landed on each of us, scrutinizing. When her gaze fell on me, I was the only one bold—or foolish—enough to meet it. Her anger darkened, and for a moment, it felt as though flames leaped between us. She gracefully lowered herself into her usual seat opposite my father.

The servants moved swiftly around the table, setting golden platters before us and revealing the morning feast: steaming porridge, savory pork, fresh fruits, and golden pastries that only adorn the plates of the men. The smell was heavenly, and my stomach churned with hunger. But, my eyes drifted to the raspberry danish on my brother's plate.

I loved sweets, and would often request a few to room midday for snacks. I slouched back in my chair, grabbing the cloth napkin that wrapped around our utensils.

He caught my eyes that lingered and my visible dismay, and he softened. He grabbed his fork, speared the danish and placed it on my plate.

"Thank you, brother," I murmured, my voice trembling

with quiet gratitude.

"Yeah," he teased softly. "I know you love these—and it's never enough."

A weak smile flickered across my lips as he leaned back, digging into the pork on his own plate. My hands were shaking. I hadn't even realized how tightly I'd been gripping Meg's hand until she tapped her fingers against mine—a silent nudge to let go.

"*Girl.*"

My mother's voice cut across the table like a whip—sharp, cold, deliberate. "You shouldn't eat those sweets. Rewards are for the obedient."

The word *girl* landed like a slap.

Was she speaking to me? Of course she was.

My chest tightened—but only for a moment. I had long since stopped expecting kindness from her. Even still... she was my mother.

I wouldn't give her the satisfaction of breaking me.

I swallowed the lump in my throat and kept my eyes on the danish.

"Call her by her name," my father said, voice low and coiled with warning.

"She is no child of mine," Mother snapped. "You're lucky I even allowed her at this table."

I didn't look up. Didn't speak. But the heat behind my eyes threatened to spill over.

"Breetun," my father growled. "You will not speak ill of any child of mine. Do I make myself clear?"

"Oh, spare me, Santu," she scoffed, crossing her arms. "You act like you raised them. Your job is King, not nurturer. Stop pretending you care about this one."

My father chuckled darkly, a sound layered with contempt. "You want to talk about jobs? Yours was to bear me an heir. That was *your* purpose."

Her eyes narrowed. "And yet it seems I've done *more* than that. Far more."

Their words sliced the air between them. Only Mother could speak to the King this way and walk away with breath still in her lungs.

A tear escaped down my cheek—hot, unbidden. It startled me. It wasn't sorrow.

It was rage.

And I let it fuel me.

"You dishonored Vitaeus," she hissed suddenly, eyes locked on me like a blade poised to strike. "You disgraced your family. Your King. Your High Priestess."

The last title rolled off her tongue like it bore the most weight.

"I—" I started, my voice cracking.

Her hand rose, silencing me.

"You ran like a coward."

"I couldn't stand by and watch you *murder* that woman's son," I said, my voice rising like flame before I could stop it.

A chill passed through the room.

The word *murder* hung in the air like smoke.

"That was an *honor*," she spat. "A sacrifice demanded by the gods."

"We hadn't seen a birth in Floos for *months*," I said, standing now, my hands trembling but my voice stronger. "And you stole the only child they had left. You slaughtered him and called it holy."

Silence.

Even the guards shifted. Milo stopped chewing. Meg's hand tightened around the back of my dress now.

A silent warning.

"Bite your tongue, you insolent child."

"You orchestrated a *murder*," I hissed. "We've been bleeding for the gods for *years*—and gained nothing. No blessings. No answers. You watched that child die for *nothing*!"

Her face twisted in fury, but her voice dropped to a venomous whisper. "You disappointment. Do you need reminding who brought this curse upon us?"

I froze.

She always found a way to make it my fault.

"Mother—" Megorna's voice broke gently through the silence, trembling. She reached for reason.

But it was too late.

The line had been crossed.

And I wasn't going back.

"Silence," my mother hissed, her voice sharp enough to split bone. Then her gaze cut back to me—her eyes onyx and glinting with something dark.

Something unnatural.

"Ganosi and Paxium warned me about you."

The words hit like a slap.

What?

I gripped the fork in my trembling hand, my chest heaving. "You blame *me*? For what reason in all of Naedorn would I bear the fault of silent, useless gods? *I'm* the one you're angry with?"

"Enough," my father's voice broke in, weary but firm. "That's enough from both of you."

But it wasn't enough. Not for me.

"Yes, I ran," I said, voice shaking—but louder now. "And I'll run every time you demand another innocent life for these gods. For nearly a decade, they've given us nothing but silence and death—and you still kneel as if that silence is sacred."

I turned to my father, desperate. "You should feel the same rage. You serve them, and they abandoned you too!"

"Kae'Dinah, stop," my father warned, eyes pleading now.

"No!" I gestured wildly to the opulence around us. "Look around! We sit at this table dripping in gold while our people starve and pray to gods who do *nothing!*"

My mother's voice dropped to a low, venomous tremble. "The land suffers... because of *you.*"

A pulse moved through the room. The shadows along the walls seemed to shudder, just for a moment—as if echoing her fury.

"Because of me?" I asked, stunned. "You think the gods punish *you* because of *me*? What have they ever done to help us?"

And then she smiled.

But not kindly.

Cold. Calculated. Amused.

She leaned forward slightly, her face still, but her eyes—her eyes black—absence of all light.

And she whispered.

Soft. Too soft. But the sound slithered into my ear anyway.

"Perhaps I should have offered *you* to Vitaeus instead of that boy."

The air around her flickered. The light dimmed, only for an instant.

It was like the room exhaled around her. Or recoiled.

44

The words struck like a blade to the ribs.

I froze.

No one reacted.

No one flinched. No gasps. No shock.

I blinked, heart hammering, scanning the room.

"M–Mother?" Megorna's voice trembled, confused. "What's wrong?"

"What did you just say?" I rasped, my throat raw.

But my mother only smiled. Sweetly now. Artificial.

Like she hadn't just spoken death over me.

"Kae'Dinah!" my father barked. "Enough of this insolence!"

Only me.

Only *I* had heard her.

Only I had seen the shadows curl around her lips and devour her words.

I turned to him, frantic. "Father, she—she just threatened me! She said—"

"Please," he sighed, waving me off. "You're exhausted. Sit down and compose yourself."

"No—you don't understand! She said she'd kill me!" I cried, pointing at her, my hands trembling.

Mother gasped, hand to her chest with feigned grace. "Fury may have touched me, but I would *never* harm my own flesh."

A bitter laugh rose in my throat, but it never left my lips.

I looked to Milo. My last hope.

"You believe me, don't you?" I whispered.

He stood slowly. Shaken.

"Kae'Dinah… breathe," he said gently, stepping forward. "Please. You're upset. Let's calm down."

His hands touched my shoulders. Warm. Familiar. But

45

they burned like betrayal.

"You think I *imagined* it?" I whispered.

"Kae'Dinah…"

"No!" I pulled back. "No one else heard her? No one saw the shadows?"

"Kae—please."

"She *spoke death* over me!" I shouted, pointing to the Queen, who looked at me now with that same serene, soulless expression.

Silence.

Judgment.

"Milo, sit down," the King ordered.

My brother hesitated. Then obeyed.

His silence hurt worse than the Queen's whisper.

"She's your *mother,* Kae'Dinah," my father said flatly. "She will not hurt you."

But she already had.

Several times, she has put her hands on me.

And she would again.

My breath shook as I stood motionless, eyes burning.

They didn't believe me.

Of course they didn't.

The shadows had swallowed the truth.

I scraped my chair back across the marble floor, the sound ringing through the room like the crack of a whip.

And then, just as I had done so many times before—

I dismissed myself.

Before anyone else could.

# Chapter 6

I burst through the doors, my breaths jagged as the bodice of my dress squeezed the air from my lungs. Each gasp felt shallow, insufficient, as though the air itself were slipping through my grasp.

I looked right—toward the staircase leading to sanctuary—then left, to the group of guards seated along the far wall, waiting for us to finish breakfast.

Captain Wilt sat among them, laughing at something another man had said. The sound was deep, unguarded—

until he saw me.

His face stiffened. His posture snapped upright as he rose to his feet.

My lips trembled. The telltale sting of tears welled in my eyes.

I turned sharply, racing up the stairs without a word, knowing he'd follow.

The sharp click of my shoes echoed against stone with each frantic step, broken only by the heavier, deliberate sound of boots behind me. He was close. Gaining. His stride steadier than my panicked flight.

Tears blurred my vision, hot streams that burned my cheeks and blurred the world. A gasping sob escaped me—

sharp and wild—like the sound of a wounded animal.

At the top of the stairs, I stopped, bending forward as I clutched my torso. My chest heaved. The corset laced tightly around my ribs left no room for air. I pressed a hand against the bodice, desperate for relief. The walls felt as if they were closing in.

"Kae'Dinah."

His voice was steady. Grounding. I couldn't see him yet.

Then his hand found my elbow—firm but not rough—guiding me away from the open landing to the shadow of a curved marble column.

He turned me, pressing my back gently to the cool stone. The chill soothed the heat of my trembling body.

My breaths came in short, uneven bursts.

Wilt reached up, pulling a leather strap from his hair. The dark coils fell forward, framing his sharp features. Then, with gentle hands, he turned me again.

"Hold still," he murmured.

I felt his fingers gather my wild, coiled hair, taming it into a tight ponytail. The motion was brisk, practical—but not unkind.

When he finished, he turned me back to face him.

"Kae'Dinah," he said softly, his hands settling on my forearms. He bent slightly, his eyes meeting mine. They were dark, steady, filled with a quiet urgency.

"You have to calm your breathing."

My chest still rose and fell in uneven, shallow bursts. My heart thundered.

"Kae'Dinah," he whispered again. My name anchored me. "You're panicking. I need you to slow down. Breathe with me."

He released one of my arms and placed his hand over his chest. He inhaled deeply, exaggerated and deliberate, his chest rising and falling in slow rhythm.

"Look at me," he urged. "Do what I'm doing."

I hesitated. Then watched his hand.

Slowly, I lifted mine, placing it over his. The steady rise and fall beneath my palm grounded me.

Wilt's hand slipped out from under mine, leaving my palm pressed to the leather of his tunic. I could feel the beat of his heart beneath it.

His hands returned to my upper arms—steady, anchoring.

"There," he murmured. "That's better."

The air came easier now. The pressure in my ribs eased.

I opened my eyes.

He was already watching me.

His expression unreadable—but intense.

There was worry. But also something else.

A territory we always stopped short of crossing.

We couldn't.

We *shouldn't*.

"I'm sorry," I whispered, the words tumbling out before I could stop them.

Captain Wilt's brow furrowed. "For what?"

"For… panicking. For breathing funny," I said with a weak laugh, glancing away.

His lips tugged into a faint grin, but his hands stayed on my arms, the grip loosening slightly. "Do not ever apologize to me for breathing, Princess," he said, voice low, the words lingering too long in the space between us.

I stiffened. My gaze dropped to the hand still resting against his chest. I could feel the steady thrum of his

49

heartbeat beneath my palm.

His nearness was overwhelming—*comforting*, yes—but too close. Too familiar.

Too much.

Captain Wilt's eyes flicked down to the eagle sigil on my bracelet. His jaw tightened.

Then, with a sigh, he stepped back, releasing me, putting space between us again.

Good.

I was still his Princess. He was just my Captain. And whatever he thought he was feeling—it had to stay unspoken.

"What happened?" he asked, voice steadier now, as if trying to reset the boundary.

But his question cracked open the fury I'd been holding down.

"My mother said it was *my fault*," I said bitterly.

Captain Wilt's expression shifted, brow drawing tight. "What was?"

"The baby boy," I spat. "The one they murdered yesterday."

His confusion deepened. "How in Ganosi's name could she twist that into *your* fault?"

I let out a broken laugh, shaking my head. "And then she *threatened* to offer me next."

"What?" His voice was sharp now—loud enough to echo.

"But no one else heard her," I said, trembling. "It was like the moment she said it, the world blinked. They only heard *me*. They looked at me like I was unraveling. But I *know* what I heard. She smiled right after. Like she knew I was the only one who would remember it."

Captain Wilt ran a hand down his face, the other resting on his hip. He looked away briefly, as if trying to reason through madness. "What do you mean only you heard her?"

"My family only responded to the words *I* shouted against the gods," I snapped. "Not a single one of them reacted to *her* threat. Not even Milo."

"Keep your voice down," he warned gently, scanning the corridor.

"I will not keep my voice down," I snapped, my voice rising again. "They told me I was tired. That I needed rest. They humored me like I was some fragile thing telling ghost stories."

Captain Wilt stepped in again, reaching toward my forehead. "Princess, are you—"

"Don't," I hissed, shoving him away with both hands. The force startled even me. "Don't *touch* me like I'm breaking. Don't question what I *know* I heard."

He held up both hands. "I'm not. It's just—"

"Just *outlandish*?" I cut in, voice sharp. "Is that what you think?"

A faint smirk threatened his lips—like he was trying to soften the moment. "She loathes you, yes. But to *sacrifice* her own daughter?"

"Yes, *Captain*," I snapped, emphasizing the title. "She would. And you know it. If Kelta hadn't stepped in yesterday, she would have choked me unconscious and laid me on that altar without flinching. Not because I'm the solution—but because I'm her failure. Her embarrassment."

Captain Wilt's face fell. "Kae'Dinah…" he said softly, reaching for me again.

But this time I saw it.

The flicker in his eyes. The doubt.

Not for my safety. But for my sanity.

51

"You don't believe me," I said coldly. "You're just like the rest of them."

"Do not say that," he said, trying to steady his voice. "I didn't mean to—"

"Don't *pretend,* Jahiel." I took a step back. "You touched me like I was sacred—and now you're looking at me like I'm cracked."

He opened his mouth to answer, but I didn't wait.

"You're unbelievable," I hissed, my voice trembling with rage and betrayal.

Then I shoved past him, stepping into the light of the corridor.

"Where are you going?" he called after me.

"Somewhere," I snapped. "I need to get away."

"You can't just walk around unguarded."

He easily caught up, his stride longer, more practiced.

"Yes, I can," I said coldly, eyes fixed forward.

"I'll come with you." His tone had shifted—too firm, too final.

"No."

"Princess—"

"I said *no!*" I whirled on him, fury surging. "I need space! Everyone's treating me like I'm mad—I just need to be *alone.*"

"I can't let you go anywhere alone."

"You could," I said, my words cutting like glass. "You could, if you remembered I'm still a royal and you're still a captain. And maybe… maybe we've been too close lately, don't you think?"

That landed.

His expression faltered, the wound visible behind his eyes.

"In fact," I continued, "I *order* you to find something else

52

to do for the next hour. After that, fine—you can come find me. But right now? Leave."

"Princess—" His voice softened. A plea.

But I cut him off.

"Please, *Captain* Wilt." My voice cracked—just once. "Go back downstairs. Give me this. Just this."

He stood still for a moment, jaw tight, eyes locked on mine. I didn't blink.

Finally, he exhaled and stepped back. He lingered, unwilling. Then, slowly, he turned and descended the stairs toward the dining hall.

Only once his footsteps vanished did I move.

I turned and walked briskly toward my wing—my pulse loud in my ears. I needed air. I needed space. I needed silence.

I needed my daggers, the open paths of the Ickree garden, and the sound of *anything* but voices that didn't believe me.

It was the only thing I trusted today.

# Chapter 7

I didn't run.

I walked—sharp, focused steps through the corridor past the main hall, my fingers brushing against the cold stone walls like a tether to reality. No one stopped me. No one asked.

They were probably too afraid to.

The garden door opened with a reluctant groan, and I stepped into a world I hadn't set foot in for years.

I paused.

It was more alive than I remembered.

The Ickree garden stretched wild under the cloud-dappled sky. Beams of light poured through the canopy, glinting off petals and stone. Moss covered the old paths like a second skin. Vines ran wild, untamed. Fireblossoms blazed red and orange through the green, defiant as ever.

It should've felt overgrown. Neglected. But it didn't.

It felt like it had been waiting. Like it understood exactly why I came.

I followed the path my feet remembered—past the broken sundial, past the bench where my father once traced ancient glyphs into my hand when I was small, teaching me how to say each one aloud.

I missed the way he used to look at me—like he believed me.

Near the garden's southern edge, I found a clearing still mostly intact. Lavender grew in tall clusters. The scent of rosemary hung thick in the air. Bees moved lazily from bloom to bloom, undisturbed by the storm brewing inside me.

I sank down onto the stone step beneath the arbor, dagger still strapped to my thigh, and drew my knees to my chest.

Captain Wilt's voice still echoed in my ears—steady, cautious, *wrong.*

And hers—my mother's—cut through it all like a shard of glass.

*"Perhaps I should have offered you to Vitaeus instead of that boy."*

I dug my nails into my arms.

She'd smiled when she said it.

She'd smiled when she threatened me.

I hated that her voice still found its way into the quiet.

I hated that *he* didn't believe me.

Megorna, pretending nothing had happened. Milo, silent. The King, detached. Wilt, worried about my *mind* instead of my *mother.*

I wasn't losing my grip. I wasn't imagining it.

And I wasn't going to beg anyone else to believe me.

That's why I came here.

Not to hide.

To remember. To choose clarity over chaos. To gather myself before the feeling inside me erupted.

A singular drop of sweat rolled down the side of my face, startling me. It was odd, the day wasn't that hot, yet I felt flustered.

A breeze moved through the trees. I closed my eyes, taking in the cooling feeling on my skin. The wind rustled a few leaves just behind me in slow, whispering waves.

Wait...

Not leaves.

Voices.

I sat up, my head snapping in the direction of the sound.

The wind passed again, curling around the trunks like fingers—but the sound remained.

A murmur. Faint. Feminine. Rhythmic.

It wasn't speech. It was a steady sound, moving with a rhythm.

I stood slowly, and reached for the dagger I had strapped to my thigh.

The garden shifted. Still beautiful—but wrong. The colors too sharp. The petals too wide, as if stretching their mouths open. The vines at the edge of the clearing curled inward, like they were watching.

There was an unfamiliar path. Had that been there when I was younger because I didn't remember it.

The whispers had picked up the tempo now, speaking faster. Matching the pace of my heartbeat.

The world grew quieter with every step. No birds. No breeze. Only the hush of that steady, whispered prayer.

And then—I saw her.

A woman knelt at the base of a blackened tree.

It was hollowed and scorched, its bark crumbling like ash. Roots coiled through the earth like snakes.

She didn't move. Just knelt there, whispering.

Something in me went still.

Her posture. The set of her shoulders. It was familiar.

She lifted her head.

And I froze. I stared into a reflection of myself. Like looking at my reflection on the surface of a lake.

It wasn't me, but it *wanted* to be.

The face was nearly mine—but burned down one side. Her mouth bent in strange places. Her eyes flickered like buried flame.

She stood in silence.

"I remembered you kinder than this," she said, voice drifting like smoke.

"You left us in the fire."

I took a step back.

She stepped forward.

"You should've burned with the rest of us."

Her hand shot out—faster than thought—and clamped around my wrist.

Pain flared instantly. Heat surged up my arm, searing through my veins.

I screamed.

Wrenched away. Fell.

The grass caught me—rough, real—but she was gone.

Gone.

"What's going on over there?" a deep voice called from just beyond the hedge.

"Me—it's Kae'dinah!" I shouted, scrambling backward, putting as much distance as I could between me and the place she had been. "Help! Quick!"

I looked down at my wrist. The skin was scorched—red, blistering.

The burn pulsed with pain.

But how?

How does something that isn't real leave a mark like this?

A moment later, General Marger appeared, blade already drawn.

His dark uniform snapped as he stepped into the clearing, eyes scanning the garden for threats.

"Are you injured?" he barked, gaze sweeping across me, then darting toward the bushes.

"I'm fine," I said quickly, cradling my wrist. "But something was here. Something grabbed me."

He froze.

His posture shifted—shoulders relaxing, stance softening. But not in a way that made me feel safer.

In a way that made my stomach drop.

"General Marger?" I called.

He didn't answer.

Just stood there. Too still.

Then his fingers shifted on the pommel of his sword. Tightened. Turned slightly toward me.

"General," I said again, this time with more force.

He turned.

And his eyes—

His eyes were black. Not dark. Not shadowed. Black.

Like polished onyx.

Like something ancient had swallowed the light.

Every hair on my arms lifted. My breath stilled in my chest.

This wasn't right.

He wasn't right.

"General Marger," I said, slowly pushing myself to a crouch, never taking my eyes off him.

His lip twitched. Just one side. A strange, creeping smile.

"General," I whispered, this time on an exhale.

He raised his sword. Not to attack.

He pointed it—directly at my wrist.

The burn.

"So… you've seen her," he said.

Only—it wasn't just his voice.

It was layered. Warped. Like many voices speaking at once.

A chorus inside a single throat.

"What the—" I gasped, drawing my dagger in one smooth motion, rising to my full height.

"What are you talking about?" I demanded, my pulse thrumming in my ears. "What's going on?"

He took a steady step toward me.

And I knew.

I was in danger.

*Give me strength.*

The words left my mind in silence, not toward the gods and goddesses I'd grown up worshiping—but to something else.

Something higher.

Someone who might still be listening.

*Please. Give me strength to fight this.*

General Marger began to pace, slow and circling. His blade rotated in his grip, catching the light.

He watched me like prey.

I crouched lower, letting instinct guide my stance.

My pulse thundered in my ears.

My dagger trembled in my hand, but I didn't back down.

He smirked—amused by the fight still in me.

Then he lunged.

Steel met steel. I blocked low, his blade scraping off mine with a metallic screech.

He struck again, harder. I deflected, dodging left.

He was stronger.

But I was faster.

His sword swung low. I jumped—barely clearing it.

My foot landed wrong. Pain shot up my leg. I stumbled, but didn't fall.

"Fight back!" he snarled.

I surged forward, slashing in rapid succession—right, left, left.

He parried every strike.

Then he drove into me with his full weight, knocking me off balance.

I hit the ground hard, the breath knocked from my lungs.

And then he was on top of me.

His sword clattered to the side as his hands pinned my wrists.

I gasped, struggling beneath him, but he didn't move.

Didn't let up.

His face hovered inches from mine, lips curled into a twisted smile.

His breath was hot—rancid—and too close.

"Now what, Princess?" he said.

Low. Guttural. Not his voice anymore.

"You're all alone. No one's coming."

He pressed closer.

"You smell like him. Pure and good," he sneered, his face too close, his voice slithering with something not human.

"Do you know what that smells like? A delicate rose."

He leaned in.

"Do you know I can't let you live now?"

His mouth twisted into a grotesque grin. "You should've burned when the others did."

My fear coiled. Hardened.

Then snapped.

*No.*

My fingers tightened around the dagger at my side.

He was too close. Too heavy.

But his weight was centered—his confidence, sloppy.

I remembered what Milo taught me.

*If you're cornered, strike where it counts.*

*Make it count.*

I twisted hard beneath him—one leg shifting, one hand jerking free.

Then I plunged the dagger into his side—deep, sharp, angled up.

Right beneath the ribs.

He gasped. Choked.

His body arched in shock, arms flailing just enough for me to push out from under him.

I scrambled to my feet, my wrist screaming in pain. Blood soaked the hilt of my blade.

The general staggered, a wet gurgle in his throat.

His hand went to the wound—then pulled away, stained dark.

"You..." he rasped, staring at me with fury and disbelief. His voice was warping again—more than one layered beneath the surface.

"I warned you," I panted, blade still raised. "Stay away from me."

He took one step—then another.

Then collapsed into the garden soil.

Face down.

Unmoving.

I backed away slowly. Breathing hard.

I didn't run.

I couldn't.

My legs trembled as I slipped back through the garden's shadowed path, one hand gripping my dagger, the other cradling my wrist. Blood still streaked my palm—some mine, most his.

My breath came in jagged bursts. My mind screamed with what-ifs and questions I wasn't ready to ask.

The castle's stone corridor reappeared through the trees like a lifeline. I pushed open the side entrance door, my shoulder catching the frame as I stumbled forward.

And there he was.

"Milo."

He turned sharply, mid-step, holding a ledger in one hand. The moment he saw me—my bloodied dress, the blood across my wrist, the trembling in my fingers—his face drained of color.

"Kae'Dinah?" The ledger hit the ground. "What—what happened?"

I opened my mouth, but no words came.

He didn't wait. He lunged forward, grabbing my shoulders, steadying me. "Who did this? Are you hurt—how bad is it?"

"It was the general," I whispered hoarsely, barely able to say it. "Mother's general. He... He's not... right. Something's wrong with him. He tried to—he—"

Milo didn't let me finish.

"GUARDS!" he bellowed, his voice echoing down the corridor like a war drum. "NOW!"

Footsteps thundered almost instantly. Four men rounded the corner, swords drawn.

And behind them—

Captain Wilt.

He froze when he saw me—his eyes landing first on the blood at my waist, then the dagger in my hand, and finally my face.

"Princess—" he started.

"Stay back," I hissed, my voice sharper than I meant it to be. But I couldn't take any more pity in his eyes. Not right now.

"She said the general attacked her," Milo said, stepping in front of me like a shield. "The one assigned to the Queen."

Captain Wilt's brows furrowed. "Marger?"

"Yes," I answered tightly. "In the Ickree garden. I stabbed him. He's down. I don't know if he's—"

"She's in shock," Milo cut in, steadying me as I swayed again. "Get a healer. And send a squad to the garden. If he's alive, I want him bound and dragged to the cells by his teeth if necessary."

Captain Wilt didn't argue. He turned sharply to the guards. "You heard him. Move!"

The men sprinted down the hall, disappearing through the garden doors.

Captain Wilt approached slowly now, his voice softer. "You're safe now, Princess."

I looked at him, and for the first time… I didn't feel it.

"I was alone," I murmured. "I asked for space. You gave it. And now look."

His jaw tensed.

"I'm not blaming you," I added. "But don't call me safe."

Milo's arm tightened protectively around me. "Come on. Let's get you cleaned up."

I tried to follow him, but my legs still shook.

Milo's eyes sweep over me. The panic etched in the lines of my face. The blood stains on my attire. The trembling of my hands.

He was furious.

I quickly broke away from his gaze and look to Captain Wilt. Only, his face wore that same rigid expression. His fists clenched at his sides, and his shoulders tense with fury.

Milo exhaled deeply and tapped his shoulder, signaling for me to wrap my arm around him.

"Get up," he barked suddenly, his voice sharp and commanding.

I jumped at the sound, startled by his sudden burst.

"Captain, help me get her up," he ordered, his tone brooking no argument. "We're going to Father."

"Prince—" Wilt began, but Milo cut him off.

"Now!"

With the help of the two men, I was lifted off my feet and into my brother's arms. The cold fury in Milo's eyes sent a shiver down my spine. I knew exactly what awaited us when we reached our father.

Retribution.

# Chapter 8

Milo stormed through the palace halls, his arms locked around me like iron. His jaw was clenched tight, his pace relentless. My blood stained his sleeve, but he didn't seem to notice—or care.

Behind us, Captain Wilt barked orders with sharp precision. "Find a healer and send them to the King's office. Now. And locate Officer Nagel—have him report there immediately."

One guard halted, startled. "What happened? Is she—"

"Do it!" Wilt snapped.

The man turned and sprinted down the corridor.

Another guard stepped forward as we neared the south wing. "Captain—what are your orders regarding General Marger?"

Wilt didn't pause. "He is to be locked away immediately. No visitors. No questions. No leniency. For the attempted murder of the Princess."

The guard froze. "Attempted—?"

"Did I stutter?" Wilt growled. "Move."

The soldier obeyed, sprinting in the opposite direction.

I barely registered any of it. My head rested weakly against Milo's chest, the world blurring at the edges. My wrists throbbed beneath my hand, still red-hot with pain. My body trembled—not from the cold, but from everything else.

Milo didn't speak. He didn't need to. His silence screamed louder than any of Wilt's commands.

I could feel his fury in the way he held me—rigid, controlled. But it was the control that scared me most. Milo rarely lost his temper… but when he did, it was never without cause.

Wilt flanked us now, a pace behind, his posture stiff. His presence was imposing, but not comforting. Not anymore.

Not after what I'd said. Not after what I'd asked of him.

Still, I could feel his eyes—watching me. Assessing. Not with doubt this time, but with something else. Anger. Guilt. Maybe both.

I didn't look back.

By the time we reached the King's wing, guards scrambled to clear the path. The polished floors echoed with boots, hurried movements, and low whispers.

"Open the doors. Now!"

Milo's voice cut through the air like a blade.

Two guards jumped, reaching for the handles to the King's chamber just as Captain Donovan appeared at the far end of the corridor, his expression tight with concern.

"What is it, Prince Milo?" Donovan asked, stepping forward, hand raised to temper the fury on my brother's face.

"We need our father," Milo hissed, his glare like daggers.

Donovan's eyes flicked to me—bloodied, bruised, and limp in Milo's arms. His gaze snapped to Wilt, alarm flashing across his features.

"Captain, what happened?"

Wilt stepped forward, posture rigid, forming a quiet shield between me and the stares closing in.

"Princess Kae'Dinah was attacked in the royal garden not long ago," he said, voice taut but steady. "She defended herself. Alone."

"Until reinforcements arrived?" Donovan asked quickly.

Wilt's jaw tensed. "There were no reinforcements."

Milo adjusted his grip on me, his arms tightening. "She nearly died."

Donovan frowned. "Who is the accused?" he asked, glancing between them.

Wilt didn't blink. "General Rove Marger."

The name struck like thunder.

Donovan's face fell. "No," he breathed, his composure cracking. "That can't be right."

Milo surged forward. "How dare you question what we saw—"

Two guards stepped between him and Donovan, halting his advance.

Donovan shook his head. "No, he was—he's trusted."

Milo's eyes burned. "He's not trusted anymore."

Wilt's voice cut through the rising tension. "The accused is in custody now. He's fighting for his life."

The weight of that settled over the corridor like smoke.

All eyes fell on me again, still in Milo's arms. I felt it in their silence—the confusion, the fear. And beneath it all... disbelief.

I straightened slightly and whispered, "Put me down."

"Kae—" Milo started.

"I can walk."

He hesitated, then slowly lowered me. My legs wobbled

but held. Wilt stepped in close, steadying me with a hand beneath my elbow.

Donovan finally found his voice. "How?"

"She brought him down," Wilt answered before I could speak. "On her own."

Disbelief flickered across Donovan's face, but he didn't argue.

"Now move," Milo barked. "We need to see our father."

He shoved open the grand double doors.

Wilt held out an arm to guide me but caught himself. Instead, he gestured silently, and I walked forward on my own, legs stiff but determined.

The King's office loomed before us—walls lined with tomes and banners, a carved table stretching through the center like a battlefield map. Green stones marked our forces. Red ones clustered in the northwest.

It was a map of Naedorn.

I shivered.

What were the red markers for? Were we at war?

"Children?" my father stood from his chair, concern overtaking his formal tone. "What brings you both up here so unexpectedly?" He set aside a stack of parchment, his brows knitting together as he took in our appearance.

My father crossed the room with long strides, the concern etched into his brow deepening with each step.

"Kae'Dinah…" His voice was softer now. Gentle. "What happened to you?"

Before I could answer, he reached for my face, brushing his thumb carefully along a streak of dried blood smeared on my cheek. His hand lingered, not with inspection—but with grief.

I felt it then. Not the weight of the crown or the authority in his voice. Just my father.

The man who once walked beside me and said I was his joy.

"I'm all right," I whispered, though we both knew it wasn't true.

He drew back slightly to study me, eyes scanning for injuries. "Who did this to you?"

Before I could respond, Milo stepped in. "General Marger," he said grimly. "She was in the garden—alone."

My father's mouth parted, disbelief flickering in his eyes.

"She asked to be alone," Milo added. "I didn't know. No one told me she went there…"

My father exhaled harshly and looked to Captain Wilt. "And you? How close were you?"

Wilt stiffened. "Not close enough."

My father's sharp gaze shifted, his expression cold and unyielding. "Why wasn't she protected, Captain? This could all have been avoided. Where were you?"

Wilt squared his shoulders, the weight of the accusation settling over him. I knew what was coming.

He was going to take the blame.

No.

"I know this, sire. I should have followed after—"

"I got away from him," I interrupted, the words spilling out before I could stop them. My friend could not take the fall for me.

"After breakfast, he escorted me to my room. I sent him to find Kelta while I waited, but I left before either of them returned. I didn't wait as he told me to. Captain Wilt and Milo found me in the halls," I admitted.

The King's hands curled into fists at his side.

"I tried to fight him off," I said quietly, forcing my voice past the knot in my throat. "But before he came—there was something else. Something in the garden. A shadow. A presence." I looked up at my father, willing him to believe me. "It disappeared. Then the general appeared. I don't know how, or why. But he was... wrong."

The King's gaze sharpened. "Wrong how?"

"He wasn't himself," I said, the words tumbling out now. "His eyes. His voice. He said things that made no sense. As if something had already taken hold of him."

My father's expression turned grave. He looked to Wilt. "What condition is he in?"

"Alive, last I heard," Wilt said, "but barely. She struck him with a fatal blow."

The King gave a short nod—but something in him shifted. His jaw flexed, and he turned his back for a moment, walking toward the map table as if to gather himself.

I followed his movement. He was quiet. Too quiet.

And then—

"She's lucky," my mother's voice cut in like silk over steel. She stepped forward, appearing from the shadows of the room, her tone falsely warm. "It's a miracle she wasn't taken from us. The general must have been under some sort of illness. Surely that would explain it."

I flinched, stepping away from her—but closer to the door.

Had she been there the entire time?

Anger coiled in my chest and gripped me with a sharp, unsettling fury.

My father didn't look at her, didn't nod, but I saw the way her words sank their teeth into his spine.

70

My breath caught.

Because I saw it.

The moment he began to retreat—not from the truth, but from me.

"What did you do?" my mother asked, her voice sharp and accusatory, her gaze piercing into me.

I blinked at her in disbelief. "What did I do?" I shot back, my voice rising. "I survived."

Her lips curled in disdain. "What if you provoked him? How do we know you didn't invite him closer—only to change your mind?"

The accusation struck like a blade.

"Does it matter?" I hissed, my voice trembling with fury. The pressure in my chest felt suffocating, and my wrist throbbed in time with the rage coursing through me.

"Please," my father murmured, looking toward my mother. Her eyes narrowed before she smirked and turned away, back to the window overlooking the city.

He turned back to me with a softer face, but his posture had changed—guarded now. Controlled.

"I'll question the general myself when the healers permit it," he said. "Until then, I want you watched."

"Watched?" Milo snapped.

"Protected," the King corrected. "She doesn't leave this wing without an escort, and that is final."

Milo exhaled hard through his nose but said nothing more.

"Captain Wilt," my father barked, his tone sharp. "Escort her to her chambers. Try not to lose her along the way. You're both dismissed."

Wilt's jaw ticked, a clear sign of his frustration. He nodded curtly, his expression unreadable. But as he moved past me to

71

open the door, I caught a glimpse of his face—stone-like and simmering. His scruffy jaw was clenched tightly, his features hard. I couldn't tell if his anger was aimed at himself... or at me.

He pushed the door open, holding it for me.

Before stepping through, I turned back to my father. Softly, I placed my wounded hand around his neck, pulling him into a hug. His strong arms wrapped around me, steady and comforting.

"I apologize for everything," he whispered into my hair. His voice carried the weight of guilt and sincerity. He didn't need to apologize like this. He didn't hurt me.

"It wasn't your fault, Father," I murmured into his chest. The fabric of his shirt was soft, carrying his familiar lemon scent. The smell pulled at old memories—sitting on his lap during military briefings, Milo and I clinging to him wherever he went. I'd shadowed him endlessly, neglecting the piano, sewing, and letter-writing lessons other girls embraced.

He glanced over his shoulder at my mother, who remained by the window, staring out at the city across the bay. Floos—the capital of Anima—stretched before her in splendor, yet her gaze seemed hollow. I couldn't tell if she was searching for something... or simply listening.

My father's eyes flicked back to mine, the faintest shadow of concern crossing his face. He leaned closer, lowering his voice.

"We'll discuss it later," he said. His words were firm, but there was something unspoken beneath them—an unease I hadn't noticed before.

I glanced once more at my mother, her silhouette stark

against the window's light.

Her stillness. Her hollow stare.

I had never felt such rage toward someone. Such heart-break.

My father's eyes met mine. He kissed my forehead softly and straightened, his attention shifting back to Wilt, who stood at rigid attention, eyes fixed straight ahead.

"Captain," my father said coolly, "what is your name and rank?"

"Captain Jahiel Wilt, sire. Second-rank captain," Wilt replied, his deep voice steady—though I recognized the rasp he had when he was near exhaustion. The dark circles beneath his eyes seemed deeper beneath my father's scrutiny.

"You're quite young for second rank, no?"

"Yes, sire. I am twenty-five. I was promoted quickly for my skill. I trained as a child."

"Nobility?"

"No, sire. Bastard-born," Wilt said without hesitation, though his head dipped slightly with the admission.

"Hm." My father narrowed his eyes.

He stepped closer to Wilt, erasing the space between them. My breath hitched—unintentional, but enough to draw his attention. He glanced at me briefly, then turned his focus back to Wilt. The intent to intimidate was unmistakable.

"Any further transgressions from you, Captain, will result in your demotion… or worse," he said, each word sharp as steel. "I mean anything. Your duty is to protect her"—he jabbed a finger in my direction without looking—"and only protect her. Do I make myself clear?"

Only protect her.

The tension strung between us wasn't as silent as I thought.

It pulsed.

"Yes, Your Majesty," Wilt answered, his voice tight.

Satisfied, my father stepped back. "Be wise, daughter. Go rest."

I nodded and exited the office.

I glanced at Wilt, but his focus remained forward, his jaw tight and movements mechanical. I turned and made my way down the corridor toward my chambers.

The thud of Wilt's boots followed close behind—steady, unrelenting. I didn't stop to greet or acknowledge anyone we passed.

My focus was singular.

Get to my room.

# Coils

*Megorna, five months before...*

S he said my power was too quiet.

"Power must speak, Megorna," Mother snapped. "It must sing when you walk into a room. Yours still whispers."

She pressed her palm to my sternum, fingers cool against my skin. "This—this softness inside you—that's her fault."

She didn't have to say her name. I knew who she meant. She always meant Kae'dinah.

But what she called softness, I had only ever known as something else... something not of this family.

Kae'dinah laughed like the sun cracked just for her. She listened when I whispered questions no one else would entertain. She remembered the names of the palace workers. She noticed when I was quiet for too long.

And sometimes... when she smiled at me, I felt like the world might be worth something after all.

I didn't know what that meant. Not exactly.

But I knew it mattered.

Still... I didn't stop the training. I never told Kae'dinah

about the chamber beneath the Queen's sanctum. About the way Mother poured oil on my skin and spoke in a foreign language until I shook with cold fire. About the voice I sometimes heard now when I closed my eyes—low and sweet and not mine.

"You were not born for shadows," Mother would whisper. "You were born to rule them."

But Kae'dinah… Kae'dinah was the one everyone watched. The one the Watchers watched as well, for reasons unclear. The one even Mother couldn't quite control.

And sometimes, in the quietest part of me, I wondered—

Was that why she hated her?

Did she envy her?

"Megorna!" my mother snapped. My head jerked toward her, fear rushing from my brain down to my spine.

"Are you listening, daughter?"

"Yes, ma'am. Always," I said, making sure to meet her gaze.

She began to pace again, her lips whispering those foreign words. The ones the shadows always answered.

The room grew colder. The edges of the chamber darkened. The shadows grew taller, thicker, until they loomed like cloaks hung from the ceiling.

My eyes widened as they began to tremble.

Then—my mother's hands. Warm. Wrapping around mine. Her thumbs stroked soft circles into my palms.

"These shadows will not hurt you, my precious girl," she whispered. "They only desire for you to wield them. To befriend them."

I looked up, watching them spiral above us, dancing like smoke along the stone ceiling.

I forced myself to calm—two deep breaths, eyes squeezed

shut.

"Of course, Mother," I murmured as I opened my eyes again.

But her nostrils flared.

Oh no.

She was upset.

I never wanted her upset with me. What had I done? Had she sensed it—my hesitation, my fear? The part of me that still reached away from the shadows?

I straightened, clearing my throat to fix it.

"Mother—"

"We're done for today," she cut in, voice cool and final. "I'll allow you to rest before dinner. Go. Relax, my girl."

She reached up and cupped my chin. Then, with a flick of her hand, the shadows vanished—dispersing in an instant at her command.

She was power.

And I had disappointed her.

I hated disappointing her.

I left the chamber in silence, the chill of the shadows still clinging to my skin like frost. My steps were quiet, but inside, I was loud—spinning, unraveling, trying to remember how to breathe without fear sitting on my chest.

The guards barely glanced up as I passed—No one ever did after leaving that chamber. They didn't see the tremble in my hands, or the shame crawling up my throat.

When I stepped into our shared chambers, I was hit by warmth. Amber candlelight danced against the stone walls. A soft rose scent floated from the oil lamp near the hearth. Kae'dinah was already inside, curled on the velvet window seat like something sacred, untouched—her book cracked gently in her lap.

Her face was bare, soft. Her hair was down—long, black coils tumbling over her shoulders like they belonged to the pages of the story she read. Her eyes flicked up when she heard me.

They always flicked up when I entered.

"You okay?" she asked, her voice a hush just above the crackling fire. She slid a ribbon between the pages and closed the book gently.

I nodded too quickly. A habit.

She studied me for a moment, then opened her arms slightly—silent invitation.

"Come here."

I didn't even pretend to resist.

I crossed the room and sat beside her. The moment our shoulders touched, I felt something shift inside me. As if the cold from earlier began to melt at the edges.

"I just started this one," she murmured. "It's about a girl who has to marry a prince but ends up falling for his younger brother instead. Very scandalous."

I smiled despite myself.

She nudged my side with her elbow. "Lie down if you want. Like before."

It was always like this after hard days. After failed lessons or long lectures. After tears we pretended we didn't shed.

We never said, "I need you."

We just… did this.

I sat on the cushion, rested a leg underneath me, then she turned to rest her head in my lap. Lying on her back, the book hovering above her head.

She kept reading, and I reached for her hair.

Thick coils spilled across her shoulders and down her back—soft, inky black, endless. I twirled one gently around my finger. Let it go. Twirled another. It was the same rhythm I used when we were children, after her piano lessons left her in tears. After I failed another test. After Mother sighed with that sharp disappointment neither of us could ever quite escape.

Kae'dinah's voice continued, smooth and warm, as she read about a girl who wasn't supposed to fall in love—but did anyway.

Her words washed over me.

I focused on the feel of her hair, the curve of her spine, the rise and fall of her breathing. She felt safe like this. We both did. In our own little world. One where love wasn't sharp, and power didn't twist inside you like a blade.

And yet...

As she read, curled against me like she always had, her voice drifting between sentences and sighs—

I wondered what would happen when I wasn't the one playing with her hair...

But wielding the shadows.

# Chapter 10

I stopped just before my door, hearing the commotion of Kelta and the other handmaids preparing for my arrival. My hand hovered over the handle, but I turned, needing to face him.

The hallway stretched empty, everyone else off performing their duties. We were alone.

Captain Wilt's eyes were fixed on the ground, his rigid posture betraying the storm of emotions simmering beneath. Anxiety. Frustration. Regret.

"Jahiel," I said softly, reaching for him.

"Do not." He raised his hands, stepping back as if my touch might burn him.

"Please, look at me," I begged, my voice barely above a whisper.

For a moment, he obeyed. His eyes lifted to mine, smoldering with emotions he couldn't allow himself to voice. Then he glanced away, jaw tight, forcing the words back down.

I scoffed, letting out a frustrated breath before turning to the door. "Follow me in."

I opened the door, stepping into the chaos of the room. The maids bustled about, their chatter fading into silence as they bowed at my entrance.

Although three of them were present, I addressed only Kelta. "Kelta, Captain Wilt needs tea—something to keep him alert and awake."

She nodded briskly, motioning to another maid, who quickly scurried out of the room.

I looked at him with eyes pleading to pick up on how I planned to empty my room. He nodded in response. We were too good at that, reading each other. Knowing what one would say without saying it.

"Have you eaten?" Wilt's voice cut through the quiet.

I hesitated, placing a hand over my stomach. The adrenaline coursing through me had muted my hunger, and it truly hadn't occurred to me that I actually hadn't eaten all day.

Wilt turned to Kelta. "Could you send the others for a spread of food? A plate for the Princess and one for myself."

"Of course, Captain," she replied cheerfully, unaware of the tension between us. She directed the remaining maids to fetch the food, leaving only Kelta.

There was a subtle pause. Only the sound of Kelta preparing bandages to clean my wounds.

"Kelta," I spoke. "We need the room for a moment."

Her brows furrowed as she glanced between Wilt and me, and then around at the empty room.

"No," she said flatly.

"Kelta, please. It's nothing absurd, I promise. You can wait in my private room. We just need to discuss the attack."

The mention of the attack softened her briefly; word of the attack traveled fast. Her hesitation lingered, though.

Finally, she sighed. "A few minutes," she said. "The walk

81

from the kitchen will take some time." She glanced over her shoulder. "Your tea should be arriving soon, though."

"Thank you," I murmured.

Kelta turned on her heel and shut the door to my private room behind her, leaving the room silent once more.

I turned to Wilt. "Speak freely."

"About what?" he snapped. His voice was low, sharp.

"About everything," I said, trying to stay calm—but the ache in my chest made my words brittle. "We couldn't speak before."

A bitter laugh escaped him. "Where do you want me to start? That I let you roam the castle alone? That you were almost killed? That the general's dying—or awaiting execution? That you took the blame for something I should've prevented and I was nearly stripped of my rank?" He shook his head. "Is that everything, Princess?"

"You weren't demoted," I muttered, frustrated. I stepped closer.

"This," he said, gesturing toward my wounded hands, "is my fault."

"No," I snapped, firmer this time. "I told you to leave. I made that decision. The general made his. Do not take what isn't yours, Jahiel."

His hands clenched at his sides as he took a step forward. Two strides and he was close—too close. The room shrank around us. His scent—leather, sweat, something warm and familiar—wrapped around me.

"You don't understand," he said, voice rough.

I could see the storm behind his eyes. Guilt. Grief. Fear.

"I almost lost you, Kae'Dinah."

He raised a hand—not forceful, but unsure—then cupped

82

my cheek like it was a question. His other hand brushed the nape of my neck, gentle, grounding.

I didn't move.

His thumb traced slow circles along my skin. "I should've stayed. I knew better."

"You couldn't have known," I whispered. My palms came up to his chest, more to steady myself than him. "It wasn't your fault."

"It doesn't matter," he said, leaning closer. His forehead rested gently against mine. "I won't leave you again."

His words sent a ripple through me—comforting and dangerous. He wasn't just a guard. He was my friend.

But we weren't what he wanted us to be.

"Jahiel…" I murmured.

"Please, Princess." His voice caught on the title.

The air between us felt like glass—fragile, one breath away from breaking.

"I forgive you," I said quietly. "But we move forward. We carry it together, or not at all."

He met my eyes. And for a moment, I saw everything he wanted to say—all the things he hadn't, all the things I couldn't give.

His lips hovered too close.

And then—my father's warning echoed, cold and sharp: *"Only protect her. Nothing more."*

I stepped back, breaking the tether between us. The space felt loud with absence.

"I won't be the reason you lose everything," I said, voice trembling. "And I won't give anyone more reason to doubt either of us."

He didn't speak, but the pain in his eyes said enough.

Just then, Kelta entered quietly. She glanced between us, reading the air before crossing to me.

"Come, miss. I've drawn a bath. It'll help with the pain," she said gently, placing her hand just above my wounds.

I nodded, letting her guide me away.

As I stepped into the doorway of my private chambers, I turned once more.

Wilt's gaze was fixed on me—still, unreadable, unwavering.

\* \* \*

The sun sank behind the western mountain, signaling that dinner would soon summon us. I sighed, my fingers brushing the edge of the book in my hands—just three pages left. Around the room, Kelta and Meg's maid, Daph, moved about lighting the lanterns, casting a soft glow against the fading daylight.

Megorna had skipped her afternoon lessons to sit with me after the incident. And that's exactly what she did—just sat. She'd grabbed her sewing things and perched across from me without asking a single question. At one point, we requested the maids bring us a tray of fruits and sweets, which they did. That's when we found our rhythm: I curled up with a book, and Meg worked on her embroidery.

Now, a few hours later, she sat across from me, squinting in concentration as she pulled her sewing closer to her face. She'd stitched a dramatic "K" onto a piece of cloth—one I was certain would belong to me. Her tongue peeked out in focus as she worked.

"Do you think your tongue will help you get it right this time?" I teased.

Her tongue slipped back into her mouth, and she shot me a vulgar gesture.

I gasped dramatically, throwing a wrapped hand over my forehead. "Oh no! Did the *Jewel* of Anima just flash me an inappropriate finger?"

She giggled, repeating the gesture. "I believe she did."

We both laughed, but then her eyes drifted to my injuries. The joy in her face dimmed, replaced by a pensive look.

"What happened?" she asked, her voice softer now.

I sighed, a long, tired breath. "I was attacked."

"I *know* that—the whole palace knows that. But, Kae'Dinah… you were nearly killed. And, you nearly killed him."

"I did kill him…" I thought back to the message Captain Wilt delivered earlier with the trays of sweets: the general's bleeding was controlled, but his execution was scheduled for dawn on the fifth day—two days from now.

"That's not funny, Kae'Dinah," she snapped.

"I'm not laughing, Meg."

"You just say it in this… sassy way, and it makes me uncomfortable."

"Oh, I'm sorry," I said, my voice sharper now. "The way I deal with trauma makes you uncomfortable. How dare I?" I pulled the book up to cover my face, needing something between us—anything.

She was quiet for a moment. I could hear her fingers dragging lightly over the threads of her embroidery cloth.

"I'm sorry," she said at last. "That was insensitive."

I lowered the book and squinted at her. "Did you just

apologize?"

"Kae'Dinah, don't make this a thing," she groaned, trying to stifle a smile. "Or I'll never do it again."

Her playfulness cracked the heaviness in the air. She tossed her sewing aside and dropped onto the couch beside me, stealing the book from my lap before I could react.

"Hey!"

"You were finished," she said, completely unbothered.

I clicked my tongue, but she was right—I had just closed the final page.

I smacked my lips in protest, but she was right—I had just finished.

"Where did your reading take you this time?" she asked, her tone curious.

Grinning, I launched into the story: a war in the Northlands, the harsh winters, and how the people survived such brutal climates. By the time I finished, her expression was flat, void of enthusiasm.

"You could at least *pretend* to be interested," I said, nudging her shoulder lightly.

"Oh, yes, I'm sorry. I forgot." She leaned forward dramatically, grinning widely in mock interest.

"You're a nuisance."

"You love me," she trilled.

She wasn't wrong. As much as she annoyed me, I loved her. It was private moments like this that cemented our bond. It was in public, particularly under our mother's gaze, that the cracks between us grew wider.

Our laughter faded, and the room grew quiet again. Meg turned toward a nearby lantern, her gaze fixed on the flickering flame.

"What's on your mind, *child*?" I asked.

"I am a woman," she said, tilting her nose in the air.

"Please. You're seventeen," I shot back.

"Mother was seventeen when she married and had Milo."

"Are you looking to marry anytime soon?" I asked, teasing.

When she didn't respond, I glanced at her. "Meg... do you want to marry?"

"Yes!" she squeaked, her voice high with excitement. "How could you not desire it?"

"I just... never thought about it." It was a lie, of course. I thought about it constantly—about who my parents might arrange for me, whether someone I found intriguing would ever be deemed suitable. But only nobility could marry into the monarchy. My mind flashed back to Father's question to Wilt.

I hadn't meant to think of him. But my mind wandered anyway—back to Father's question to Wilt, to the tension in the room that hadn't belonged to me.

I didn't know what it was that had shifted between us. Captain Wilt was constant. Steady. Expected. The warmth of a fire—reliable, even comforting. But lately... that warmth had lingered too long. Like a stare held one second too many. Like the way his voice softened when he said my name.

I wasn't naive. I knew what it meant.

His feelings for me were more than *friendship*.

But I didn't want that.

Whatever affection stirred in him was not returned. Not in the way he might hope. And maybe I'd been cruel in not naming it sooner. Maybe it was easier not to name it at all.

"Well, you should," Meg said, shoving me gently. "You're not that young."

"Stop that," I said, swatting her hands away as I stood and stretched my arms above my head. My evening dress—a soft cream—mirrored Meg's in cut, but not in color. Hers was a modest blue, covering her arms and neck, while mine left my shoulders bare.

"Where are you going?" she asked.

"To the library for another book. All your talk of marriage has me in the mood for a good love story."

"Have you not read them all yet?"

"Maybe I have. And if I have, I'll read them all again," I said with a smirk, grabbing my satchel. "Nothing else for me to do in this gods-forsaken castle now that I'm to be watched."

She shook her head as I dipped into a mocking curtsy. Meg clapped slowly and deliberately, pulling a laugh from my throat.

"Wow," she said, grinning. "I didn't know you had such manners in you. That was impressive."

"Please. I mastered that before you could even run," I scoffed. "Walk with me?"

"No, dinner's soon, and I can't miss it." Her head lowered again as she returned to the cloth she'd been stitching for me. Without looking up, she added, "Father said you're excused, if you'd like to be."

"Oh, I'd *like* to be," I said, and we both chuckled softly. The weight of the day, and the tight reins our parents held over us, pressed in again—quiet but ever-present.

I backed toward the door, grabbing my brown satchel—the one that held both my studies and my comforts. "Thank you for spending time with me, Meg."

"You're most welcome," she said, her smile soft and warm, but quiet. Her eyes lingered on me. A subtle sheen glimmered in their corners.

"I'm glad you're alive, Kae'Dinah," she whispered. "I'm not sure what I'd do without you."

I sighed, her words wrapping around me like a shawl. "You won't ever have to wonder," I said. "Because I'll be right here. I love you."

"I love you, sister," Megorna replied, and I stepped back through the door.

# Chapter 11

I stepped out of my chambers, expecting to find a familiar set of brown eyes waiting for me. Instead, I was met with piercing blue. Captain Nagel,

He was an older man in his late thirties, and he stood just as tall as the others in our guard.

"Do you need anything, Highness?" he asked.

"Oh, I thought Captain Wilt would be here," I said, careful to keep my tone steady.

"No, we switched earlier. He'd been up and needed to rest," Nagel responded.

"Of course," I replied, sharing a small smile. It was good that he was finally getting the rest he needed. "Could you escort me to the library?"

"Yes, Your Highness." Captain Nagel stood, sliding the familiar wooden stool back against the wall before motioning for me to lead the way.

"Thank you, Captain," I said with a polite smile, stepping into the corridor.

The curtains along the windows were drawn tight, muting the morning light. Warm lamplight glowed against the stone walls, softening the silence between us.

We passed Milo's quarters. His guard stood at attention,

but when I nodded in greeting, his return was stiff—too sharp, too quick. The kind of gesture meant to fulfill duty, not respect.

My chest tightened.

That man's jaw was clenched so tightly I feared it might snap. His glare didn't hide what he felt: anger. Contempt.

I had nearly killed a respected member of the royal guard. Perhaps they all had ties to General Marger. Friends. Brothers-in-arms. I hadn't stopped to think what he meant to *them*—only what he had become to *me*.

Captain Nagel seemed to notice too. As we walked, he shifted slightly to my side, his voice low and steady. "Don't let their silence trouble you, Princess," he said. "You did what you had to do. And while others may not say it—I will. I'm proud of your strength. And I'll make sure you're protected."

I didn't respond at first. But the words anchored something loose inside me.

He gave a soft grunt, clearing his throat as we rounded the next corridor. "I believe I saw a few new books being shelved in the library a few days ago," he added casually, his tone easing into something gentler. "Might be worth seeing if any caught your interest."

"Really?" I asked, glancing back at him as we walked.

Captain Nagel had always felt like a distant uncle—warm and loyal, though occasionally scatterbrained when it came to anything outside military affairs. His stories of battle strategy had once filled the lull of long travel days, offering a kind of puzzle I always looked forward to. He'd pull me aside, challenge me with impossible scenarios, ask what route I'd take or how I'd respond to an ambush.

Mother said it was a waste of my time. But Father—Father

always smiled at my answers. He never praised me the way he did Milo, not aloud. But when my plans made more sense than my brother's, the warmth in his eyes said enough.

"Yes, I know you like that sort of thing," he replied. "But there are no new history books or anything."

"I suppose romance books will have to do tonight. Do you know where they were imported from?"

"Malcert and Aatier, I believe," he said casually.

He didn't need to guess. Those were the only two countries we ever traded with. The Queen had banned imports from the rest—only our allies were considered clean. Only those who shared our beliefs were worth dealing with. The others, scattered across the continent, were lost. Or so my parents claimed.

Scarcity plagued their lands. Corruption ran through their streets.

Mother often spoke of them with a pitying tone, but always with certainty—none of their filth would ever breach our borders. My tutors warned that even reading their texts could bring something worse than death. That was why the borders were locked. That was why only Malcert and Aatier were welcome.

But what truly was worse than death... when we were the ones issuing it?

I knew the rhetoric. I'd heard it all my life. But I had my doubts.

If these nations were as broken as we were told—why were they so silent? If they suffered so deeply, why didn't they reach out? We were too close—river to river, coast to coast—for their need not to touch us. No famine or collapse stays behind one fence forever.

I'd studied every map of the continent I could find. Committed the lines, the markers, the borders to memory. I knew Naedorn. Every sigil.

Aatier, the fox.

Malcert, the bear.

Syx, the whale.

Valdeen, the wolf.

Jouse, the cobra.

Purmee, the barracuda.

And Anima—our home—the eagle.

I used to repeat them like a prayer. Now, they surfaced on their own—unbidden but constant. They clung to me like tar, like everything else I read. I didn't know why they stayed with me, only that they always did.

We turned a final corner, and the scent of parchment and old leather drifted out to meet me. The library.

By day, it belonged to scholars, healers, and nobles. But at night... it was mine.

Silent. Warm. A place where knowledge didn't lie to me. Still, tonight, even the stillness unsettled me.

"Do you know what you're looking for?" Nagel's voice boomed beside me, sharp and sudden against the quiet.

I jumped.

He reached out, squeezing my shoulder with a remorseful expression. "I'm sorry, Princess. That was too loud."

"It's fine," I said quickly, forcing a breath out. "I was... just lost in thought."

But I wasn't fine. Not really.

My eyes darted across the shadowed corners of the hallway, scanning for movement even when I knew there's be none. The echo of General Marger's voice still clung to my memory—his weight on top of me, his eyes, hollow and black.

Then there was the face that mirrored mine. The one that disappeared.

A flicker of nausea stirred in my chest, but I swallowed it down.

"I promise you're safe," Nagel said gently, noticing the tension in my posture. "No one will lay a hand on you. Not while I'm near."

I nodded once, grateful for the assurance but unable to speak around the lump forming in my throat.

"Just a love story tonight," I murmured, trying to keep my voice light. "Nothing else."

"I understand," he said, his tone softening. When we reached the doors, he pushed open the stained-glass panels with ease and retrieved a lantern from the wall. "I'll light the way."

He moved with careful purpose, using the lantern to ignite the specialized library lamps—each encased in glass to keep flame from reaching the shelves. Their warm glow filled the cavernous space slowly, pushing back the dark.

The scent of parchment and ink drifted toward me. Familiar. Calming. Still… I stayed close to Nagel's side.

The library usually felt like a second home. But tonight, even its silence had teeth.

"I believe the love stories are on row eleven," I said after a moment, my voice steadier now.

Nagel turned to me with a nod. "I trust your directions more than my own," he said with a smile, his presence grounding me in a way I hadn't realized I needed.

And so we walked forward—him with his lantern, and me

with my heartbeat finally beginning to slow.

Row six.

Row nine.

Row eleven.

I turned down the aisle, raising the lantern to scan the spines. A bright red book caught my eye. Its velvet cover was luxurious beneath my fingers, and I read the title aloud.

"*Forbidden Love?*"

I chuckled. "What are they teaching their people in Aatier?"

"They have very... open morals over there," Nagel replied with a slight smirk.

Before I could respond, a loud crash echoed from the library's entrance. We both froze. Nagel's head whipped toward the sound, the light from his lantern straining to reach the far end of the room. His posture shifted immediately—battle-hardened—and he drew his sword.

"Do you have your daggers?" he asked urgently.

I nodded, crouching to pull the twin blades from the hidden sheath beneath my dress. The ones I had tucked away after Kelta dressed me and cleaned my wounds.

I made a silent promise in that moment: I would never be unarmed again.

"Good." His tone was firm. "Stay here. I'll check the entrance. If someone's here—scream, and I'll come back. If I don't return... don't hesitate to kill. Do you understand, Princess?"

"Yes," I whispered, gripping the daggers as tightly as fear gripped me.

Nagel disappeared into the shadows, moving swiftly and silently toward the entrance. His lantern cast eerie silhouettes along the shelves, then vanished as he rounded the far corner.

And I was alone.

The silence that followed was deafening. Every small creak, every shifting shadow seemed louder, heavier. The once-comforting library now pressed in around me.

My eyes darted to the corners, scanning for movement even though I knew—hoped—there'd be none. But the echo of General Marger's voice clung to me still. His weight pinning me. His hollow, black eyes.

And the other face—the one that mirrored mine—gone in an instant.

I tightened my grip on the daggers, the cool steel grounding me. The library flickered with warm light, but even that couldn't chase away the chill crawling up my neck.

What if someone was after me?

What if Nagel didn't come back?

What if *she* returned?

My chest tightened. I shouldn't have left my room.

The hairs on my arms stood on end—just like in the garden. I turned instinctively, scanning the shadows behind me.

Nothing.

Then, like a blanket, something unseen settled over me.

Not heavy. Not cruel. But... calming.

My body straightened. My breath slowed. I should've panicked—but I couldn't. Something willed my fear away.

*What is this?*

*"Kae'dinah."*

The voice whispered my name, soft and steady. It moved through the room like a breeze through trees—unseen, but felt.

I stepped back from the sound. Fear tried to rise again,

climbing up my spine.

*"My child, come to me."*

My child?

I froze. The voice again. Gentle. Familiar. This one reached *through* something.

My child.

Something in those words tugged at my chest like a thread. As if part of me already knew it. Against every instinct—I stepped toward it.

Daggers raised.

Heart pounding.

In the dim lantern light, I caught the faint glow of Nagel's lamp further down the main aisle. He was moving steadily, checking each row. To my left, his light bobbed faintly in the dark. To my right, shadows stretched deep into the library's vast expanse.

A soft wind brushed beneath my chin, tilting my head gently to the right.

*"This way,"* it whispered.

A strange warmth bloomed in my chest—like a fire catching in dry kindling. My legs carried me forward, step by step.

*What am I doing?* I should be running. I should be terrified. But I wasn't.

The voice was alien... and yet familiar. A stranger to my ears, but somehow a citizen to my heart.

It felt more right than anything had ever felt in my life.

I didn't know how to explain it. Couldn't justify it.

But moving with that voice in my ears felt truer than any plea to the gods.

An inexplicable peace settled over me, wrapping itself

around my shoulders like a warm cloak.

It made no sense—yet I *knew* I would be unharmed.

I lowered one dagger and slid the red book into my satchel. Though my instincts felt still, I kept the second blade in hand.

I wasn't foolish enough to let my guard fall entirely.

"*Stop*," the voice whispered—sharp and urgent. "I am here. Find me. Quickly."

I lifted my lantern, taking cautious steps forward.

Row fifteen.

I hesitated, heart pounding as I crept another step ahead.

"Quickly… find me," the voice sang—lilting and persistent.

I turned sharply into the aisle, swinging the lantern left and right. Shadows danced wildly across the shelves, but nothing revealed itself.

Then my mind slowed.

Whatever this is… it's making requests of me. But how do I know it's not another trick? Another mirror?

"Show yourself," I whispered, desperate now. "Help me find you."

"*As you request,*" the voice hissed.

A soft *thud* echoed behind me.

I spun around.

There, on the lowest shelf, lay a brown, worn book. My eyes darted down the aisle, searching for anyone—or *anything*—watching. But I was alone.

I had to be alone. I heard no steps. I saw no other lights. I was alone… right?

Cautiously, I crouched. The book's spine read *Tried by Fire*, with strange symbols etched beneath the words—symbols I didn't recognize.

"*Hide me,*" the voice whispered again.

Before I could react, a violent wind tore through the aisle. It snatched the breath from my lungs.

My hair whipped across my face.

The lantern's flame vanished—extinguished in an instant—leaving only darkness.

I opened my mouth to scream, but the wind swallowed the sound.

My hands shot up to shield my face, my neck—anything exposed.

I crouched low, trying to withstand the storm of it—

Then everything stopped.

"Princess."

Nagel's voice—familiar, real—cut through the silence like a blade.

I gasped for air, chest heaving. The world felt off-kilter, spinning.

My lantern lay on the floor beside me.

My daggers were back in their sheaths.

And in my hands...

I clutched the velvet red book.

The love story I had picked up earlier.

Nagel appeared at the end of the aisle, his calm demeanor starkly out of place. "It's secure," he said. "A metal flower vase tipped over near the entrance. Spilled some water, but no harm done." He looked at me, his brow furrowing at my pale expression. "Are you all right, Princess?"

"You saw no one?" I asked faintly.

"No one," he replied. Concern weaved between the aging lines of his face. "Are you sure you're okay?"

"Right," I murmured, crouching to collect a few random books and shove them into my satchel to hide my confusion.

As I opened the bag, my breath caught in my throat.

The brown, worn cover of Tried by Fire stared back at me.

"What is going on?" I whispered, frozen.

"Do you need help?" Nagel asked, his voice pulling me back to the present.

*"Hide me,"* the voice whispered again, this time within my mind. It rang like a warning, urgent and insistent.

I jumped.

"Oh," I gasped, slamming the satchel shut. "No, I've got it." Rising too quickly, dizziness swept over me, but I steadied myself.

Nagel's brow lifted slightly, but he nodded and motioned toward the central aisle. "This way."

I followed, casting one last glance over my shoulder at the rows of books behind me.

My eyes caught the carved sign above the aisle I'd just left. *Row Eleven.*

My stomach dropped.

*No... how am I back here?*

I turned slowly to the right, peering down the long corridor of bookshelves.

"How?" I whispered.

Nagel's voice was calm but alert. "Princess, do you see someone?"

"No, I just..." I faltered.

*What do I say? That the library rearranged itself around me? That I ended up somewhere I hadn't returned to?*

I said nothing more, only clutched my satchel tighter and walked toward the grand doors.

Nagel didn't press me. He walked quietly at my side, but I knew he saw it—the tension in my shoulders, the unsteadiness in my steps. When we reached my room, I nodded to him.

"Goodnight," I murmured, voice thin.

"Goodnight." His brows drew together slightly in concern. "If you need anything at all tonight, I'm right here."

His gaze held mine—steady, protective.

"I know," I whispered.

He gave me a warm smile, then turned away as the door closed behind me.

I stepped inside.

Kelta was already there, bent over a golden tray. Her hands moved with practiced grace as she rearranged a platter of fruit beside two steaming bowls of stew and a gleaming glass of wine. The firelight danced across her tightly braided hair, casting soft shadows against the stone walls.

She glanced up as I entered, her expression bright. "What did you find this time in the library?"

I froze.

Her words felt like a test.

Like a dare.

What did I find?

My mouth opened, but the truth snagged somewhere behind my teeth.

That book. That voice. That wind. Had I imagined it? Had it truly spoken? Moved me? Placed something in my hands I don't remember picking up?

My fingers flexed, feeling the weight of the book still in my satchel—solid and real.

"Princess?" Kelta's voice cut through the fog. I startled slightly.

She straightened, frowning. "Did you hear me?"

101

"I... I'm fine," I managed, forcing a smile that didn't reach my eyes. "Just tired."

Her concern didn't fade. "What did you find, though? You always bring back treasures from those dusty shelves."

I hesitated, "A new love story from Aatier. It must've arrived a few days ago."

Her expression softened. "Oh, that sounds lovely. We can read it together after dinner." She uncovered the bowls. "The kitchen made rabbit stew tonight. Smells wonderful."

"I think I'll eat in my room." I avoided her gaze as I made my way toward my private room. "I'm exhausted, but I promise I won't start the story without you."

Her disappointment flickered across her face, but she nodded. "Alright, if you're sure." She gathered the tray, removing her own bowl of stew. "I'll wait until tomorrow, then."

As she placed the tray on my desk, I stepped out of my boots. Then removed my daggers.

Kelta sighed. "I hate those things."

"My daggers?" I asked absently.

"Yes." She laughed softly.

*"Hide me."*

The voice rippled through the room, soft yet undeniable. I froze, a chill snaking down my spine.

"Kae'dinah?" Kelta asked, her voice distant as I turned abruptly, just in time to see her reaching for my satchel.

"No!" The word tore from my throat as I lunged forward, snatching the bag from her hands.

"Oh!" She stumbled back, clutching her chest. "My apologies! I didn't mean—"

"You can leave now." My voice was tight, sharper than I'd

intended. "I'll manage on my own tonight."

"Princess, let me at least—"

"Kelta, you're dismissed," I said, softer this time but still firm. Her eyes searched mine for a long moment before she bowed and left the room.

When I heard the final door of our shared living space close, I collapsed into the chair by the fire.

Alone.

I clutched the satchel against my chest. My heart pounded as I slowly opened it, the strange book within seeming heavier than before. The brown leather was worn, ripped, and frayed along the edges. The title was handwritten, not printed. I ran my fingers over the parchment—old, browned with age—and opened to the first page.

At the bottom, in a scrawling hand, were words that made my blood run cold:

*Shaunsa of Temoi, son of Syx.*

I gasped, flinging the fragile book across the floor. It landed just beside my bed. My chest rose and fell so hard I had to place a hand over my racing heart to calm myself.

Son of Syx? The Syx? One of the first mortal men? No, it couldn't be. That book would have to be hundreds of years old.

Scrambling to my feet, I stumbled toward the book, nearly tripping in my haste. Kneeling, I picked it up carefully, examining the edges and silently cursing myself for throwing it. To my relief, it was intact.

I sank to the floor, legs folded beneath me, and opened the book again. My hands trembled as I turned the pages.

The next contained handwritten words—no, a letter:

*Dear brother or sister, or whomever finds and reads this,*

*I have been instructed to write to you. To share with you the journey I am to take. A journey that I'm currently on alone. But I have been told that I won't be for long. As I prepare to embark on the journey, I pray that Highest assists me with every endeavor. I also pray that however, or whenever, my words find you, you are in a better state than I. Until our next write...*

*Highest, ignite what sleeps within me. Burn away all that is false. Lead me, and I will follow—even into the fire.*

*3 A.R. – Shaunsa of Temoi, son of Syx.*

3 A.R.?

I lightly traced the imprint of the words, my breath catching. I had never seen that abbreviation before, not in all the books I'd read—history, military strategy, romance, adventure. I flipped to the next page. Blank. Then another. Also blank.

"What?" I said, standing abruptly and pacing the cool floor of my room. "This is it?"

I turned back to my bed, my gaze fixed on the satchel. The question spilled out of me, desperate and unbidden: "Is this it? Is this what you wanted me to find?"

Silence.

I flipped through the pages again, frantic, but there was nothing more. No answers. Just blank parchment.

"Until our next write," I murmured, my voice echoing faintly in the room. My fingers tightened around the book.

"Highest, ignite what sleeps within me. Burn away all that is false. Lead me, and I will follow—even into the fire."

The words came effortlessly, like breath I didn't know I'd been holding. As they left my lips, a strange warmth unfurled in my chest—a calm so deep it spread through my limbs like balm, chasing tension away. I placed a hand over my heart, stunned by the sensation.

Then the air changed. Thickened.

The silence was no longer empty, but full.

Charged.

Shadows recoiled, as though the firelight had swelled with new life. My breath caught. It only lasted a moment, a flicker—

But something had shifted.

And I felt it.

My hand trembled as I clutched the book to my chest, heart hammering.

"I don't understand," I whispered to the empty room.

The calm didn't leave—it sank deeper. My body, once alert, now felt impossibly heavy. As though whatever had just happened had taken something in return. Not painfully. Not cruelly. Just... necessarily.

Like it borrowed from me.

A yawn broke through my lips, uninvited.

I rubbed my eyes, the book still clutched to my chest. My feet carried me to the bed without thought. The journal dropped beside the pillow, the covers pulled around me

before I could even reason through the movement.
   Whatever had happened,
   Could wait.
   Sleep took me before the fear could return.

# Temple of Cado

*Amias, two months before...*

A light breeze from the mountains whipped around the prominent pillars of the temple's entrance. I leaned forward onto the stone-railed balcony overlooking the city's lights twinkling in the distance. The scents of pine and foliage ruffled my nose. Cado, the city hidden in the mountainside of the West Realmwall, felt unusually calm.

My mouth extended in an exhausted yawn. I was tired. Not just physically but mentally and... emotionally. I sighed. The space above my lungs felt strangely hollow. I regretted waking up early to spar with Jon. I didn't know he would come at me with everything he had this morning. The training was brutal but necessary. I stood straight, stretching my aching limbs toward the domed stone ceilings.

The foyer of The Holy Place was calm and eerily empty. Cool air filled the space around. The temperature vastly contrasted with the warm, humid air I had just left a few moments before. Cado's Holy Place was carved into the side of a mountain.

I pivoted on my feet to scan the room again.

No one was here.

My eyes continued to search the space. I walked away from the railing. The foyer's stone floors clanked below my filthy boots. I was covered in sweat and dirt. My all-black fighting leathers exposed my arms. Dust coated the coils of my black, wool hair. I stood out amongst the clean gray walls and shiny stone floors.

My eyes roamed around the room until they snagged on the carved foot of something large. I craned my neck upward to look at the entirety of the piece. The exposed rock looked as if an artist had chiseled away an image of a Guardian; it was massive. I took a few steps toward the guardian on the wall and craned my head back to admire the craftsmanship of the sculpture.

My mother loved guardians.

She'd paint them and decorate the halls of our living quarters with their beauty. She'd say that they'd visit her in her dreams. She told me stories of their diversity and painted every shade and encounter.

My throat bobbed as I gulped down the reality of the thoughts.

I would never see another new portrait of those guardians again.

I heard the small taps of footsteps approaching me from the northern hallway. The steps were light and small. I knew it was a more petite woman before I saw her. Long ago, my father had noticed this gift that Highest had blessed me with, the gift of heightened senses and discerning people. He taught me how to use it, and it helped me become the warrior I'd always dreamt of being.

She cleared her throat, "Prince Harth," the petite veiled woman whispered from beside me, staring up at me while I continued to gape at the guardian. My eyes slid to her briefly before fixating back on the artwork.

"This carving was created over 260 years ago. The sculptor was a member of The Blessed of Lana. She was reported to have carvings in cities like Floos, Por, Temoi, Scala, and even Ellarum. I'm unsure if his carvings are still erected in most of those places."

Ellarum. It's been months since I've seen it.

The mention of where I was born caused me to turn my attention back to the woman. Her face was concealed by a cream-colored veil, with only her brown eyes visible. The cream fabric covered her from her head to her toes. I couldn't tell her age, but I saw no wrinkles or creases on her face; she could be reasonably young by that view alone. A tight coil of dark brown hair peeked from the side of her veil.

I glanced at her again; the contrast was vast. I towered over her by at least a foot.

"I don't think I ever noticed anything this incredible at the Holy Place in Ellarum." My low voice rumbled through the space, causing her to step back. She stared down at the floor bashfully.

"It's there, Your Highness. You'd need only to look up when you return home. It is there," she chimed. Her voice was sure but shy.

I smirked, nodding, "I'll do just that."

"This way," she sang and pivoted towards a narrow hallway. I slid my hands into the familiar resting place of my pockets and strode down the hall after her.

The halls were lined with candles, and the melted wax

109

dripped down the sides of the white stone walls, which had years and years of build-up. As if they just continued to stack years and years' worth of fresh candles upon one another. My mother had visited this Holy Place many times. Of all the locations, Cado was her favorite. I'd never visited with her in the city where she grew up. I never could, as I was constantly training with the army. Constantly going to classes taught on strategy and history. Many invites were unintentionally ignored.

Invites I'd never have the opportunity to accept or decline again.

The further we moved down the hall, the less light from outside illuminated the space. Soon, the only light was that of candles.

I glanced around.

We had been walking for some time.

Coming here alone... had that been a stupid idea? I nervously cleared my throat.

The woman turned to glance over her shoulder. "It's ahead, Your Highness," she said, still walking forward. I saw the light of day reaching around the hallway's corner. Relief cooled my body. "Up ahead is our private prayer room reserved for our most honorable guest." I have no reason to be afraid here, I'm amongst my people. I'm safe here.

The hallway soon turned into steps sloping down into a great mouth that opened towards half a cave wall, wet from the runoff from the mountain. The other half is open to the view of the city of Cado, perched adjacent to us on the cliffside. I stopped, my breath escaping my lungs in shock. The view was stunning. These mountains were the most beautiful thing I'd ever seen. The steps continued down to a narrow balcony, and I gladly followed. The view stole my focus. The clouds seemed close enough to touch and thick enough to stand on. The mountain peaks weren't visible, but you could see the twinkling lights of the distant city. I leaned forward onto the stone railing.

"I will leave you here to pray or…" she paused to choose her following words carefully, "or… to mourn however long you'd like. The bells on both sides of the space alert us all." the woman shared, pulling me back from the dream of the landscape to the reality of why I even requested the room.

She pointed left and right to show me the woven tassel that hung from the wall. My eyes trailed the braided navy cords. They were strung through a hole, which must have been some way of alerting people outside of this room.

Directly in the room's center lay a fire pit with small coals glowing, bringing some light to the room. Its heat warmed the entire space. I slowly turned, looking at the other amenities the room offered. Chairs lined with velvet cushions were placed sporadically around the room. A stream of water trickled down from beside the wall on the far east side until it cascaded off the side of the mountain. I swallowed, thirst from the journey finally making itself known. She tracked the movement of my eyes. "Oh, yes. I'll go get you water," she said, turning quickly and running up the stairs.

I heard her steps gradually fade into the distance.

This was the first time I'd visited the temples in far too long. The weight of the loss was beginning to press down again, heavier than before. I rubbed the curve of my neck, trying to release the tension gathering at the base of my skull. The silence felt foreign—unfamiliar and uncomfortable.

I took the nearest seat, elbows on my knees, and covered my face with my hands. Another deep breath. Another one that didn't help.

I could still feel the phantom tug of the collar she used to correct me with. Still hear the trill in her voice when I returned home from training with Father.

She was always so proud of me.

Always so encouraging.

Always so full of love.

My father was strength and logic—everything hard and unwavering. She was warmth and softness. Nurturing goodness. Together, they created a home that felt whole. Balanced. Loved.

I had been their only child. They tried for more, but it never happened. I knew it broke her a little. But she'd always say, *"Highest put everything I ever wanted in a child within you."* Then she'd squeeze my cheek and pat my head.

I used to stare into her eyes and wonder how a face could be that beautiful. That round and gentle and kind.

I miss her.

"What am I supposed to do now?" I spoke aloud into my hands. The question was bigger than one answer.

Her death blindsided me. I hadn't stopped to really think about it. Not fully. Not honestly.

Because thinking meant feeling.

And I wasn't ready for that.

Her death brought new dreams. Vivid ones.

She was in every one.

Pointing. Directing. Guiding my eyes to details I never would've noticed.

One dream told me I had to go to the land of the eagle. So

I left.

We left. My men and I.

My father—Highest, strengthen his grieving heart—was reluctant to see me go. But he trusted what I saw.

Especially if it was her showing me where to look.

*"Highest will protect you,"* he said as I left him behind in our empty estate.

Without his bride. Without his best friend.

I shook my head as a fresh wave of sadness clawed at my throat.

She died without meeting my bride.

Without holding a grandchild.

Without leaving me instructions on how to live without her.

No little ones to soak up her goodness.

She was my best friend, too.

My eyes burned. I am not as close to my father.

The more I reflect on her absence, the more I feel it.

The more I ache.

Uncertainty was never a friend of mine.

And grief is full of it.

A single tear escaped before I could stop it.

A nervous chuckle broke the stillness.

"I can't believe I let you make me cry first this time," I whispered, brushing the tear away.

"We used to bet on that, remember?"

It was always her.

"Father would tell me sensitivity isn't strength," I said with a broken laugh.

More chuckles bubbled up—soft, bitter things.

"Well," I exhaled, the laugh falling flat in my throat, "neither is dying."

The words hung there for a beat too long.

*He'll crawl first, Harth.*

She told my father that often. *He'll crawl, then he'll walk, then he'll run for sure.*

I could still hear her saying it, still feel the warmth of her hand on my back, always intercepting my father's sharpness with gentleness. She believed in my future even when I stumbled.

"I'll crawl first," I murmured, grounding myself in the words. "Thanks for the gentle reminder."

I stood, stretching out the ache in my back, and stepped toward the far end of the cavernous room. The air was damp, cooler near the stream that cut across the temple floor. I stopped just short of the pit—a hollowed stone circle where offerings and prayers had long been spoken.

The silence pressed in again. This time, I didn't resist it.

I dropped to one knee.

No flame. No ritual. Just my voice.

"Eternal Flame," I whispered to the ceiling. "Highest above, I submit to You."

The old words came easily, spoken by every Harth who came before me. But I couldn't stop there. My voice cracked as something deeper began to rise.

"As Prince of Valdeen, I surrender what strength I have left. I don't know what I'm doing without her. So if You're listening... help me to see what I need to see. Help me to lead. Help me to carry this weight before it crushes me."

I swallowed hard. "Because I don't have her anymore. And it's heavier than I thought."

A breeze stirred from somewhere behind me. Not cold—

just sudden. Sharp. Like the air had changed its mind.

I straightened.

Then it came again. Louder. Fiercer. Whipping around the cavern with impossible force.

Dust lifted from the corners. Stones trembled in their place.

I rose to my feet, bracing myself.

Then a voice—loud, deep, and far too close.

"Run."

I spun around, hand flying to the dagger at my waist. But the room was empty.

I scanned the shadows, the upper ledges, even the slivered path above the stream.

Nothing.

Still, I wasn't alone.

"Amias," the voice boomed again, this time to my left.

I turned fast—too fast. My foot slipped on a loose stone slick with water. I stumbled backward, arms flailing, and slammed into the edge of a carved chair. A blinding pain cracked against my skull.

Then—

Only darkness.

* * *

I awoke to fierce, deep, primal growls circling me like predators sizing up their prey. I was no longer in the temple. Gone were the stone floors and sacred air. Now, I lay in a clearing surrounded by dense woods. Darkness blanketed the world, save for the pale light of a full moon high above, casting an eerie silver glow over the space.

"Get up, young king," a voice growled, low and guttural.

King? The word twisted in my mind. "Stand to your feet!" another voice commanded, harsh and unyielding.

I sat up, disoriented, and counted seven pairs of eyes in the shadows. They watched me, unblinking, their golden orbs like embers in the dark. The growls rumbled on all sides, a menacing chorus.

I reached instinctively for my weapon, but my hand met empty air. My leathers, my blade—everything was gone. Looking down, I saw only a black tunic and loose-fitting pants.

"What is this?" I whispered, taking a step back.

The creatures around me snickered, a low, mocking sound. "You're not in danger here, Prince," one said, its voice rich with amusement.

But their growls persisted, coming closer, then fading, only to return from another direction. I turned, scanning the darkness, tensing as I instinctively fell into a defensive stance. My bare hands would have to suffice if it came to a fight.

"Prince Harth," one voice broke through the growls, layered with an almost regal authority, "we did not come to harm you, but to warn you."

The words struck me like a blow. A warning?

"In the coming months," the voice continued, "your world will be knocked off balance. Boldness will falter. Fear will rise. Peace will crumble, leaving conflict in its place. Darkness will stretch across the land, choking out the light. A darkness so deep it will consume all hope unless you find it."

"Find what?" I demanded, my voice trembling. "Is war

coming to Valdeen?"

"Protect the Light, young King," the voice boomed. "A light that will burn bright like the sun. It will illuminate the way for many. It is the only light that will survive in Naedorn for years to come, until the land is restored."

I stepped toward the voice, desperate for clarity. "Yes, I hear you, but what does this mean? Is war coming? How long do I have before—"

A sudden, unseen force slammed into me, knocking me to the ground. I landed hard, the breath leaving my chest. A massive creature emerged from the shadows, its brown eyes glowing. Its black fur shimmered under the moonlight, and its teeth gleamed in a snarl.

A wolf.

I froze, my back pressed against the ground as it prowled closer. Its saliva dripped onto my boots, each drop like molten lead. Around me, the other growls grew louder, deeper. My heart thundered in my chest.

Wolves.

The realization struck me. Wolves, the sacred symbol of Valdeen. This was no ordinary dream.

"Highest, help me," I whispered, my voice a prayer barely audible over the growls.

Another wolf inched closer, its snarl softening. Its glowing hazel eyes locked onto mine, holding me captive in an intense stare. For a moment, the world fell silent.

"You've crawled enough, boy," the wolf said, its voice suddenly softer, more feminine. It didn't speak aloud—the words resonated in my mind, clear and unmistakable. "Stand and run. Do what must be done before all hell breaks loose."

The voice was familiar, laced with warmth and unwavering

care—the kind that had guided me all my life.

I gasped, staring into the wolf's eyes as they began to shift. The hazel faded, replaced by a deep, rich brown, warm like pools of cocoa. My breath caught.

"Mother?" I whispered, disbelief and awe colliding in my chest.

The wolf's gaze softened, and it dipped its head in a small, deliberate bow before turning away. Its powerful frame moved silently as it retreated into the woods, the shadows swallowing it whole.

*  *  *

I jolted upright as ice-cold water splashed against my face, shocking me awake. I gasped, the chill biting into my skin and stealing my breath. Two firm hands gripped my shoulders, steadying me as I flailed.

"Amias, open your eyes! Say something!" A familiar voice grounded me, deep and commanding.

I blinked hard, my vision adjusting to the dim glow of candlelight. The sacred chamber of the temple came into focus. Jon's sharp features hovered over me, his strong hands still holding me in place.

"What… what happened?" I rasped, my voice raw.

"You fell and hit your head, Prince," a soft, measured voice answered from my right. I turned to see the veiled woman standing close, who offered me a wet towel.

The dull throb in my skull surged to life as I pressed my hand to my head. My fingers grazed a swollen knot, and I hissed through clenched teeth.

"Great," I muttered, the pain sharp enough to draw a curse.

The veiled woman's eyes widened, though her expression remained otherwise composed.

Jon let out a sharp laugh, already amused. "He's fine," he said dryly, standing and extending a hand to me.

I grasped his hand, using his pull and my legs' unsteady push to rise. Jon's hand shifted to steady my arm as I swayed slightly.

"I'm fine," I assured him, though my wobbling said otherwise.

He raised an eyebrow, skeptical.

"I am," I repeated, this time more firmly, though I winced again as the cool towel pressed against my head.

"Good," the veiled woman said quietly, withdrawing something from the folds of her robes. "This arrived for you moments before I found you." She held out a sealed letter. "The ravens brought it."

I took the letter, noting the absence of any wax seal or sigil. She bowed deeply and left with a quiet grace, the light sound of her steps fading quickly.

"I wonder what she looks like under all that cloth," Jon murmured, stepping closer.

"Stop it," I snapped, narrowing my eyes at him. "Be respectful."

"What?" he said, feigning innocence. "From what I could see, her eyes look young. It's a shame the Blessed volunteer so early. She's probably pretty."

"Jon, please," I said firmly, meeting his gaze. "It's impolite."

He held up his hands in mock surrender, a smirk tugging at his lips. "As you wish, Prince."

Ignoring him, I ran my fingers over the plain envelope,

feeling the coarse parchment. Something about it felt urgent, ominous. Without hesitation, I tore it open.

Jon leaned over my shoulder as I unfolded the letter. "What is it?" he asked.

"It's from Anima," I said, my voice tight. "More people asking for help."

Together, we scanned the message.

Refugees.

Hundreds of them. They'd fled across borders, over mountains, and through treacherous waters to escape the Watchers' Rebellion. Entire families fleeing persecution—executed for refusing to worship Vitaeus, one of the false gods. Beheadings. Burnings. The people who wrote this letter had risked everything, their faith in the Highest their only protection.

They were pleading with Valdeen for help.

I folded the letter, pressing the edge against my palm as the weight of the words settled on me.

"I saw things while I was unconscious," I murmured, still reeling. "Like a vision."

Jon's lips quirked into a knowing smirk. "It's not like Highest to stay silent when a Harth gets involved."

He wasn't wrong.

My mother had seen and heard so many things our natural eyes didn't.

I exhaled sharply, the memory of the wolves from my dream resurfacing: their glowing eyes and growled warnings.

"I think it's happening, Jon," I said, my voice low but firm. "The purification… It's happening in Naedorn."

Jon's expression darkened. "Then it's no coincidence

120

you've been shown this."

"We have to go find something," I said, the weight of it pressing against my chest. "We need to prepare the Wolves. Our journey may be longer than we thought."

Jon placed both hands on my shoulders and guided me toward the exit. The faint metallic scent of the temple mixed with the words from the vision that now echoed in my mind.

Protect the light. Protect the land.

There was no time to waste.

# Chapter 13

D arkness.
Complete and suffocating.
A void that stretched endlessly, cold and unrelenting.

I crouched on the stone floor, my breath steady despite the icy chill that seeped into my skin. My mind raced, but I forced my hands to move methodically, brushing over my face. My hair was loose, cascading in untamed black wavy, coils down my back and curling around my waist.

The fabric on my body was unfamiliar—light, soft, and undoubtedly luxurious. My fingers lingered over the embroidery, tracing what felt like gemstones sewn into the material. A dress, fitted to perfection.

My hands moved upward, and I froze as they met the weight around my neck. Gems—cool and smooth—pressed into my skin, set into a chain I couldn't immediately identify. Something else rested on my head, heavy and cold, but before I could examine it further, I felt the metallic bite of restraints on my wounded wrists.

Not jewelry. Shackles.

I paused, testing the movement of my arms. Each shift rattled the chains softly in the silence. The bracelets weren't just for show; they tightened as I moved, pulling me toward the ground with deliberate force.

I gritted my teeth and planted my knees more firmly on the floor, refusing to give in to the pull. "What is this?" I muttered, my voice low and sharp, a challenge aimed at the void itself.

The chains responded. Without warning, they yanked hard, dragging me down. My torso slammed against the cold stone, but I refused to cry out. The rough surface scraped against my exposed skin, and the gems on my necklace bit into my neck as the pressure increased.

"No—no. What is this?" I hissed through clenched teeth. My pulse thundered in my ears. I pressed my palms flat against the floor, trying to push myself up, but the restraints tightened further, forcing me back down.

Fine.

I'll let the darkness think it could win.

"Enough," I growled, my tone steady despite the weight pressing me to the ground. I tilted my head slightly, glancing in the direction of the force that bound me. "If you think I'm going to beg, you're wasting your time."

The chains rattled in response, but I stayed silent, my mind racing for answers. Where was I? What was this place?

Fear gnawed at the edges of my resolve, but I locked it away, burying it deep. Whatever this was, whoever—or whatever—was responsible, they would regret underestimating me.

"What did you dress her in?" a woman's voice echoed, both close and distant, as if ricocheting off invisible walls. The warmth of bodies moved around me, though I couldn't see them. A gust of air brushed my skin as people rushed past me.

The chains loosened so I stood quickly, muscles tensed, reaching instinctively for daggers I knew wouldn't be there.

"I put her in the gown crafted and imported from Aartier," another familiar voice responded. My heart clenched. I knew that voice. "The one custom-made for her. Then we styled her hair down her back. Her natural curls have been soaked in goat's milk and honey."

"Kelta," I whispered, panic rising in my chest. Her voice sounded so near, as though she stood just to my left. But when I turned, nothing greeted me—only darkness stretching infinitely. "Kelta, can you hear me?" I yelled, my voice trembling.

"Well done," another voice boomed, sharp and cruel. "You actually did something right for once. You're not worthless."

A touch—cold and invasive—grazed my chin, lifting my face upward.

I snarled, thrashing in place. "Get off me!" I shouted, trying to shove the invisible force away, but I couldn't move. Shackles bound me tightly, their weight unyielding.

"You powdered her face well," the voice continued, now with a sickening amusement. "And here too," she grabbed my wrist. "You can barely see the injury."

It tilted my hands to the side, examining me like a doll.

I scanned the void, desperate for a hint of light, but saw nothing. Was I blind here?

The force gripped my chin again, yanking my face forward. Hot, rancid breath washed over me.

"Those damned eyes," it hissed, low and venomous, a whisper meant only for me.

"What was that, Your Majesty?" Kelta's voice interrupted, her tone cautious.

Your Majesty?

Realization struck, chilling my blood. The familiarity of the voice... it was the queen.

"Some days, I wish we burned those things out," she chuckled, the sound rich with malice.

Anger and betrayal stung my eyes. I strained against the chains, but they held fast.

"Your Majesty?" Kelta gasped, her voice tinged with alarm.

"Oh, Kelta, it was a joke. Paxium bless you," my mother said, the mockery thinly veiled beneath her words.

Her grip tightened on my chin, forcing me to meet the darkness where her presence loomed. "You must know I love my daughter," she cooed, her tone dripping with false affection. "I'd *never* hurt her."

Then she shoved me backward.

And I fell.

The chains vanished, the weight of the jewels and crown gone as I plummeted into the endless dark. My stomach twisted, and the air tore past me, but there was no ground, no end—Until suddenly, I landed in the soft down of my bed.

I jolted upright, my chest heaving as sunlight spilled through the windows, illuminating the bay outside. Sweat clung to my skin, but I wasn't cold anymore. Only burning from the inside.

# Ickree Palace

*Amias*

Ablanket of mist cloaked the rolling, golden hills of Anima. I wrapped my fingers around the medallion hanging from it—the wolf sigil of Valdeen etched into its surface, dulled by the dirt and sweat of travel. I rubbed my thumb over the symbol as if the touch might summon clarity.

"Why am I here, Highest?" I whispered to the sky, my voice carried off by the breeze. The medallion's weight pressed into my palm as I clenched my fist around it. The dreams and signs had brought me to this land of false gods and fallen alliances. I only prayed they hadn't led me to my death.

"Amias," a gravelly voice interrupted behind me. I released the chain and turned to see Jon.

"Ian and Tavin have returned," he said, his tone steady but edged with unease. "Ickree will see you. He's gathering an audience."

"An audience?" I arched a brow.

Jon's expression remained stony, but a flicker of worry tightened his jaw. "I don't know why. But I have my

126

suspicions."

I frowned. "Then share them."

He hesitated, his gaze drifting toward the palace. "If Ickree's not behind it, the Queen might be. She could use the opportunity to... make an example."

"An example?" My lip curled. "You mean a show of loyalty. Bowing to a golden goddess."

"Yes." His voice was flat. "Exactly that."

I exhaled sharply and rose to my feet, accepting his outstretched hand. The grass whispered against my boots as I stretched, rolling tension from my shoulders.

"This will be fun," I said dryly.

Jon's face darkened. "Are you sure this is the Highest's will, Harth? We step into their nest with no guarantee of leaving alive."

"I saw an eagle with golden eyes," I said, my voice low.

"Most eagles have golden eyes," he countered, his skepticism plain.

"No, it was different. There was fire in these eyes." I met his gaze, searching for understanding. "Its voice was firm, melodic. Its speech... southern. That's why we're here."

Jon studied me, his features drawn with concern. "I don't know Harth. We could turn back. Take some refugees and leave."

I shook my head. "The dream wasn't a mistake. We're here for a reason. And we'll find that reason within those walls."

Jon followed my gaze to the palace, his jaw tightening. "I'll prepare our men to go with you."

"Two will stay outside the palace."

"Yes sir."

"If we're not out by dusk, they leave."

"Harth—"

"No questions." I snapped. "We all leave tomorrow."

Jon's mouth pressed into a thin line, but he nodded. "Yes, sir."

As he strode away, I turned back toward the palace, the wind tugging insistently at my cloak. For better or worse, Highest had called me to this diseased land. And I would answer.

\* \* \*

The stone beneath my boots was pristine, polished to a perfect finish. I pulled my black coat closer around my shoulders, adjusting the collars and cuff links to maintain a semblance of royalty. Days without a proper bath had made the effort nearly futile, but appearance mattered now more than ever.

I inhaled deeply, centering myself before ascending the grand stairs leading to the palace. Jon and twelve other men followed closely behind, their boots a quiet cadence against the stone. I'd instructed them to keep their hands away from the pommels of their weapons. We would not present ourselves as a threat—not yet.

Four Animaian guards awaited us at the second landing, their green-and-gold uniforms crisp and their stances rigid. "Gentlemen," I greeted with a curt nod. They returned the gesture in silence, and we proceeded up the final steps in unison.

The vast and magnificent palace loomed before us. Towering stone pillars stretched skyward, and the sprawling gardens surrounding the structure were a testament to meticulous care and attention. Ivy vines spiraled up the white stone walls, weaving a striking contrast of green against the gleaming surface. This was nothing like what we'd seen in the city surrounding this fortress.

I paused, tilting my head to take in the sheer size of the palace.

"Your Highness?" Jon's voice cut through my observations, a quiet reminder of the eyes on us. He shifted uneasily, his gaze darting between the guards flanking us and those stationed along the palace walls.

I glanced back at the men behind me, their anxious expressions waiting for my next move. With a sharp exhale, I resumed my stride, my boots clicking against the stone. The disparity was jarring.

Outside the palace, Animaian people suffered.

Inside these walls, the opulence was staggering.

The massive wooden doors ahead creaked as they opened, pushed laboriously by a team of servants. I blinked as we stepped inside, my eyes adjusting to the dimmer light. Emerald-clad guards lined the grand entryway, their postures as rigid as the ones outside.

From the far end of the room, a man emerged. His crown of gold feathers rested lightly atop braided hair that hung to his shoulders. A single sword hung at his side, though the confident stride with which he approached suggested he didn't feel the need to use it.

We stopped mere feet apart, neither of us speaking at first. His sharp, dark eyes assessed me, lingering on the pommels of my weapons.

Counting them.

I smirked.

His gaze rose to meet mine, and I took the opportunity to study him. The family sigil over his heart marked him as Ickree blood—royalty. Though shorter than I by a few inches, he was broad-shouldered and strong. A second glance revealed the dagger tucked into his boot. He was armed but likely unfamiliar with how to wield his strength effectively.

"My name is Prince Santu Milo Ickree, Fifth of my name," he declared, his tone measured.

I inclined my head in acknowledgment, my men offering slight nods behind me. I caught the flicker of displeasure on his face. We only bow fully to a Harth or to Highest.

"Pleasure to meet you, Prince," I said, the corner of my mouth twitching into a smirk. "I am Prince Amias Dai Harth, Third of my name. Seems our fathers lacked imagination."

A tense silence followed. His jaw tightened. "I don't consider my name a burden but an honor," he replied sharply, stepping closer. "Four men before me bore this title and achieved exceptional things for the country you stand in now. A reminder, Prince Harth... you are a guest in my house, and you require my permission to enter further and speak with an audience."

The tension was palpable. From the corner of my eye, I saw Jon shift, his hand inching toward his blade. I met his gaze briefly, silently hearing his voice in my head: Apologize, Harth. Now isn't the time.

I turned back to Prince Milo, ready to concede. "My apologies, Prince Ickree. I didn't mean to—"

Laughter erupted, cutting me off.

A deep, booming sound that caught me entirely off guard.

Before I could react, Milo clapped a hand on my shoulder, his amusement evident.

"Loosen up, Prince Amias," he said, grinning broadly. "It was a joke. I pray you aren't always so serious, or this visit will be insufferable."

I smirked, silently conceding that I'd walked straight into his trap. "Prince Santu," I extended my hand, a gesture of camaraderie. "Well played. You fooled us all."

He grasped my hand firmly, his grin widening. "Please, call me Prince Milo. Now, let's get you to the guest suite before my mother sees you like this."

Just the mention of the infamous queen sent a chill down my spine. "Thank you, Prince Milo," I replied, glancing at my travel-worn attire. "Now I'm insulted."

"Better me than her." Milo chuckled, gesturing toward the hall.

"If your intentions are pure, you'll be just fine," he said, his tone light, though his gaze lingered, searching. "I pray the gods allow you to stay long. I rarely get to converse with other heirs."

*The gods.*

The very phrase that separated us. Their idols and rituals, the endless cycle of reverence for Vitaeus and her pantheon— that belief system had unleashed the Watchers' Rebellion upon the world decades ago. A grim reminder of what happens when mortals worship the wrong powers.

"Yes," I replied, my voice steady. "Highest help us all."

The effect was immediate.

The Prince froze, his confident expression slipping into one of confusion and guarded curiosity. His eyes locked onto mine, the air between us charged with tension. "Highest?" he

131

repeated, slow and deliberate, as if testing its weight. "That phrase has only been written in history—"

"Your Highness," a voice interrupted, sharp and controlled, cutting through the room like a blade.

A woman emerged from the shadows to Milo's right, her hair streaked with gray and styled into a curly bun atop her head. She wore a deep emerald gown with a tan apron tied neatly at her waist, her stately and utilitarian appearance.

A servant—but nothing about her felt lowly.

Though petite, her posture radiated authority, and her presence was immediately protective as she moved to Milo's side. Her eyes, sharp and unyielding, flicked to me with suspicion.

"Prince Harth," she said, her tone measured but firm. "My daughter, Daph, will escort you to your chambers. You'll have time to prepare before the court assembles."

A young woman stepped forward at her mother's nod. She moved with quiet efficiency, her tan skin and dusty brown hair reflecting her mother's features.

"Your Highness," the girl said softly, dipping into a modest curtsy. Her voice was quiet but carried an undercurrent of resolve. "This way, quickly. You don't have much time."

Without waiting for a response, Daph turned and began leading the way down a corridor opposite the Prince. Her long skirt swayed with each brisk step, the motion purposeful and deliberate.

Jon glanced at me before issuing quick orders to the men. He, along with Asher, Fran, and Tye, fell into step behind us as we followed the young handmaid. Fran was born here in Anima and would be helpful. Asher, from Aartier, grew up exposed to the gods, both countries served. Smart move.

The walk was silent save for the faint echo of boots on the polished stone floor. Daph didn't look back once, her focus fixed ahead as she navigated the palace halls with precision. Despite her composure, I couldn't help but notice the slight tremor in her hands as she opened doors and gestured the way.

"This is where you can rest for a moment," she said, her voice low. Her gaze stayed fixed on the ground as she motioned toward the room, her hands trembling slightly. The nervous energy radiating off her was palpable.

I gestured to Jon, who turned to the men behind us. They entered the room without hesitation, the sound of rummaging soon filling the air as they searched for threats. Leaning against the frame of the door, I studied the hand-maid carefully. Her posture was submissive, her chin dipped.

I cleared my throat, breaking the silence. Her eyes darted up briefly before returning to the floor.

"Daph, is it?"

"Yes, Your Highness," she replied, her words hurried and faint.

"Do you have any advice for our audience this morning?"

She hesitated, the barest flicker of something—fear, perhaps—crossing her face. "Ahh... none that I can think of at the moment."

I tilted my head, unconvinced. "I'm sure there's something," I pressed, crossing my arms as I glanced briefly into the room to gauge the progress of my men.

Her voice, when it came, was softer but steadier. "Well... I would keep my mouth closed about your outdated god."

"Outdated?" My eyebrows rose.

"Yes, sire," she said, her voice no louder than a whisper.

We said nothing for a moment, letting the silence stretch.

Curious, I stepped closer, the soft light catching the faint sheen of sweat on her brow. The shift in proximity allowed me to study her more closely. Her features were delicate—round cheekbones and full lips—but the marks of labor were unmistakable. Calloused hands and faint shadows under her eyes dulled what might have been radiant beauty under different circumstances. As she stood before me, a weary handmaid with averted eyes, her timid exterior couldn't quite hide the flicker of defiance beneath.

"Daph," I said, my voice firm but calm, "I will not shy away from who I believe in. Highest is the one who sent me here, and Highest is the one I will always acknowledge."

Her head lifted, her gaze meeting mine at last. The courage it took was visible in the set of her jaw, in the way her trembling hands stilled. "Then Highest will be the one to get you killed," she said, her words measured but heavy with meaning.

She stepped back, the distance between us growing with each retreating step. Her composure cracked for just a moment—a shake of her head, a flicker of exasperation—before she turned toward the hall we'd just come from.

"I'll return for you shortly," she said over her shoulder, her voice softer now, almost regretful.

And then she was gone, her footsteps fading into the silence of the palace.

# Chapter 15

"Kae'Dinah!"

The sharp call of my name sliced through the air. I jolted upright. My chest rose and fell in ragged gasps as I tried to find the line between sleep and waking.

My mother's voice—it always struck something deep, something ancient. And for a moment, it made me feel small again.

But not today.

I blinked rapidly, disoriented by the sunlight stretching across my sweat-soaked sheets. I hadn't meant to fall back asleep—not after that nightmare.

The dream still clung to my skin like ash.

The voice. The shackles. Her.

And yet—something else burned deeper.

Not from the nightmare. From the journal.

Those words—his *prayer*—were still echoing inside me. Stirring something I couldn't fully name.

I could feel it rising. Just beneath the surface of my skin.

Footsteps approached—hers. Sharp. Certain. Heavy with power.

Fear began to reach for me, familiar and practiced.

But I caught it mid-lunge.

*No.*

I drew in a breath, steadying myself. My palms pressed into the mattress. My spine straightened.

I would not let her break me again.

Not after what she'd done.

Not after the general and the garden.

Not after what I now *felt.*

The door slammed open, crashing against the stone wall. She appeared in the doorway, draped in green silks that gleamed like the jungle under sunlight. Gold jewels hung heavily around her neck, and her crown—a magnificent headdress of golden feathers interwoven with diamonds and pearls—sat perfectly atop her head. It mirrored the ones made for Megorna and me, but hers, of course, outshone them both.

"Get up and get dressed. Now."

I didn't flinch.

I didn't rise.

"Why?"

The question left my lips sharp as flint. Dry. Controlled.

Not a protest.

A challenge.

She scoffed, stepping further into the room, the scent of her jasmine perfume suffocating the air between us. "I'm only waking you because your father demanded it. Megorna is already dressed, and the court is nearly assembled."

"I won't be part of another sacrifice."

"You disrespectful girl," she hissed, storming to my armoire and yanking it open with practiced fury. "It's no sacrifice. We have guests present." She pulled a brush from the shelves, grabbed a jar of water, and stalked toward me, her sharp movements a predator's warning. "The prince from Valdeen is here. Your father insists everyone be present."

Valdeen? We have no relations with the country. No trades. No agreements. Not even bad blood.

She reached for a handful of my curls, and I flinched, shrinking away instinctively.

She chuckled, a low sound that set my teeth on edge, and continued her task. "Kelta!" she barked, her voice cutting through the stillness of my thoughts like a butcher's knife.

My handmaid entered immediately, carrying a dress so stunning I froze. The green fabric shimmered with every movement, embroidered with threads of gold and silver that sparkled like sunlight on water. Stones adorned the neckline, promising to frame my face with their brilliance. The bodice was tailored tight, to highlight my curves—elegant, commanding, unmistakably regal.

I gaped at its beauty, my throat tight. "What is this all for?" I whispered, my voice hoarse, the dream's lingering grip still clinging to me.

She lightly poured the water on my hair. Her hands worked through the mane with painful precision, the brush catching at my scalp with every stroke. "The prince has delivered no motives yet, but the possibility of a union—even with *you*—is too great to ignore."

"I won't marry him," I said, my voice steady but quiet, a warning carried on its edges.

"You will."

"I will not." My gaze lifted to meet hers, steady and unyielding. "I am no child of yours, remember?"

The brush stopped mid-stroke.

Kelta eyed me nervously as she prepared my dress.

137

She rounded to face me, her expression sharp enough to cut, her silks rustling with the movement. Slowly, she crouched before me, her crown catching the morning light. Her eyes, molten and unrelenting, locked onto mine as she leaned closer.

"Do not mistake my mercy for my weakness," she said, her voice low, dangerous. "I have spared you from damning consequences too many times. That does not permit you to disobey me in perpetuity. "

The hair on my arms stood on end, causing an armful of chills to rise on my arms. The weight of her words pressed down on me, cold and suffocating, like the iron shackles that had once chained me in the darkness. It was like I could still smell the metallic rusted iron from my dream. My wrists ached with the phantom heaviness, though they remained wrapped.

The past few days had been too much—too many feelings, too many threats and terrors.

Too many unexplainable occurrences.

I no longer desired to please her, her will, or *her gods*.

The defiance in me begot an ember—a fire of my own. One that would not be soothed. I straightened, squaring my shoulders, refusing to let her shadow diminish me anymore.

"I do not want to go," I growled.

She chuckled, low and unamused, her lips curving into something between disdain and amusement. Kelta, standing nearby, eyed me with furrowed brows, her suspicion clear.

"Please," my mother scoffed. "You have no choice."

"I have all the choice," I snarled back.

Her eyes darkened, a storm brewing behind them. "Oh, is that so? When will you finally accept that I am the one in control here? Not just over you—over our family, our country, and the entire gods-damned world." Her voice hissed like venom, sharp and biting. "You will go. You will be silent. You will smile in that Prince's face. You will leap even if I demand it."

Her disgust was palpable, but my heartbeat slowed, stronger with every beat. My voice turned to steel, steady and unflinching.

I smirked. "When will you accept that the control you think you have over me is like trying to hold back a wildfire?"

The words startled even me. For a heartbeat, I nearly apologized.

But then—I saw it.

A crack in her mask.

Fear.

It flashed across her face—barely there, but unmistakable. A fleeting emotion she would never have shown to anyone else.

*I saw it.*

*I saw it.*

*I know I did.* I had never seen that look on my mother's face. Ever.

And just as quickly as it came, it vanished, replaced by the commanding, unshakable Queen of Anima.

"Kelta," she snapped, her voice sharp, her eyes never leaving mine. "We begin in half an hour. See that she's in the room, or it's your life at risk."

I flinched away from her threats towards my friend. But threatening her life only made me want to oppose her more. I have never felt like this. Not in all of my life had I dreamed of pushing back openly like that, but I did.

I watched her rise and turn away, her crown tilted slightly as though its weight pressed heavier than usual. I stayed seated, breathing deeply.

Kelta gave a hurried nod as she turned to leave. Then fled to untie the sleep garments I wore from behind me. My mother lingered for a heartbeat longer, her back turned to me. Then she spun around, her gaze sharp, trying to cut through my defiance and sweep from the room, her silks trailing behind her like a shadow.

*I saw her mask crack.*

*I saw fear.*

She cocked her head to the side, then slammed the door shut.

I exhaled, my chest tight with a mix of anger and resolve, and... what was this? Confidence?

"What is wrong with you, Princess?" Kelta snapped, her voice low and sharp. She glanced toward the door as if fearing the Queen still lingered, her hands already working to strip me of my sleep garments.

"Nothing," I said flatly. I had nothing more to say. Nothing was wrong with me—not anymore. I felt like a caged bird set free, but I had no clue who had opened the door. I honestly didn't care who opened the damned thing.

"Do you want to be punished?" she hissed, her movements brisk, almost frantic.

I shook my head, "If she wanted to punish me, she would have done it already."

Kelta froze, her fingers hovering over the fabric for a moment too long. "She could still. Don't be foolish." She knelt to help me step into the emerald-green dress, her tone softening just a fraction. "You're walking a fine line,

Kae'dinah. Not just with her, but with the gods."

"The gods?" I laughed bitterly. "I don't care for them either."

Her hands stilled. "You don't mean that."

"I do." I did mean it, and Kelta should know that more than anyone else. The gods killed that baby, and the gods nearly got me killed. I meant it.

The silence between us stretched thin, the tension like a cord pulled too tight. Kelta resumed lacing the back of my gown, her movements slower, almost hesitant now.

"I know you're angry," she said finally, her voice carrying a note of desperation. "The sacrifice, the attack—it's shaken you. But you're making dangerous choices. You think you're untouchable, but you're not. Your mother sees everything, Kae'dinah. And the gods—"

"The gods?" I cut her off, the fire in my chest flaring again. "They've done nothing. They watched as I nearly died, as our women stay bare. If they exist, they deserve no reverence from me."

Her gasp was sharp, almost a rebuke in itself. "Princess," she whispered, her voice trembling with warning. "Do not speak like this. You're inviting ruin. Not just for you—for all of us."

I met her gaze in the mirror, her reflection heavy with concern and something deeper. Love, maybe. Devotion. The very things that bound her to me also tied her to my mother and the gods I despised.

"Kelta," I said softly, yet with an edge, "I will walk whatever line I choose. And it will be my choice. She won't hurt you. I won't allow it. I will tell my father, and she won't have anything to hold over me because I will have done nothing wrong. She only finds faults in me because she holds everything I do under a damned magnifying glass."

She stared at me, stricken, her hands faltering on the last lace. "And the Captain?" she asked, her voice barely above a whisper, as if the words themselves might condemn us both.

I stiffened. Why would she bring him up? We were nothing more than friends, one of my closest ones, but just that. "He's my *friend*."

"Is he?" She moved to face me, her expression shifting from worry to judgment. "Friends don't leave the scent of each other lingering on their clothing. Friends don't request the room, don't—"

"Kelta." My voice was sharp, cutting her off. So she saw it too, what I was afraid to accept. I couldn't risk his life for my curiosity.

She frowned but didn't retreat. "You're walking a thin line, Princess, between dishonor and defiance. Your mother won't tolerate it. Neither will the gods."

Her words settled over me like ash, choking but hollow. I straightened, forcing the fire within me to burn hotter, brighter.

"You've kept my secrets, Kelta. Cleaned my wounds, soothed my fears. But I no longer care who watches me or what rules I break. The gods have taken enough from me, from everyone. My mother has taken enough as well. I'll not yield more—not to her, not to you."

Her mouth parted slightly as if I'd struck her, but she recovered quickly, her eyes narrowing. "I made vows," she said, her voice low and trembling with restrained anger. "To your family. To the gods. To you. I will not let you throw everything away—not after all I've done to protect you."

I turned from her, unwilling to meet the weight of her stare. "I never asked for your protection," I muttered.

"And yet you've needed it," she snapped. She grabbed my arm, spinning me to face her. "You will go to the Great Hall. Not just for my sake, for yours. You will smile at the prince, and you will forget whatever foolish rebellion is stewing in you. If you don't, so help me Paxium, I will tell your mother everything I know."

I stared at her, disbelief and fury twisting in my chest. Remnants of the dream began to whisper back into my mind. The blindness had restricted me from truly seeing and directing my own life. It's been two women, pushing me about like a puppet. "You wouldn't," I growled.

"Try me," she said, releasing me and storming toward the shared living space.

"Kelta," I hissed, following her.

"We're already late," she said without turning, her voice clipped.

Everyone wanted control—my mother, the gods, even Kelta. But I had none left to yield. I wouldn't be blind to this again.

# Chapter 16

K elta, Captain Wilt, and I stepped into the corridor, the sound of our footsteps swallowed by the wide, polished halls. The palace was already awake—servants rushing in silence, guards stationed at every archway. They all knew what today meant. So did I.

I smoothed the skirt of my gown with one hand, barely recognizing the girl reflected in the golden mirrors we passed. Gold thread wove through the fabric, catching the morning light, but it felt like a costume. A distraction.

I clenched my fists.

Behind me, I could sense Wilt's presence—not intrusive, just... there. But I didn't look back. Not today.

"Kae'Dinah," he said gently.

I didn't respond.

His voice was too soft. Too knowing. And I didn't want kindness right now.

I was still aching in places I hadn't named yet. My skin still bore bruises from the garden, and my spirit had been scraped raw.

I kept walking, spine tall, chin level.

Ahead, Kelta adjusted the shawl around her shoulders, stealing glances over her shoulder to check that I hadn't run off.

I almost wanted to.

Every instinct in me screamed to run—not from the gathering, but *to something*. A pull. A weight I couldn't explain. It sat low in my belly, urging my steps faster, harder, toward the Great Hall. Toward… what?

I didn't know. But something was waiting for me there.

My pace quickened. I didn't wait for Wilt or Kelta to catch up.

"Kae—Princess," Wilt corrected himself. "You're walking too fast."

"I'm fine," I snapped. My voice was sharper than I intended, but I didn't apologize. I couldn't.

The hem of my gown tangled slightly at my feet, and I stumbled forward. Wilt's hand shot out to steady me, fingers brushing my elbow.

*"Focus."*

"I can't focus," I yelped, trying to still the flimsy shoe back onto my foot. "I don't need you to tell me constantly."

"I said nothing, Princess," Wilt spoke, still holding one hand for me to lean against as I balanced on one foot.

"You didn't say—"

*"Focus."* The voice had returned. I froze, staring down the stairs. I could hear the faint chatter of people gathered in the Great Hall.

"Princess," Wilt's deep voice boomed from my left. "You heard something?" he eyed me suspiciously.

"No," I snapped. "Let's get there before the prince enters." I quickly trot down the remaining stairs.

The echoes of our feet striking stone were all I could hear as I hurried through the halls of our palace. The rhythm of the clicks quickened with my racing heartbeat.

I heard the voice again.

*What triggered it?*

*Why didn't the voice return last night?*

The sun was a quarter of the way above the sky, casting pale light through the high windows. The palace had awakened earlier than usual to receive these visitors from Valdeen—a rarity in my lifetime.

The closer we got, the more the same questions rolled around in my head.

*Why did they come?*

*How are they truly different from us?*

*Why have we not been allies for so long?*

Valdeen is separated by the treacherous mountain range to our west. My father always spoke of just how dangerous the range is. Years ago, men were sent into the mountains and were unable to scale them. Many died. But yet, somehow these men were here. No doubt, experts in the terrain.

We were *very* late.

Mother had awakened me later than my sister, no doubt an intentional slight. Kelta moved to the space behind me, standing next to Wilt. She followed, lifting the small train of my gown to let me move faster. Despite my efforts to tread lightly, my shoes clattered noisily against the floor, each step betraying my presence.

My heart raced with an unusual excitement.

*What's wrong with you? Calm down.*

Still, something gnawed at me, pulling me forward with a strange urgency. A visitor had come from a distant land. This was something that I may never get the opportunity to experience again. And yet, beneath my excitement, there was an unshakable gravity to it all. Why had this visitor commanded the attention of the entire court?

I stopped just outside the side entrance to the Great Hall, and inhaled deeply.

Click.

Exhale.

Click.

I reached for the door and opened it. Wilt pushed past me, making a clear path from the side entrance to the dais. Megorna stood to the side, quickly motioning me to join her. Our dresses were nearly identical, just like our crowns. I rushed up the few stairs and to her side. Only to look down at the men assembled before us.

A unit of Valdeenian men stood in the midst of our great gathering. Each one dressed in all black, armed with a range of weaponry. One held a large axe, a few with two large swords across their backs, some with bows and arrows, and another with a morning star. Each man carried a unique weapon along with a sword sheathed at their side.

Every single fact that I had learned about the country came spewing to the forefront of my mind. Valdeen was a country renowned for its skilled fighters and a military that could take whatever they wanted. They just never came down from their mountains. We know nothing of their economic state but that they mine gems. They grew grapes from prized vineyards. From this impression alone, I knew the books were actual in that regard. They looked like they lacked nothing.

The men were all tall—taller even than Milo, who stood just over six feet. Their skin tones spanned a wide spectrum, but the three at the front shared something striking: deep, dark complexions that shimmered with a brilliance and beauty unfamiliar to me. Just a shade lighter than the black leather they wore, their presence commanded attention.

They were, without question, handsome.

From the center of the tight rectangular formation, one stepped forward. His black hair was cropped close at the sides, leaving a crown of soft, tightly coiled texture—like sheep's wool—no more than two inches high. A neatly trimmed line of scruff traced his chiseled jaw, connecting to a full mustache above his lips.

And his eyes—

Not brown. Not gray. But a deep, stormy blend of both. A color I'd never seen before.

He was stunning.

He strode forward as my father rose from his decorated throne—broad-shouldered and commanding, his presence impossible to ignore. His black beard, streaked salt and pepper, seemed grayer than it had just days ago. He lifted his hands, a gesture to calm the murmuring crowd.

"Fear not," his deep voice echoed. "We've assembled you all here today because Valdeen has sent us a significant gift." He paused, then turned toward Megorna and me. She grabbed my hand, squeezing it in excitement. I rolled my eyes.

"The possible gift… of an alliance?"

*An alliance?*

The thought turned my stomach. And judging by the man standing before us, he hadn't come here to hand over anything, much less himself. I arched a brow. *Well, that eliminates the theory of marriage.*

"No, Your Majesty," the man said, his voice deep, raspy, and smooth. It held an accent I'd never heard before—warm and clipped at once. "We are here to—"

"Bow," hissed my mother from her identical throne beside my father.

He turned to face her.

Her eyes blazed with something close to hatred, burning into him like a hawk sizing up prey. Megorna's grip tightened around my hand. Our mother's fury was immediate, but confusing. The man had barely spoken. He hadn't refused a proposal. He hadn't issued a threat. What could have provoked her already?

The visitor straightened, squaring his broad, muscular shoulders.

"I bow fully only to my deity and my king... respectfully," he said, his tone measured, firm.

A smirk crept to the corner of my mouth.

Meg nudged me gently and dropped my hand with a huff.

We were both quietly relieved: the prince had a spine.

Father's gaze snapped to our mother. "He is permitted to honor the rules of his land here." His tone left no room for argument. Then, shifting back to the man, he nodded. "Please. Go on. State your affairs."

He inhaled and paused, no doubt carefully constructing his words. "My name is Prince Amias Dai Harth, third of my name," he began, his voice strong but deliberate. "I've come here to deliver a message to you all."

Father raised an eyebrow and turned to walk back and rest on his throne. "Just a message?" he questioned, his tone skeptical.

He nodded, holding his ground. "Yes, Your Majesty."

"Hmm," I sounded. Causing my sisters to lean into me.

"What do you think?" she whispered.

"I like his confidence," I whispered, never taking my eyes off the men.

"Yes, and," Meg groaned softly. "How do you think they look. I've never seen men more handsome. Well, besides Captain Wilt and that one man training to be a healer with the nice fitting pants."

I whipped my head to her and gaped, "Meg, please spare me inappropriate thoughts."

"Please, you admire Captain Wilt all the time," she whispered.

"Stop it," I hissed. "The Prince is handsome. Now, quiet, so we can see why they're here."

"Was a raven too much to send?" Mother quipped, her voice dripping with mockery.

Laughter rippled through the gathered assembly, casual and complicit.

He smiled to himself, taking another small step towards the dais. "I find great value in your acceptance of my invitation today. It is with extreme gratitude that you've gathered your royal courts to hear the words of a prince from a distant land." He raised his voice, causing it to resonate through the grand cathedral. It was firm, authoritative, and commanding, and by the looks of those gathered, they were thinking the same thing about the foreigner's voice.

He turned, surveying the assembly before us: a sea of wealth and power, cloaked in fine silks and shimmering jewels. They had all put on their best today.

"We've traveled long days and nights to ensure that our brothers and sisters west of the mountains hear the declarations entrusted to us," he declared.

"Consider it a great honor to host you, all the way from

Valdeen," Father interjected, his voice a low rumble that filled the room. He shifted slightly in his throne of steel and stone—but his words faltered the moment the Queen's slender fingers trailed across his resting hand.

The court fell silent.

I inhaled, and once again the familiar scent of rusted iron filled my lungs. I turned toward my mother. Her smile was no longer simply beautiful—it was a masterstroke of control, seductive and calculated. With a single touch, she had silenced a king.

*What in the gods' name is going on?*

*Had she always done that?*

I tilted my head slightly, studying them. The way they sat. The way she looked at him. The way he obeyed without protest. It was always strange, how easily she could silence him. How often she did.

My movement must've drawn attention, because one of the Valdeenian entourage shifted his gaze toward me. His eyes narrowed briefly before turning to observe my parents, too—his expression unreadable.

Father hesitated, his eyes narrowing as he regarded her, but he said nothing more. He sank back into his throne, while she sat victorious, her smirk cutting like a blade. Her sharp, glaring gaze shifted to me, then Megorna, then back to the Prince. She gave a subtle gesture, bidding him to continue.

"I greatly appreciate the hospitality, Your Majesty," he said smoothly, forcing a kind smile.

"Get on with it," she interrupted, her tone laced with mock respect. Then, with a smirk, she added, "Respectfully," throwing his own words back at me.

I scoffed, earning a jab from Meg.

I looked at her and shrugged, "Mother is an ass."

"Kae'Dinah!" She whisper-yelled, silencing me. I chewed on the side of my lip to keep quiet.

"I was given a dream," He began, my head shot back in his direction. A dream? Curiosity taking complete control.

He continued, "A great bird, ablaze with fire, descended from a mountain range. It was massive, its presence commanding, with one eye of golden grain and the other an inferno of flame."

His words silenced the light whispers around us, the weight of the vision drawing me into a tense stillness. Even Mother, whose biting humor had filled the air only moments ago, sat frozen. Her expression shifted—no longer amused, but stunned.

I wasn't sure how to interpret her reaction.

Was it fear?

Skepticism?

Awe?

That would be the second time she let her mask slip. She quickly glanced at me again before turning back to the Prince, like she sensed my accusations of her.

He took a step closer to the dais, "At first, the bird soared high, admired by all who beheld it. People praised it, casting their wealth before it as a show of reverence. They marveled at its beauty and power, a sight that seemed almost divine.

"But then, the bird did something no one expected. It began to fly lower, skimming the earth, and everywhere it passed, flames erupted. Great winds set fields of crops ablaze before the bird, reducing the golden harvest to ash. Barns and storehouses ignited in an instant, along with cattle and mules. The land itself began to burn.

"It didn't stop there. I saw the great bird fly over towns, its fire consuming everything in its path. People fled into the streets, screaming, but they could not escape. Even those who bowed in reverence were engulfed by the flames. Nothing and no one was spared.

"I saw golden gods—great statues with the heads of great beasts," He paused, inhaling then blowing it out to steady himself. He looked up, meeting my mother's stare with a tense one of his own. Mother's body sat tight, her composure faltering yet again. But he straightened his stance, emanating confidence and assurance.

I knew whatever words he prepared next would offend her most of all, "They melted under the intensity of the bird's flames. These statues, once revered, stood no chance. The flame showed no mercy. It had no opponent. It carried no remorse.

"It burned even the stone—the stone we believed could not be touched by fire—leaving it blackened and cracked in its wake. This bird carried judgment upon its wings, tasked to cleanse the land of its disease and refine it through destruction.

"That was my dream. That is why I am here. This is your warning, Anima."

The room felt frozen. Stunned by the weight of his warning.

The seconds that passed felt like hours.

Then, Milo stepped forward, now standing fully beside our father, who sat silently on his throne. "Who sent you with this vision?" he asked, his tone sharp with skepticism.

Before he could answer, our mother's voice sliced through the room like a blade. "You're filled with delusion, boy," she

153

said, rising from her seat to address the court. "The gods won't simply burn. The gods cannot and have not failed us ever!"

The Prince chuckled, an exhausted sound. "You all in this room live comfortably here in Floos, while the land around you is barren and suffering," he said. I could visibly see the restraint in the veins of his neck as he forced himself to remain calm. "I've seen it with my own eyes on our journey here. Nothing has been done for you or your people."

"Watch your tongue!" she hissed, stepping closer to the edge of the dais, her fury palpable—the metallic smell of iron wisping by me yet again.

He stepped forward as well, undeterred. "Your people cry out for help! They've fled west and south for refuge, begging for aid. Crops won't grow. Illness and starvation have asphyxiated your citizens. Yet here you sit, thriving off what little can be reaped! Your people begged us to bring word to their king, to plead for their lives. And here you are, turning a blind eye to their suffering. Dressed in wealth, bodies full of abundance."

Father rose abruptly, his deep brown eyes blazing with frustration. "You have no right to cast judgment in our country!"

"You're right, King," he shouted back, voice echoing through the chamber. "I don't." he stepped back, deeper into the protective confines of my guards.

Not a move out of fear, but of wisdom.

He paused before leaving, his final words slicing through the tension. "That's why I'm here—to tell you that Highest sent me. He is the omnipotent judge."

His words landed like a thunderclap. A ripple of gasps

swept the room, followed by the low hum of frantic whispers.

*Highest.*

The words from the journal.

I rolled the name around in my mind, repeating it like a mantra.

*"Kae'Dinah?"*

I heard the voice whisper my name. I turned sharply to look at those around me. The muffled chaos of the room faded, muted to my ears, and my name rang out again.

*"Kae'Dinah!"*

I glanced at Meg, Milo, and Kelta. Their mouths remained shut, and every eye in the room was fixed on the man sent from Valdeen. Not one of them had spoken my name. And not one of them was hearing what I was.

The voice called again, insistent.

*"Kae'Dinah."*

*"Kae'Dinah."*

*"Kae'Dinah."*

*"Kae'Dinah."*

I pressed my hands over my ears, the repetition unbearable.

"Kae'Dinah?" Meg asked cautiously.

I stepped out of her outstretched hands to the center of the dais and shouted, "Stop!"

The room froze, and every eye turned toward me, their stares sharp and questioning.

*"The people suffer,"* the voice whispered again, its tone softer but no less piercing.

"What is it that he speaks? Our people suffer?" I asked, my voice trembling as I stared blankly in my father's direction. The voice knocking on the doors of a feeling stored deep inside me. Turning to my mother, I spoke again, this time

155

louder. "Our people suffer, and all you hear are insults to gods, Mother?"

Gasps rippled through the room. Whispers erupted in the crowd as the weight of my words settled. The Prince's eyes fell on me as I strolled past her.

The Queen spun toward me, her eyes dark with fury. "Silence!" she hissed, closing the distance between us.

I refused to cower. I scanned the room. Could it be true? Were people suffering beyond these walls—people we claimed to love and protect—while we lived in abundance?

I turned to my father, desperation creeping into my voice. "Father?" My plea cracked slightly. "The people are suffering? Fleeing? We've known nothing of this, right? Tell me you've known nothing of this."

Anger swelled in my chest, mingling with helplessness. Tears pricked my eyes, hot and stinging.

Behind me, my mother's venomous tone sliced through the tension. "I should've locked you away years ago," she spat.

Her words cut, but I refused to let them control me. Refuse to wonder when she first had the thought. Turning back to my father, I called again, more urgently this time. "Father? Tell me." A tear slipped free, falling from the corner of my eye.

He remained silent, his gaze fixed ahead as the guards moved to encircle the Valdeenian prince.

I turned to the men dressed in silver armor and emerald accents. I looked at Wilt, whose eyes were fixed on every move that I made. I looked back at my father. The guards were about to act. He would have them kill the prince—not because he wanted to, but because my mother wasn't pleased with it. There was a familiar glass over his eyes, as if he sat before me physically but not mentally. "No," I whispered, disbelief anchoring me to the spot.

I rushed toward him, grabbing his arm. "Father, if you let our men kill him, we will all perish. We don't have the military strength to face Valdeen," I whispered, urgency pushing my words. "Literature says they have the strongest armies in the world. If you kill him, you've killed all of us."

My father's gaze finally shifted to me. His large brown eyes softened, and for a moment, he looked at me as he once had. His gaze dropped to my wrist, where I still wore the bandages covering wounds from my attack.

He raised his hand, halting the guards. "Everyone, quiet!"

"But darling, he has dishonored the g—"

"Silence!" my father thundered, cutting my mother off. She gaped at him.

Then he turned his attention to the prince.

For the first time, I truly saw him. His dark mahogany skin glowed under the sunlight. He stood tall, broad-shouldered, and powerful, his black leather accentuating his muscular frame, and his jacket strained against his movements. He looked as though he belonged to the mountains themselves, a man shaped by their strength and elegance.

My father's voice was firm. "You will be out of Floos by sunrise tomorrow. No harm will come to you until then. But at first light, you are no longer under my protection."

I let out a deep breath, a strange relief flooding me despite the tension that lingered.

*"Go to him,"* the voice whispered, calm and commanding. What? I couldn't walk to him in front of all of the nobility?

*"Go to him."*

157

I stood, shaking slightly, but for the first time in a while... I obeyed.

My cautious legs carried me down the dais stairs toward the prince. I looked in Wilt's direction, his eyes wide enough to fall from his face. He stepped towards me, coming closer to me as I moved closer to the Prince. I held up a hand, halting him, and his jaw ticked in frustration.

The Prince watched each step I took. His eyes moved from my exposed leg to my face. My chest tightened as another wave of heat bloomed within me. It spread from my core to my limbs, leaving me breathless. I pressed a hand to my chest, trying to ease the burn.

He stared back, his storm-gray eyes meeting my golden ones.

His full, shaggy eyebrows furrowed, and he shook his head side to side with confusion.

Then, to my shock, he fell to his knees before me.

Gasps erupted around the room. His guards stiffened, some glancing at me with suspicion, others gripping their weapons, ready to strike.

"Kae'Dinah," my father warned from behind me, his voice low.

I raised my hands in a calming gesture, turning toward the prince. My mind raced. Why would he kneel before me while refusing to acknowledge my parents?

"Prince Harth, please rise," I begged, still remaining a comfortable distance away for my own safety.

"I can't believe this," his deep tone felt like brass. The accent made his words hard to decipher in his panic. "I can't believe you stand before me."

"What?" I chuckled nervously, "What are you saying,

Prince?" My voice was now trembling. "Prince, why do you bow before me after refusing my parents? Please, rise now."

He didn't move, his eyes searching my face as though I held all the answers. A tear fell from his eye, tracing a slow path down his cheek. His breathing was rapid, and the smile on his face was almost crazed.

"You are the reason I am here," he murmured, the word barely escaping his lips. His gray eyes crashed into my golden eyes, and he whispered, "Vikastees."

Then, before I could ask another question, his body went still. Too still.

His eyes glazed over—not unconscious, but no longer present. As if something—or someone—had seized his thoughts.

Then his knees buckled, and he collapsed onto the floor.

# Chapter 17

I was consumed everywhere. The burning within me, once a flicker, now roared through every part of my body. I screamed, staggering back, gasping for air.

The room turned to chaos.

His guards rushed to his side, panic mirroring my own.

Wilt was at my side in seconds, Nagel not far behind, both with swords drawn.

"Who touched her?" Captain Wilt roared, his voice cutting through the chaos.

"What did you do?" one of the Valdeenian guards demanded of me.

"What did he say?" another barked sharply.

"Captain, stop!" I yelled, struggling to focus. "No one touched me. He only... spoke a word."

"What word?" the same guard snapped, his tone sharp and desperate.

The word escaped my lips instinctively, foreign yet familiar. "Vikastees."

The Valdeenian guards froze. One shook his head, his face shocked.

"Her eyes," someone murmured. They all turned to

look, their gazes shifting quickly to one another with silent gestures I didn't understand. Without another word, they lifted the prince and retreated toward the exit, the Anima guards holding the doors open wide.

"Wait!" I called, my voice breaking. My desperation was swallowed by the room's growing murmurs.

Wilt grabbed me, his grip firm but steady. "You need to calm down. He could have killed you."

One Valdeenian lingered near the door, casting a brief glance at the dais where my parents stood. The noise from the crowd grew louder, anger and confusion rippling through the nobility.

And still, I stood there, the word "Vikastees" burning in my mind like a benediction.

"I want his head!" my mother growled, her voice slicing through the chaos as the doors slammed shut behind the Valdeenians.

Shouts of agreement erupted from the crowd.

"Enough!" my father whispered, though his quiet tone carried a deadly edge.

"I want his head served on a golden tray, garnished with his lies!" my mother shrieked.

"EVERYONE OUT!" my father bellowed. "Leave only my family!"

Wilt's hands dropped from me, hesitation flickering across his face. His body tensed, torn between staying and obeying orders.

The room erupted as guests and guards scrambled to leave. Amid the chaos, a nobleman in gold bumped into my shoulder. Wilt shoved him back, his protective instincts flaring.

161

"Watch where you're going!" Wilt growled, then turned to meet my gaze. "As soon as you're done here, I'll be right outside."

I nodded, trying to steady my breathing. "Okay."

My eyes fluttered to the ground as the people emptied the room.

*Vikastees.*

The word was foreign. A word I'd never heard before. Yet, it fluttered around my mind and wound itself around my torso. The word claimed me as if it had hands and a will of its own.

*Vikastees.*

A word so powerful that it made the large prince once before me fall to the ground. I could see the scene replaying right before my eyes again. He looked upon my face, spoke the words, and an emotion that I couldn't quite name covered his face before he lost all consciousness.

What in the gods' name?

What power did that word hold?

The doors shut with a large thud. Causing me to jump and leaving an eerie silence behind. My mother's rapid breaths were the only sound, sharp and uneven.

"How dare you grant him immunity?" she hissed, her voice trembling with fury. "The gods demand his blood! I must have his head on my altar!"

"Please, Mother," Milo began, stepping down from the dais toward me. "Kae'dinah, are you okay?"

"I need it. I need him dead!" my mother seethed. The scent of iron wafted through the air, sharp and nauseating. How could she so soon demand the blood of someone else? Has she not had enough?

My nose scrunched at the nauseating smell that wafts by me again. "Do you smell that?" I murmured, my words catching in my throat.

"What did he say to you?" Milo demanded, his hands gripping my elbows. "Did he threaten you?" Milo's eyes met mine, they were frantic and laced with so much fear that it made my heart rip.

"I don't know," I whispered, my voice shaking. I tried to ease my voice to let him know that I was physically fine and that he didn't need to worry anymore. But I'm afraid that I couldn't even convince myself that I was fine.

"It wasn't foreign," my father interjected, his eyes fixed on the doors. He paused. His admission caused us to turn in his direction. "It was ancient. From long ago."

The tension thickened as we all continued to stare at him.

"Ancient?" Milo asked, stepping closer to our father and releasing his hold on me.

"Yes," he replied, his voice low. "The word spoken—'Vikastees.'"

My mother froze mid-step. Her eyes, once brown, gleamed an unnatural black as she turned toward us.

An unnatural black that I had seen before. My core tightened.

My stance shifted almost on instinct, an instinct to defend myself.

"Mother?" I whispered, my heart racing.

Her lips curled into a smile, her gaze locking on me with twisted delight. "You," she said, her voice dripping with malice. "Finally."

* * *

The room warped. The air shifted, bending reality itself.

My torso stretched in the most unnatural way. Leaving behind a nauseating headache.

I blinked, trying to clear the dizziness that had just fallen upon me, and found myself back in Wilt's hands.

I look around the room frantically. The crowds were beginning to exit the room... Again. But they had already cleared the room. What the hell was going on?

The Valdeenian guards were carrying the prince from the room again. The nobleman in gold brushed past me once more.

Wait... that had already happened.

Wilt tensed, his hand tightening on my arm.

"I want his head!" my mother's voice rang out, calm and knowing this time.

I looked at her. She was watching me, smiling, her expression filled with cruel satisfaction.

"What is this?" I whispered, my voice trembling as I stared down at the black marble floors. This had already happened.

"EVERYONE OUT!" my father roared again.

This time, I stepped out of the nobleman's path before he could touch me. Wilt's eyes darted to mine, confusion etched on his face.

"Princess," he began, but I cut him off, my voice low and urgent. I look back to my mother, her eyes had never left me. It was almost as if she was watching me, waiting for me to realize...

My eyes widened as the thoughts finally caught up.

"You'll be right outside those doors, I know you will," I said firmly. My hands clutched his upper arm and squeezed. His eyes shot in my hands and worry found his face. "Don't leave without me. If I don't come out, find me."

He hesitated and search my eyes. Then his eyes roamed to the space on his arms that I clung to so desperately, and he nodded. " I will do just as you ask, but I don't understand."

"Neither do I," I whispered, glancing at my mother's knowing smile. "But trust me. Stay close."

He backed away from me, his steps hesitant, before turning to escort the remaining guests out. The royal guard followed suit, ushering the last of them through the heavy doors. With a resounding thud, the doors shut, sealing us in.

Silence.

A silence heavier, longer, and more foreboding than before.

I turned toward the dais.

Father stood motionless, staring at the closed doors. Milo's eyes were on me, sharp with concern, while Megorna watched our mother with a furrowed brow. Her usual composure was gone, replaced by a confusion that mirrored my own.

"Kae'dinah, are you okay?" Milo asked, stepping down from the dais and closing the distance between us.

I didn't answer. My focus shifted to my mother as she approached Father. Rising on her toes, she whispered a string of words into his ear. His face twisted with shock, and he shook his head violently.

"Kae'dinah," Milo tried again, gripping my arms to steady me. But I was too busy trying to look around him."What did he say to you? What did he say? Did he threaten you?"

The sharp metallic scent from earlier wafted between us again, stopping Milo's questions. I turned towards my brother, his worried features shifted into something closer

165

to anger.

"Milo, do you smell that?" I whispered, my voice barely audible.

"Did he put his hands on you?" he demanded, his voice rising. "You have to know something, Kae'dinah!" His hands were on my shoulders now, shaking me, trying to get me to recall whatever information he thought I had forgotten.

"I don't know!" I yelled back, my voice cracking under the weight of my emotions. Tears of anger blurred my vision. "Do you hear me?"

"You're the curse," Father said suddenly, his voice thick with sorrow.

"What?" I turned to look up at the face of my father, and there, deep in the pools of his brown eyes, I read something I had never seen before.

Sorrow.

Pain.

Remorse.

Anger.

That look alone took my breath away. That look cause my chest to slowly rise and fall more intensely, pulling in more air with each inhale.

"You're the one in the dream he spoke of." He sank onto the edge of his seat, with a plop. Like his body couldn't bear the weight of the words he spoke. His hands were trembling as they ran through his beard. "You're the one with golden eyes. Who else could it be?"

"Father, that's not—" I protested.

"I heard his words, Kae'dinah," he snapped.

"Maybe you interpreted them wrong!" I retorted.

"Silence!" he roared, his anger sharp and sudden. "Your

rebellion has festered into something uncontrollable, girl!"

*Girl.*

I had never shown an ounce of rebellion towards him. He was my father, and everything he spoke to me, I obeyed. I trusted him, so I obeyed.

*He's my father.*

This wasn't right. This wasn't what happened before. I turned to our mother and caught the faintest tug of a smile at the corners of her lips.

She was smiling? Why?

*She did this.*

She had fed him lies, and he believed her.

"What did you do?" I shouted, storming toward the dais.

Milo's strong arm caught me by the waist before I could ascend the stairs, his grip firm.

Mother scurried to my father's side feigning a look of fear. She turned and motioned for my sister to join them in the safety behind my father.

Her eyes widened as she looked from me to our mother.

"Meg, don't!" I pleaded. She hesitated, biting her lip. Her head rapidly turning from me to our parents and then back again.

"Something is happening. She's luring you all some how. This isn't right!"

Megorna wavered, her gaze flickering between us before stepping in my parents' direction.

"I'm sorry," she whispered, then crossed the room to stand by Mother's side.

My heart sank. I shouldn't be surprised. She was the favored. She was obedient. She was the jewel of our country. The center of my mother's attention. The perfect heir to her title.

"She's been the destruction of our land this entire time, my dear," Mother murmured, her voice calm and calculated.

"What are you saying, Bree?" Father asked, desperation lacing his tone.

"We've lived in desperation for too long" she replied, stepping away from him.

"How could you possibly know that?" Milo interjected, his voice sharp with defiance. My brother still stood at my side with his fist, clinch tightly, unsure of what to believe. I could see it all over his face. The doubt the defensiveness.

She turned back to Father. "How could we have been so blind?"

I gaped at her, my mind racing.

"What do we do?" Father whispered, his eyes now fixed on me as Milo's hand reached for mine and tightened. There was fear in his gaze—but was it for me, or of me?

"She's the one who should have been on the altar to Vitaeus," Mother said, her voice flat and unyielding. Her dark, hollow eyes swept over me. "Not the baby boy." She hung her head in mock sorrow on my father's shoulder.

A cold, paralyzing fear coursed through me.

I couldn't breathe.

Couldn't think.

She'd kill me.

Tears burned hot trails down my face.

My very own mother would kill me. Place me on an altar and offer me to her gods. My chest heaved up and down rapidly as the thought slowly sank in. She would really kill me. And as the words begin to click together in my head. I finally realized that she would kill me the same way that she killed that boy.

As a burning offering to a greedy goddess.

"You won't," Father stammered, his voice trembling. "You won't put our daughter on the altar."

"She is the curse, Santu," Mother insisted, falling to her knees before him. Her hands clutched his robes, her expression one of desperate conviction. "Think about it! When did this all begin?"

"It's her, my love," she whispered, bowing her head fully at his feet.

"Breetun, you must be mad if you think—"

"What is one for many?" she interrupted, her words cutting through him. "You said it yourself when we gave the baby boy to Vitaeus. You said those words. You love our people, don't you?"

"Mother," Milo interjected, his voice steady but firm. A warning almost. A warning not to push our father and not to push him. Because I knew my brother would protect me or at least try to.

She spun on him, her eyes feral. "Quiet!" she hissed.

Milo flinched, retreating a step. The anchor on my mother's face in that moment with something of true terror.

"Mother, Kae'dinah should not be put to de—"

Her glare silenced him instantly.

"She is the answer to our healing," Mother said, her voice dripping with false sorrow. Her gaze fell on me, and for a moment, she seemed genuinely pained. But I knew better. She was acting, playing her role flawlessly, as if my death truly grieved her. And even though I heard her words come from her very own mouth, I couldn't believe that they were happening. She was actually suggesting that my death be the solution. She was actually considering giving one of her very own.

It was in this moment that I saw her for who she really was. She'd do anything to have everyone fall before her and worship her. To be the answer for our country's healing. To be the one who has sacrificed the most to be considered the most honorable.

Her pride was disgusting.

She bowed her head in mock resignation. "Yes, the cost is great for us, but the reward for all of Anima—and even eastern Naedorn—would be immeasurable."

"You're evil," I spat, lunging toward her.

That metallic scent filled the air again, coiling around me like an unseen chain. Milo's grip slackened at my hand, and I turned to him in confusion. His face was pale, his wide eyes staring at me—not with love, but with terror.

I froze.

"Milo!" I yelled in shock.

The smell. The change. It was doing something. To Milo. To Father. Twisting them, turning them against me.

"Milo?" My heart plummeted as I realized the truth.

"Your eyes," he muttered.

"Milo," I whispered. He shoved me completely, and I stumbled to the floor. My hands hit the cold stone, and pain shot through my bandaged wrists. I stayed there, shaking, breathing heavily.

No.

I dragged myself to my feet, pushing my gown aside as I rose. I faced my family—the people I had loved and trusted all my life—and saw nothing familiar in their expressions.

Fear.

Disgust.

Confusion.

"Milo, please," I begged, reaching for him. He flinched as if my touch might burn him.

"Don't let them do this to me, brother," I pleaded. My heart felt like it was breaking completely in half. Because the look on my brother's face was the final blow to my destruction. "I love you. I am your sister." Tears blurred my vision, and I struggled to see his face through the haze.

"What is the proclamation?" Milo's voice cracked, his fear palpable. But he couldn't even look at me.

My knees buckled again, and I sank to the floor. This can't be real. This has to be a dream.

"The fate of our world rests upon your decision, my king," my mother purred, her words dripping with triumph.

Through my tears, I lifted my head to meet my father's gaze.

"Father, please," the plea escaped me on a trembling lip. I had never felt a brokenness so heavy. An isolation so empty and a rejection so intense. The way he looked at me. It was as if his decision had already been made. A finality in his eyes that already said their goodbyes to me.

His jaw trembled, and a single tear slipped down his face.

No.

No, no, no.

"One for many," he said, his voice breaking.

A wail tore from me, raw and unrecognizable. A sob so violent that I know it burned the lining of my throat. I could feel it. The foundation of my world crumbled beneath me.

"You sentence me to death?" I sobbed, my voice shaking.

"GUARDS!" Mother barked, her voice sharp, quick, and

unrelenting.

The doors burst open, and guards flooded the room, their boots pounding against the stone floor.

"You sentence me to death?" I screamed again, my voice hoarse. Father turned away from me, his shoulders hunched. He couldn't face me. But he would, I rushed to my feet and made my way to the dais, intentionally placing myself in the line of his vision so that he had to see me.

"Do you think killing me will save this kingdom?" I cried, my footsteps moving quicker now as the words cut through my throbbing head.

"Don't let her near us!" mother shrieked.

The guards hesitated.

"She's lying about me!" I yelled, my voice desperate and raw. "Father, please don't let her do this to me!"

But he wouldn't even look at me.

Coward. He was a coward.

The guards grabbed my arms, their grips like iron. I fought them, thrashing with every ounce of strength I had.

"Don't touch me!" I screamed; I would not go, not without a fight. I yelled again, throwing an elbow into one guard's stomach. He doubled over with a groan. I grabbed his sword and spun, waving it before me.

The other guards circled me cautiously. They had every right to fear me, after seeing me train. After killing the general.

"She is to remain unharmed," mother commanded.

"Come any closer, and I swear I'll kill you!" I snarled, my hands trembling.

From the left of my vision, A figure stepped forward. I recognized the steady, deliberate stride even before I turned fully.

Captain Wilt.

His dark brown eyes locked with mine, steady and calm.

"Lower the sword," he said, his voice firm.

"I'll kill you if I have to," I whispered, trembling.

But could I? Could I really harm my friend?

"You won't," he said, his tone unwavering. He knew I couldn't hurt him, and I hated that he knew that.

The hurt in his voice sliced through me. I faltered, my grip on the sword loosening.

"Lower the sword," he said again, stepping closer.

The final ounce of something inside me shattered. I had no more left to hold onto. He wasn't going to help me. He was going to stand with them. He was going to let them take me. He was just going to obey and ask no questions.

My throat tightened as the tears came again, spilling down my face. "You're just like them?" I choked. My hands trembled under the weight of the metal sword. He saw the moment of weakness when my stance slackened.

And, he lunged.

The sword clattered to the ground as he twisted my arms behind my back.

"You're a liar and a coward!" I shouted, thrashing against him.

The guards approached again, emboldened by my disarmament. Wilt's grip tightened, and his voice dropped to a whisper, meant only for me.

"I'll get you out of here, I promise. It's you or no one, Kae'dinah. I will get you out."

I stilled, my breath hitching.

"Keep fighting," he murmured. "Make it real."

A sob of relief tore from my chest, but I obeyed, thrashing against him as if his words hadn't reached me. "You're all cowards!" I screamed. "I'm your child! Your blood!"

Seconds stretched into eternity.

"Milo!" I cried, looking towards my brother. But he refused to look at me. Then I turned my gaze to my father and called for him. "Father!"

Neither of them looked at me. Milo stormed toward the exit, his face twisted in anguish.

"Meg!" My voice broke. I caught her tear-streaked face as she knelt, sobbing into her hands.

Her lip trembled as she whispered, "I'm sorry."

I felt as if I couldn't breathe. As if the woman who gave birth to me had taken her very own dagger and ripped my heart clean out. The room seemed to spin air seemed to vanish.

The guards hauled me toward the doors, dragging me across the cold stone floor. "Father!" I screamed, my voice raw and desperate.

He didn't turn. His shoulders just shook violently as silent sobs emptied him.

The queen's voice rang out as the doors closed. "Prepare her to be sacrificed."

Wilt's jaw clenched as he followed, his eyes meeting mine for a fleeting second.

I turned one last time towards my family on the dais in between the closing doors, Mother's face gleaming with triumph. Her lips twisted into a cruel smile.

"I will kill you," I growled towards her, thrashing against the hold of my guards yet again.

"Vitaeus honors you." she said and the doors slammed

shut, sealing me inside another nightmare.

# Chapter 18

I made them drag me.

I refused their commands to walk or move forward after being locked away for hours.

To the depths with them. To the depths with her. To the depths with the gods.

These people.

My family?

How easily they cast me aside. How easily she convinced them to rid themselves of me.

They are no family to me.

The thought burned, rolling endlessly through my mind as the two guards carried me, one beneath each arm, up the grand stairway toward my private quarters.

I let myself hang there, suspended between the arms of two familiar men whose names I didn't even know.

The one on my left glanced at me, his eyes filled with something that almost looked like worry. But the one on the right... His face twisted with a revolting pride. He carried me as if it were an honor to escort me to my death.

All for Vitaeus.

*Vitaeus honors you.*

Her words echoed in my mind like a dagger twisting deeper

with every syllable. It makes me sick.

*For Vitaeus.*

Well, death to her. Death to all the gods. Death to my mother.

A tear slipped down my cheek, slow and warm, as I finally let the thought settle in: there was no hope. Whatever thread of hope remained between my mother and me had long since frayed. She's hated me for so long. No matter what I did, it was never enough for her.

The painted portraits hanging in the master hallway flashed in my mind—our family frozen in false perfection. My cries came unbidden, a wail so guttural and raw that I didn't even realize it was me at first.

The guard on my right dropped me.

I fell hard, the stone floor biting into my knees and palms. Pain flared sharply in my body, but I barely felt it over the weight in my chest.

"Get up!" the man barked.

I didn't answer. My sobs came harder, shaking me as I pressed my hands against the cold stone. My father. My brother. My sister. Did they deserve death, too? Or was it fear that kept them in line? Fear that forced them to say nothing? To comply?

"I said, get up!" he snapped again, nudging me with his boot.

"No," I croaked, my voice breaking. Just a few more cracks until total brokenness.

The man crouched, his voice lowering to a growl. "You're no better than the stray dogs we chase from the city streets, now. I'll drag you myself if I have to."

Drag me? I'd like to see him try. I lifted my head, my glare

177

hot and unrelenting, every ounce of fire I had left blazing in my gaze. "Then drag me, coward!" I roared.

He stilled with terror. His eyes met mine. But my words seemed to strip away the last of his patience, replacing it with pure hatred. His hand shot forward, grabbing a fistful of my hair.

"No!" I screamed, the searing pain like a thousand needles piercing my scalp. My hands clawed at his, desperation flooding me. "Please!"

My vision blurred as the nausea in my gut churned violently, threatening to pull me under. The ache in my body was nothing compared to the betrayal tearing me apart inside. I had been reduced to a status of nothing. I was losing my family. My home. My title. My honor. My life.

"Enough!"

Wilt's voice boomed down the hallway, a deep, commanding sound that froze the air around us. His heavy steps thundered closer, joined by another.

The guard's hand released my hair. The pain ebbed immediately, leaving me trembling. I pressed my forehead to the floor, my tears hot and endless, as the guards' voices tangled in heated argument.

"The queen said unharmed," Nagel.

Captain Nagel was here. I could hear the tone of his voice. He was very upset.

"She wouldn't move," the guard muttered, his earlier arrogance replaced by a wary defensiveness. They outranked him.

"Then carry her there," Nagel growled through clenched teeth.

My body shook as I pushed myself up, but when I opened

my eyes and looked forward, it wasn't the cold stone hall that met my gaze. It was Wilt's.

His dark brown eyes softened as they fell on me. His outstretched hand lingered in the space between us, a silent offer of help.

For a moment, I stared at him, wondering how someone so familiar could feel so alien. He stood here now, just as compliant as the rest of them, delivering me to my death under my mother's orders.

So, I spat at his hand.

Wilt pulled it back slowly, his jaw tightening as he wiped the spit off on his pants. His mask didn't falter, though the subtle flicker of frustration crossed his face as his tongue pressed against the inside of his cheek.

"Get up," he said, his voice calm, almost too controlled.

"I can't," I muttered, my voice barely a whisper.

"Are you hurt?"

"Yes." My words trembled, cracking under the weight of my emotions.

"Where?" he pressed, his hand brushing the scruff of his jaw as he glanced at the other guards still arguing a few paces away.

"Everywhere." My tears fell freely now, unbidden and unstoppable. "I hurt everywhere. Everything is broken."

For a moment, he didn't move. But his eyes softened, and I saw the faintest trace of understanding pass through him. He knew what I meant—that the pain wasn't just in my body but radiated from everywhere, cutting deeper than any blade ever could.

A loose breath escaped him before he reached down and placed his hands under my arms, hoisting me to my feet in one smooth motion. The guards stiffened, their eyes wide in stunned silence. Then, before anyone could object, Wilt shifted forward, slipping an arm beneath my knees while the other cradled my back.

I clung to his neck instinctively, resting my face against his shoulder as the sobs racked through me.

I wanted to give up—because fighting while broken felt like I was only scattering the pieces of myself further and further away.

"Captain," the guard who had been on my left stammered, hurrying to keep pace with Wilt's long strides. "Do you think it's appropriate to carry her like this?"

"Do you think it was appropriate to drag her by her hair?" Wilt's voice was sharp, biting, but he didn't even glance in the man's direction.

"No," the guard replied quietly, shame in his tone.

"Get out of my sight." Wilt snapped. "Your orders were to get her ready for the ritual, and you can't even manage to get her to the room."

"My apologies, Captain." The man fell back, cowed by the reprimand, leaving Wilt to carry me the rest of the way alone.

Wilt's voice dropped to a whisper, barely audible over the soft echoes of our footsteps. "Do you think Kelta would help?"

My eyes widened.

"What?" I mumbled against his shoulder, unsure if I'd heard him right.

"Kelta." His tone was insistent, though his stride slowed slightly as he gave me more time to respond. "Would she help me get you out of here?"

Get me out? I glanced at him, his eyes still fixed forward.

He would be risking everything? And, Kelta. My handmaid, my confidante—someone who spoke love and reverence for the gods, just as she spoke love for me.

"No," I muttered, the answer weighing heavily in my chest. I knew she wouldn't.

Wilt sighed, his arms tightening around me briefly before we reached the door to my chambers. Two new guards stood watch, their gazes flicking nervously between Wilt and me. One retrieved a heavy key of black iron from his pocket and unlocked the door, pushing it open to reveal what awaited inside.

He carried me in and set me down gently on the chaise, his movements careful, almost tender.

I glanced around the room, once vibrant and filled with Meg's and my possessions. Now, everything was shoved to the walls, leaving the center bare and stark. A line of handmaids stood waiting, their hands still at their sides, their expressions impassive—except for one.

Kelta wouldn't meet my eyes. Her tears held back, her betrayal louder for it.

"You can chain her there," a sharp voice cut through the silence, drawing my attention.

I turned to see a woman step forward, her dark, graying hair coiled tightly into a high bun. Her heavyset frame and stern features exuded an air of authority. Recognition hit me like a slap—Kelta's mother, the queen's personal maid.

"Chains?" I asked, snapping my head toward Wilt.

"Yes, chains," the woman replied, her voice smooth but laced with malice. "You killed a general. You didn't think we'd leave you unrestrained, did you?" Her smile was tight, venomous.

181

"I wouldn't hurt *them*," I said, lifting my chin toward Kelta and the other maids.

"We don't know that," she countered coolly. "We can't take any chances." She turned to Wilt, dismissing me entirely. "Captain, chain her by her wrists to that pillar." She gestured to a pile of iron cuffs at the base of one of the room's ornate pillars.

Wilt's jaw clenched as his eyes darted to me, then to the pile of chains. He hesitated for a heartbeat before stepping forward to retrieve them.

He crouched in front of me, holding out his hand. "Your wrists," he said quietly, his voice softer than before.

Kelta's mother scoffed, rolling her eyes as she turned to bark orders at the maids. "Warm water for the bath. Goat's milk, honey, and roses. Fetch the blood robes for her to wear to bed."

I placed my trembling hands in Wilt's, his fingers working carefully around the bandages on my wrists. He set each ring I wore on the cushion beside me before running his thumb lightly over the cloth on my skin. His touch lingered, hesitant, before he reached for the shackles.

The cool iron snapped closed around my wrists with a heavy finality.

"Jahiel," I whispered.

"Yes?" he murmured, his eyes fixed on his work as he fastened the chains.

"I'm scared."

"Me too," he exhaled, the admission so quiet I almost didn't hear it.

He tightened the last clasp and stood in one fluid motion, crossing the room to Kelta's mother. "She's shackled," he said, his voice void of emotion. "Anything else you need?"

"No," she said, her tone sharp. "We'll take it from here."

Wilt's gaze flicked back to me, just for a moment, before he turned and left the room.

# Chapter 19

They washed me for an hour. Warm water mixed with goat's milk and crushed roses ran over my skin and through my hair. They scrubbed under my fingernails, each movement precise and methodical. My hair was brushed until it gleamed, causing my black coils to bounce all the more. The fragrant oils they worked into my scalp, left a bittersweet aroma I couldn't ignore. The sacrificial priest arrived, his voice steady as he read sacred text over me, but the words blurred together into meaningless sounds.

I heard nothing.

I felt nothing.

I barely heard what they said, barely comprehended their requests, though they tugged and positioned me like a doll. I had no clue of the time or just how long I've been prepped.

Now I sat at the edge of my bed, the white silk sheets beneath me pristine and cold, a cruel contrast to the suffocating weight of the iron shackles on my wrists and ankles. Kelta and Daph knelt before me, massaging oils into my legs with careful precision, their touch routine but detached.

"Will I sleep with these shackles?" I asked, my voice raw from disuse.

Kelta's hands faltered. Her eyes met mine briefly, then darted away as she resumed the task.

"Kelta," I repeated, louder this time. My tone startled Daph, whose hands paused mid-motion.

"Yes?" Kelta's voice was tense, her focus fixed on my leg.

"Will I sleep in these shackles?" I demanded, my voice breaking. "I asked you a question."

Her fingers stilled completely. She took a sharp breath before responding. "I'm not obliged to answer your questions anymore."

The statement hit like a slap. I flinched, inhaling shakily. "What am I to you now, friend, that you can't even look at me... Answer me."

Her gaze dropped, and for a brief moment, her expression cracked. She wiped at her sleeve, catching a tear before it could fall. Then she turned back to her task, silent and rigid.

I turned away from her, unable to look at the stranger she'd become. "Daph," I said softly. "Will I sleep in these shackles?"

Daph hesitated, her eyes flickering between Kelta and me. Finally, she rose, rinsing her hands in the water trough before drying them on a cloth. She moved with deliberate slowness, as if trying to delay the inevitable answer.

"You will sleep in the shackles," she said, her voice careful but final. "Guards will come to escort you at dawn."

I exhaled shakily, my breath hitching in my chest.

*Dawn.*

How soon was dawn?

"What time is it?" I whispered, the words catching in my throat.

Daph searched my face before answering. "It's just after midnight. We're about to leave." She gestured toward the maids bustling quietly around the room.

I nodded absently, the weight of her words pressing down on me. "Will—"

Three sharp knocks sounded from the other side of the door, stealing the question from my lips. My stomach twisted. I knew instantly who it was.

Kelta hurried to the door, her expression pinched with agitation. She cracked it open, leaning out slightly. "Yes?"

"I know you've readied her for bed," Wilt's voice came low and urgent. "I just need to see her. Please."

"You can't be in here, Captain," Kelta hissed, her tone clipped.

"I know," he said quickly, "but I only have hours. After tonight, we'll never have this conversation again."

Kelta sputtered, her lips tightening.

"Let him in," Daph said calmly, stepping past Kelta to address the room. "As long as he doesn't touch her, it's fine. We'll know if he does."

Kelta swallowed hard, her jaw tight. With a curt nod, she turned to the other maids. "You have five minutes," she muttered before they all grabbed their things to leave.

The door clicked shut behind Wilt as he strode quickly to my side.

"Don't touch me," I said sharply, shrinking back. "They'll smell the oil on you."

"I'm getting you out of here," he said, crouching in front of me. His hands moved to the chains on my ankles as he pulled a small dagger from his belt and began working at the locks.

"Jahiel," I whispered, my voice unsteady, "how do you expect to get me out of this building?"

"I don't know," he admitted, his focus fixed on the chains.

"We need a plan. How will we get past the maids?"

"I don't know, Kae'dinah."

"Do you even have a plan?"

He exhaled sharply as the first lock clicked open. "No."

"So what are we doing?" I hissed, flexing my freed wrist. "I can't just run around the castle. They'll kill you, Jahiel!"

"And you'll be dead by morning," he snapped, his voice rising. "What does it matter? At least we tried. I'd rather die trying than sit here while they prepare you for slaughter."

"I don't want your life at risk because of me! You've worked too hard—"

"My life means nothing if you're gone," he hissed, voice cracking.

"You don't mean that."

"I do," he said, quieter now, but certain. He reached for my hand, gripping it tightly. "I'm not a man of nobility. There's nothing else for me to achieve here. And you... you're my closest friend, my reason. That's why I'm risking everything." He gestured between us. "So please. Let me try. Let me do something."

I opened my mouth to respond, but the words never came. His hands rose to my face—gentle, trembling—and then his lips were on mine.

I froze.

Then, hesitantly, I leaned into him. The kiss was soft, hesitant, hopeful. But it didn't feel right. It didn't feel *true*. His kiss didn't pull something out of me—it pressed something down. I'd imagined this moment once, long ago, when the world was gentler and we were still innocent. But this wasn't a love story. Not mine, anyway.

His head tilted, his tongue brushing over my lips, his hand slipping into my hair—down, further, to my back.

I flinched.

The spell broke.

I pulled away, breathless but not breathless in the way stories described. Jahiel stepped back, wiping a hand across his mouth, avoiding my gaze. My chest ached, but not from longing—from the weight of clarity.

I had read love story after love story, where the kiss was always the moment everything changed. But this... this proved something else.

I didn't want to be kissed like I was a decision made out of desperation. I didn't want to feel relief when it ended.

"Change into pants. Something warm," he muttered, his voice rough. "You won't make it far in that dress."

He turned away like it meant nothing.

Did it?

I numbly peeled off the blood-red gown, replacing it with dark cotton leggings and thick leather pants. My hands trembled as I dressed. The tunic, the vest, the wool-lined cloak. I strapped on my boots. Fastened my daggers. Readied myself for escape.

*"Take me,"* a familiar voice whispered in my ear.

I froze, whipping my head toward the satchel by the fireplace. The journal inside seemed to hum with energy, its presence palpable. Without hesitation, I grabbed it, slinging the strap across my shoulder. I raced to my vanity and began to throw my things in the satchel.

"Let's go," Wilt whispered, his sword drawn.

I took a step toward him, but a small scream rang out from the adjoining room, sharp and brief. The sound was cut off with terrifying finality.

Wilt's stance shifted, his grip tightening on the hilt of his sword. "Stay behind me," he said, his voice low and deadly.

I drew my dagger. We moved to the door, opening it cautiously.

The scene before me was hard to process. My gaze fell first to the main hallway door, where the two guards who had been stationed outside my door now lay motionless on the floor.

My breath caught as I scanned the room. Each maid was trembling, their breathing rapid, while shadowy figures dressed in black held knives to their throats.

I clapped a hand over my mouth to muffle a gasp. Wilt reached back, his free hand gripping mine, grounding me in the chaos. From the shadows, a tall figure emerged, his presence commanding and cold.

I tightened my grip on the pommel of my dagger as his masked face turned toward me. His dark eyes bore into mine.

"We're here for you," he said, his voice calm yet firm.

I let out a gasp.

"Who the hell are you?" Wilt barked, his tone sharp and unwavering.

The man ignored the question, his gaze fixed on me. "We've come to save the Princess."

That accent.

The booming authority in his voice stirred something familiar in me. I blinked, my heartbeat thundering as recognition sparked. I had heard this voice. I heard him in the Great Hall early today.

Wilt stepped forward. "I'll ask again: who are you?"

Releasing Wilt's hand, I stepped from behind him, placing myself between the two men.

"I know who you are," I said, my voice steadier than I felt.

The masked man straightened. "We don't have time for this. Are you coming?"

"Yes," I answered without hesitation.

"What?" Wilt turned to me, his voice rising in disbelief.

"You can stay behind," the man in black said curtly, his tone dismissive. "We will deal with the witnesses."

"No!" I yelped, the panic sharp in my voice. "Don't kill the maids."

The six men exchanged glances, silently assessing the situation. Finally, the leader nodded. "Knock them out."

Before I could protest further, the men moved with precision. Each maid was subdued as gloved hands clamped over their mouth. Kelta's wide eyes locked with mine before rolling back as she collapsed unconscious.

"What about him?" one of the masked men asked, nodding toward Wilt.

"He stays with me," I said firmly, stepping in front of Wilt. "He freed me from my shackles."

The leader's eyes lingered on Wilt, assessing him coldly. Then, with a series of rapid hand signals, he communicated silently with his team.

Another man emerged from the shadows, holding a solid black scarves.

"Wrap these around your head, Princess," he instructed.

I obeyed without question, tying the scarves tightly around my face and loose hair.

The leader turned to me, blinking rapidly before asking his next question. "Do you have the book?"

Shock rippled through me. "How do you know about the book?"

"Do you have it?" he repeated, his tone sharp.

"Yes," I said hesitantly.

"Good." He turned without another word, striding toward the door. "Then we're exactly where we're supposed to be."

I hurried after him, lowering my voice to a whisper. "How do you know about the book?"

He didn't respond.

"Prince!" I hissed, the realization hitting me and him like a thunderclap. Yes, I was sure it was him now.

He froze, spinning back toward me in one swift motion. Before I could say another word, he pressed me firmly against the door frame with his forearm, his gloved finger pressed to my lips, silencing me.

Wilt's blade was drawn in an instant, the tip pointed directly at the man's chest. "Get your hands off her," Wilt growled.

The man didn't flinch, his eyes locked on mine. "Tell her to keep her mouth shut," he said coolly, addressing Wilt without breaking his eyes from mine. His eyes were deep gray, like the familiar storm clouds I had seen earlier. "If anyone in this Highest-forsaken house hears who I am, this will be another kind of war."

"I know it's you," I whispered, my voice trembling despite the defiance in my words. "I know your voice from earlier today. You're the Prince of Valdeen."

He exhaled sharply, his hand dropping from my face. Wilt hesitated for a moment before lowering his blade.

The prince straightened, removing his face cover and pulling back his hood. "Yes, I am," he admitted, his voice firm. "I believe I was sent here for you. But we have to move… Now."

# Chapter 20

Four of the Valdeenian men walked briskly ahead, their feet making no sound. The cool, silent stone halls stretched long before us. The eerie silence of the space pressed heavily on me. Once familiar, this palace now felt disconnected from my soul. It now felt like a skeleton, as if all the things that once made this place warm and alive were now gone and stripped away, leaving bones sharpened to kill.

I had to breathe deeply in order to keep myself moving and stay grounded.

I looked around at the men who quietly assessed every hall we moved down. I observed how they all silently moved, and I wonder… how did they know to come and find me? And why would they risk so much to rescue me?

My thoughts swarmed my head like an agitated hive. Questions flew, searching for answers that would not come. Answers from my family. Answers from my Jahiel. Answers from these men and their prince.

I took in another deep pull of air. We were nearing the exit.

Almost to freedom.

Almost out of this place—the place I had called home for

the entirety of my life. It had been my sanctuary, my safe place. The weight of that realization settled over me like a shroud as we crept toward the palace's private, sacrificial quarters. A side door to the city lies just on the other side. Of course, this would be the exit we'd need to take to the city. Now that everything had been prepared here, there were the least amount of people, as everyone was exhausted and had left the area for their rooms. Suddenly, the men signaled us to stop.

Jahiel's hand moved to his sword hilt, his shoulders stiffening. He tilted his head toward the voices drifting through the hall ahead.

"I won't allow this!" Milo's voice rang out, sharp and furious, echoing down the stone halls. My heart leapt, my brother. Why was he down here so late in the night?

"Please, spare yourself the humiliation of begging, son," the Queen replied, her tone clipped and dripping with disdain. "It's unbecoming of you. It's especially unbecoming of a king."

My breath caught. Her voice sent chills down my spine. My forehead, already moist with sweat, seemed to produce even more in the presence of her voice alone.

"The Queen," I mouthed to Prince, who was now looking back at the Captain and I. He nodded silently, his expression grim, and moved to confer with the men at the front of our line.

"I'm not begging," Milo shot back, his voice rising with indignation. "I'm demanding. This is my sister! Your daughter!"

My heart seemed to constrict as I listened to the pleas of my brother. Tears began to pull in my eyes as I leaned my

194

body against the stone wall behind me. Just like he always had, Milo was defending me. He was here. He was trying.

"My daughter?" The Queen's words dripped with venom. "I have one daughter, and she is the only one who deserves my protection. The only one deserving of all of this."

I froze, every muscle in my body tightening, even though she had told me before I no longer belonged to her, her words still pierced through me like a jagged sword. Jahiel placed a steadying hand on my arm, his face unreadable.

"This is madness!" Milo snapped, a maddening laugh bubbling from him. "You're condemning her for what? To appease the gods? To save your own ambition? Mother, if you are so favored by our gods, why don't you ask them for another way!"

The Queen's laughter echoed down the hall, cold and mirthless. "You're so naïve, Milo. Do you think ambition alone has kept this family in power for generations? Do you think the favor of one is enough to save an entire region? Sacrifices must be made. Kae'dinah... is simply fulfilling her role, her only purpose. To die on behalf of the freedom of others. "

"Role?" Milo's voice cracked with disbelief. "Her role is to die so that we can get crops? Mother, it has to be something else. Maybe we can send scribes and scientists out to the land to see why it won't yield a harvest. Perhaps we should slow down and consider alternative approaches. You would sacrifice your blood for what? Temporary reprieve? What happens if this problem happens again? Will it be one of my children on that altar?

"You are a foolish boy. The gods ensure our survival forever. She is not just the answer to this season but the answer to their survival forever," the Queen replied, her voice now low and dangerous. "And they see more clearly than you ever could. They see our future. So I only beg them to have mercy on your behalf, for you are clueless. I pray that they teach you how to rule a kingdom when it's your turn to sit upon the throne."

"This is a disgrace," Milo growled. "You're tearing our family apart! Kae'dinah is worth more than all the gods' promises combined."

The Queen let out a derisive snort. "*Your* sister is worthless to me, Milo. Your heart isn't in the right space to see that yet, though. I had to make her worthless to me to take this step for Anima. Learn how to or the land will suffer."

"You lie too well for your own good, mother." Milo hissed. The tone of his voice taking on something more lethal than I had ever heard from him before. "Admit it, you never found worth in her. That's the real reason she's been killed."

I heard the click of the queen's heels to the stone, as if she were taking slow, careful steps towards my brother. My hands squeezed into fists so tight that I could feel my pulse pumping in my palms.

"You want my truth, son? She has never held any space in my heart. She has always been a weak-willed, insubordinate child who never understood her place. Those children are the ones who destroy kingdoms, and I couldn't have that."

Jahiel's grip on my arm returned, tightening as though sensing I might crumble under the weight of her words. I bit my lip hard enough to draw blood, refusing to cry.

"And yet you call Meg worthy? She was born in the same womb as us. It seems to me that the cause of that lies on your shoulders, not Kae'Dinah's." Milo spat, his fury boiling over.

196

"Oh boy, you were so young. Now please leave from here, the more you beg, the more I favor your sister."

Milo scoffs, "You are disgusting. I hate that I even call you mother."

"And I hate that I will have to call you king. Maybe I should fix that too?"

"Is that a threat?"

The queen laughed as her shoes clicked away from Milo and away from us.

I could sense Milo's rage, "I am the heir. I've trained for this all my life. And you—" He shuttered. "You insult me by threatening my ascension to my father's throne. By denying my demands?"

"Your father's throne?" She was laughing louder now.

"You don't think my father would wonder how the third in line took the throne so quickly?"

The Queen paused. The silence was deafening.

"Meg is obedient. She listens. She doesn't question the will of the gods—or mine. Unlike you and your sister, Milo, she knows when to bow. And no, I don't think he'd wonder anything."

"You're always defiant, always clinging to foolish ideals that have no place in our country," she continued. "The gods have already seen your weakness, Milo. Don't make me prove them right. Now, be a good boy and leave before I have you prepared alongside *your* sister."

Milo's breathing grew heavy, his rage barely contained. "You're no Queen. You're a coward and a witch."

The Queen's voice dropped to a deadly whisper. "Be careful, Milo. You may think you're protected, but the gods' patience is not infinite. Cross me again, and I will see to it that Meg becomes the heir within the year."

"I won't stand by tomorrow," Milo declared. "I won't participate in this... this—"

"You'll do as you're told, you stand tall at the front supporting this to show solidarity for our family and kingdom," the Queen snapped. "The ceremony will proceed, and you will be there. That's not a request."

The conversation had ended. I exhaled as the tears I hadn't noticed continued to cascade down my face.

He had tried. My brother had tried on my behalf. I didn't know where my father was. I hadn't seen Meg, but Milo had tried.

A wave of restorative love washed over me. My brother tried.

The Queen's footsteps faded, but Milo's sharp stride approached us.

We all tensed and looked towards each other.

Then, Jahiel motioned for us to retreat further into the shadows, weapons drawn, but my chest tightened. The Prince shook his head, stopping us in our steps, but instead signaled for his men to draw their weapons.

They couldn't hurt Milo.

Not my brother.

Not the one person still fighting for me.

I moved forward, my hand lightly touching the pommel of the prince's sword, and shook my head, no.

His eyes widened with confusion, then Milo strode around the corner, muttering curses under his breath. He didn't see us immediately, his focus fixed on the ground. The Valdeenians remained poised, their weapons ready. I don't know what made him look but when he finally noticed us, his hand darted to his sword, his face paling with shock. His eyes scanned the men, calculating the threat.

I took a shaky step forward, lifting both hands in surrender, then my brother's eyes locked onto me. His hand froze on his sword. Our gazes met.

My own narrowed, daring him to call for help, to summon guards to stop us. A single tear trailed from the corner. His eyes followed it, and my brother visibly softened before us.

His mouth snapped shut as he stepped back. His hands mirroring mine in surrender. His gaze moved deliberately over the men, then to the Captain, and finally back to me. He took a deep breath, his posture relieved, before nodding.

He understood. He understood what was happening, that these people were getting me out and getting me away from the death waiting for me at sunrise.

He knew this was my way to freedom. Without a word, he placed a hand over his heart and bowed.

I shook my head and took two more steps towards him.

Jahiel grabbed my arm, pulling me back as Milo shook his head at my advance.

He pointed to his head, both fingers resting on his temples. *Use my head.*

I knew the gesture; it was familiar. It was the way he told me to think before I acted. He moved towards us, out of the moonlight and into the shadows.

Then he placed his fist back on his heart and thrummed twice.

*Follow your heart.*

Then he pulled the small dagger from his pocket. The one I had made for his fiftieth birthday, engraved with an M. It wasn't big enough for combat, but he often kept it to peel an apple or open a letter. My tears were now uncontrollable. It's a wonder how I could even see him, still see anything.

The tears almost seemed to melt away the anger I had towards the world, towards my family. Like a smoke, that calmed the bees once raging.

I raised a trembling hand to my mouth, trying to hold back my own cries.

He was giving me the dagger.

I shook my head, but he nodded yes. Grabbed my hands and placed he small dagger in them. His calloused hands covered mine, warm and firm. He briefly rested his forehead on mine before looking up at the group behind me.

"Valdeen," he whispered to himself. Noting the attire of the men who were getting me out. "Okay, I'll call my men away. You exit through the side door and head towards the city. You have maybe an hour before they're in your chambers again."

He looked at the men again, his head bobbing up and down with confirmation as if telling himself that these men could actually free me.

"I love you." Milo pulled me into a tight embrace, and I had to push my face into his torso to keep from sobbing loudly and giving us all away.

"I love you." He straightened quickly, pushing me away. I gazed up at his unreadable face. Milo turned and wiped his face quickly, his steps growing heavier as he masked his hurt and disappeared down the cold stone hall.

We waited until we heard him call for assistance from a few of his guards.

"Let's go," Jahiel whispered, his hand brushing mine to pull me forward.

I looked at the dagger in my palm. Squeezing its pommel before tucking it away.

My brother...

I sighed, then turned towards the men, who looked at me and nodded. We moved in perfect silence, the air thick with the weight of the severance of this house, this family, and land.

# Chapter 21

The scent of water, soil, and rot clung to the air—an unpleasant combination that turned my stomach. The streets of Floos were far less dazzling than I had been told. They'd fed us lies.

I wasn't sure how much my family truly knew, but I had been completely blind.

The capital city of Anima was drowning in poverty. We wound through narrow alleys lined with crumbling brick huts, moving so quickly I could barely keep pace. Jahiel gripped my hand—firm, unrelenting—as he pulled me along.

We passed hunched figures begging for coin, their voices thin and desperate. And among the poor stood others who wore their desires like crowns. Dressed in sheer silks and delicate lace, a group of men and women leaned against the pillars of a brothel, their bodies as exposed as their intentions.

"Keep your head down," the Prince warned, his voice low as we passed. From within the building came the moans and cries of sex workers, their pleasure loud and exaggerated. Some called out to us from the doorway, beckoning with outstretched arms and painted smiles.

Out of the corner of my eye, I caught two harlots sauntering toward the men who had freed me, their hips swaying with calculated grace, hoping to intercept us.

"What's the rush, boys?" one of them purred.

No one answered. No one looked. We kept moving.

Jahiel's hand pressed harder into the small of my back, urging me forward.

"You look tense, darling. Come join us," the other cooed, bold and bare beneath gauzy fabric. They were brazen—shameless in their seduction, their bodies on display like offerings, their smiles both charming and cruel.

Jahiel gave a sharp shake of his head and followed the Valdeen men down another alleyway. I looked back just once, catching the two women as they turned to one another and began to kiss, their laughter echoing behind us.

I swallowed hard.

The brothels thrived, while the streets begged for mercy. Pleasure glittered in their eyes the same way it did in the eyes of the nobles. Even my own family.

Pleasure ruled here. And that drive alone—it was deadly.

Pleasure and power would make us do just about anything.

This was Floos.

This was Anima.

This was how the gods wanted us—

Blind to what truly mattered.

Bile rose in my throat.

At last, the two men leading us slowed as we approached an alehouse. I exhaled, praying whatever came next would be nothing like what we'd just left behind.

Outside, a man dressed in familiar black leathers stood waiting. In the pale moonlight, I noticed that all the men wore the same dark attire—a uniform, perhaps?

The Prince pulled back his hood, removed his gloves, and tucked them into his pocket. Silver chains hung around his neck, and a wolf-shaped ring glinted on his finger. He extended a hand to the waiting man—a gesture of camaraderie.

"Can we rest safely here?" His voice, deep and measured, broke the silence.

The man nodded, his eyes darting over our group. "Yes, sir. The owner's been paid for his silence tonight. He'll only serve those I allow in." His gaze lingered on the familiar faces of the squad before landing on me. But it was when they landed on Jahiel that his brow furrowed in confusion before he turned back to the Prince.

"An hour's all we'll have with our new guests," he said, chuckling as he brushed past the Prince, patting his back on the way into the alehouse.

"Sir, that's one more than we planned for," the man said quietly as they disappeared inside.

Jahiel glanced at me, the corner of his mouth lifting in a faint smirk as his grip on my hand tightened. "How are you feeling?"

"Alive," I said softly—the only word that felt true. My body ached, pain crawling from my ankles up through my thighs after the frantic escape. My mind couldn't begin to piece together everything that had just happened. All I could do was breathe—and cling to the strange, fragile sense of gratitude taking root in me. These men were risking everything to save me.

The Prince returned, expression unreadable. He extended a hand to Jahiel, clasping it with a firm nod.

"Let's speak inside," he said. "Princess, keep your scarf

up and your head down. Your eyes are... uncommon. I'm certain your people would recognize you."

I looked to Jahiel. He was the only one here I knew—the only thread of familiarity in a world unraveling. He held my gaze, then gave a small nod, leaving the choice to me.

I turned back to the Prince and nodded without speaking, then followed him and the others into the building.

The door creaked as it shut behind us. I kept my gaze low, just as he instructed. The floor beneath my feet was dirt—at least I hoped it was dirt. It might've been something worse, so caked and dark that it mimicked earth.

This was what I was meant to stare at now?

From polished black stone to... this.

But I was alive.

I was free.

That would have to be enough.

That would be my mantra, my anchor.

Jahiel guided me through the space—past empty tables and uneven stools. The low murmur of a voice filtered in from somewhere behind the counter. Probably the alehouse owner who'd agreed to shelter us.

The Prince pushed open another door, leading us into a narrow back room where more Valdeenian men waited. Weapons and sacks were propped against walls, and the scent of ale, sweat, and stew hung heavy in the air.

The men who'd pulled me from the castle exhaled deeply as they entered, pulling down their hoods. Up close, I could see not all of them bore the radiant dark skin I'd first noticed. Their tones varied—some lighter, some darker than my own—but all moved with the same quiet intensity. As they loosened their cloaks and shrugged off gear, their shoulders relaxed. A breath of relief passed through the group, unspoken but shared.

I lifted my eyes from the floor fully, letting myself believe I might be safe here too.

"What have you dragged us into now, Prince?" one of them asked, skepticism tightening his voice.

"I have no idea what you mean," the Prince replied, a half-smile tugging at his lips as he stuffed his gloves into a worn sack.

Another crewman chuckled, his eyes darting between Jahiel and me. "And who are they?"

The Prince ignored him, turning to me instead. "You're safe here," he said, his voice low, warm. "You can remove the scarf."

I hesitated, glancing at Jahiel, who stood tense beside me, his eyes sweeping the room with measured caution. When I looked back, the Prince's gaze hadn't shifted. His eyes were dark and steady.

Slowly, I reached up and pulled the scarf from my head. The fabric slipped down my back in a soft rustle as I pushed it behind me.

The room changed.

The man who'd asked the question took a step back. Others froze mid-motion—spoons paused inches from mouths, hands suspended in the act of pulling off cloaks. Silence descended.

"This is astonishing," the Prince said, clapping a hand on the stunned man's shoulder.

"You… you stole the princess?" the man stammered, looking between the two of us like he couldn't decide whether to kneel or flee.

"Rescued," the Prince corrected, his grin crooked. "But... I suppose you could say it like that."

All eyes turned to me. Their awe was sharp enough to slice through bone, and I shifted, suddenly unsteady under the weight of it.

"Your dream—"

"I know," the Prince cut in, sinking onto a stool and lifting a water skin to his lips.

Still gripping Jahiel's arm, I studied the men—each one staring at me like I was something between a legend and a warning. Carefully, I stepped forward and let go of him. The scarf balled into my hands, knotted tight by my restless fingers.

"Thank you," I said quietly, "for what you did for me tonight."

"The most beautiful part," the Prince murmured, "is that she doesn't even realize the significance."

My eyes snapped to him.

He was still watching me.

His storm-colored gaze studied every line of my face—pausing at the coils of my hair, the slope of my cheek, the shape of my lips. When his eyes lingered too long, I bit my lip and looked away, heat rising in my throat.Their awe was suffocating.

His stare was worse.

"You carry daggers," one of them said, his voice curious. "Are you skilled in using them?"

"Yes," I replied, eyes narrowing slightly. The question caught me off guard.

"Why were you coming for her?" Jahiel snapped, stepping forward. His arm blocked their view of me, pulling me behind him—placing my body between his and the door.

"I was going to ask you the same," the Prince retorted. "You would've been executed for treason if caught with her. And you could've made it ten times harder for us to save her. Did you even have a plan?"

My gaze shifted from the Prince to Jahiel. Then back again.

The silence said everything.

Jahiel's jaw was clenched tight, his eyes unreadable. He hadn't thought beyond breaking me free—that much was clear. I had wondered the same thing myself, ever since the chains fell from my wrists.

The Prince shook his head slowly, like one might to a child who'd spilled something important. "That's what I thought," he said. "We started planning the moment we left the Great Hall… well, the moment I awoke. We knew we had to get your princess out of there. So I considered everything— personal tours of the royal library, a dinner with her siblings, even a marriage proposal."

My head jerked up, eyes locking on his.

Marriage?

The smirk he wore faltered slightly, darkening into something more serious. His gaze drifted to the far wall, no longer seeing the room around him.

"We didn't expect it to become a rescue," he murmured. "We didn't anticipate your queen was that far gone… that she would actually plan to sacrifice her own daughter."

He had been planning to save me.

But why?

Why would a prince of Valdeen—of all lands—risk so much? Strategize for an entire evening just to get *me* away?

I stepped out from behind Jahiel, placing myself in full

view of the men once more. No longer hidden. No longer shielded.

"Why, Prince?" I asked, voice steady. "Why did you feel the need to rescue me?"

He looked up from the wall he'd been staring at, eyes locking onto mine.

"You say *me*," he said softly, "as if you hold no value apart from the kingdom."

"My thoughts have been chasing themselves—round and around—trying to figure out why you all did this for me!" My voice cracked on the last word.

Because every time I said *me*, it felt like there should be a better reason than just... *me*. I felt like I alone wasn't enough—for these men to risk their lives, for a nation to risk its peace.

I wasn't enough. I knew it. And I hated it.

The Prince nodded, as if he could see exactly what I hadn't said aloud.

"I believe you were the reason we were sent here, Princess," he said, stepping forward. He towered over me now, his smirk somehow both reassuring and unsettling.

"I didn't realize it at first. The dreams were foggy. But I saw your eyes. When I saw you—" he paused, rubbing a hand through his short, wool-textured hair, "—when I saw you and spoke the holy words, it brought me to my knees."

My breath caught. I took a step back. His words crashed into me. His gaze pinned me.

"What?" I stammered. "What does that even mean? What does any of this mean?"

Anger sparked—hot, unrelenting. A flame flaring to life.

"Why do you say I'm the reason you're here? I've never

heard of allies from Valdeen. I don't even know how your people *interact* with the rest of us!"

My voice rose with the pressure behind my ribs. "You need to start making sense, Prince, because right now... right now it seems like you all showed up—and my life *imploded*!"

"Princess—" he began, reaching a hand out as if to calm me.

"No!" I snapped.

And just like that, something in me cracked wide open.

A surge moved inside me—new and unfamiliar. Too many emotions I had always been too scared to show.

"Why did you show up? And how do you know about the book?" My voice dropped to a growl, my rage burning, alive.

He knew about the book. The one that found me. The one no one else should know existed.

The Prince chuckled.

A low, maddening sound.

He rubbed his chin, eyes gleaming with awe.

"Captain," he said, motioning for Jahiel to step beside him. "Have you ever seen her like this? She's stunning."

"Are you serious?" I barked. "Don't talk about me like I didn't just ask you *several* questions!"

"Captain," he said again, ignoring me, eyes still on me. "Look at her."

My heart was racing. My throat burned.

And my eyes—

"Kae'dinah," Jahiel breathed, stepping back. "Your eyes..."

"Now you see," the Prince murmured, arms crossed. "Does she always do this?"

I turned between them, panic blooming.

"What are you talking about?"

"Your eyes, Princess," a man near the wall said. "They're glowing. Like embers."

"What?" I shouted, spinning to face the others. "What are you talking about?"

"Eyes glowing like fire," the Prince said quietly. "It's faint, but it's there."

He exhaled, reverent and shaken.

"Highest save us all."

Jahiel winced at the mention of the name, his eyes darting between me and the Prince. Then, without warning, he stormed toward me, snatching the scarf from my hands and holding it up in front of my face.

"Put this on. We're leaving."

I stared at him—his usual awe shattered, the Captain's mask firmly back in place.

"What is going on?" I asked, voice low and wary.

"We are leaving," he snapped, sharp and unyielding.

"Where will you go?" the Prince crooned, amusement curling through his voice. "You had no plan before."

Jahiel ignored him, snatching my satchel and thrusting it toward me. I barely caught it before it hit the ground.

"Put the scarf on!" he barked again.

"Jahiel," I snapped, stepping toward him. "What did you see?"

"He can't explain what he saw," the Prince answered instead, stepping closer.

"He can't explain it—and that terrifies him. So, like the protector he swore to be, he's taking you away from the threat. Which, I assume, he thinks is us."

The Prince gave Jahiel a small nod. "I'd do the same. But in this case, it's a mistake."

"Are you ready?" Jahiel growled, grabbing my forearm.

"No! What? Jahiel, slow down."

"We're leaving. *Now!*" His voice rose, near frantic.

"Where will we go? What will we do?" I shot back.

"We can't stay in Anima. They'll realize I'm missing any moment—and they'll search every house from the palace to the gates."

My eyes flicked to the Prince. He was maddeningly calm. Behind him, his men were already moving—tightening packs, adjusting weapons.

I leaned closer to Jahiel, my voice barely above a whisper. "What did you *see?*"

His frantic gaze met mine. His chest heaved.

"I don't know."

"If my understanding of the law and prophecy is correct," the Prince said smoothly, adjusting the strap of his pack and the blade across his back, "then *I* do."

I turned toward him, breath caught.

His tone was steady. Certain. Unshaken.

"I know who you are. I know what you are. Highest must've sent me here to retrieve you."

His dark eyes locked with mine.

"I also know you have the journal. And I know…"

He stepped forward, his voice low, almost reverent.

"…that you are everyone's salvation, Princess."

The room held its breath.

"You are in danger here. And we have to get you out. Leave with us now, and I vow to tell you everything else you wish to know."

I swallowed hard, his words a torrent in my mind, fighting to find meaning.

212

*Salvation*

*Me? How?*

In all of my training, I knew better than to trust him. He was a stranger from a foreign land. He could hold me for ransom. He could use me as a pawn.

Yet, He knew things—things I hadn't told anyone. Spoke like he truly recognized me from a dream. He and these men made me feel safer than I ever had before. Made me feel like the answers I craved were just on the cusp of my *yes*.

My gaze shifted to Jahiel, whose eyes pleaded with me to trust him instead. His fear was palpable, his loyalty unwavering. But his answers... he had none.

The anger simmering in my chest faded, replaced by something calmer, sharper. I blinked rapidly, as if clearing fog from my vision.

"There she is," the Prince murmured, his lips curving into a smile that revealed startlingly perfect teeth. I turned away from him and faced Jahiel—my friend, my protector.

"Jahiel—"

"No, we're leaving now," he cut in, his voice trembling with frustration.

"We have no plan," I said firmly. "I know you want to protect me, but we can't just improvise this!"

"This could be a trap! They could be working for your mother!" he argued, his voice rising. "They could take you hostage, demand payment from the King—" He spoke my thoughts. We were weighing our fate with the same pieces.

"There's an idea," the Prince interjected with a mocking grin.

I narrowed my eyes at him, and he raised his hands in mock surrender.

I sighed and squeezed my eyes shut before opening them again. I looked at the face of my friend. "We're going with them," I declared.

"No, we're not, we've heard nothing of his *plans* either," Jahiel snapped.

He was right. I had no clue what the prince wanted from me, but my core told me I could trust him. Like I'd known him for years. "Well," I paused, my tone softening as I made my final decision. "I'm going with them."

Jahiel's expression darkened, his voice breaking as he boomed, "So what? I destroyed my life for you, and now you abandon me?" His words fell like a dagger to my chest.

"No," I said, my voice firm but quiet. "*My* life was destroyed—mine, not ours. You made this decision on your own, and I admire you for it; you know I do. But this," I gestured to the Prince and his men, "this feels right. I can't explain it, but I know they're our best option. You just have to trust *me*. Do you trust me, Jahiel?"

He rubbed his hands over his face, his frustration evident. He turned to pace the floor. Then turned to look at the men around us. Finally, he nodded, his voice low. "I do."

"Good," I said softly. "Because leaving you behind would be the final blow to break me. You're all I have left."

His jaw ticked as he looked around the room again, then back at me. He exhaled deeply and gave a small, reluctant nod.

The Prince stepped forward, extending his hand toward me. I hesitated before taking it, his touch firm and steady.

"I'll show you everything you need to know. I promise," he said, his voice reassuring. "We'll discuss more on the ship. But we must leave now."

"The ship?" I echoed, confused. "Where would we travel by boat? The great river flows south, but Valdeen is to the west."

"Yes," the Prince replied, squeezing my hand slightly before I yanked it back. He smiled, unfazed. " We will ride south to get your answers and to avoid them finding us if they think you stowed away with us. We'll forgo titles until we're safely off Anima's territory. My name is Amias. And yours again, Princess?"

"Kae'Dinah," I answered.

"That's a beautiful name, feels regal and powerful," he mused. "I like Kae. I'll call you Kae."

"Excuse me?" I gasped, my brow furrowing. He shortened my name?

"You, sir," he said, turning to Jahiel. "You must be Jahiel."

Jahiel nodded silently, still visibly distressed. I understood his concern—it mirrored the storm inside me. But despite the chaos, this decision felt inexplicably right.

I couldn't ignore it.

# Chapter 22

I had never been on a ship before.
Horseback, yes. Carriage, often.
But water?

The books I read had never warned me about the way it moves beneath your feet—constantly shifting, like the world is always tilting one way or another. Especially at this speed.

The great river of Naedorn stretched wide on both sides, so wide I couldn't see the opposite bank. I'd once read that merchants used this river to ferry goods from Jouse to the northern borders of Anima and up toward the Gulf coast of Aartier. That felt like a lifetime ago—when learning about trade routes was part of my duty, not my survival.

We moved fast, cloaked under the guise of a merchant vessel and the early morning sky.

I didn't ask questions when Prince Amias handed over a pouch heavy enough to buy the boat outright.

I didn't ask questions when, under the cover of darkness, forty people—men, women, and children—were hurried onto the ship alongside us.

They were dressed plainly, faces wrapped and lowered, their belongings bundled in cloth or carried in their arms. Refugees.

I didn't ask where they came from or why they were fleeing.

Because how could I?

I didn't even have all the answers for myself.

Below deck, it was crowded.

The hold was low and narrow, and the air thick with too many bodies and not enough space. Prince Amias had brought a small unit of his finest soldiers—he'd said it with a pride that didn't match the weight of the moment. Now they sat among the others, guards disguised as weary travelers.

The refugees stayed close together, wrapped in silence and shadow. Mothers curled around sleeping children. Men sat upright, eyes open and alert, as if ready to run even now. There was grief in the hold.

Grief, and exhaustion.

Jahiel slept beside me. His head rested against the wooden wall, his hand still close to mine, even in rest.

We wouldn't have made it on our own.

That much I knew now.

Jahiel had told me to run. But we had no money, no food, no water. Just a few jewels, I'm sure, would've led the guards straight to me.

Our plan was desperation.

This—this was strategy.

This was survival. But I couldn't sleep. Not while the hum of fear still throbbed through the dark. I reached for my satchel, pulling it gently into my lap.

On top was *Forbidden Love*, the book I hadn't touched in days.

A sharp ache bloomed in my chest.

Megorna. Kelta. My sister and my friend.

217

Kelta denied me. And Meg… she hadn't even come to see me.

Not once.

I shoved the book back inside too quickly, the sting of memory too loud in my ears. My fingers brushed something soft—Meg's handkerchief. The one she embroidered just for me. A green "K" stitched into the center like a signature.

I bit down on a sob, folded the cloth back into the bag, and pushed it away.

The wooden ceiling above me creaked with the sound of movement.

Carefully, I stood, stooping under the low beams as I made my way toward the ladder. The rungs were slick from damp air, but I climbed anyway, needing space. Needing light. Needing anything that wasn't shadows and silence.

The hatch pushed open, and dawn's sunlight poured through like a slap.

I squinted into it, crawling out onto the deck. The wind hit my face, sharp with morning chill, but I welcomed the bite. Behind me, too many people breathed in too little air. I needed to breathe something different.

They would have noticed I was gone by now.

My mother would unleash everything waiting in the depths when she learned the truth. The gods might even tremble before her rage .

I finished the ascent until I stood on the unsteady deck.

Laughter greeted me—booming and carefree, snapping me out of my thoughts. It came from the Prince and another man near the helm. As I closed the heavy, creaky hatch behind me, the faint click of the latch made Amias turn, catching me off guard.

He straightened, rotating his shoulder and smiling at me.

"Did you rest, Kae?" he asked, his voice lighter than I expected. He seemed to be genuinely concerned.

"I couldn't rest at all," I admitted.

"Why is that?" asked the man steering the ship.

"Of all the books I've read," I replied, trying to keep my voice steady, "none of them ever mentioned how upset your stomach can get on these waters."

From behind me, Amias let out a low whistle. "Oh," he whispered to the man, one eyebrow raised, "she reads?"

"Do not insult me, Your Highness."

He only flashed a pearly white smirk in response.

"This?" The man at the wheel grinned, throwing up his hands. "This is nothing compared to the ocean."

"Really?" I asked, raising an eyebrow, the corners of my mouth twitching.

"Yes. The ocean is far worse. Get your sea legs now while you can."

"Thank you for that advice," I replied, my voice heavy with sarcasm.

He laughed. "We'll get you some ginger at our next time. I'm Jon Midland." He extended a hand, and I clasped it gently. "His right-hand man. Second in charge when he's off doing... whatever it is he does."

Jon Midland was just as tall as the other Valdeenians, with long limbs and broad shoulders. His rich, dark skin gleamed in the morning light, and he wore his hair shaved close. A small hook curved through the lobe of his ear.

Amias leaned against the railing, casual as ever. "He's rarely in charge," he said with a chuckle. "Because I'm always around. But I let him think that—for his ego."

"Nice to meet you, Jon," I said warmly.

He offered a parting smile and returned his attention to the wheel. I turned back to Amias just in time to catch him mid-yawn.

"Have you gotten any rest?"

He grimaced. "Nah. I don't like being below deck. Too dark. Too crowded. Too tight."

"Your Highness? The big bad Wolf is afraid of the dark?"

"First," he paused. "Stop calling me that. And second, I'm terrified, actually."

"Ah," I said, nodding with mock seriousness. "Noted. I'll revisit that subject when I get more answers out of you."

He laughed under his breath. "So when do I get to be interrogated?"

"Now, if you're brave enough," I teased.

He gestured dramatically. "Ask away."

My questions scrambled over one another in my mind, all jostling to be asked first. I tried to pin one down.

"Alright," I said slowly. "Who are the other people below deck?"

"Refugees," he replied, resting his elbows on the wooden banister.

"Refugees?" I echoed, brows knitting. "From where?"

"From Anima."

I blinked, stunned. "Wait... the people are fleeing?"

He nodded, his expression hardening. "Yes. Anima isn't what you've been told. Every day, people are in danger if they don't... comply."

"Comply?"

"Obey. Serve. Submit. However you want to hear it."

"Obey what, exactly?"

He hesitated, then looked out across the glittering river. "Obey your family."

The hatch slammed open behind us, making me jump. My head snapped toward the noise, but my thoughts clung to his words.

*Obey.*

It wasn't foreign. But how far had things gone for people to risk everything just to leave?

I furrowed my brows, shaking my head like I could shake away the rising questions. How long had the Ickree name inspired fear more than loyalty?

Amias glanced at me. "We don't have to talk about them. The ones who could escape are here now. They're safe."

"But how many couldn't leave?" I asked quietly. "How many were left behind?"

His face fell. "That's a heavy subject. I'd rather not weigh you down more than you already are."

I scoffed. "You'd think I'd understand them better than anyone else at this point."

A small smile tugged at his lips, then faded. "Okay," he said, rubbing the back of his neck. "Enough of that. What other questions do you have?"

I paused, nibbling my lower lip, unsure where to begin. I wanted answers, but Jahiel's warnings lingered in my mind like a shadow. We knew nothing about these men or their true character or intentions.

"Tell me about yourself," I said carefully. "Your hobbies. Skills. What you do when you're not sneaking around countries and estates."

Amias blinked, clearly thrown. Then a low chuckle slipped past his lips.

"That's not the kind of information I promised to share."

"You didn't specify," I said, allowing a sly smile.

He tilted his head, studying me with a glint of humor in his eyes. "Fair enough. Amias Dai Harth the Third. Twenty-four. I like long walks on the Ellarum's coast, wine, and a good fight. And you?"

"Oh gods," I laughed. "Kae'dinah Lex Ickree. Twenty-two. That's all you get for now."

His expression softened, something unreadable flickering in his gaze as he leaned back against the railing again.

"Kae'dinah Lex. The reader. The girl with the daggers and motion sickness." He said it slowly, like it tasted interesting on his tongue.

I nodded, barely suppressing a smile.

"Can I call you Kae?"

I narrowed my eyes. "Oh, now you ask?"

His grin widened, all confidence and charm. "You don't like it? I think it suits you."

I rolled my eyes but couldn't quite stop a small smile of my own as I turned to the water. The river stretched endlessly, reflecting the sun in shimmering ripples. "Tell me about Highest, I read about him in the journal," I said after a moment. "You speak of him—or it—often."

"*That's* a real question," he said, his voice softening. His gaze drifted to the horizon as if searching for the words. "Highest isn't a 'what.' Highest is a 'who.' The creator of all things. He's everywhere, all the time. He's… everything."

He glanced at me then, his expression serious and searching. "It's not something I can fully explain. It's something you have to *experience*."

I frowned, the weight of his words settling over me like

an invisible mantle. An all-powerful being. Was he anything like the gods I had been taught to revere? Or was he… more?

"So like the gods?" I asked, my eyebrows rising.

"No, *nothing* like the gods you had in Floos." He hisses. His words were spiced with disgust. "Highest created them. Highest does all things. He doesn't just rule in one area like harvest, fertility, the sun, or the moon. Highest is all of those things at the same time. Accessible at any time. He's much bigger than what you've experienced."

I continue to look out over the sun moving above the waters. Highest was much bigger than what I had experienced. How? The idea of something better than the gods I had been raised around was incomprehensible.

"How does that answer make you feel?" he asked suddenly. I exhaled while my eyes flicked to his.

I hesitated, "I'm… unsure," I admitted finally. "I've only ever known the gods."

He scoffed, his voice low but sharp. "The gods? You mean the Watchers? *They* are no gods. They are chaos. They made a mess of things many centuries ago."

"Mess?" I echoed, the unfamiliar words mingling with what I knew to be truth. Making the air feel heavy between us.

"Yes, the rebellion? The Watchers' Rebellion," he said, his brows knitting together in disbelief. "You've never heard of it?"

I shook my head. "No."

"What did they teach you in Anima?" he asked, his voice laced with incredulity.

"They taught us that the Great Liberation of Naedorn was over 700 years ago," I replied cautiously, unsure if my answer would satisfy him—or provoke him.

His laugh was loud, sharp, and bitter. It startled me. "The Great Liberation?" He shook his head, leaning forward as if the sheer absurdity of my words needed closer examination. "Wow. They really fed you that nonsense, didn't they?"

I flinched back. His words slapped me like the insult they truly were.

"It's not nonsense," I said defensively, straightening. "It's history."

"History?" He scoffed again, this time with more force. "Let me guess—they told you the Watchers freed Naedorn from some great enemy? That they brought peace and prosperity?"

"Yes," I said slowly. "They saved us from chaos. From destruction."

Amias gave a humorless laugh. "Saved you? Kae, the Watchers didn't save Naedorn. They *enslaved* it."

The word hit like a blade. My stomach twisted violently. "That's not true." I wanted to believe it wasn't. I *needed* to believe it wasn't. I hated them—I *did*—but all of it, the festivals, the offerings, the prayers… it couldn't all have been for *nothing*.

"It *is*," he said, his voice sharp. "The Watchers rebelled against Highest. They weren't gods—they were traitors. Jealous. Power-hungry. And when they couldn't take his throne, they came for us. They twisted everything. Made themselves gods. And they've ruled your people through fear ever since."

I took a step back. "If that's true—then why? Why lie? Why teach us to worship them, to *die* for them?"

"Because they *feed* on it, Kae. On fear. On loyalty. On

224

blood." His tone was like flint against steel. "They don't just want your worship. They want your *soul*. They've wrapped your kingdom in chains and dressed it in gold to make you forget you were bound."

My throat tightened. I couldn't breathe. Couldn't *think*. "Why would my family—why would my *mother*—do that?"

"Because they serve the Watchers. Willingly or not."

I staggered back a step, the words burning hotter than fire.

"That's not true," I said, too fast. Too loud. Too *frantic*. "You don't know her. You don't know my family. You weren't there. You didn't—"

*They tried to kill me.*

The thought exploded through me, loud and cold and final. My voice faltered, and I gripped the railing until my palms stung. "They... were going to kill me. Just to please them."

Everything inside me fractured.

"You call them traitors, liars, monsters," I said, voice breaking. "And maybe they are. But don't you dare act like this is just *information* to me. You're asking me to see my entire life as a lie. You're asking me to stand here and agree with you while the people I love—my *sister*, my *father*, my *friend*—are still there, living under those lies. Still calling those monsters gods."

"Kae—"

"You think it's that simple?" I hissed. "That I'll just wake up and say, *oh, well then—guess I've been serving impostors this whole time!*" I laughed bitterly. "Is that what you want? For me to just tear my whole world apart in a single breath?"

"No," he said quietly. "I want you to remember what you already *felt*."

I froze.

"You knew it was wrong," he said, stepping closer. "You *hated* the sacrifices. You *wept* for that child. You flinched when your mother spoke their names. You've already turned from them in your heart. You just haven't said it out loud."

I stared at him. My hands were trembling. My lips parted, but I couldn't speak. Because he was right.

And I hated that he was right.

"I *tried* to stay silent. I *tried* to be good. I tried to follow every rule. I kept my head down. And for what?" My voice broke. "So they could bind me to an altar like livestock and call it *honor?*"

"I'm sorry," Amias said, and this time his voice was low. Real. "You didn't deserve that."

I let the silence stretch, thick and pulsing.

Then finally, I asked, "And what about your Highest? How do I know he's not just another god behind a mask?"

His gaze didn't waver. "You don't," he said. "But he doesn't ask you to prove yourself. He doesn't demand your blood. He just asks you to *trust*—even if it's trembling. Even if it's not complete."

He stepped forward, so close I could feel the warmth of him, the steadiness I didn't want to want.

"He gives you everything he has," Amias said. "For your yes."

I looked away, my grip on the railing loosening.

*Everything... for *my* yes?*

As if it were simple. As if yes could rise clean from the ashes of what I'd just escaped.

Trust.

That word again.

I couldn't even say it in my mind without flinching. If I

couldn't trust the gods I'd served since I could speak, if I couldn't trust my own *mother* not to betray me—how could I trust his Highest?

But something about the way Amias said it wasn't a command.

It sounded like a memory. A wound. A vow.

His voice didn't carry doctrine—it carried devotion. And that made it harder to dismiss.

"You don't have to believe me now," he said. "But in time, you'll see. And when you do, you'll understand why Highest sent me to find you. You'll see just how powerful he is to orchestrate our paths the way he is."

I turned back to him, eyes burning. "Why did he send you? What does he *want* from me?"

Of all the questions clawing their way through my ribs, that was the one that mattered.

*Why me? Why not someone else?*

What made me worth the trials?

"That," Amias said, voice dropping into a hush, "is something we will have to hear from him. But for now, trust this—Highest has a plan for you, Kae. One the Watchers fear."

He stepped closer.

"And that's why they want you dead."

My breath seized in my lungs.

*"They wanted me dead?"*

"Want," he corrected, nodding, the gravity in his voice undeniable. "The sacrifice they prepared for you—it wasn't random. It wasn't just your mother's twisted will. It was mischief. Prompted by them. The Watchers. They knew what you are. What you could become. Even if you don't."

227

I could feel it then. Something crawling beneath my skin. An awareness.

As if something inside me recognized the truth before my mind could form it.

"They won't stop trying to stop you."

The words coiled around my spine and pressed in.

Not *my mother*. Not *the court*.

*Them.*

"They won't stop…" I echoed under my breath, the air thinning. "Trying to stop me from what?"

I looked up at him. My voice broke before I could steady it. "What am I, Amias?"

He held my gaze. But his silence was answer enough.

He didn't know.

Or he did—and feared saying it aloud.

I swallowed hard, forcing myself not to shake. "Where are we going now?"

"To Syx," he said simply, like the word should mean something to me.

"To Syx?" I repeated, frowning.

"Yes." A hint of a smile tugged at the corners of his mouth. "The Holy Lands. Where else would we go to get your answers?"

I stared at him, unsure whether to feel relieved or even more afraid.

Syx—the Holy Lands.

A place I'd only ever read about in passing, its significance watered down in Anima's teachings, treated like a myth wrapped in suspicion.

Now it was supposed to hold the truth I'd been denied my entire life?

Amias smiled again, that maddening half-smile of his. "Highest help us all," he murmured with a quiet chuckle, shaking his head. "You really don't know anything, do you?"

My brow twitched. "They taught us *their* truth in Anima," I muttered. It came out quieter than I meant, and it made me hate how small it sounded.

"Don't be ashamed," he said, his tone dipping to something softer. He leaned in slightly. "You're not the first person they've lied to. And you won't be the last. But you…"

His gaze lingered on me, like he was searching for something more than just a response.

"Your heart's different. Almost as if Highest plowed the soil Himself, long before I ever showed up."

I stiffened slightly, unsure if that was a compliment or… something else entirely.

Then his smile shifted—lighter now, teasing—and something in the air between us cracked just enough for me to breathe again.

"You know," he added, tone lilting, "if I'd known you were this beautiful, I'd have come sooner. Though I imagine convincing you might've required more than prophecy and stolen plans."

Wait.

What?

If I'd known you were this beautiful…

My heart stuttered. My mouth parted. I should've snapped back. Brushed it off.

But I didn't.

Maybe because the way he said it wasn't laced with arrogance.

It was… honest. And confusing.

229

And maybe I didn't feel the need to run from it.

I looked at him. Really looked.

His words should've made me feel bare. Vulnerable. But instead, they steadied something inside me—something trembling beneath the weight of truth and betrayal.

"I—" I started, but the words disappeared somewhere between his smirk and the way the light played along the sharp lines of his face.

He laughed, deep and unbothered, the sound wrapping around me like warmth.

"Then again," he said, glancing toward the hatch with a shake of his head, "Highest's timing is always perfect. So… here we are."

I straightened, determined not to show the heat rising to my cheeks.

That's when I realized how easily he could disarm me. How quickly he turned my world upside down—and now, apparently, made my pulse misbehave.

"You're staring," he said casually, glancing back with mischief in his eyes.

"I'm not," I replied quickly—too quickly. And far too unconvincingly.

His chuckle was low and knowing. "It's alright. I am, too."

He leaned just enough to close the distance between us. "Though, if we both keep doing it, it might get awkward."

I blinked hard. That broke the spell.

"Don't be ridiculous." I stepped back from the railing, shaking my head as a reluctant smile tugged at the corners of my lips. "I think I'm done talking to you for today, Amias."

"We'll see. The day's just begun," he said with a wink, resuming his place against the railing.

"I doubt it," I muttered, turning from him.

As I walked toward Jon—who stood near the mainmast pretending not to have overheard anything—my stomach let out a loud growl.

Jon raised an eyebrow without turning his head. "Hungry?"

I winced. "Sorry."

He waved it off with a smile. "Don't be. I imagine escaping death and unraveling your entire belief system works up an appetite." He nodded toward the hatch. "Ike and a few others are stirring below. He'll fix you something."

I gave a grateful nod and turned toward the hatch. The creak of wood underfoot and the low murmurs of voices drifted up through the floorboards—refugees. Survivors.

And me.

I paused at the hatch, glancing back just once.

Amias was still there, his gaze fixed on me.

I looked away before I could overthink it and dropped through the open hatch.

Warm light from a lantern below spilled up to greet me. I descended the ladder slowly. The air was thick with the smell of sweat, wood, and salt—underscored by the faint scent of something edible. I'd take anything at this point.

A few sat in quiet conversation. Others still slept, bundled beneath thin, worn blankets. My gaze drifted toward the corner where I'd sat beside Jahiel. He was awake now, chewing quietly.

I cleared my throat. "Who's Ike?"

My voice echoed louder than I intended.

The room paused.

All awakened eyes turned to me—some shifting where they sat, others simply staring. For a breath, I regretted disturbing the peace. I was certain some of them recognized me. What I wasn't sure of… was whether they still saw me as an enemy or a companion.

A tall, slender man rose from a bench near the wall. His locs hung down to his waist, moving as he did. His gait was slow, deliberate, shoulders hunched slightly forward.

"I'm Ike," he said, his voice low and calm.

He stopped in front of me and held out a cloth bundle. I took it cautiously, fingers brushing rough cheesecloth.

"Thank you," I murmured, unwrapping the bundle. Inside were a few strips of dried meat and a pale, flat bread.

"That's manneh," Ike said, tone flat. "And dried turkey. Keeps well. Travels easy."

"Manneh?" I echoed, brow furrowed as I studied the bread.

"Bread we've eaten for centuries," he said, crossing his arms. "Flat. No rise. Not like the soft stuff you're used to."

His sharp gaze lingered on me while I examined the food.

"It's safe to eat," he added, a flicker of impatience sneaking into his voice. "Might not be a royal feast from Floos, but it'll quiet your stomach."

"Oh, I wasn't judging the rations," I said quickly, a flush of embarrassment prickling my neck. "I've just… never had it before. Or even heard of it."

"Well," he said, reaching for the bundle, "I'll take it back if you don't want it."

"No!" I clutched the cloth tightly to my chest. "I want it. Thank you, Ike."

He paused, raising an eyebrow. A faint smirk tugged at his mouth.

"You're welcome, Princess—" He caught himself, glancing around at the quiet eyes still watching us. He tilted his head, thoughtful. "Wait. What do we call you again?"

I hesitated.

Then the words tumbled out before I could stop them. "You can call me Kae."

The second they left my lips, I froze.

Why did I say that?

My chest tightened at the realization. Not just of what I'd said, but what it meant. I'd accepted it—this new name. This new self.

Ike blinked, then gave a small bow. "Kae, then."

I turned and made my way toward Jahiel. Leaning my back against the curved wooden wall, I slid to the floor, still cradling the bundle of food.

"Where were you?" Jahiel asked, tearing off a piece of manneh and turkey, tossing it into his mouth.

"I needed some air," I replied, carefully unwrapping the cloth to peer at the unfamiliar food again. My stomach growled fiercely, loud enough to draw Jahiel's attention.

He glanced at me, then at the food, before arching an eyebrow. "Eat," he said, a hint of command in his voice.

"Yes, sir. I will," I promised, eyeing the dried meat and bread hesitantly. I tore a small piece of the manneh, its edges crumbly and dry. Lifting the jerky to my nose, I inhaled its smoky, savory scent.

"Don't make a show of it—just eat," Jahiel pressed, his tone sharper this time.

I turned to him with a glare. "Could you relax? I'm eating," I snapped, tearing the jerky with my teeth. "You're quite bossy in the mornings."

From the corner of my eyes I could see him rolling his. I brought my hand to my mouth, tossing the food inside. The flavor surprised me. It was smoky, rich, and savory, melting across my tongue. My shoulders sagged slightly in relief as the hunger clawing at me eased.

Jahiel chuckled beside me, and I elbowed him playfully.

"Ow," he said, mock offended, rubbing his arm. "Careful, that's my fighting arm!"

"Please," I muttered, taking another eager bite of the jerky.

"Try the manneh," he said, nudging me.

I glanced at the bread, its pale surface dry and cracked. With a sigh, I took a cautious bite. Though tough to chew, the flavor was unexpectedly pleasant—salty and slightly sweet. It made my mouth water for another bite.

"Wow," I murmured, quickly tearing off another piece of bread and following it with a bite of jerky. Then, I repeated the process before I swallowed the first bite.

"Easy," Jahiel teased. "It's good, I get it—but don't choke on it."

"I'm sorry that I'm hungry," I said, laughing as I swatted his arm. I inhaled another bite, barely pausing between chews. If my stomach could purr from the feeling of this food, it would. I was starving. I thought back to my last meal. I thought back to my last real meal—the stew I ate alone in my room while flipping through the foreign journal. I didn't get to eat the following morning, due to the hurried assembly with the prince. Then, all the food they offered me was custom sacrificial meals, and I refused to eat out of fear that they were trying to sedate me. I shook those thoughts away. I didn't want to think back to that. "Do you have water?" I turned to ask Jahiel.

He handed me a water skin, and I took a long drink before the vessel was snatched away.

"Hey!" I yelped, glaring at him.

"We have to ration this," he said with a smirk, capping the water. "You'll need to learn how to get by with less. This isn't the castle where you're given more than enough."

"I know that!"

"Well, drink like you know that," Jahiel tucked the water away in his satchel. While wrapping what was left of his food up for later.

I rolled my eyes. "Well, I don't have much of a choice now, do I?"

He laughed softly, leaning his head back against the wall. The warmth of his gaze dimmed as his expression grew serious. "Have you rested?"

"No," I admitted quietly. My mind had been plagued by nightmares—the attack in the garden, the haunting memories of my family, and my mother's cruel eyes. Sleep came in short, restless bursts, often interrupted by every creak or sound that startled me awake.

"You need to rest," he said firmly, though his own exhaustion was clear. Dark shadows framed his eyes.

I pointed at him accusingly. "*You* need to rest, too."

He shrugged. "I've tried. These wooden floors don't exactly make it easy."

"We should reach Syx soon, right?"

"Syx," he said, though his tone faltered slightly.

"Yes, have you ever traveled outside of Anima?" I asked, but my words fell short as I looked at his face. He seemed to be deep in thought. I frowned. "What is it?"

Jahiel hesitated, his brows furrowing deeply. After a long pause, he asked, "Would you stay there?"

"In Syx?"

He nodded, staring straight ahead. "Would you stay there with me... if I had a plan?"

My chest tightened, and I turned to him, but his eyes remained fixed on the empty space before us. His question brought back the memory of our rushed kiss in my room before we fled. Jahiel was my friend, my only friend now. But I didn't think we saw the same future. I believed he imagined us building something steady and lasting—while I couldn't even picture tomorrow, much less who would be in it.

"I don't know, Jahiel," I whispered. "Amias says we're heading to the Holy Lands. He believes we'll find answers there."

"Answers to what?" His hidden frustration bled through his words, though he tried to keep his tone steady.

I didn't have the strength to explain—not the dreams, the journal, nor Amias's cryptic words. "Questions," I said simply.

Jahiel exhaled sharply, his patience wearing thin, as it often did. "Alright," he said curtly, ending the conversation.

I sighed and slid down until my back was flat against the floor. Jahiel handed me his blanket before rising and heading toward the ladder.

He climbed to the deck and exited the hold, slamming the door shut behind him.

"Well... that's over," I whispered.

"Windy waters above, but it's messier down here, huh?" a voice said from nearby.

Startled, I turned to see a man sitting diagonally from me. His braided hair hung over his shoulders, and though his accent wasn't Valdeenian, he wore the black and wolf sigil of Valdeen.

He smirked and crawled closer, extending a hand. "Tavin," he said. "Nice to meet you, Kae."

I glanced at his hand but didn't take it, instead clutching the blanket tighter.

"You're with Amias?"

He laughed and withdrew his hand. "Alright, no handshake. Fair enough. But it's still nice to meet you, Kae. And yes—I am."

"Who told you to call me Kae?" I asked, suspicious.

"I heard you say it to Ike. Was that wrong?"

"No," I muttered, using my arms to pull myself upright. "I'm sorry. I'm just… skeptical and confused."

His laugh was warm, a deep, melodic sound. "I'd be too."

I rolled my eyes and turned away, pulling the blanket over my shoulders. "I'm going to sleep, Tavin."

"Sleep tight, darlin'," he said, amusement clear in his tone. "Don't worry. I'll keep you safe."

"No need," I replied with a sigh.

He chuckled. "The Prince was clear—you're not to be left unprotected. Those were his strict orders."

I froze.

Under strict orders? To protect me?

"Aren't you all here for the same purpose?" I asked sarcastically.

Tavin shifted, leaning closer. His voice dropped to a whisper meant only for me. "Yeah, but staying ready is better than getting ready," he said with a wink.

I stared at him, trying to decide whether he meant it seriously… or if I was meant to laugh.

He smiled again. "Sleep," he said gently.

The floor creaked as he moved to sit beside me. My gaze lingered for just a moment longer.

Protection?

I rolled back over, pulling the blanket over my head, and decided to take whatever sleep Highest might give me.

*If that's something He gives at all.*

# Chapter 23

My eyes snapped open to find myself surrounded by darkness.

I must've dozed off. Judging by the silence and the stillness of the ship, it was night. Everyone else slept soundly around me. How long had I been asleep? I pressed a hand to my chest, feeling the rapid but steady beat of my heart. If I had to guess, I'd slept most of the day. And for once, I slept dreamless—no tormenting memories, no haunting visions.

Just peace.

*"Kae'Dinah."*

The familiar, commanding voice emerged from my satchel—low and insistent. My heart quickened as I sat up, fumbling silently through my belongings to find the worn, leather-bound journal.

The voice came again, clearer this time. Almost tangible. It no longer felt like a distant echo or a whisper carried by wind. I could almost see the face it belonged to—sharp, authoritative—lingering at the edge of my mind.

But was it only in my mind?

A shiver crawled down my spine. I turned abruptly, stretching a hand along the wooden wall beside me. My fingers met only smooth, cold planks.

No one was there.

The steady sound of breathing from my left reminded me Jahiel was still beside me. But I knew his voice—and this wasn't his.

I returned to my task, but rummaging in the dark was futile. My satchel was stuffed with whatever I'd managed to grab during our escape. With a frustrated huff, I slung it over my shoulder and stood.

The cramped space below deck was littered with sleeping bodies, their outlines faint under the pale light seeping through the small circular windows.

At the ladder, I grabbed the creaky rungs, skipping the loudest one. I pressed against the hatch door and pushed—

It barely budged.

I sighed, adjusting the satchel straps. Bracing myself again, I leaned into the effort—

This time, it swung open effortlessly.

Above me, Amias's silhouette crouched in the moonlight. He smirked, holding the hatch open with ease, and extended a hand down to me.

I looked at it briefly, then took it. His grip was warm, steady, and startlingly strong—he lifted me out of the hold like I weighed nothing at all.

I staggered slightly as my feet touched the deck and instinctively grabbed his upper arm for balance.

"Thanks," I whispered, careful not to wake anyone below.

Amias just shook his head and quietly closed the hatch behind me.

Then he turned and strolled toward the helm.

I finally caught my breath—

And lost it again.

The sky stretched above us in a vast, glittering sea of navy. Stars blanketed the heavens in a way I'd never seen at home. And the moon—

It loomed impossibly large. I could make out every crater, every ridge. Its silvery light shimmered across the river, casting the ship in a glow that made the world look... otherworldly.

"Such rare beauty," Amias murmured beside me. His voice was soft, his nearness cutting the chill in the air.

"I've never seen it like this before," I said, tilting my head back. "The moon... it's almost magnified. Like I could reach out and touch it."

I turned. He wasn't looking at the moon. He was looking at me.

After a beat, Amias smirked. "Oh, the *moon*." He feigned surprise. "It does look lovely... too."

Heat rose to my face.

The prince was a shameless flirt. I was sure he flirted with every woman he got near.

He chuckled and walked toward the wheel. The glow of moonlight traced the sharp lines of his back and neck. His tunic hung loose, the ties undone just enough to reveal a sliver of his chest.

The familiar wolf ring, once on his finger, now hung from a chain around his neck, swaying with each step.

I shook my head, tearing my thoughts away from him— and the way his words lingered in the air.

*The journal.*

That was why I'd come.

The voice had called me, pulled me from my dreams.

I scanned the deck and spotted a large wooden crate secured near the bow. It looked sturdy enough to sit and read. Really, it was the *only* place to sit and read.

Before I could walk that way, my eyes caught on movement near the railing.

Amias was now talking with someone I recognized... sort of.

The man—Tavin?—leaned casually against the rail, arms crossed.

But something was off. His face was familiar, yet not. His smile was too sharp. Too mischievous.

I approached. "Hello again," I said slowly, watching him. "It's Tavin, right?"

The man exchanged a quick glance with Amias—humor flashing between them.

"Sure," he replied, dragging the word out like a punchline. His lips twitched, barely containing laughter.

I frowned. "Okay...?" My confusion deepened. "Do you think it's safe to sit over there?" I asked, gesturing to the crate by the bow.

Amias arched an eyebrow. "What do *you* think?"

I glanced at the ropes. They were tight—secure. The crate hadn't moved the entire journey, even with the rocking.

"You already know the answer," Amias said, his tone playful. "You've examined the ropes twice now." He leaned in slightly, lowering his voice. "You're beautifully intelligent, Kae. Do you really need my opinion?"

I scoffed, unsure whether to be flattered or annoyed.

The other man chuckled—a deeper, richer version of Tavin's voice.

"Maybe she just wanted a second opinion."

I froze. My eyes narrowed.

"You're not Tavin, are you?"

He smirked. "Caught on, did you?"

"I knew something was off," I muttered, stepping back. "Who are you?"

He extended a hand, all wolfish grin. "Tye. Tavin's twin."

I crossed my arms, ignoring the gesture. "And why didn't either of you *say* anything?"

Tye laughed, the sound smooth and unbothered. "It's more fun this way. You'd have figured it out eventually."

"Uh-huh," I huffed, turning back to Amias and doing my best to ignore the imposter steering the ship.

*Tavin—the protective, responsible one.*

*Tye—the opposite.*

*Noted.*

"I'm going to sit up there," I announced.

Amias stepped aside. I crossed the wide deck, weaving between crates and barrels—no doubt part of the ship's disguise as a trade vessel.

One box was stamped with a familiar mark: linen shipments from Aartier.

Someone in Floos was going to be upset when their fabric didn't arrive.

At last, I reached my chosen destination. The crate was covered in a thick net of rope, knotted tight. I slipped my fingers through one of the loops and tugged lightly to test if it would hold my weight.

"You need another hand?"

Amias's voice startled me. I yelped and pressed my forehead against the crate.

"Please don't do that again," I panted, turning to face him.

"Do what?" he asked, feigning innocence with maddening ease.

"You scared me."

"My apologies." He held up his hands in mock surrender. "What brings you topside in the middle of the night?"

He leaned casually against the crate, one arm resting just above my head. It took all my self-control not to glance at his bicep—or the way his shirt gaped at the collar.

I had to admit, the prince was distractingly handsome.

"Oh," I stammered. The journal. "I couldn't sleep, so I came out to read."

"The journal?" he asked, tilting his head.

"You never told me how you knew about my journal."

"Not *your* journal. *The* Journal." His brow arched, tone playful.

"That's basically what I said."

"You didn't specify." He hummed, mocking my earlier deflections with irritating accuracy.

"You're an ass, Prince," I muttered, crouching down to rummage through my satchel. The moonlight made it easier to see, thankfully.

"Ouch." He dropped beside me, patting his chest like I'd wounded him. I ignored it.

As I searched, his hand reached past mine, plucking the dagger scabbard from the bag.

"Throwing knives?" he asked, turning them over.

"Yes. One of many."

"Are you accurate?"

"Always."

He gave a quiet hum, placing the scabbard aside. Then— before I could stop him—he pulled something else out.

His whole demeanor shifted.

"*Forbidden Love?*" he asked, lifting the book with a raised brow.

My stomach dropped. "Give me that," I said, lunging for it.

But his arms were too long. He leaned back, easily keeping it out of reach.

"This seems interesting," he teased, flipping it over to read the back. "Very romantic. Lots of feelings. You and the captain read this together back in the palace? Is *that* why he was so eager to free you?"

I froze. My whole body went still.

"Give. It. Back." My voice was sharper than I intended.

Amias tilted his head, a glint of something unreadable in his eyes. "Why do I feel like you're hiding something?"

"I'm not hiding anything." I snatched the book the second he let go. "You're just nosy."

He chuckled as I turned away, the sound low and smug. A flutter rose in my chest—unwelcome and annoying.

*Get it together, Kae'Dinah.*

I stepped a few paces away. I needed air. Space. Something to remind me why I came up here in the first place.

"Is there something between you and the captain?" he asked suddenly—faster than I expected, like the question had been waiting on his tongue.

I turned back, eyes narrowing. "Is that your business?"

Amias shrugged, leaning casually against the crate I'd picked. Not planning to leave. His smirk returned—infuriating and magnetic.

"If you're not reading with him," he said, "we could start reading together." He laughed.

"No!" I snapped. "Can you just—"

245

But my voice faltered.

My words trailed off, caught in a wave of memories. Suddenly, I was back in the palace, curled up with Meg as we read the book together, whispering and laughing over the adventures. I thought of her delighted giggles as I recounted the stories to one another, how we'd dream of living those wild escapades ourselves.

The memories hit me like a storm, tightening my chest and sending tears welling into my eyes.

"Kae?"

His teasing tone was gone, replaced by quiet concern. He leaned closer, his voice softer. "I didn't mean to upset you."

I shook my head, covering my face with my hands as the tears spilled over. "It's not you… Well, it is kind of, but… It's just…" My voice broke, and I couldn't finish.

"I'm sorry," he said after a beat of silence. "I shouldn't have bothered you. I can go."

"No," I hissed, surprising both of us with the intensity of my response. I didn't want to be alone. "Just… can you sit there and shut up? I just need a moment."

Amias nodded and stayed where he was. I shifted back, lowering myself to sit fully on the deck, my back resting against the wooden crate. I gathered my knives and the red velvet book, holding one in each hand.

I held the knives out, showing him the pommels. Each one was adorned with a brilliant emerald and engraved with an intricate "I." Then, I reached into my satchel and removed the smallest of them all. The one I gave Milo, which he returned to me.

"My brother gave these throwing knives to me," I said, a small smile tugging at my lips. "It was the first time I out-threw him. He told me I deserved them more than he did. He was always better with a sword and hand-to-hand combat anyway. He's built for up-close combat. I'm better at a distance—knives, bows."

"Your father let you train?"

"Yes," I said, the memory of my father's warm, encouraging smile filling my mind. "Against my mother's advice, of course. He saw how naturally it came to me. After so much begging, he couldn't tell me no anymore."

"Most women in eastern royal families don't get that kind of freedom," he said thoughtfully.

"I know." I squeezed the pommel of my brother's dagger, as if trying to keep the good memories firmly in place. "I bought this blade for Milo, it's so small because we were young when I got it for him. I had to tell our maid to find someone to get it made custom by a blacksmith." I smiled at the cool metal.

I turned to the red velvet book, maneuvering it from one hand to the other, letting the soft fabric rub against my fingertips.

"And this," I began, holding up the book, "is a romance novel from Aartier."

"Ah," he said with a knowing look. "Aartier has no morals. Books like that are banned in Valdeen."

"Really?" I murmured. He nods. I twisted my wrist to flip the book from front to back. I exhaled slowly. "That's interesting, I was supposed to read this with my sister and my handmaid the night you all saved me." My voice cracked, a tear slipping down my cheek. "The night they were preparing…"

The words came out quietly, almost to myself. I sniffed,

covering my mouth to stifle the sob that broke free.

Amias didn't say anything at first. Instead, he scooted closer until he was right beside me. After a moment's hesitation, I felt the weight of his arm drape across my shoulders.

His quiet comfort only intensified the tears.

People I had known my whole life. Grew up with. Laughed with. Ate with. People I had grown to love, cherish, and admire. Those very people were the ones who dragged me down the halls of my home. Rid my body of dirt unpleasing to the gods and prepared me for slaughter like I was an animal.

So I cried, and he let me cry.

He didn't try to stop me or fill the silence with words. He simply waited, his presence steady and grounding. I appreciated it more than I could say. Because for the first time in my life, I felt like I was alone. But this prince's presence was somehow healing me. His silence was loud as he sat and comforted my still-breaking heart.

I don't know how long I sat there, but by the time I lifted my head, my vision was blurred from the tears. I glanced over my shoulder at Amias, his head resting against the crates as he gazed out across the water.

Straightening, I rolled my neck, trying to ease the stiffness that had settled in. "Thank you," I whispered.

"No need," he said, smiling warmly. "I was the trigger; the least I could do is be the comfort too."

I let out a weak chuckle. "This *is* all your fault."

He laughed softly, the sound low and rich.

I reached over his outstretched legs and pulled the worn, brown leather-bound journal from my bag. Holding it in both hands, I looked at him again. His eyes, wide with awe and curiosity, were fixed on it.

"This is *the* journal, the one that found me, " I said, offering it to him.

Amias didn't take it. Instead, he gently removed his arm from my shoulders and leaned back. "Tried by Fire," he murmured, almost reverently.

"Do you want it?"

"No," he said, shaking his head, his eyes never leaving the cover.

"How do you know about it anyway?" I asked, turning it over in my hands.

"Well, I suspected," he admitted, rubbing his chin thoughtfully. "I didn't know, but I assumed that if you were who we believed you were, you'd have it. And here it is."

"It called me by my name," I said, my voice quiet as I turned toward him. His gaze shifted from the journal to my face, and I felt a sudden intensity in his eyes.

"What?" I asked.

"Nothing."

"No, it's something. Look, I know you probably think I'm crazy, but it jumped off the shelf to get to me."

He laughed again, "Kae, relax. It's just something we'll have confirmed in Syx," he replied, his tone suddenly guarded. "We should be there by noon, tomorrow."

I tilted my head, curious about his vague response, but decided not to push further.

Turning back to the book, I untied the leather strap. Running my thumb along the spine, I let my fingers glide over the pages. "I wish I knew more about it," I mused. "The journal only had one entry the last time I—"

My words faltered as my thumb stopped on the pages.
There were now three entries.

"Impossible."

"What is it?" Amias asked, his voice sharp with curiosity.

"When I first read this, there was only one entry. Now
there are three." My voice shook. "It's been with me the
entire time. How is this even possible?"

"The sacred always reveals itself in layers," he said simply.

"What?"

"That's how holy things work—they wait for the right
moment. He can reveal what He wants *when* He wants,"
Amias explained, his tone reverent.

I opened to the second entry, my fingers trembling as they
traced the indented strokes of ink on the page.

Amias suddenly stood, leaving a cool space beside me.

"Where are you going?" I asked, glancing up at him.

"The journal found *you*," he said firmly, both hands pressing gently on my shoulders. "The words are for you alone.
Remember that."

I pressed my lips into a tight line and nodded.

"I'll be at the wheel with Tye if you need me," he said,
turning and walking quickly around the crate.

I listened as his footsteps grew quieter and quieter. Exhaling slowly, I looked back down at the journal and began to
read.

> *Dear Heir,*
>
> *The land seems to groan and beg for relief. The
> Watchers continue to operate under the guise of gods.
> Though they have power, they are not all-powerful. Do
> not be deceived by their schemes and vices. They fear*

250

*us more than we fear them.*

*I have also received word that the people in the East have begun to offer human life in place of livestock and foul for sacrifice. Stating the gods find the aroma more pleasing. It is sickening to hear such a thing.*

*I must move quickly, I desire to move now. But, I must wait patiently for Highest's instruction.*

*Highest, ignite what sleeps within me. Burn away all that is false. Lead me, and I will follow—even into the fire.*

*3 A.R. – Shaunsa of Temoi, son of Syx*

I gasped, the weight of the words crushing me.

Human sacrifice, just like in Floos.

It was the practice I despised most, the one that had driven me to flee that day. And here, written clearly, it says that practice goes against the will of the Highest. Yet the gods demanded it. They demanded it often. So what does that say about the two?

I exhaled shakily, the information hitting me like a perfectly aimed arrow.

My trembling fingers turned the page to the following entry:

*Words from my heart.*

*I fear, for my enemies wield power wicked in the light of You. I fear, for they grow in their disregard for morality—killing just to kill, abusing their power, draining the poor.*

*Oh Highest, my body fears. But my spirit is strengthened, for I know You will heal the land that groans for Your goodness.*

*Strengthen me in mind, body, and soul. Illuminate my enemies.*

*Highest, ignite what sleeps within me. Burn away all that is false. Lead me, and I will follow—even into the fire.*

*3 A.R. – Shaunsa of Temoi, son of Syx*

The words on the page burned into my mind, their weight both heavy and invigorating. This wasn't just a journal—it was too real, too close.

I stood abruptly, shoving the journal into my satchel before practically sprinting across the deck.

"Amias!" I called out sharply.

He turned away from Tye and strode toward me, his brow creased with alarm. "What's wrong? Are you okay?"

"Yes, I just need to ask you something," I replied, my voice quick and clipped. "What is 3 A.R.? It was written after the signature on each journal entry."

His body stiffened, his expression darkening. "Are you certain it said 3 A.R.?" he asked, stepping closer, his voice dropping to a hushed whisper.

I nodded, concern etching itself deeper into my face. "Yes, I'm sure."

"A.R. stands for After Rebellion, it's the date. Like a year marker," he said, his voice low but weighted.

"What *year* are we in now?" My heartbeat quickened as the gravity of his reaction settled in.

His jaw tightened, and when he finally spoke, the words felt like a blow. "The year is 699 A.R."

"What?" I stumbled back, the air feeling thinner with every

252

passing second. "Nearly 700 years? I... I don't understand. How is that even possible?"

"We have to get to Syx faster," he mused, almost to himself.

Then, with no further explanation, he spun around, bolting toward Tye at the wheel.

"Amias!" I called after him, but he didn't stop.

I stood frozen for a moment, my thoughts swirling like the waves below. Seven hundred years. Nearly seven hundred years since these words were written, and yet they had found their way to me.

Why?

My fingers brushed the satchel at my side. The journal now sat, tucked securely hidden, its secrets yet to be fully revealed. I turned to face the horizon, its endless expanse mirroring the questions now raging within me.

The answers lay ahead in Syx.

# Chapter 24

The waves lapped over my ankles.

I pushed myself up from the shore, brushing sand from my backside. My bare feet sank into the white sand, soft and warm beneath me. Looking across the water, I noticed something shimmering in the distance—a flicker of light, bright as a lantern.

I turned my gaze to the shoreline, surrounded by lush green palms and thick vines. The water was the most brilliant shade of turquoise I had ever seen, glistening under the sunlight. Waves crashed against the shore, their sound mingling with the cawing of distant birds.

I stood, instinctively patting my body for a weapon. My hands came up empty.

*"Walk here,"* a voice called. It sounded like one voice and many all at once, drifting toward me from a narrow path between the trees.

"Hello?" I called back, my voice shaky. Only the wind through the leaves answered.

I sighed and began walking, my steps slow and hesitant. The sand gave way to a narrow uphill path lined with greenery, guiding me into the dense forest.

The trail opened into a clearing, and my breath caught.

Before me stood sixteen swords, their blades buried in the earth, arranged in a half-circle. Each one gleamed with brilliant metals and adorned with intricate gems. They were works of art, crafted with impossible beauty.

In the center stood two swords taller than the rest, their pommels twined with golden vines. One shimmered with onyx, the other with emerald.

I stepped forward, drawn to the weapons. But as soon as I moved, a violent gust of wind knocked me to the ground, stealing the air from my lungs.

Dark clouds rolled in overhead, thunder rumbling in my ears. Lightning lit the sky, casting jagged shadows across the clearing.

Heat surged through my chest and limbs, like a fire igniting beneath my skin. I clawed at my chest as I lay on my back, gasping.

The clouds hovered ominously, then burst apart as four pillars of fire struck the ground like lightning, engulfing the outermost swords. Flames roared, with a heat so intense that the blades and gems melted into pools of molten iron.

I hadn't realized I was panting until the sound broke through my shock. My body trembled, paralyzed by the scene before me. Slowly, I rose to my knees, waiting for the dizziness to pass before standing.

The ground where the swords had burned was scorched black, the air heavy with the acrid scent of melted metal.

"Why?" I whispered, staring up at the retreating clouds.

A gentle breeze stirred the air, brushing my hair and raising goosebumps along my arms. I turned toward the sensation, my body tensing.

The breeze tugged at my hair again, pulling it back from

my ear.

*"They are among you,"* a voice whispered.

* * *

I screamed.

Then jolted awake.

My chest heaved as I scrambled upright, sweat clinging to my skin. The flickering shadows of a crate loomed above me, and the roar of fire was gone—replaced by the low, steady lap of water against the ship's hull.

"Hey. Hey." Jahiel's hands were on my shoulders, steadying me. "Kae—breathe. You're safe. It was just a dream."

My hands gripped his forearms. "It felt so real…"

"It's gone now. You're alright."

The air around us was thick with heat. I could hear others stirring nearby, though no one spoke.

Then another voice cut through the dark. Calm. Controlled.

"What happened?" Amias stepped around the crate. His eyes locked on me, sharp and searching.

"She had a nightmare," Jahiel said, curtly. He didn't turn to look at him.

"What did you see?" Amias asked, directing the question to me.

Jahiel rose slightly, his shoulders squaring. "Can it wait?"

Amias kept his gaze on me. "It might not be just a nightmare. It could be something we need to understand."

"She needs rest," Jahiel snapped. "Not riddles and prophecy."

"I'm not giving riddles," Amias replied, his voice still level.

"I'm giving respect to the fact that she might be hearing something important."

"That's not your place to decide," Jahiel muttered, now fully between us. "You don't even know her."

"And yet here I am," Amias said softly. "Listening. Which is more than some do."

The air between them pulsed—neither loud, but both locked in a tension I hadn't expected.

"Enough," I said, more breath than voice. I rubbed my temples, then looked at them both. "Please. I don't need protection if it turns into a fight."

Silence.

Then Amias spoke again. Gentler. "We'll be in Scala by noon. When we get there, you'll have choices. Just... remember they're yours."

His eyes lingered on mine, then flicked to Jahiel. He gave the smallest nod, then turned and walked back toward the bow.

Jahiel stared after him. His voice was low when he finally spoke. "Did I miss something?"

I swallowed, already weary. "Jahiel, please don't—"

"No." He stepped closer, keeping his voice quiet but tense. "Tell me. Tell me what I don't know. What you've shared with him that you haven't with me."

I looked away. "I don't think you'd understand."

"Then give me the chance to try." His tone cracked slightly. "I left everything behind for you. I need to know it meant something."

I hesitated. "I'm not asking for your sacrifice, Jahiel. I didn't ask for any of this."

"You didn't have to." His voice was bitter now, his fists

clenched. "I watched them drag you to the altar. I heard your mother name you as the offering. And no one moved. Not even your father. So I did."

My throat tightened. "I know."

"Do you?" he asked. "Because sometimes I think you've already left me behind."

I stared at him, heart pounding. "Tell me something, then. Tell me you left with me because you care—because there's more than just duty."

He was quiet. The only sound between us was the ship's slow groan against the river's pull.

Finally, he whispered, "I didn't leave because of duty. I left because when they called me to the Great Room, and I saw the guards surrounding you like you were prey… something in me broke."

I blinked.

"I don't know what that makes me," he said, looking down at our hands, "but I know what I *would've become* if I let them kill you."

He took my hands gently, his thumbs brushing across my palms—steady, familiar. "You were never just my assignment, Kae'dinah."

I didn't flinch. I'd always known that.

Even if he never said it aloud, the way he looked at me sometimes… I knew. I just never asked him to name it.

Because once something is named, it can't be unspoken.

"I figured as much," I murmured, eyes low.

He hesitated, like he hadn't expected me to admit it so easily. Like part of him still hoped it would land softer—mean more.

"I thought you already knew," he said.

"I did," I replied. Quiet. Careful. Honest.

And still—I didn't know what to do with it.

Because even outside the palace walls, even in a world that had turned upside down, *he* hadn't shifted. He was still Jahiel. My guard. My shadow. My friend. The only one who knew every version of me and never once turned away.

I trusted him with my life… but love?

That kind of love?

I didn't know how to offer something I wasn't sure I could feel for him. Not without rewriting everything I'd ever known about us. And maybe… I wasn't ready to.

He must've seen it on my face. His voice softened, retreating a step before I could.

"You don't have to say anything. I just wanted you to hear it. Finally."

I nodded—barely. "Thank you," I whispered. Not for the words. But for the grace in letting them settle gently between us.

Then he asked, voice quieter now, "Will you tell me what you've learned? About the journal. About all of it."

That—I could give him.

So I did.

I nodded, grateful for the shift, for the space to think.

And I told him.

I told him everything—about the boy who died in the square, the black eyes of the General who tried to kill me. The journal that seemed to write itself. The visions, the fire. The voice I heard but didn't understand. The betrayal of my family. The way Amias had spoken of the world beyond Anima, of truth I'd never been allowed to know.

I told him all of it—except the pages only I could see.

By the time I finished, the sun had begun to rise. The waters shimmered ahead, and the cliffs of Scala's harbor came into view.

Jahiel leaned against the crate beside me, quiet.

"That's why I have... questions," I said, my voice trembling slightly. "This Highest they speak of has chosen me for something. I need to know what all this means."

Jahiel turned to look at me, and I expected confusion... maybe even concern. But what I saw instead made me still. There was something shuttered in his eyes, something unreadable. Not anger. Not pain. Something colder.

Like he didn't recognize me.

"Okay," he said, barely above a whisper.

Not *supportive.* Not *encouraging.*

Just... okay.

The word hit harder than it should have. It wasn't what he said—it was how he looked at me. Like I'd slipped too far out of reach.

"Okay?" I echoed, my voice cracking slightly. "Is that all you have to say?"

He inhaled sharply, his brow furrowing. "I don't know what else to say to you," he said, and his voice was honest— but distant. "You're talking about visions. A god I don't know. Things I don't understand. I'm trying to keep up."

I flinched—not because he shouted. He didn't. But because I could hear the ache underneath.

I stepped forward, needing to bridge the space between us. "Then *try.* With me. I'm not asking for answers—I'm asking for you to stand beside me while I look for them."

He dropped his gaze to the deck, jaw tight. "The Prince already made that promise," he muttered.

260

And there it was—the bitterness.

I didn't want to believe it, but I heard it plain.

"No," I said firmly. "You don't get to tap out when it gets hard. Not after everything. Not when I've never once turned my back on you."

He stared at the city ahead, silent.

I stepped closer, my voice low. "It would break me if we had to part ways, Jahiel."

His shoulders stiffened.

"I'm not asking you to stay because of your oath. I'm asking because you know me. Because I trust you. And because... I don't want to face all of this without my friend."

He finally looked at me again—and this time, I saw the storm. The conflict. Not rejection... but fear. Pain.

"This is just so much more than I expected," he admitted, voice raw.

I nodded slowly. "I know. It is for me, too."

I reached for my satchel, needing space now. Needing breath. Our hands brushed—then dropped.

And without another word, he turned and walked toward the others.

# Chapter 25

The port teemed with life, a cacophony of voices, movement, and color and the sun had just peeked above the horizon. White stone platforms jutted into the turquoise sea, their surfaces bustling with port workers in pale blue uniforms. Long hooks extended from the docks, latching onto the sides of our ship to guide it smoothly into a designated space.

The air buzzed with energy—men and women carried crates and boxes, bags brimming with spices, and nets full of glistening fish. The vibrant hues of their clothing swirled through the crowd like strokes of paint on a moving canvas. Vendors called out their wares, their voices rising above the crashing waves and squawking seagulls. Every step, every gesture, radiated urgency.

Amias gestured for me to step closer to him, his gaze scanning the crowds. I hesitated, glancing over my shoulder. Jahiel lingered on deck, his arms crossed tightly as he watched me move.

Amias turned toward me, his voice calm yet firm. "As soon as we're allowed to disembark, I'll arrange for horses to take us to the temples. If that's not possible, we'll move quickly on foot. There's no leisure strolling in Scala's port. Everyone here has a purpose. They either want to sell or buy."

The ship shuddered to a halt as port workers leapt aboard, ropes in hand, securing the vessel with practiced speed.

Behind us, someone cleared his throat. "Amias."

We turned to see Jon standing with a man clad in the same pale blue uniform. His sleeveless shirt revealed muscled, tattooed arms, and a curved sword hung at his side. White linen wrapped his head, held in place by a golden belt adorned with the sigil of Syx—a gleaming whale.

The portsmen stepped forward, flanked by two others in blue. "Name and business?" he demanded, his accent unfamiliar and sharp. They moved quickly, just like he said. When did they even have time to board the ship?

Amias straightened, his tone measured. "I am Prince Amias Dai Harth of Valdeen, and we seek spiritual guidance and refuge."

The man's eyebrows rose. His comrades exchanged looks before he spoke again, suspicion thick in his voice. "Refuge? For all of you? What trouble could a Prince have caused in Valdeen to earn exile?"

"We've done nothing wrong, sir. The refuge is for the woman and her people," Amias replied smoothly. His confidence carried weight, each word precise and controlled.

The portsman's gaze snapped to me, his dark eyes narrowing. "Who is she?"

Amias stepped aside, leaving the question hanging in the charged air. His meaning was clear—he wanted me to answer.

My pulse quickened as I glanced at him. His expression was steady, almost encouraging. "Tell them," he said, his

263

voice low. "Tell them who you are."

Drawing a deep breath, I stepped forward. "My name is Kae'Dinah Lex Ickree, princess of Anima."

The men stiffened, their hands instinctively moving to their swords. I could see Jahiel edging closer to me from the corner of my eye, his posture tense, protective.

"Easy," Amias said, raising a hand in a calming gesture.

The leader's eyes remained locked on me. "Why are you here?"

Amias answered before I could speak. "Highest instructed us to rescue her," he said, his voice ringing with authority. The portsmen flinched at the name, recognition flashing across their faces. "Her family was preparing *her* for sacrifice. She would be dead if we didn't step in."

The men's expressions shifted, sympathy mixing with unease.

I would be dead by now.

The feeling dropped to my belly like a stone in a stream. I'd be dead right now if these men didn't get me out.

I gulped down the nausea,

Amias pressed on. "Look at her. Her eyes—" He gestured toward me, and I felt their scrutiny as they leaned forward, examining my face. Their gazes lingered on my eyes before all three stepped back, their expressions shaken.

"Highest bless," the leader murmured. He turned to Amias, nodding stiffly. "We will arrange transport. Stay aboard your ship. Someone will bring you fresh water while we secure proper vessels and guards, Prince."

"How far is the journey on foot?" Amias asked, his tone practical.

The portsman frowned, calculating. "An hour, perhaps.

But it's dangerous without proper protection."

"I have my men. People tend to avoid those from Valdeen," Amias replied, his calm demeanor unshaken.

The man hesitated. "And if you or she are recognized?"

"We'll keep our faces covered," Amias said, mouth twitching.

I watched their exchange, biting my lip to suppress a grin. He handled it well, his confidence radiating reassurance.

As the portsmen turned to carry out their tasks, Amias glanced at me. "Rest while you can. We'll move swiftly once we're allowed to disembark."

Jahiel stepped closer, his presence looming like a shadow. His jaw was tight, but he said nothing at first, his eyes darting between me and Amias.

"Where are we headed?" Jahiel asked finally, his tone clipped.

Amias turned to him slowly, like he'd only just realized Jahiel stood there. His face was unreadable. "To the temple of Scala. There's a priest who might offer insight or direction."

He glanced down at me.

"They need to see her," he added. "She might be the answer to things they've only guessed."

Jahiel's jaw tightened. "More information than you've already shared?" The irritation in his voice cut sharper than it should have.

Both Amias and I turned to him. I met Jahiel's anger with a soft look—pleading, almost. He had every right to be unsettled. Everything I'd just told him reshaped the world he thought he understood. But this wasn't Amias's fault.

"Jahiel," I said gently, laying a hand on his crossed arms.

Amias's gaze flicked to the touch. He nodded, curt and

265

unreadable. "Get ready to disembark," he said, eyes meeting Jahiel's in a silent warning before turning and walking off.

I exhaled, pressing my fingers to my temple before crouching to tighten my boots. The heat wrapped around me like a wool blanket—humid, suffocating. When I stood, I noticed how Jahiel's sleeves were rolled, his hair damp against his forehead.

"Are you ready? Do you have everything?" I asked.

"Just this bag," he muttered, lifting the worn strap on his shoulder.

I scoffed softly and reached to gather my curls, lifting them from my neck.

Before I could secure them, Jahiel stepped behind me. He slipped a leather strap from his wrist and gently swept my hair back, tying it high with practiced ease.

"Thank you," I murmured.

He didn't answer at first. But then—quietly, almost to himself—he exhaled,

"Why do I feel like I'm competing?"

"What?" I turned slightly, brow furrowing.

"Nothing," he said quickly, but I'd heard it. Competing.

I wiped my face, the heaviness of the air pressing in again. The heat made everything feel louder, thicker. I stretched my arms above my head, desperate to shake it off.

"It's so hot here," I muttered. "But really—thank you. For the hair."

He gave a faint smile. "You're welcome. I wish we'd packed lighter clothes."

"Do you think we'll see the royal family?" He asked.

"Not likely," I said, watching the market beyond the dock. "The royals of Syx live on the western end. In Suemana."

My vision swam briefly, the colors around me blurring at the edges. I blinked hard, steadying myself.

"Are you alright?" Jahiel's voice snapped sharp with concern.

"It's just the heat," I lied.

"Hmm," he grunted, unconvinced. "How do you know so much about this place? Did Amias tell you?"

"No," I said sharply, offended. "You act like you didn't watch me read books for years."

"On geography?"

"Yes," I replied, fanning myself with my hands. "I read books on history, geography, adventure, romance, poetry—I liked it all."

"Liked?" he asked, raising an eyebrow.

I sighed. "I don't know if I still enjoy it. My usual reading partners are a world away now." A hollow smile tugged at my lips.

Jahiel placed a firm hand on my shoulder and squeezed, offering a small drop of comfort.

"We're good to go!" The shout came from Tavin—or was it Tye?—standing at the top of the ramp leading to the docks. The crew began moving, Amias descending first, clapping each of his men on the back as they disembarked.

Jahiel reached the ramp and hesitated, testing its sturdiness even though we'd just watched several large men descend without issue. Satisfied, he motioned for me to follow.

The ramp was sturdier than I expected, and I couldn't help but look around at the port city as I descended. The people of Syx were vibrant and lively, their voices rising in a melody of bartering and laughter. The land was nothing like the streets of Floos—here, everything thrived.

"Wow," I breathed, awestruck.

"It's quite a sight," Jahiel admitted from ahead of me.

He stepped off the ramp, pointedly avoiding Amias's outstretched hand. I flinched at the tension between them.

Amias sighed audibly and turned his attention to me. "Princess," he said, extending his hand.

"I'm sorry," I whispered, grabbing his hand for stability. The dizziness from earlier had returned.

*"Now we begin,"* a voice cried faintly from my satchel.

"What?" I murmured aloud.

Amias squeezed my hand. "What did you say?" His face searched mine, concern etched into his features.

*"Now,"* the voice said again, louder this time. My chest heaved, and fire burned just beneath my skin. Sweat poured from my face as I stumbled forward, stepping fully onto the stone platform.

I hissed, clutching Amias's arm. "Now we begin," I whispered hoarsely.

His eyes widened, but before he could respond, the world tilted. My vision blurred, and the oppressive heat suffocated me.

"Princess!" Amias's voice called, but it was too late.

My legs buckled, and darkness swallowed me whole.

# Flicker

*Maeve, one month before...*

I never quite understood why we were called seers, when we were born without the gift of sight.

Yes, we could perceive dreams and decipher visions, but the visible beauty of Highest's creation was a wonder I couldn't imagine being stripped of.

I sat cross-legged on the stone platform just outside the Holy Place as the sun began its slow ascent over the horizon. Hues of vermilion, gold, and soft rose bloomed across the surface of the water, glinting as the waves lapped gently against the stone ledge beneath me.

The others couldn't see this.

They could only feel the sun's warmth on their skin, inhale the salt of the sea, and trace the smoothness of the white Scala stone. But not this—not the shimmer of light as it kissed the waves or the lavender haze that lingered at the edge of dawn.

They couldn't see what I was given partial favor to witness.

And for that, they despised me.

I rose quickly, letting the folds of my sage-green robe fall in quiet waves around my ankles before turning and hurrying inside.

The High Priest would be delivering new letters from the other holy sanctuaries—correspondences for me to transcribe and add to the ever-evolving chronicle of Naedorn.

*The true record of our history.*

I moved swiftly through the inner halls, weaving past the Blessed as they carried water, incense, and scrolls, their heads bowed in reverence. Their devotion was voluntary. They were here by choice, offering their lives in service to Highest.

Unlike us seers.

Well—half-seer, in my case.

I arrived at the scribes' chamber before the priests, unsurprisingly. The Blessed had already escorted the others in—seven of them, seated obediently on their benches, hands folded, lips pursed.

"Maeve?" one of them called out.

I considered not answering. I nearly denied them the luxury of acknowledging my presence—but I knew they could smell the sea on me.

"Yes?" I replied, feigning innocence with careful poise.

"You smell like the ocean," he said, his tone steeped in disdain.

"She always smells like an animal," another muttered, a woman this time.

I rolled my good eye, letting their words pass over me like smoke. I knew the truth. I knew they loathed me because I had more than they did. Because I could see.

I pulled fresh parchment from the table and began writing, capturing every detail of my most recent dream with swift precision.

*Flames.*

*Everything burned.*

Lately, my nights were awash in fire—cities devoured, skies thick with smoke. I didn't understand why. I only knew it frightened me enough to keep it to myself.

The chamber was quiet for a while—save for the scratch of my quill.

It was always like this in scribes' chambers: thick stone walls that swallowed speech, velvet drapes that silenced the breeze, and seers who only dared to speak when summoned.

Every temple had a scribe assigned to its High Priests, but Scala was favored, and I served them with my quill and sight. My talents secured me that favor. My literacy earned me that trust.

I dipped my quill into the inkwell, letting the ink drip slowly before setting the tip against the parchment. My eye—the one that still served me—followed the flicker of candlelight as it danced across the page.

My blind eye pulsed—a warning behind its lid.

A warning. A stir.

Something always came after that ache.

I looked up just as Priestess Edith entered the room, robes trailing behind her like smoke. She carried a small stack of sealed letters, which she handed to me with a nod before moving to her place.

"Seers," she called out, "I require an interpretation. A vision came to me this morning—urgent, I believe."

The others straightened in attention, nodding in agreement like well-trained dogs.

I did not.

My attention was already fixed on the correspondence.

Five letters today—each marked with the sacred seal of urgency.

Jouse.

Malcert.

Syx.

Valdeen.

Purmee.

My hand hovered over them all, desiring to use my other advantage on each one. The one that was a secret. Highest had given me the abilities beyond interpretation and vision. I could hear the voices. I could listen to the murmurs of the author.

I chose Purmee.

I pressed my palm flat to the parchment, closed my eye, and inhaled.

The echo came like a whisper across my cheek.

*"Every single one of our seers had the same dream last night. If you don't think that elevates this as an urgent cry to Syx, then I must question your judgment."*

My lashes fluttered. My heart did not.

Purmee's High Priest was frightened. His fear trembled through the ink like a storm waiting to break.

It pulsed through my blood as though the man had shouted at me directly.

I set the Purmee letter aside, the echo still humming faintly in my ears.

My fingers hovered over the next seal—this one from Jouse, wax cracked but still clinging like a secret not meant to be passed.

I pressed my palm to the parchment and let my mind fall quiet. The echo unraveled slowly, like ink blooming in water.

"The girl was not touched by gods," a man said—his voice low, strained. "She was born of pure power of Highest."

Another voice answered—steadier, female, older. "Her eyes, Brother. Have you seen them?"

A pause.

"Golden. Flickering. As if fire were alive inside her. I could not look too long upon her face."

My breath hitched.

I had seen those eyes. Not in waking. Not yet, but amongst the visions of fire. Eyes like coals kissed by Highest's breath.

Eyes that burned.

"It's not awake yet. She does not yet know what she carries," the man continued. "But the Watchers do. They fear her. Which means she is important."

"She is a girl," the woman insisted.

"She is indeed," the man murmured.

I pulled my hand away as if burned.

My pulse fluttered beneath my skin. I stared at the letter, at the ink dry on the parchment, as if it might move, might spell her name in the curling lines of someone else's worry.

The girl with fire in her eyes.

She wasn't just a vision.

She was real.

And whatever she carried—whatever she was destined to do—the Watchers feared it.

That meant something.

That meant everything.

My fingers twitched. My chest tightened.

The dream didn't wait for sleep.

It took me—right there in the scribe's chamber, while the others whispered and Edith recited.

The candlelight blurred.
The floor fell.

*　*　*

Stone. Sky. Smoke.

I stood in a place I'd never seen before—drenched in crimson light. The wind howled like it carried secrets too heavy to bear.

And there she was.

A girl with fire in her eyes.

Her curls whipped around her face—long, wild, black as oil—and her skin was streaked with ash and tears. She struggled against hands that gripped her arms, guards dragging her toward a stone altar. Her mouth was open, screaming—but I couldn't hear her voice.

Just the beat of wings.

The eagle.

It circled overhead once, then dove. Its talons tore through cloud and flame, and suddenly—it split. The bird opened not like flesh but like sky—and from within its chest, it coughed her up.

The girl with the eyes of fire.

She fell—down, down, toward the altar.

She was a sacrifice.

I tried to scream.

But another voice filled my head instead. Soft and heavy as thunder.

"From Anima."

I gasped. My hands trembled.

* * *

I came to with a cry, the vision tearing away from me like skin.

I was no longer in the dream. I was on the stone floor of the scribe's room, breath ragged, body slick with sweat.

The room had gone still.

The seven other seers had risen, some stepping away from me as if I were contagious.

"Her mouth," one of them whispered. "She was speaking in another language."

"She was thrashing," another priest spoke. He must have entered when I saw her. "She nearly knocked over the ink well."

Priestess Edith stood frozen, letters clutched in one hand, her other raised as if to ward me off. "Maeve—what did you see?"

I sat up slowly. My hands were still trembling.

"Anima," I said, my voice thin and hoarse.

"Anima?" Edith's eyes narrowed.

"There's a girl," I murmured. "Golden eyes, like fire. She's being taken. There's an altar. A sacrifice. The eagle—Anima's sigil—it carried her. It delivered her."

Silence.

"She is the fire," I whispered.

"No," one of the seers hissed. "Not from Anima. That place is cursed. They offer human life for favor. If someone's on the altar now—it's too late. You know that."

"You saw it too late," another muttered. "Once the altar is in view, the judgment has already passed."

"She's doomed," someone whispered.

275

"That's not a vision," one scoffed. "That's a nightmare."

I was still on the floor, breath shallow, sweat cooling against my temples. No one moved toward me. No one asked if I was alright.

Just their voices, circling like flies.

"She said Anima," one seer hissed. "Does that mean salvation will come from Anima?"

Snickers followed. Quiet, bitter.

Even Priestess Edith said nothing. She simply turned away, rifling through her scrolls, as if what I had seen hadn't happened at all.

I rose slowly, as if any sudden motion might make the dream return. My legs felt like stone. My mouth was dry.

I returned to my writing desk.

My parchment sat blank.

I dipped my quill and hovered it above the page. I could still feel the girl's eyes—burning, beautiful, full of something I couldn't name.

But the echo was gone.

The voice was gone.

The vision was fading at the edges like ash in wind.

"She's too proud of that one eye," someone whispered behind me. "Maybe it's driving her mad."

They chuckled.

I didn't turn around. I just sat there, frozen in that moment between knowing and not. Because I had seen it. I was certain I had.

And still—

A slow, small voice crept in beneath the silence, What if I'd been wrong all along?

What if the fire I saw wasn't prophecy... But the last flicker of a gift that was leaving me?

# Chapter 27

I woke to a cool breeze drifting in from an open window. Sheer cream curtains fluttered, revealing glimpses of swaying palm trees and a brilliant sun hanging low in the sky.

Late afternoon.

Did I faint?

Sitting up, I glanced around the room, my eyes adjusting to the dim light filtering through the curtains. The tiled floor gleamed, and the walls, a soft cream, were adorned with potted plants. The table beside the bed displayed colorful glass pieces, their surfaces catching the sunlight. A golden cup of water sat next to my daggers.

I shifted, the silk sheets sliding off my legs, and moved to the edge of the bed. My feet touched the cool tile, a sharp contrast to the sweltering heat I'd felt earlier. My clothes were draped neatly over a straw chair in the corner. My satchel rested beside them. I looked down quickly.

Someone had changed me.

The high-waisted, wide-legged cream pants I now wore fell loosely around my legs, while a peach-colored cropped tunic rose just above my belly button. My hair, freshly braided, brushed my back.

Heat rushed to my cheeks as I considered the care it must have taken to braid my hair. Who had seen me like this?

Shaking the thought away, I reached for the note beside the water.

> Drink all of this. We're waiting in the gathering room.
> —A

A for Amias, I assumed. The corners of my mouth tugged upward before I quickly swallowed the smile. I drained the cup in one gulp, the water cool and soothing against the dryness of my throat. Then I slid into a pair of peach slippers waiting beside the bed. They fit perfectly.

I walked over to my things, and I tucked a small throwing knife into the waistline of the pants.

"Just in case," I murmured.

The door creaked slightly as I pushed it open. Paintings lined the hallway, each depicting majestic winged beings in various poses: teaching, fighting, protecting. Their beauty was striking, their eyes almost alive, following me as I walked.

"Guardians," Amias's voice broke through my awe.

I jumped slightly and turned to see him approaching, a golden cup of water in hand. "Hi," he said, extending the cup.

"Hi." I took it, gulping the new water gratefully.

"These beings were charged with teaching and protecting us," he explained, motioning to the murals. "They were powerful, created by Highest to guide humanity."

I paused, my gaze lingering on a mural where a Guardian's face twisted into something almost... wrong. My heart quickened. "They're beautiful."

"They are," Amias agreed, his voice soft. His eyes lingered on mine before I turned my attention away from him. He cleared his throat, "That beauty is what made their rebellion so seductive," he continued. "The Watchers were once like them."

The weight of his words settled on me, but I forced myself to keep walking.

Ahead, the hallway opened into a large room filled with voices. The men of Valdeen lounged in fresh clothing, cups in hand, laughing and mingling with strangers. The heat from outside seemed muted here, the air cooler, though still tinged with humidity.

I accidentally brushed into a woman as I passed, her presence sudden and unfamiliar. She was shorter than me, draped in a veil that cascaded to the floor, obscuring her face completely.

"I'm so sorry," I said quickly, steadying her.

"No, forgive me, Your Highness," she replied, her voice low and measured. Her eyes met mine, widening with intensity. She blinked twice before her eyes slid downward. She curtsied before hurrying away, her steps light yet purposeful.

Amias turned, eyes following her as she retreated. "That is one of the Blessed," Amias explained, stepping closer. "They dedicate their lives to serving Highest. Sacrificing the possibility of a family, covering their bodies and faces as a symbol of humility. *They* cared for you earlier."

I blinked, staring after her. "Oh." Relief, relaxing my tense shoulders.

He handed me another cup of water, and I drank it without hesitation.

Amias watched me closely. "You fainted the moment you stepped onto the land," he said. "I carried you here to the temples. The priests think the connection between you and this place may have overwhelmed you."

"You carried me?" The thought of a man fighting the scolding heat for miles with me in his arms. Made me feel a way I was unprepared to feel. I asked, lowering the cup, the moment his second sentence registered. "Wait—what connection?"

He eyed me, then his gaze fell on the room. He hesitated, then exhaled. "Follow me."

He extended his elbow, and I looked at the invitation. Unsure if that kind of proximity would be ill-advised. My mind drifted to Jahiel, who was nowhere to be found. And after a brief pause, I took it. The warmth of his arm was steady, grounding me as we walked deeper into another hall.

Murals were painted on this hall too, seeming as if they grew larger. The Guardians loomed above us, their expressions a mix of serenity and power. I couldn't shake the feeling that their painted eyes watched me too closely, as if waiting for something.

"Hm," I murmured, staring up. "They're magnificent. But also…"

"Terrifying," he finished, his chuckle light.

I nodded, laughing softly. "Yeah."

He turned to look at me, his eyes filled with a warmth that caught me off guard. "You should laugh more. It suits you."

"Stop," I said, swatting his arm playfully. My fingers brushed against the hard muscle beneath his sleeve, and my heart gave a small, traitorous lurch.

*Focus.*

281

"You've had a rough few days. I just never heard you laugh—it's like a song."

"Amias, really, we've just met. Of course you've never heard me laugh," I said, trying to hide how breathless I felt.

"I guess you're right." He smiled, then looked ahead again. "Still. I hope I hear it again."

Silence fell between us, but it was a warm one—unexpectedly gentle.

As we continued down the hall, the murals seemed to grow taller. The Guardians stared down from the walls, their painted forms massive and still, yet somehow watching. Waiting.

"I used to be afraid of them," he said suddenly, his voice quiet.

I glanced at him, surprised.

"Not because they were terrifying," he went on. "But because they *weren't*. Because they saw everything. Even what I did in the dark."

I followed his gaze to the closest mural. "These on the walls don't feel like paintings for some reason. They feel like they could step down from the wall at any moment."

He hesitated, as if weighing how much to say. "My mother... used to paint them in Ellarum. Not like this—these are another artist's interpretation. Hers were different. Wilder. Colorful. More alive."

"She saw them?"

He nodded. "In visions. Dreams. She'd wake up and start sketching or painting before she even spoke. Said they came to her with news. I used to sit with her while she painted."

I didn't speak—his tone had changed. There was a heaviness behind it.

"She passed away last winter," he added softly. "It was sudden. Too sudden."

"I'm sorry," I said, and I meant it.

He nodded once, eyes fixed on the mural ahead. "It's strange. Seeing them again. Her paintings were so beautiful, these here aren't even comparable."

I watched him for a moment. There was grief there—open, unguarded. Not loud, but deep. And he wasn't trying to hide it.

"She would've liked you," he said after a beat, then gave a small, crooked smile. "She believed in prophecy more than anyone I knew."

A lump rose in my throat. "You think she'd believe in me?"

He looked at me then—really looked. "I think she'd say you were sent for such a time as this."

We reached the door. The air seemed heavier here. Holier. More final.

He stopped and turned to face me, and the warmth from before faded into a quiet intensity.

"Inside are three high priests and a few seers. They've gathered to meet you, to hear of your visions or dreams, and to answer your questions. They told me to escort you here as soon as you woke."

They had been waiting on me? While I slept?

The weight of their expectations pressed against my shoulders. What if I didn't measure up?

Amias must've seen the shift in my expression. He took a small step closer, brows knitting. "Hey. It's alright. This is your chance to seek clarity, to learn as much as you can. I'll be right outside this door when you're finished."

"Are you not coming in with me?" I asked, my voice smaller

than I meant it to be.

He hesitated. "This is your meeting, Kae'dinah. I'm just—"

"No," I said, reaching for his arm before I could think better of it. "I don't know anything about them. What if I offend them? Or they say something I don't understand. I need you with me."

His expression softened again, and for a second, I thought I saw that grief again—less raw now, but familiar. A shared ache.

Finally, he exhaled, rubbing a hand across the back of his neck. "Alright. But I'll let you lead and only speak when necessary."

I nodded, loosening my grip. "Sorry," I whispered. "I didn't mean to grab you so hard."

"It's fine," he said. "You're not the only one who's nervous."

Then, he knocked on the wooden door. It creaked open a moment later, and a veiled woman greeted us with her hands pressed together in silent acknowledgment.

As we stepped inside, a faint hum filled the air, reverberating like a heartbeat. The room was vast, its atmosphere heavy, charged with an energy that made my skin warm. Mounted high above a stone fireplace were two large tablets, their surfaces carved with intricate symbols. I didn't recognize them, yet I understood them instinctively—rules, laws, ancient and unyielding.

Ten separate points. Numbered.

This was no ordinary meeting, and no ordinary room.

Three priests stood at the center of the room, Amias leading the way toward them. Two men and one woman were dressed in flowing white robes embroidered with golden threads that glinted in the firelight. Amias nodded to them before extending an arm toward me, silently inviting me forward.

My stomach tightened. My bottom lip slipped between my teeth, an old habit I'd yet to shake when I was nervous. With measured steps, I approached, my gaze shifting to the eight other figures standing silently behind the priests. Dressed in plain green tunics that fell to their knees, they wore matching pants and kept their hands clasped in front of them.

"Hello," I managed, my voice barely more than a whisper.

The woman priest's gaze locked onto mine, her expression softening with wonder. "Highest, your eyes," she whispered. "There is no doubting you now."

"Magnificent," one of the male priests said, turning to the other. "Is there any record of a woman being among the heirs?"

"No record," the second priest replied. Stunned or confused.

I cleared my throat, annoyance prickling at the edges of my nerves. "I said hello." My voice carried more force this time, and I noticed Amias biting back a smile.

"Hello, Princess," the woman said warmly. She gestured to a cushioned chair at the center of the room. "Please, take a seat. We are honored to have you here. It has been so long."

"So long since what?" I asked as I rounded the chair, lowering myself into it deliberately, my chin held high and shoulders squared, just as I'd been raised.

The priests exchanged a confused glance, then turned their eyes toward Amias.

"We rescued Princess Kae'Dinah from Anima," he said, his voice steady.

Suddenly, a woman in green stood, her fiery orange-brown

285

hair tumbling wildly around her shoulders. Glowing with excitement, she strode toward me, her eyes—one vivid green, the other cloudy white—locking onto mine.

"I saw it," she said, her voice rough with emotion and thick with a different accent. "I saw you. The salvation coming from Anima. The eagle, coughing you up on the altar. Everyone thought I was mad, but I knew what Highest showed me. You are the truth. You are here, standing before me."

Her hair was unlike anything I'd ever seen—fiery, wild. She was stunning—petite, with a tawny, freckled face.

The first priest turned to her, his tone sharp. "Seer Maeve, your vision was... unusual. Nothing like it has ever come to pass."

"And you said she was on an altar in your vision," the woman priest added softly. "We didn't dare hope."

"My mother, the Queen of Anima—"

"She is not your mother," Seer Maeve interjected quickly, the words slicing through the air.

"What?" I breathed, my body going rigid.

"Please continue, Your Highness," the first priest said, his voice tense with impatience.

I drew in a steadying breath, trying to reorganize my thoughts. So many had seen me.

I eyed every single one of them before continuing.

"The Queen offered my life to her gods as a sacrifice. I would have been killed if the Prince and his men hadn't rescued me."

All eyes turned to Amias, who nodded solemnly before shifting his gaze back to me.

Maeve continued to stare, her expression reverent—like a

disciple awaiting her prophecy's fulfillment.

"Seer Maeve," the second priest snapped. "Take your seat. You've said enough."

Maeve bowed deeply before retreating to her place, her wild hair glowing in the firelight.

"Forgive me," I said, gesturing vaguely to the room. "I don't understand any of this. I didn't grow up following Highest, but somehow... He brought me here."

The woman priest leaned forward. "Do you even know who you are?"

I shook my head. "No... But I'm listening—and willing to be taught."

Another silence passed, thick with meaning. Finally, the woman priest spoke.

"Nearly 700 years ago, the Watchers rebelled," she began. "Their corruption spread like a disease, changing humanity and leading us away from Highest. Prophets, Messengers, and Seers were sent to warn the people, but after 20 years of pleading, the corruption only deepened." She paused, her eyes gleaming with something between hope and awe. "Then, a child was born of a woman of The Blessed—a child with eyes of fire. Highest sent this child, imbued with His power, to judge the land and lead His people out of deception."

The words struck me like a physical blow. I swallowed hard, my eyes instinctively seeking Amias's steady gaze. He nodded, his expression soft but unreadable.

The priestess continued, her voice reverent. "That child was the first heir. They brought judgment, cleansing the land of its wickedness. Prophecy tells us the heir is marked by their eyes—eyes like yours. You are the first heir in nearly 220 years."

I leaned back, the weight of her words crashing over me. My hands trembled, and heat simmered beneath my skin.

"Kae'Dinah?" Amias's voice was soft but steady.

"I'm fine," I muttered, though my vision blurred.

"Your eyes, Your Highness," the second priest said cautiously. "They're glowing—like flames, embers"

"What?" My head snapped up, panic lacing my voice. My chest tightened as the warmth within me swelled, threatening to overtake me. Was it possible that fire truly burned inside me?

I pressed a hand over my chest, inhaling deeply to steady myself. Slowly, the heat subsided, and my vision cleared.

A few silent moments passed.

No one spoke.

Everyone just looked… at me.

"So, I'm an heir?" I asked, my voice low and trembling.

"Yes," the priestess said, her tone heavy with meaning. "You are a judge—the cleanser of our world."

I exhaled, a short, stunned laugh escaping before I could stop it.

"You're joking."

The collective gasp was immediate. The priestess didn't smile.

I slapped a hand over my mouth. "I'm so sorry. That was—I didn't mean to offend. It's just… a lot."

The priests nodded in unison, their disapproval practically vibrating in the silence.

Amias coughed into his fist—poorly masking the grin pulling at his mouth.

I shot him a glare before facing the others again.

"What does this mean for me?" I asked, my voice firm

despite the swirl of emotions inside. "What do I need to do now?"

The room still crackled with tension as I fought to absorb what I'd just heard. My head buzzed with questions, dozens of them, clambering for space at the forefront of my mind.

The priests exchanged glances, their faces a mixture of reverence and unease. Finally, the first priest—the man who'd first spoken—raised a hand, his expression placating.

"Princess, there is much for you to learn," he said, his voice calm but heavy with significance. "But it must wait now."

"Wait?" I repeated, my brow furrowing.

"The Festival of Strings begins at sunset," the woman priest explained, her tone soft but resolute, as her eyes cut to the sky outside the window. "It is one of our most sacred celebrations, a time of music, praise, and unity in honor of Highest. During this time, no work may be done. Not even for you."

I clenched my jaw, frustration bubbling to the surface. "But you've just told me I'm supposed to be this… judge, this salvation, and now you want me to sit and wait? How can I—"

"Princess." Amias's voice cut through my protest, low and soothing. When I turned to him, his eyes held a quiet steadiness that calmed me, despite myself. "This is how we honor Highest," he said, stepping closer. " I know you're eager to learn more, and you will. But for now, *patience* is the lesson."

I opened my mouth to argue but stopped when I saw the slight quirk of his lips—a faint, mischievous smile that softened the sternness of his words. What in the world was so amusing to him now?

Despite myself, I felt a tug of curiosity and something that attracted me. I turned away from him, shaking my head like I could dispel the feeling.

"I'll wait, then," I said, arching a very impatient eyebrow.

The priests visibly relaxed, though seer Maeve's intense gaze still lingered on me from the corner of the room.

"It is settled," the first Priest said, relief evident in his tone. "At sunset tomorrow, we will resume. But tonight, you will celebrate with us. You will feel the joy of Highest and the unity of Syx. We are truly honored to host you, heiress."

The priests rose, their movements deliberate and reverent as they began to leave the chamber, one by one. Maeve was the last to depart, pausing at the door to glance back at me with a strange, knowing look.

When the room was empty except for Amias and me, I exhaled a long breath and looked at him.

"Well," I said, folding my arms. "What now? Do I just sit in awe of my glowing eyes until tomorrow night?"

I couldn't tell if I wanted to cry or scream.

Amias chuckled softly, a sound that warmed the air more than the fire behind him. "That wouldn't be a bad recommendation," he said, stepping closer. "But I think you'll find the evening more... *enjoyable* than you expect."

I arched a brow. "Enjoyable? I've just been told I'm the judge, and now I'm supposed to... relax?"

He paused, his expression softening. "You've been through more than anyone should endure in a lifetime. I know how much you want answers, but trust me, the Festival of Strings will give you more than you think. I had honestly forgotten about it with my travels."

I frowned, not entirely convinced. "And if I don't feel like

290

celebrating?"

He smiled, the faintest curve of his lips that felt almost conspiratorial. "You might change your mind when you hear the music. *I* wanted to offer you a dance, but—"

The words hung between us, weighted. Like bait set in a snare, he laid out for me so perfectly.

"A dance?" I repeated, my tone laced with incredulity.

"Yes," he said, his confidence growing as he held my gaze. "It's tradition, of course, for honored guests to join in. And since you're the most honored among us..."

His voice trailed off, his meaning clear.

For a moment, I was at a loss for words, caught between skepticism and the fluttering in my chest. So was the dance for his benefit, or just a simple gesture of hospitality for an honored guest?

"I suppose it would be rude to refuse," I said lightly, though my pulse quickened.

"Very rude," he replied, his tone teasing but his eyes serious. I could see it now, the way he searched my face for an answer before my words came out. He was solely asking for his own benefit. He was asking because he simply wanted to dance with me.

Our gazes locked for a moment too long, and I quickly looked away, brushing my hands over my pants as if to smooth away the tension. Why was he so... persistent? So upfront?

"Well, then," I said briskly, my voice steadying. "I'll be sure to prepare myself for this grand festival. And one dance, just one."

Amias inclined his head, his smirk widening just enough to reveal a dimple in his cheek. "Just one. I'll hold you to

291

that."

He turned and headed for the door, pausing briefly to glance over his shoulder.

"The Blessed will come in to escort you back to your guest room. They'll also help you get dressed for tonight," he said, turning back around. "Sunset, Princess. You'll hear the crowds before you see them."

His words faded as the door gently closed.

Before I could respond, he was gone—leaving me alone in the room with my thoughts and the lingering warmth of his voice.

I sighed, sinking back into the chair behind me. Tonight would be a distraction, one I wasn't sure I needed—but as much as I hated to admit it, a part of me was already looking forward to it.

And maybe… to seeing him again.

There was something about Amias that unsettled me—but not in a way I feared. It was quieter than that.

# Chapter 28

"Do others dress like this?" I asked, staring at my reflection in the floor-to-ceiling mirror in my guest room. The Blessed had arrived shortly after the priests and Amias left me in the meeting room. Four of them, veiled and serene, escorted me silently down the halls, their steps soft and purposeful. Behind the closed doors, I could hear the faint hum of voices as the palace began to fill with eager guests.

The Blessed wasted no time. They bathed me in what was undoubtedly the most luxurious bath of my life. The water was the perfect temperature, infused with scents that calmed and rejuvenated. I could have stayed there for hours, letting the heat soak away my worries, but they gently insisted I rise.

Afterward, they stood me on a small pedestal before the mirror and began their meticulous work. Their hands were swift and steady as they dressed me in what they deemed traditional attire.

"Yes, ma'am," one answered simply, sewing the waistline of my skirts to fit perfectly.

The others worked in near silence. One polished a golden necklace to a brilliant sheen. It was stunning, with opaque egg-shaped gems set in a row of gold. Glittering chains cushioned the gems above and below, creating a piece that felt regal yet overwhelming.

Another Blessed woman affixed a golden belt to the top hem of my skirt. Its gems—deep reds, blues, golds, and familiar emeralds—sparkled in the light. They moved with practiced precision, adjusting layers of satin and embroidery until I looked as though I belonged here.

But I didn't.

I exhaled slowly, turning back to the mirror. Five days. It had only been five days, and yet my entire world had unraveled.

My gaze dropped to their hands as they worked. For a brief moment, I thought of my handmaids back in Anima—Kelta and Daph. Would they be punished for my escape? I prayed not.

I prayed to Highest that they would be safe.

I prayed to Highest, and it felt natural. It felt right. It felt like he actually heard me. I could sense it down in my heart that he could. With all the people who'd heard of me, with even the unnatural timing of Amias' visit, I could feel that everything happening was orchestrated and intentional.

So I closed my eyes and prayed for my former servants.

And Meg.

Sweet Meg, did she miss me? Had she cried when she realized I was gone? Did my father?

A sharp pang shot through my chest, and my lips trembled. No matter the amount of hurt they caused me, I knew that I still loved them immensely. And no matter how much their rejection broke me, I couldn't find it in my heart to break them back. My hands balled into fists at my sides as I took a deep breath and whispered words for them as well.

One of the Blessed appeared at my side, holding a small polished clay cup and a towel. She extended the items toward me.

"What is this?" I asked, motioning to the cup.

"A tea to help you relax," she replied, her voice soft and soothing. "Your mind seems troubled."

I grabbed the warm cup.

She retreated to the table, her movements graceful as she retrieved the jewels they had prepared for me.

I brought the cup to my nose, inhaling the warm herbal aroma. My stomach twisted violently.

*Jasmine.*

The scent struck me like a blade. Jasmine, the Queen's scent. It lingered in every room she graced, clinging to the air like a ghost. It was her presence, her power. A sharp memory of her hands on my neck, her eyes cold and calculating, flashed in my mind.

"No," I gasped, the word escaping my lips before I could stop it.

The Blessed paused, confusion flickering across their veiled faces.

"No jasmine," I repeated, lowering the cup and extending it back toward one of them. My voice was firmer this time. "Please, no jasmine. Not ever."

They exchanged glances before one finally nodded. "Of course. No jasmine."

The woman motioned for the others to continue, their hands resuming their quiet work.

"I apologize," I murmured, running my palms over the satin material of my skirts in an attempt to ground myself.

The Blessed only nodded, their silence returning.

* * *

The Blessed spent another half an hour dressing me, styling my hair, and decorating my face before they dismissed themselves.

I stared into the mirror.

I had never been transformed like this. The powders of gold and dark browns applied to my eyes intensified the golden irises staring back at me. My eyes were no longer a dull yellow but a sharp, piercing gold, hazel flecks appearing at certain angles.

I had never seen them look like this.

"Wow," I whispered to myself, my lips sticking together slightly from the colored substance they had applied.

*I* had never looked like this before.

The outfit clung to me in ways that felt both foreign and powerful. The golden belt rested snugly over my belly button, the sheer sleeves floating down to my shoulders like a whisper. The heavy necklace of layered gems and glittering gold adorned my neck, covering most of the open square neckline of my soft top.

I tilted my head side to side, smiling faintly as the jewels sparkled in the candlelight.

I backed away from my reflection, walking to my daggers. I grabbed the smallest of my leather holsters, wrapped it around my thigh, under my skirt. Then I sheathed two blades.

Just in case.

Three knocks sounded in a familiar pattern at the door.

I stared at the door, already knowing who it was.

I moved briskly to the other side of the room, the skirts flowing around my feet like I was walking on water. Opening the door, I was greeted by Jahiel, his hair pulled into a high bun, his tawny skin clean and glowing. His face was freshly shaven except for the shadow above his upper lip. He looked good.

He wore a dark green tunic and pants set with matching green-and-gold slipper-like shoes. No doubt a nod to the life we lived just a week ago.

I crinkled my nose, feigning disgust as I fanned at the air. "Oh no. What is that smell? Is that…florals? No way—bring back the grime and hard labor. That's the Jahiel I know. "

He laughed, stepping into the room fully. I matched his retreat, moving back to give him space as I closed the door.

"I'm sorry—who are you? I thought this was where the Princess slept," he said, turning toward me. His eyes roamed over every inch of my outfit—the exposed skin, the jewels on my neck, the color on my lips, and then finally, my eyes. "You do not *look* like the Princess, I've known all these years."

Heat rushed to my face as I turned away, walking back to the mirror to stare at my reflection again.

He was right.

I didn't look like the Princess he knew anymore.

I looked… more powerful now. More confident.

And honestly, I wasn't sure if I even wanted the title anymore.

"I'm not sure I *want* to look like her," I said softly. Jahiel took slow, deliberate steps toward my side, his hands clasped behind his back like he was restraining himself.

I turned to him, finding his eyes fixed on my lips.

"Jahiel," I said softly, uncertain what I was warning him from—me, this moment, or something heavier behind his eyes.

His gaze flicked to mine, then drifted across my face again. Familiar. Too familiar.

"Yes," he whispered, his voice warm and low—the same voice that once comforted me after long days in the court, or made me laugh when the world felt too cruel.

But now that warmth felt like pressure. Like something expected of me.

I stepped back, needing distance—space to breathe, to think.

"Jahiel," I said again, a little firmer this time.

His eyes met mine fully, and I saw something break in them. Then he stepped forward, hands brushing against my arms, fingers wrapping gently around my elbows like he used to when I was upset.

"You are the most beautiful woman I've ever seen," he said, his voice weighted with something he'd never dared say out loud before. "You always have been."

I blinked.

The words hit me like a misstep on stairs—sudden, jarring, off-balance.

He'd never said that before. Never in that way.

"Jahiel…" I breathed, but he didn't wait.

He leaned in, brushing his lips softly against my collarbone.

Heat bloomed across my skin, but it wasn't desire.

It was shock. Guilt. Discomfort.

I didn't pull away fast enough.

He kissed me again, slower this time, drawing a quiet sound from my throat—not longing, but confusion.

He moved up, lips ghosting just beneath my ear. It was gentle, yes.

But not right. Not for me. Not for us.

This wasn't the stolen breath of a storybook kiss.

It was the unraveling of something I'd never meant to tangle.

"Jahiel," I gasped, trying to pull my mind back into my body.

"You smell divine, Princess," he murmured.

That word.

It struck deep—like a chain trying to reattach itself.

Princess.

I flinched.

I wasn't her anymore. I didn't want to be.

I stepped back, the haze breaking like glass around me.

This wasn't love.

This wasn't home.

"No," I said, pulling away completely now, my voice low but steady.

He froze, the air between us thick with disbelief.

"We can't," I said.

"We could," he whispered, still reaching, still hoping.

"No, Jahiel. We can't."

"Why not?" he asked, frustration creeping into his voice. "There are no rules here. No eyes watching. We don't have to hide anymore."

"I know that."

"Then why do you run from me, *Princess*?" he asked, and this time it felt like a weapon.

"Do not call me that again."

My voice rose sharply—fire pulsing beneath my skin.

He flinched. "Isn't that who you are?"

"No," I said, my voice shaking now with anger and clarity. "I stopped being her the day they offered me up on that altar. That title was buried with who I used to be. So don't call me Princess."

Something stirred inside me—warm and electric—rising through my chest and into my limbs. I felt it building, pulsing in my hands, flaring behind my eyes.

Jahiel took a step back. His shoulders tensed.

"Then what are you now?" he asked, voice softer, eyes wide.

I looked past him and caught my reflection in the mirror.

My eyes glowed faintly—flickers of gold and fire dancing in their depths.

Unfamiliar. Otherworldly.

*What are you now?*

The question echoed in my mind, not with accusation, but revelation.

I walked toward the mirror, passing Jahiel without another word.

I stared at the girl—no, the woman—who stared back.

Her face was mine.

But she didn't belong to Anima anymore.

And she didn't belong to him.

I turned to face him once more. "I don't know," I said softly. "But I know I'm not your princess. I never was."

His face fell.

A bitter chuckle slipped out of him, raw and disbelieving.

"Why are you laughing?" I asked, tired now.

"Because you barely know these people," he said, shaking his head. "And yet you're letting them pull you further and further away from yourself."

I wanted to tell him the truth:

That I wasn't being pulled away.

I was finally stepping into who I was meant to be.

"Jahiel, I'm clearly not myself," I said, motioning toward my reflection in the mirror—toward the version of me I didn't fully recognize yet.

"Yes, but—"

A series of knocks cut him off. Sharp. Deliberate.

"Kae?"

The voice through the door made my heart stutter.

Amias.

At just the sound of his voice, something inside me exhaled. My mind whispered safety, and my body responded before I could stop it—shoulders relaxing, breath steadying.

Jahiel's eyes narrowed.

He saw the change in me. I knew he did.

I shook my head and turned from him, crossing the room with long, deliberate strides.

I opened the door.

Amias stood there in a navy tunic and matching pants, silver chains resting against his chest. His wolf-sigil ring glinted in the candlelight as his dark eyes swept over me.

But his didn't *roam* like Jahiel's had.

His gaze landed—intentionally—on my face. My frown. My unspoken plea.

"What's wrong?" he asked, his voice low and steady. He didn't ask out of courtesy—he knew something was wrong. He felt it.

His eyes flicked past me—and landed on Jahiel.

I watched his expression shift, sharpening like a drawn

301

blade.

Without a word, Amias placed both hands on my shoulders, steady but sure, and gently moved around me.

He stepped into the room, placing himself between me and Jahiel with a quiet authority that didn't need announcing.

His body was tense.

Protective. A shield I hadn't asked for… but wanted all the same.

"Why are you in her room?" he demanded, his voice like steel.

"Why are *you*?" Jahiel threw back, his voice sharp.

"I wasn't unaccompanied," Amias shot back, his tone cold.

I turned quickly, nearly colliding with Tavin and Tye as they stepped into the large door frame behind him.

"You should not be in her room—accompanied or not," Amias said tightly, his gaze darkening.

Jahiel scoffed. "Please. She's not a child. She can have whomever she wants in her bedroom."

"Oh, I know that," Amias growled. "But it's not her actions I'm questioning. It's yours. She is not just a woman anymore. She is the most important person in our world. So perhaps you could muster a little restraint when it comes to sating your own physical needs for her."

Jahiel's eyes narrowed, his jaw tightening. "You have no grounds to speak on her behalf."

"I do, actually," Amias said, his voice unwavering. "Highest sent me to her for that very reason. This is bigger than you or me, my friend."

Jahiel took a step closer, his voice low and brimming with defiance. "I spent my life in Anima protecting her, knowing her. You've known her for days, and you think you know

302

what's best?"

Amias's eyes flashed with disdain. "Anima wanted to kill her. The fact that you still reference that cursed land with any reverence sickens me. She's not who you once knew her as."

Jahiel clenched his fists at his sides, his frustration palpable. "Then who is she now, Prince?"

Amias met his glare with steely determination. "More," he said firmly, his voice ringing with finality. "So much more than you can imagine."

I exhaled the breath I hadn't realized I was holding as the two men slowly closed the space between them, tension crackling in the air like a storm waiting to break.

Jahiel's eyes slid to mine, dark and conflicted, his chest rising and falling with sharp breaths, as if he were struggling to contain the storm building inside him.

"You see this, don't you?" he asked, voice quieter but laced with urgency. "You see how quickly they're trying to change everything about you—your face, your title, your identity. And now they tell me—me—that I no longer know you."

"Jahiel, it's not like that," I said softly, my voice cracking slightly.

"Then what is it like?" he pressed, stepping closer, his tone raw. Not demanding—pleading. Needing an answer I didn't know how to give without breaking something.

Amias shifted again, unyielding. A silent wall between us. "She doesn't owe you an explanation."

Jahiel's lips parted, his pain twisting into something sharper. "She doesn't owe you anything either, Prince," he growled. "You think a vision from Highest gives you claim over her? It doesn't. She's not yours to direct or protect."

"I never said she was mine," Amias replied, his voice level and steady. "But she's also not yours. You speak of knowing her, of protecting her—but where was that protection when Anima condemned her? Where was your defiance when her life was traded for the approval of false gods?"

The words landed hard.

Jahiel staggered under their weight, the truth in them undeniable. He looked at me then—really looked—and I saw it. The hurt. The betrayal. The unraveling of a story he'd written alone.

"I did defy them," he said, voice low and shaking. "I defied everything I was taught—everything I believed—to keep her alive. So don't stand there and question my loyalty... or my love for her."

"Love?" Amias repeated, sharp and cold, like the crack of a whip.

The word stunned the room into silence.

Even the flames in the sconces seemed to flicker quieter.

I took a slow step forward, heart thudding. My hands trembled as I reached for Amias's arm—not to stop him, but to anchor myself.

"Amias," I said softly, "let me speak to him. Alone."

His head snapped toward me, silver-gray eyes narrowing. "You don't need to—"

"Please," I interrupted gently, but firmly. "I need to. Not you. At this rate, things will only get worse."

He studied me for a moment, jaw clenched. Then he nodded once—reluctantly—and stepped back. With a glance at Jahiel that could have cut through steel, Amias turned and gestured for Tavin and Tye to follow him out.

"I'll be right outside," he said as he stepped into the hall, the door closing behind him.

I turned to Jahiel, meeting his storm of a gaze with my own. "Jahiel…" I began, voice steady despite the ache behind my ribs. "You're right about one thing. We've known each other for most of our lives. You've always been… safe to me. Constant."

I took another breath. "But I never saw you the way you saw me."

He flinched, almost imperceptibly.

"You are my best friend," I said gently, honestly. "You matter to me. But not like that. Not the way you want."

He blinked, and for a moment, all the fire left him. Just a man grieving the story he'd built in his mind.

"I didn't mean to mislead you," I added. "But I can't give you something I never had."

He hesitated for a long moment before finally nodding, though his posture stayed tense.

The silence that followed was suffocating. Jahiel stood motionless, his eyes locked on mine, like he was trying to read something deeper than I could offer.

"I'm not the same person I was in Anima," I said, my voice barely above a whisper.

"You keep saying that," he bit back, jaw clenched. "But you still haven't told me who you are now."

"I don't know," I admitted, the confession slipping out before I could stop it. "I don't know who I am or who I'm supposed to be. But the person you're holding onto—the princess you protected—she's gone. She died the moment they decided I was worth sacrificing."

His face twisted with pain. His hands curled into fists at

his sides.

"You think I don't know that?" he said, voice breaking. "You think I don't blame myself every day for what happened to you? For how she treated you? I couldn't save you then—but I can now."

I shook my head, tears stinging the edges of my eyes.

"Saving me doesn't mean holding me in the past, Jahiel. It means letting me change into whatever comes next."

The words seemed to crush him. His shoulders sagged as though their weight was too much to bear. For a moment, I thought he'd argue, fight the truth I was trying to give him. But instead, he let out a shaky breath and stepped back.

"I vowed to protect you with everything in me," he said. "I'm afraid, Kae'dinah. I'm afraid that accepting what they say about you will paint a target on your back. I'm afraid I won't be able to stop them—if the whole world decides to come for you."

*The whole world.*

I looked at him—at the one I'd held close like a brother, closer. His eyes were wide, searching every inch of my face, like he was trying to memorize what he might soon lose. He was terrified. Not of me. But of everything beyond me.

And yet... I wasn't afraid.

Deep in my chest, I felt it: the steady, unshakable sense that this—whatever *this* was—was right.

But how could I explain that?

"I know," I said softly. "But you have to trust me. Trust your friend. I can't see the future, but something inside me keeps screaming not to go back. So I won't. And you can't either. If we keep clinging to who I was, you'll never see who I'm becoming. A week ago, I was a princess who needed your protection. But now..."

I swallowed.

"I'm not sure I need you as that anymore."

He stared at me for a long time, his gaze searching mine for something I couldn't name. Finally, he nodded—slow, reluctant, but real.

"What do you need me as?" he asked, voice barely above a whisper.

The question caught me off guard. I didn't have the answer—not yet. But before I could even try to form one, the door creaked open behind him.

Amias stepped inside. His eyes immediately locked onto mine.

"Is everything all right?" he asked, his voice cautious but firm.

"Yes," I snapped, the tension spilling over. "Everything's fine."

Amias nodded, though his gaze lingered on Jahiel for a long beat before returning to me. "It's time for the festivities. Dinner is being served first."

He motioned toward the door.

I hesitated, glancing at Jahiel one last time. His eyes met mine—still sad, but gentler now. A glimmer of understanding.

"Go," he said quietly. "You deserve to enjoy this."

I paused, the words unspoken still crowding my throat. I didn't want to leave like this. But he looked back at me like the conversation was already over. Like he'd already let me go.

So I nodded, stepped past Amias's extended arm, and walked into the glowing warmth of the evening.

# Chapter 29

I followed Amias as we descended into a grand room bathed in the warm flicker of candlelight. To our right, four towering arches opened onto a courtyard, where guests in jewel-toned garments drifted like falling petals. Amias stepped forward, his posture regal as he bowed to a cluster of dignitaries near a buffet glistening with ripe fruit. I moved to his side, flanked by Tavin and Tye—ever silent, ever watchful.

The garden beyond shimmered in the moonlight, its beauty undisturbed by the hum of conversation. Shadows of flowers danced in the breeze, oblivious to the chaos unraveling inside me.

I inhaled—slow, shallow. This, I could do. I had been trained for this.

Smile. Stand tall. Speak with grace.

Disarm with charm.

My body moved on instinct, sculpted by years of royal expectation. But inside, I was cracking. Every breath felt rehearsed. Every movement felt like betrayal.

The crowd welcomed Amias with knowing smiles. Some called him *prince* like they'd known him since birth. When those same smiles turned toward me, polite, curious, too careful.

But some did more than smile.

Their gazes lingered—too long. Not at my dress, or my posture, but… my eyes.

A woman dropped her gaze the moment I met it.

A child clung tighter to her father's leg, and someone—an older man—bowed a fraction deeper than he had to.

I kept my chin high, my gaze forward, like I hadn't just been cracked open.

But Jahiel's voice echoed through me like a bell struck in a hollow room.

He *loved* me.

Not in protection. Not in friendship.

In silence. In shadow. In a way I never asked for and never returned. It wasn't a confession. It was a revelation. A truth that had always lived between us, now made unbearable by the fact that I could not carry it with him.

*He loved me...*

And I didn't know what to do with that.

Once, those words might've been everything. A balm. A gift.

The air thickened in my throat. I blinked hard. The heat behind my eyes rose with every step, every whispered greeting, every carefully measured smile.

One of the twins caught my eye.

"I'm fine," I muttered before he could ask.

He smirked—unconvinced—but said nothing.

But I wasn't fine. I was breaking, and everything around me—the music, the silks, the candles—it all made it worse.

Because I remembered.

I remembered standing like this beside my siblings, shoulder to shoulder at endless banquets. We made faces behind goblets, whispered insults about suitors, counted the minutes until we could escape together. We were a trio once.

*Were.*

Tears threatened. I bit them back. I wouldn't cry here.

Not where they could see me.

Not where I was supposed to be poised, elegant, whole.

But my body no longer cared what I was supposed to be.

Memories came sharp and fast.

Milo's wide, terrified eyes. Megorna, still and pale. My father, unmoving. Silent.

None of them stood.

None of them fought.

Not one said, *She cannot be sacrificed.*

*She cannot be sacrificed.*

The words echoed louder in my head than they ever had aloud.

They were silent, every last one of them.

While I was prepared to be offered to gods I never believed in.

I swallowed a sob that clawed at my throat. The effort tasted bitter, and through the ache, another memory surged—

I scoffed—too loud—nearly choking on the tears begging to fall.

Heads turned. Eyes found me. I froze.

I forced a smile. Bowed. Whispered an apology I didn't mean. And turned away before anyone could see too much.

These thoughts—these cursed thoughts—they tore at me.

Love and abandonment. Devotion and silence. Loyalty and betrayal.

All of it unraveling me with every breath.

Every step I took. Every word I spoke. Every memory I had once cherished now rose like a ghost to mock me.

My legs moved faster than my mind. I pushed through the crowd, unsteady.

I reached the wine table, grabbed a goblet.

A servant stilled as I approached, his eyes flicking to mine—and staying there.

His breath caught.

Not fear. Not admiration.

Awe.

I downed the wine without a word.

It burned. Sweet and sharp.

I fled to the courtyard before I shattered in front of them all.

The night was chilled. Wind scraped at my skin like punishment. Fire pits flickered around the stone path, but their warmth didn't reach me. Couldn't touch what was breaking inside.

I wrapped my arms around myself—trembling, hollow, burning.

For a moment, I just stood there, frozen in the courtyard's quiet. The distant laughter from inside faded beneath the rush of blood in my ears. I turned slightly, confirming that I was alone—far enough from the crowd, from the curious stares, from anyone who might see me unravel.

And then I let go.

The tears came suddenly, spilling over like a storm I could no longer hold back. Hot, desperate sobs wracked my chest, tearing through me with the kind of grief that didn't care who I used to be. I didn't try to stop them. I couldn't. I bent forward slightly, one hand braced against the cold stone wall as the weight of it all—everything I had lost, everything I had been forced to become—poured from me.

And then—*Tssss...*

I froze.

One of my tears had struck the ground and sizzled, steam curling into the air like breath from a flame.

I blinked hard, another tear falling—and again, *Tsssss.* The sound sharper now. My hand flew to my cheek, fingertips pressing into my damp skin.

No pain. No sting. Only heat.

My tears weren't just falling.

They were burning.

"Hey?"

Amias' voice slipped into the quiet like a gentle tide—deep, steady, and full of concern.

I didn't move at first. I simply lifted a trembling hand to stop him from coming closer, my body still crouched low to the stone path. I needed to see it again. Needed to prove to myself that I hadn't imagined it.

Another blink. Another tear.

*Tsssss...*

It hit the ground and sizzled.

A sound no tear should ever make.

My stomach twisted. My breath faltered.

"What is happening to me?" I whispered, more to the wind than to him.

"Kae?"

That name again. Steady in his mouth. My name—but somehow softer when he said it.

I stood slowly, rolling my shoulders as if that could press

the chaos back into place. When I turned, I found him already watching me, his storm-gray eyes roving over my face—not searching for flaws, but trying to understand.

His voice was calm, gentle. "Are you okay? Do you want to talk about it?"

No, I thought. I want to disappear. I want to scream. I want to run back to the part of me that existed before everything cracked open.

But I didn't say any of that. I couldn't.

Amias stepped closer, and with him came a strange sense of warmth—like the firelight had followed him. Citrus and cedar drifted from his skin. Grounding. Familiar. Like a memory I didn't know I had.

And just like that, the heaviness inside me shifted. Not vanished. But... softened.

I looked up at him, eyes half-lidded, caught in the storm he carried behind his gaze. And still, I stepped back. I had to. I didn't understand what this was. I didn't understand him.

Because every time he was near, my thoughts unraveled— like my guard didn't know how to hold its shape.

He smiled then, something quiet and nonthreatening. A real smile. One that didn't push, didn't press.

Just... offered.

And he stepped closer.

"What is it?" he asked. "You can tell me. I won't yell or be upset. You've been through a lot since arriving in Scala."

His voice threaded through the chaos in my mind, pulling loose the tangled knots of thought I hadn't realized were binding me. The more he spoke, the less I felt like I had to hold everything alone.

Why does your presence make it easier to breathe? I

wanted to ask. Why do the words fall out of me when you're near?

I swallowed instead. "I can be honest?"

He tilted his head slightly, those storm-gray eyes steady and sure. "With me? Always."

I hesitated, casting a glance toward the lights of the feast beyond him. The people. The party. The expectations. All of it dulled in his shadow.

I exhaled. Not just air—but something tight, something unseen.

"People say they want honesty," I murmured. "But they rarely mean it. It's too easy to get hurt."

He didn't flinch. Didn't deny it. He only nodded like he knew that truth already and still stood before me anyway.

And in that moment, I realized something I hadn't wanted to admit.

I don't know why I trust you.

I don't know why your presence feels like peace when my life is anything but.

But it does.

The storm in his eyes calmed the storm in my mind.

And I hated how much I wanted to stay in that calm a little longer.

He chuckled—a low, quiet sound that somehow managed to loosen something in my chest. "Tell you what," he said, reaching up to toy with a coil of hair resting against my shoulder. "Let's play a game."

The gesture startled me—gentle, almost reverent. But then his hand fell back to his side, as if he realized the intimacy of it too late.

He didn't apologize. Just let it fall away, like the moment

had passed.

Did he feel it too? That pull? That strange peace that lingered between us like something old and familiar, though we barely knew each other?

I arched a brow, folding my arms as if I could protect myself from whatever was unraveling inside me. "A game?"

He nodded, a smile tugging at the corner of his mouth. "One minute of brutal honesty. No interruptions. No judging. No solving. Just… listening."

I let out a breathy laugh, though it didn't reach my eyes. "You really think you can handle my truths?"

He lifted a brow. "I'm not afraid of honesty. And I think mine might surprise you more than yours will surprise me."

His voice was steady, but something behind it flickered— like he wasn't as unaffected as he pretended to be.

"You go first," he added, too casually.

"Why do I have to go first?"

"Because it was my idea. And I'm trying to be brave."

I hesitated, a knot forming in my chest. My mind flicked to that place where my tears had scorched stone—like embers from a dying fire.

"…Okay," I said softly.

I stared at the cobblestones. The words gathered at the edge of my throat but refused to move.

"If I'm being honest," I began, "I'm exhausted. Not just tired—*soul-deep* worn. The last few days have been too much. I have too many emotions I haven't sorted through. I found out I'm something I never asked to be. And the world expects me to carry a burden I don't even understand."

I paused, my breath catching.

"And instead of breaking down over that, I'm here crying

over a family that abandoned me… and a man who said he loved me."

I didn't dare look up.

"Jahiel. He's protected me. Given so much of himself for me. But now I wonder—did I miss the moment when his loyalty became love? Have I been holding him in my hands without even realizing it?"

I exhaled slowly. "And somewhere in the middle of all that, my tears started burning through stone like they were boiling. Like even my grief isn't familiar anymore."

I shook my head. "I haven't had time to process what that means. I don't know if I'm breaking… or becoming."

I swallowed.

"And then there's you."

Finally, I met his eyes.

"Every time you're near, something inside me stirs. It's… uninvited. Unsettling. Beautiful. I don't know why your presence calms me when I feel like I'm falling apart. I don't know why the words fall out of me when you're close—but they do."

I clenched my jaw, a whisper of guilt curling in my chest. "I want to push you away just to prove I can. Just to prove that I'm still in control of something. But I keep standing here."

I breathed in shakily. "And I think… I miss my brother. More than anything. And that grief is bleeding into everything else, and I don't know where one emotion ends and the next begins."

I turned away for a moment, staring out at the fire pits. "How's that for honesty?"

He was quiet.

Too quiet.

When I looked back, he wasn't smiling. Not teasing. His eyes had softened, something unreadable flickering beneath the gray.

"Kae..." he started.

I held up a hand. "No solving. No judging. Just listening. That's the rule, remember?"

He nodded, lips twitching faintly in surrender. "Fair enough."

He took a breath, dragging a hand through his curls.

"My turn," he murmured.

Then he looked at me—and there was no pretending left in him.

"I don't like Jahiel," he said.

I blinked, caught off guard.

"I don't trust his intentions," he continued. "I don't like the way he watches you, or the way you look at him like he might still have a claim on your heart. It's hard for me to leave you alone with him, and that feeling—it makes me uncomfortable. And jealous."

He exhaled. "And I hate that I feel that way."

I couldn't look away. His voice wasn't bitter. Just... honest.

"I see how tightly you hold everything inside. Like you've trained yourself to never be too much or ask for too much. I don't know if someone taught you that, or if life did, but I want you to know this..."

His voice softened, slowed.

"You don't have to wear every emotion like armor. If something hurts, let it hurt. If something brings you joy, feel it fully. You don't have to edit yourself around me."

A muscle ticked in his jaw.

"And... honestly?"

He hesitated—just for a beat.

"I wasn't expecting you to be so beautiful," he said, voice low, reverent.

It wasn't just flattery. It was honest. Unfiltered. A confession wrapped in wonder.

"When I saw the eyes in my dream, I thought they belonged to someone distant. Untouchable. Powerful. But now... Now you're here. And I can't seem to look away."

He blinked, his gaze holding mine.

"You weren't supposed to be someone who makes it harder to separate obedience from desire."

He looked down for a breath, collecting himself, then back at me.

"I want to be a guide to you. A protector. A friend. But I'd be lying if I didn't admit..." He gave a soft laugh. "Your presence unravels me, too."

I stared at him—confused, undone, seen.

We stood there, still just a breath apart, saying nothing more.

Then, slowly, Amias cleared his throat and smiled. A gentle, almost bashful thing. "They're saving us seats for dinner."

He extended his elbow for me to grab.

I hesitated.

"Well, I can't hold your arm over there," I said softly, half-teasing. "What will people think of me?"

He chuckled, the sound warm and low. "Fair enough."

He didn't offer his hand again. He just waited.

And somehow, that restraint felt more intimate than touch.

We turned toward the party, but before we could take a step, he paused.

"Wait."

I nearly collided with his back. "What?"

He turned slightly, brow furrowed. "Did you say... your tears were boiling?"

I swallowed. "...Yes."

A beat of silence passed.

"Interesting," he murmured, almost to himself. "We'll ask the priests about it tomorrow."

"Fantastic. Let's go now before I start steaming again."

He huffed a quiet laugh, and we continued toward the table—side by side, like nothing had changed.

But something had.

And we both felt it.

# Chapter 30

F amiliar faces from his entourage greeted me as I slid onto the long wooden bench between Amias and one of the twins. The banquet spread before us was magnificent—roasted chickens, golden potatoes spiced with herbs, woven baskets of ripe fruit, pitchers of wine and water, and the familiar flatbread, manneh, stacked in generous portions. The rich aroma made my stomach clench with hunger. I couldn't remember the last time I'd had a meal like this.

Laughter and conversation hummed around us. Nine other long tables stretched across the great hall, filled with people indulging without restraint. No begging. No hunger. Just abundance.

"Eat something," the voice to my left said.

It was Tye—I recognized the raspy edge in his tone now. He smirked, revealing the single golden tooth that distinguished him from his twin. His plate was already stacked high, a ridiculous mountain of food.

"When did you even have time to pile that much?" I asked, incredulous.

Tye only chuckled and grabbed a basket of manneh, holding it out to me. "Here."

I took two pieces, murmuring a thanks, and was about to reach for the chicken when Amias tore off a leg and placed it on my plate with a wink.

I rolled my eyes, turning away as he chuckled behind me.

"Just know," Tye continued, scooping something creamy onto my plate without asking, "when you eat with us, you better move fast. We devour. No leftovers."

"Got it." I smiled, cutting into the chicken with my knife.

Across from me, a man I hadn't spoken to yet furrowed his brow. "What are you doing?"

I paused mid-bite. "Eating?"

"With a fork and knife?"

Tye laughed. "Vance, relax—she's a former princess."

"Former." Vance scoffed. "Key word. At that pace, she'll be here all night just finishing that plate."

I frowned, glancing around. Most of the men were eating with their hands, tearing into the chicken, scooping potatoes with bread. Instinct had guided me to use utensils, but now, under Vance's scrutiny, I felt absurdly prim.

"Does it bother you?" I asked, arching a brow.

"Yes." His lips quirked. "Just pick it up. Or is the princess too delicate to get her fingers dirty?"

My back stiffened. My mother's voice echoed in my head—her scolding, the sharp sting of correction whenever I failed to eat with perfect form. I had been trained for years to suppress any childish, improper tendencies. Now, the expectation was the opposite.

I was the opposite.

"Vance," Amias warned, pausing on his own plate to come to my defense.

Slowly, I relaxed my shoulders, pushed up the sheer sleeves

of my blouse, and leaned forward, elbows on the table like the men around me. Then, without breaking eye contact with Vance, I grabbed the chicken leg and bit into it.

Tye let out a laugh. "Oh, I like her."

I rolled my eyes again.

Vance only shrugged, unbothered.

Before I could respond, a firm voice interrupted.

"Excuse me. Is there space for me here?"

I looked up to see a familiar freckled face.

Maeve, the seer from earlier.

She stood between Jon and Vance, one hand gripping her plate, the other resting on her hip. Her wild coils were now tamed into a low bun, her eyes—one dazzling green, the other clouded—scanning the group with mild impatience. Her voice seemed to purr out of her. There was something distinct about the way she spoke—some dialect I couldn't place. Not from Syx. Not from anywhere I knew.

The men stared at her, dumbfounded.

I understood why. Maeve had that kind of beauty—the kind that made you look twice without realizing you were staring. Her features didn't match the women of Syx— brownish freckles dusted across light brown skin, one eye clouded, the other vivid green. High cheekbones, a strong nose, and full lips softened by youth. She looked nothing like the older seers I'd glimpsed in passing. She was younger. Sharper. Easier to notice.

"Well?" she huffed. "Can I sit here, or not?"

Jon and Vance scrambled, parting like the sea. She stepped over the bench and flopped down across from me. Her outfit mirrored mine—a skirt and top set—but in the muted sage of the seers, unadorned by the jewels or embroidery mine carried.

"Thank you," she muttered, adjusting herself. Then she turned to me. "Hello again."

I nodded slowly, uncertain where this was going.

"I saw you over here, surrounded by these men, and figured you might need some actual conversation." She smirked.

The men, once full of chatter, fell uncharacteristically silent.

I studied her—measured, guarded. She was charming. Too charming. And I wasn't ready to decide if I liked that yet.

"Thank you for rescuing me, Seer Maeve," I offered, voice playful but distant.

She laughed, and from the corner of my eye, I caught Tavin elbowing Tye as they exchanged quiet remarks.

"You all can just call me Maeve," Maeve said, more casually than the words warranted. "I saw you storm off earlier. Did the Prince have to talk you off the ledge?"

I stiffened.

How long had she been watching me? And why did it feel like she already knew more than she should?

"You were watching me?" I asked, keeping my tone flat.

"I noticed. I notice a lot, actually," she shrugged. "I would've checked on you myself, but Prince Harth got to you first. I know hearing the call on your life can be... overwhelming."

"Amias, please," he offered from beside me, using that careful, princely voice he reserved for new acquaintances.

"Yes, of course. Amias," she replied politely, then turned her attention back to me.

I narrowed my eyes slightly. "So you understand the weight I feel now? How so?"

323

"Yes. Being a seer is a tremendous amount of pressure."

"More pressure than the judge?"

She didn't flinch. "No. But I know what it's like to be doubted. To have to fight harder for respect because you're different. Foreign."

Her words struck something buried beneath my ribs—another ache I had to wrestle. But I shoved it down.

"A path you'll have to walk soon enough," she added gently.

I exhaled sharply through my nose. "Did Highest tell you that, or is this your own observation?"

Maeve tilted her head, eyes steady on mine. "I came over here to offer support, not to disagree with you."

"You assume I need support?"

Her lips pressed into a thin line. "I assume you don't have many people who understand what you're about to face."

That landed harder than I expected.

I scoffed to hide the crack in my armor. "No one here is like me. I'm from a foreign country. A former worshiper of false gods. My own family tried to kill me. And now I'm a judge—a woman judge. How exactly are we alike?"

Maeve didn't flinch.

"I, too, am from a foreign country. My family didn't want to deal with me, so they sent me away as a child on a trade ship. I was called to be a seer because of the visions I had, but they still doubted me. The other seers—" she hesitated, just briefly, "—were all completely blind. I wasn't. So they tested me. Challenged me. Constantly questioned my abilities. Then… they cast me out."

Her voice wavered, just slightly. Enough for me to catch it.

And something in me shifted. I recognized that flicker.

That need to hide the pain even while speaking it aloud.

"I had to prove myself," she continued, voice quieter now. "To make them believe I belonged."

Silence settled between us like a cloak. The men exchanged awkward glances, unsure if they should speak or stay quiet.

"So no," she said finally, "you're not alone. You might feel like it, but you're not." She began to push back from the table, as if preparing to leave.

Something twisted inside me—sharp, urgent. I didn't want her to go. Not yet. Not like that.

"No."

The word escaped before I could think to stop it.

Maeve paused, watching me.

I rubbed my brow. "I'm sorry."

A beat. Then—her lips curved into a knowing smile.

"Apology accepted." She settled back in her seat. "Now, eat your food before these men take the rest."

Friendships built on shared struggle. I wasn't used to that. I wasn't used to too many friends at all.

Her command to eat sounded too casual, too familiar—but not in the way that stung like my mother's tone. No, Maeve sounded more like...

Milo.

I blinked the thought away.

"So, seers are supposed to be fully blind?" I asked, carefully picking up a piece of manneh and dipping it into the orange paste Tye had added to my plate. I had seen the men do it, but my attempt felt clumsy and unsure.

Maeve's eyes twinkled with amusement as she watched me fumble. She giggled softly, then reached across the table for the bowl of mush in front of the twins.

"These," she said, lifting the bowl, "are smashed beans with herbs and olive oil."

She pinched a piece of manneh, folded it, scooped up a bite, and popped it into her mouth.

I mimicked her quickly, rushing the food to my lips before it could drop.

"Perfect," she praised, beaming as I reached for another.

The flavors surprised me—rich, spiced, warm. A soft sound escaped my throat.

"Wow," I murmured through the bite.

"What did she try?" Amias asked.

Maeve smirked, clearly enjoying the show.

Amias's eyes flicked between us, then landed on my face. His grin tugged into that crooked shape I was beginning to recognize—dimple and all.

"Never mind," he said. "You've got orange on your mouth. Here."

He held out a cloth napkin. I snatched it from him before he could think about wiping it himself.

"You're always laughing at me," I muttered.

"Yes," he said easily. "Or maybe I'm just happy to be looking at you."

I stilled.

The way he leaned in, the softness in his voice—it was too smooth. Too real.

Across the table, Maeve tossed a few grapes into her mouth, chewing slowly, her eyes all-too-knowing.

"Well," Amias said lightly, "if you're finished with her, Maeve, I'd like to steal her for a moment."

Maeve didn't answer immediately. Her gaze lingered on mine for a beat longer than necessary—like she already knew we would be friends. Like she saw it before I did.

She nodded. "That's fine. We'll have more time later."

I smirked back at her.

"Perfect." Amias stood, stepping over the bench before extending his hand.

I eyed him warily. "Where are you taking me?"

"To give you the dance I promised."

I hesitated—just for a moment—before slipping my hand into his and letting him lead me into the thrumming cele-bration.

* * *

The festival unfolded around us in a golden glow—lanterns swinging above, performers weaving through the crowd, people laughing, drinking, dancing. The air buzzed with life.

"Beautiful," I breathed, taking it all in.

Amias' gaze flickered to me. "Yes, it is."

When I met his eyes, my stomach clenched. I wasn't sure if he meant the scenery or me... I wasn't sure how I felt since his confession. But he wasn't hiding a thing.

He took a slow step closer.

"I'm a bit jealous that you get to see and celebrate this often," I said.

He chuckled, taking yet another step closer to me. "Oh, you were referring to the festivities. Yes, they are nice too."

"Shameless," I countered, turning to him. "And you seem way too practiced for me to be impressed any longer."

That startled a laugh from him. A full, head-thrown-back kind of laugh. He clutched his stomach as if I'd wounded him.

327

"Too practiced?" he repeated.

"Yes. You say the most practiced things—like these are the same words you use on every *interesting* young woman that crosses your path." I took a step back, putting space between us. Then I deepened my voice in a loose imitation of him, and I smirked. *"Oh, you were referring to the festivities. Yes, they are nice too.* Definitely seen it written in a few books."

Amias blinked, then grinned. "That's how I sound?"

"Oh, wait, let me try again." I switched to a rough approximation of a Valdeenian accent, arching my brow. *"Is that how I sound?"*

His smile widened, his head shaking in disbelief.

"You know," he mused, walking backward now, "that wasn't too bad."

I narrowed my eyes, watching him.

"We can work on it later," he added, still retreating. "For now, you owe me a dance."

I scoffed. "Oh, I'm not finished. First, you leave me a note, then you demand that I drink and eat, and now—" I waved dramatically toward him "—you're claiming your promised dance. Just a whole list of demands, all storybook cliches. Notes, drinks, food, annoying compliments—"

I beamed at him, and to my absolute shock, the Prince rolled his eyes.

*Actually rolled his eyes at me.*

I giggled.

"Highest bless," he murmured, glancing toward the musicians as a slow melody drifted through the night. "One of my favorite songs." His eyes flicked to mine, glinting in the firelight, "and obviously you know I mean the sound of you laughing, right?"

328

"Stop it," I snapped.

"Stop what?"

"The compliments."

"I will not."

"Why?"

"Because you deserve them."

My breath hitched, and I sighed.

We stood there, caught the same untitled feelings and stares as before. His lips curved—not into his usual grin, but something softer, something unreadable.

I exhaled, rolling my eyes to break the moment. "Shameless flirt," I said, walking away.

His smirk returned. "Modest bully."

I spun so fast my hair moved like a black wave—smacking him square in the face.

I gasped.

He laughed. A full, unrestrained laugh as he rubbed his chin.

And then, just as smoothly, he turned on his heel and walked off—heading toward the dancing circle, leaving me standing there.

Still smiling.

# Chapter 31

Amias weaved through the dancing crowds effort-lessly, glancing back every few feet to make sure I was still following—which I was. People danced around us, in between us, rushing past in flurries of color. Laughter of varying pitches swarmed my ears like a chorus of buzzing bees.

The joy of it all made my smile grow.

"This way," he called over the music, his voice almost lost beneath the rhythm of drums and strings.

I stumbled forward, caught in the tide of movement, the rush of bodies and music pressing in from every side.

"Kae!"

I turned left toward his voice, but he wasn't there.

Just more blurred shapes, figures shifting like reflections in rippling water.

"This way!"

I whipped my head right, but again—nothing.

A game?

He was playing a game?

But something felt wrong. My balance tipped, my footing unsure. The world around me twisted, too fast, too loud. My breath came quicker, my chest tightening.

Then—cold.

A whisper of something not-quite-there slid past me, sending a shiver down my spine. My head snapped in the direction of the sensation, but nothing greeted me. Only shadow from the fires around stretching in unnatural ways.

Then I saw it.

A figure loomed, impossibly tall, its form shifting like ink dissolving in water. It took a step forward, its movements smooth, deliberate. Feminine. The sway of its hips was eerily graceful, almost seductive.

My stomach clenched.

I staggered back, but my feet felt rooted, as if the ground had claimed them. Around me, the festival still roared on—dancers twirling, instruments playing, voices laughing. But, in a muffled way. Like I was there but looking from a veil. No one saw it. Fear curled around my ribs, clawing up my throat.

> *"Though they have power, they are not all-powerful.*
> *Do not be deceived by their schemes and vices."*

The words from the journal rang in my mind. They struck something deep within me, something ancient.

A warmth ignited in my chest.

Embers flared at my fingertips.

The shadow halted.

I lifted my hands, fingers spread wide, a silent invitation to the darkness. Power pulsed beneath my skin, hot and alive.

The creature cocked its head, a motion too human, too knowing. It took a slow step back.

I advanced.

The colors around me dimmed, the movement of the crowd slowing until they became nothing more than drifting figures in the periphery. Only the shadow and I remained, locked in a silent battle.

The fire in me surged.

The darkness recoiled.

It shrank, compressing inward, its towering form dwindling until it stood merely six feet tall.

"Leave," I commanded, my voice reverberating through the space—not just sound, but force. A power not entirely my own.

The shadow hissed. Then, in a ripple of black, it fractured, splintering into four separate pieces that slithered into the crowd and disappeared.

A new sound cracked through the space, in echoes.

My name?

"Kae'Dinah!"

The world around me was returning extremely slow, in pieces—screams, muffled and warped. Voices layered over one another.

Then—Amias. I could just make out his frame.

He was before me now, his hands hovering near my shoulders but not touching. "Kae, listen to me. You have to come back."

He was there again. His presence grounding me, again. But the world still felt wrong.

I couldn't see his face.

Only the outline of him, like a shadow against firelight. And beside him—a smaller silhouette. One shorter than me.

Maeve.

She turned toward me, her voice steady, unwavering.

"Kae'Dinah?" A pause. "Come back, heiress."

Something stirred at her words. A pull. A tether.

Chaos rippled to my right, but my body wouldn't turn.

"Let me speak to her!"

The voice was sharp, cutting through the noise.

Jahiel.

He shoved past the growing circle of onlookers, stepping toward me.

"Get back!" Amias snapped.

Jahiel didn't stop.

"You get back, Prince." His voice was fierce, steady.

Amias' posture bristled. "I'm warning you. Her skin—"

Jahiel cut him off, wincing as he withdrew his hand from my arm.

He stepped closer, voice low, urgent. "Kae'Dinah," he murmured, his tone stripped of its usual formality. "Come back."

I stared past him, past all of them.

"Please," Jahiel pleaded. "You have to snap out of this." A beat. "Or people will get hurt."

*People.*

The people here at the festival had stopped moving.

Because they were watching me.

They couldn't see the shadows—only me.

And yet—I saw them as if from another world. A place slightly off from theirs. Close enough to touch, but untouchable all the same.

All the people who had danced so joyously only moments ago. The music had stopped. The laughter had ceased— everything had slowed.

Because of me.

Not because I had frozen them.

But because they had froze to watch.

My breath shuddered.

The fire inside me flickered and just like that—the world rushed back in.

I inhaled sharply, knees buckling as I collapsed to the ground. The cold earth bit into my skin, grounding me in reality. Maeve was there in an instant, kneeling before me while Amias and Jahiel set up a protective perimeter around us.

"Wolves!" Amias bellowed over the crowd.

I lifted my gaze to Maeve. She let out a breath of relief, her chest rising and falling with exhaustion. "There you are," she panted. "We have to get you out of here."

But my body remained frozen. My senses prickled.

"It's still out there," I murmured, the growl low and vicious, rasped from my throat like an untamed beast.

Maeve blinked. "What?" She leaned closer.

"It's still out there!" I roared.

Jahiel and Amias snapped their heads toward me.

Maeve hesitated, searching my face as if trying to understand what I meant. Then, she nodded. "Okay. We need to move." She rose, careful to touch only the fabric covering my skin as she helped me to my feet.

Eyes bore into me from all around. Some were filled with awe. Others fear.

"Wolves!" Amias called again, his voice cutting through the air like steel. A vein bulged along his neck as figures began emerging from the crowd.

Tavin and Tye arrived first, followed closely by Ike, Vance, Jon, and the others—all of them moving with precision. The moment Amias had called for them, they knew what to do. His men. His warriors.

They reached the edge of our protective circle.

"Get these people back!" Amias commanded. "We need a path to the temple chambers—now!"

Tavin and Jon immediately set to work, barking orders as the Wolves spread out, hands resting on the pommels of their swords. No longer concealed. No longer cautious.

Jahiel appeared beside me, offering a blanket.

"She's burning up, man!" Maeve scolded, shooing it away.

"He's just trying to help," I whispered to her before turning to Jahiel. "Thank you."

Something flickered in his eyes, but he nodded in silent acknowledgment.

Maeve looped her arm around mine, shouldering some of my weight as we began moving forward. The festival, once alive with movement, now felt like a stage—every pair of eyes tracking my steps, watching me with a mix of reverence and wariness.

As we passed Amias' men, I nodded in silent gratitude.

Then—something caught my eye.

The glint of metal.

The all too *familiar* pommel of a sword.

I inhaled sharply, my gaze snapping to the man holding the weapon. His grip tensed beneath my scrutiny. "They are among you," I whispered to myself.

"What Kae?" Maeve responded. Leaning in closer to hear my whispers.

My chest clenched.

"You," I said, extending a trembling finger toward him.

The man shook his head, feigning confusion. "I don't know

what you're talking about."

But I knew.

"You were in my dream," I hissed.

And he was on our ship.

His stance shifted. His breathing steadied.

Then—his eyes darkened. Onyx black.

Everything happened at once.

I shoved Maeve to the ground just as the man drew his sword.

"Death to you, *heiress*!" he roared, lunging for me.

Jahiel crashed into him like a battering ram, knocking him off his feet before he got any closer to me to strike.

A sharp war cry rang out from behind me.

I spun just as another man charged—his eyes, too, black as night. His sword gleamed, raised high, ready to cut me down.

Amias stepped between us. His blade met the attacker's with a resounding clang.

"What are you doing, friend?" Amias demanded, his voice a mix of anger and betrayal. The man he fought was with us. He was with us the whole time. He was one of the few who escaped Floos.

"She can't live!" The man bellowed through clenched teeth.

Tye moved swiftly to Amias' side, slicing through the man before he could advance on the Prince. Blood sprayed across the garden grass.

"What the depths is happening?" Tye questioned, pivoting to a crouching defensive stance beside me, his blade dripping crimson.

Swords clashed behind us.

I turned just in time to see Jon drive his blade into a man

Ike held before him. Ike dropped him as he bled, turning quickly to hurl a sword to Jahiel, who caught it effortlessly, spinning and striking down the first attacker.

Amias' voice cut through the chaos. "What is going on?"

"I had a dream," I gasped, my mind racing. His eyes shot to mine. "The shadows split… Four swords were struck down. There were four of them, Amias."

Maeve's eyes widened. "That means—"

"There's one more." I panted.

A wave of silence passed through the men.

Then, all at once, they turned, scanning the crowd.

The people shifted, shrinking back, fear coiling in their expressions.

Somewhere, hidden among them, the last assassin was waiting.

I searched frantically, my eyes darting from face to face. Then—movement.

A figure, still and unassuming, subtly shifted his weight. His hand crept toward the hilt of his blade.

My stomach dropped.

He stood just behind Amias.

"No," I whispered. My gaze locked on him.

"Amias, no!" I screamed.

The last assassin drew his sword and lunged—straight for Amias' unguarded back.

I didn't think. Didn't have time to.

My hand flew to the slit in my skirt.

In one motion, I freed my daggers and in the next… I threw them.

Twin flashes of silver cut through the air, whizzing past Amias' head. One struck the man's throat. The other embedded itself into his eye, burying deep into the onyx black void.

His body crumpled.

Silence.

I stood frozen, my breath ragged.

Every single wolf turned their gaze towards me

The world blurred at the edges. My heartbeat thundered in my ears.

My gaze dropped to the bleeding man on the ground.

"I said there were four," I murmured.

Maeve looked at me, a slow smirk spreading across her face.

Relief crashed over me like a wave.

It was over.

I took a step toward the body, but then my vision wobbled. The grand garden—the towering trees, the cascading floral trellises, the glowing lanterns still swaying from the chaos—blurred and rippled like water disturbed by a stone. It wasn't the world that was rocking; it was me.

I reached out instinctively, but there was nothing to hold onto.

Amias was suddenly there, gray eyes sharp with alarm as he dropped to his knees before me. His hands cradled my face, unnaturally cool against my fevered skin. My breath hitched at the sensation.

"Kae, don't sleep," he commanded, voice taut with urgency. "Do you hear me?"

I tried to nod, but even that felt like too much effort. A sharp pain lanced through my chest, blooming beneath my palm as I clutched at it. My body was failing me, the fire inside flickering, dimming.

"Ow," I gasped, my knees buckling.

Maeve was at my side instantly, catching me before I hit the ground. "Prince, we need to get her inside. Now!" she barked, her jaw clenched.

Amias inhaled sharply, eyes darting toward the growing crowd. He released me and surged to his feet. "Everyone, back! Now!" His voice carried through the garden, a command that sent murmurs rippling through the onlookers. "Make a path!"

Jon, already reading his intent, signaled the Wolves. The warriors dispersed, forming a tight, unbreakable perimeter around us.

Jahiel knelt beside me, eyes flicking to Maeve. "On three, we lift. Understood?"

She nodded, shifting for a better hold beneath my arms.

"One... two... three."

They hoisted me upright. My body sagged against Jahiel, his grip firm, steady.

"Kae'Dinah, talk to me," he murmured, his voice quieter now. "Can you move?"

I forced my toes to wiggle, flexed my calves. Weakness coursed through me, my limbs leaden. "A little," I managed. "But I don't know for how much longer."

"Then we go as far as you can, as fast as you can." His tone left no room for hesitation.

Maeve moved in closer, wrapping my other arm around her shoulders. With them half-carrying, half-dragging me, we moved swiftly across the garden, winding through the veiled paths to the Temple House. Amias strode ahead, leading the retreat, his back rigid with fury. His sword remained unsheathed at his side.

Eyes followed us from the shadows of the festival, wide with fear, whispering among themselves. But I had no strength left to meet their gazes.

# Chapter 32

"What is the meaning of this?" The High Priestess's voice cut through the chamber like a blade.

I lay stretched on a chaise in a room lit by dozens of candles, my skin fevered despite the cool cloths the Blessed pressed to my temples. Their hands were gentle, their whispered prayers like murmurs in a storm. It soothed the heaviness settling into my bones.

The Priestess glared at Amias. "Death, during the Festival of Strings?" she seethed. "Prince, you know the sanctity of this day. You know how much it means to us to keep the peace!"

Amias scoffed. "With all due respect, Priestess, I don't believe Vitaeus or the other gods, cares much for the Festival of Strings."

Her expression faltered, the color draining from her face. Her gaze snapped to me, confusion furrowing her brow.

"The Watchers haven't set foot on our shores in centuries," she said slowly. "What are you talking about?"

Amias took a step forward, his presence suffocating. "They were here. Their eyes—black as midnight. And they were coming for her." His finger jabbed toward me. "I didn't come here to spill blood today, but I'm certain Highest will forgive me in the name of protecting His Heiress."

The chamber was silent. The air thick.

"You carried blades to the celebration!" a second priest boomed, stepping from the shadows.

"When do we not?" Jon shot back, arms crossed. "And thank Highest for that. If we hadn't, the Prince and the Heiress would be dead, and our world would have no chance at redemption."

Jon perched on the arm of my chair, his presence grounding me. I exhaled, slowly, before turning to the priests. My voice was hoarse but steady.

"What were they?" My fingers dug into the fabric of my dress. "And why were they in my dreams?"

The Priestess hesitated. "We told you we would educate you after the festival."

I shook my head. "We can't afford to wait any longer."

Her lips pressed into a thin line. "You were attacked, yes. But you are not dead, Heiress. We should be rejoicing."

A sharp, bitter laugh escaped me. "And what happens when I step outside? How do I know I won't be attacked again?"

The second priest's face remained impassive. "We don't."

The honesty was almost cruel.

My hands curled into fists. Desperation clawed at my chest. I turned sharply to the Priestess. "Where can I seek Him?"

"Excuse me?" she asked sharply.

I hesitated. Had I overstepped? Was I even worthy of demanding an audience with Highest Himself?

"Don't douse," Amias murmured from beside me.

I turned to him. His gray eyes, so often unreadable, were firm now—unyielding. He gave a slow, deliberate nod.

*Don't douse.*

*Don't extinguish.*

His words fueled my boldness like oil to a flame.

I turned back to the Priestess, spine straightening, dragging my body upright. Causing the blessed to flinch back as they cooled me. "I demand to know how to seek Highest. Now."

"You don't get to make demands—" the priest by the door began, his tone sharp.

The Priestess silenced him with a single raised hand. Her gaze met mine, burning with something unspoken. "You already have His ear. And His words."

I stilled. His ear and His words?

The journal.

A sharp inhale escaped me as I realized what I had hidden in my room. The Priestess nodded ever so slightly, as if acknowledging my silent revelation.

Disgruntled voices rose from the courtyard beyond the open window, the tension of the crowd palpable. We all turned toward the sound.

"Calm the people," I ordered, my voice steady despite my exhaustion. My eyes swept across the priests. "I'm guessing the Watchers would want nothing more than to sow confusion and unrest. That's what they do in Floos. They take a small splinter and infect minds with doubt. Stop it here. Tell them who I am. Tell them what those creatures were."

Silence stretched through the room. The priests stared at me, some in shock, some in wary contemplation. Maeve's lips parted slightly, surprised. Amias and Jahiel, however, regarded me with something else entirely—pride.

A soft chuckle broke the stillness.

343

Tavin.

Tye elbowed him sharply, but Tavin ignored the warning, grinning. "Well? You heard her. Our Heiress has spoken." His voice was light, teasing, but his eyes held something deeper—approval.

The priests stiffened before exchanging quick glances. Then, without another word, they summoned the remaining women of the Blessed and hurried from the room, leaving only myself, Jahiel, Maeve, Amias, and the Wolves.

A sharp clatter shattered the quiet.

I flinched as Amias knocked a metal pitcher off the table, sending it skidding across the floor. No one moved.

His breaths were measured but heavy, his brows drawn tight as he paced before us. A storm rolled in his gray eyes.

"This is my fault," he ground out, each word clipped, seething. "They were hidden among *my* ship."

"Prince," Jon warned.

But Amias wasn't listening. His fists clenched, his anger barely restrained. "I thought we vetted them," he spat, gesturing around the room. "Better than this, Jon."

"We did," Jon snapped.

"Clearly, we didn't," Amias growled, his voice raw—more a snarl than words.

A chill settled over me. This was a side of him I hadn't seen before.

Fury.

"Amias," I called his name softly. His head snapped toward me, those stormy gray eyes now ablaze.

Jahiel moved off the wall, stepping closer, his body tense.

"That wasn't them," I continued. "They weren't themselves. They—"

"They were possessed by the Caligo," Maeve interjected. "Offspring of the Watchers. They're called Shadows. They go after the weakest in spirit when they possess."

Amias' breath hitched, and his eyes narrowed on me.

"But you knew," he accused, his voice cutting through the air like a blade. "You knew this would happen and didn't warn us."

He stepped toward me, frustration radiating off him in waves. Jahiel matched him, closing the distance between us. They were less than a yard apart now.

Ike stirred from his spot, but instead of siding with Amias, he moved to my side.

Amias' gaze bore into mine, demanding an answer.

He told me not to douse—so I wouldn't.

I pushed myself up from the cushions. Knocking the cool cloths from my arms and forehead.

"How in the world do you expect me to know my dreams have significance when no one will answer my questions?" I countered, my voice rising.

Amias scoffed. "You never spoke of any dreams like this."

"You told me to tell no one. You said my answers were in Syx, so I held them in."

"But death and betrayal should be something you have the wits to communicate!"

His words landed like a slap.

"The wits?" I flinched, my breath catching in my throat. For a brief second, regret flickered in his expression, but he didn't take the words back.

I lifted my chin. "Do not insult my wits. The vision wasn't clear, and no one helped me decipher it."

"Easy," Jahiel growled towards Amias, one hand resting on

the pommel of his sword.

Amias turned his gaze on him and chuckled darkly. Not threatened, not moved.

"The vision was metaphoric?" Maeve asked, her voice more cautious now.

"Yes," I answered, then turned back to Amias, my frustration boiling over. "I am not one of your wolves, Prince. I will not accept reprimands or cruel corrections. You will not speak to me like a child. And you will not insult my intelligence."

I shakily stepped forward, voice unwavering. "The blame is on none of us in this room. These are the splinters I spoke of. So stop this... this *tantrum* and help me next time I ask for it."

A muscle feathered in Amias' jaw. He took a slow step back, blinking rapidly—as if suddenly realizing what he had said, what he had done.

Maeve crossed her arms. "Strengthen your *spirit*, Prince."

Jon exhaled sharply, stepping forward to clasp Amias' shoulders. "Anger never helped you achieve anything. Control does."

Amias clenched his jaw, then nodded. Eyes closing for a brief moment, he exhaled, grounding himself. When he opened them again, his voice was low, raw. "My apologies. To everyone."

His gaze locked on mine. "Kae—"

"No!" My voice cracked, and everyone flinched.

His eyes widened.

"You know this is difficult for me," I continued, voice shaking with exhaustion. "Weeks ago, I wasn't having dreams or visions. I knew nothing of the Shadows. Nothing

346

of Highest. This is the world you were all born into. I *wasn't*."

I sucked in a breath, hands trembling. "So give me grace, Prince. I haven't even fully accepted who I am."

Amias exhaled, then said quietly, "You can't change that—"

"Just shut up for a moment!"

The room stilled.

Eyes widened.

Jon suppressed an impressed smile. Tavin turned away to hide his laugh. Even Tye blinked in surprise.

I inhaled, closing my eyes for a moment. When I opened them, Amias' gray gaze was locked onto my face, unreadable.

I turned to the room, my heart pounding.

Doubt crept into my chest, twisting and clawing. Did I even want this? Could I deny it? Run from it? Was I truly the hope they believed me to be?

"I can do this," I whispered, pressing my hands to my face. "I have to do this."

"Kae—" Amias tried again.

"You've said enough," Jahiel interrupted, his voice like iron.

The weight of his words settled over the room, thick with unspoken tension.

Amias slowly turned toward him, his gaze dangerous. "Have you been vetted, Captain?" His tone was razor-sharp. "Whom do you serve now?"

Jahiel's body tensed. "Amias, for Highest's sake," Jon interjected.

"No." Amias' voice cut through the air. "He was on our ships. He was among the people. He once served those gods. He once sent people to the sacrificial pits."

Jahiel's jaw clenched. "I am loyal to no gods."

"Then where is your loyalty?"

Jahiel's breath hitched. Then, slowly, he stepped forward, towards Amias.

"My loyalty?" His voice was steady, unwavering. "My loyalty is to her. Only her. No one else. Nothing else."

The air grew impossibly still.

"Whatever she commands, I will do." Jahiel drew his sword in one fluid motion, the blade gleaming. He leveled it at Amias. "If she says to run, I run. If she says to kill, I will."

Steel rang out as swords left their sheaths—every blade in the room now directed at Jahiel.

Tavin was the first to break the silence. He tilted his head, watching Jahiel with something like curiosity. "He's still our prince," he mused. "Even if he speaks recklessly."

"Lower your blades," I ordered.

Jahiel didn't move.

Then, one by one, every sword in the room dropped.

I stared at them.

Maeve smirked. "She is the highest power in the room. And you all know it." She looked around. "You all fight for her. And now, whether you like it or not, you all fight for Highest. So let's end this ego duel here."

Maeve exhaled sharply, and placed her hands on her hips. "This *tension* is suffocating." She said, as she waved one hand around the air, "Everyone, go to bed."

The Wolves exchanged glances, then slowly sheathed their weapons.

Then slowly the room emptied, but as I stood in the lingering silence, I knew one thing for certain.

There was no turning back now.

\* \* \*

348

That night, after all the bed preparation. After the blessed and Maeve left my room.

Sleep did not come easily.

Even after the crowd quieted. Even after the tension bled from the walls. Even after everything—there was a tremble still pulsing beneath my skin.

Because I knew what the Priestess meant.

I already had His ear. And his words, the journal.

As the moon arched high above Scala, I curled beneath the cream satin sheets of my bed, whispering to myself and Highest, who had been described as always listening.

"I need answers… Why is all of this happening, Highest? Why does it have to be me?"

I stared at the ceiling until darkness thickened behind my eyes.

And then—

*A hum.*

It wasn't sound. Not fully. It was vibration, thrumming low and alive, rippling through my chest like the distant echo of thunder.

A door appeared before me—golden, radiant, humming so violently with power that the very air around it shimmered. The wall that held it was made of the same gold. Not gilded. Solid. Endless. Unmovable. Pure.

The door itself seemed to breathe, pulsing like a heartbeat.

I stepped forward, breath catching in my throat.

The moment my fingertips brushed the surface, warmth surged into my palm—not heat, fire. Fire that did not consume, only awakened. My body leaned in instinctively. The door opened.

I stepped through.

The room beyond was still. Silent. Perfect.

The walls were endless and bright, yet not blinding. Not until—

He was there.

I didn't see Him walk in. He had always been there in the center of the room. Light poured from Him, cascading in waves that seemed to bend time itself.

I couldn't look directly at Him.

I could only see just enough to make out the outline of a figure. Humanoid, but not entirely. Like light had chosen form, not flesh.

His presence was too vast. Too bright. Like staring into the core of a star.

Thunder and whisper.

Ocean and ember.

The feeling of it all shook me down to the marrow, and yet—I was not afraid.

I squinted, then lowered my gaze instinctively, shielding my eyes with one hand. My knees bent beneath me—not in fear, not yet. In reverence.

The presence was weight. A divine gravity that stilled my soul and silenced every question I'd carried like armor.

*"Lift your head, Daughter."*

# Seal

She came to Me.

Faltering, weary, trembling beneath the weight of what had been laid upon her shoulders—but she came.

Even as sleep pulled her under, her spirit reached for Me. Even in confusion, she knew where to look.

I was already waiting.

She entered the place where time does not bend, because time does not rule Me. The door appeared before her—not summoned, but revealed. Its golden frame hummed with the power she carries but does not yet understand. She lifted her hand, fingers brushing against eternal flame housed in mortal skin.

And still, she did not flinch.

*Brave girl.*

She stepped into My presence, and light flooded around her.

She could not look at Me.

Not yet.

She squinted, then shielded her eyes, knees bending beneath the weight of My nearness. Not fear. Reverence.

Her spirit recognized Me before her words could form.

I watched her. The one who questioned altars soaked in blood. The one who wept for the innocent while the rest of her world feasted. The one who internally asked Me why I had been silent while the Watchers schemed.

She did not know I had been with her the whole time.

"Lift your head, Daughter," I said—not in sound, but in truth.

She obeyed, slowly, her hand still shielding her gaze. Her voice trembled, unsure.

"I don't know what's happening to me."

I do. Because I placed it in you.

"You carry what I placed in you," I told her. "You are aflame because I am aflame. My fire runs through you."

She lowered her hand further. Still blinking. Still adjusting.

But she did not back away.

She sat.

Not as one defiant, but as one willing to stay—willing to burn and ask Me how to wield the flame instead of begging for it to go out.

"You must not fear what burns within you," I said. "Train it. Wield it. It is not here to destroy you. It is Me in you."

Tears welled in her eyes.

"Why me?" she asked—not with pride, but with awe.

Why not you?

"Because you were willing to question what others blindly accepted," I answered. "Because you wept over injustice. Because you stood when it would have been easier to stay silent."

She could not see it yet, but the light within her had begun to steady. What flickered before now glowed—uncontrolled, but no longer wild.

"And because even now," I added, "when the world offers you power, you still ask Me where to walk."

She lowered her head again—not out of shame.

Out of surrender.

The fire responded, flickering gently around her.

"I am with you, Kae'dinah," I said. "I will be with you in fire, in silence, in war, in stillness. You are *My* judge. Not the world's. Not even your own."

She breathed Me in.

The room pulsed. The flame sealed within her spine. Not a mark. Not a scar.

A beginning.

"Train the fire," I whispered. "And trust Me."

She said nothing—but her spirit answered.

And when she awoke, her pillow was wet, her chest warm. But she did not cry for fear.

She cried because she knew...

She was never alone.

# Chapter 34

I woke before the sun had fully risen over the eastern horizon. Rubbing the sleep from my eyes, I stared at the ceiling, still foggy with the remnants of my dream. My hands moved to my hair, scratching my scalp beneath the intricate braid the Blessed had assembled the night before. They had oiled my scalp carefully before bed, then changed my pillows to satin-covered ones, ensuring every detail of my care was accounted for.

As I sat up, I felt a weight beside me.

*Maeve.*

A small smile tugged at my lips. I wasn't sure when she came back or even if this was the role of a Seer, but after last night, she had been more than just an advisor—she had been a friend.

Slowly, I moved my legs to the edge of the bed, the silk nightclothes the Blessed had dressed me in gliding over my skin—the finest fabric I had ever worn. I slid my feet into the perfectly fitted, plush slippers they had left at my bedside, shielding myself from the coolness of the tiled floor. Moving carefully, I made my way to the connected bathing room, shutting the door quietly behind me.

Inside, a single candle flickered. I took it and lit the larger oil lamp, casting a warm glow across the room. My fingers moved to the braid, unweaving it slowly. The moment my hair fell free, cascading past my back, I marveled at the sheen it now carried.

They really know how to care for me here.

I ran my fingers through the thick waves, massaging my scalp as I did. The sensation was soothing, reminding me of how Meg and I would take turns tending to each other's hair after long days.

But it wasn't just the past pressing on me.

Last night still clung to my skin, even beneath the oil and silk.

The memory of heat—*too much heat*—boiling beneath my ribs. My body had screamed with fire I couldn't control, power that nearly consumed me. I had felt myself tipping, unmade by my own gift.

And someone had died.

Because of me.

Or maybe, *through* me.

He would've killed Amias first. I knew that. He was already reaching. But my instincts didn't wait for permission. It leapt. It ended him.

The Watchers had sent him. I could still see them—like shadows curling around the corners of my thoughts. They wanted me gone. They had tried to kill me—not with brute force, but with strategy. With possession. With lies.

I pressed a hand to my chest, suddenly unsure if I was trembling... or still burning.

I squeezed my eyes shut and breathed.

*I can't keep dwelling on the past. I will not live as if I'm afraid. I cannot be afraid.*

I inhaled. Exhaled.

Then I turned to relieve myself.

When I emerged, I hesitated, peering around the room to see if Maeve was still asleep. The sunlight had crept further in, softening the darkness. She remained curled beneath the blankets, her head at the foot of the bed.

I walked around the bed to find the journal I'd hidden away in my bag. The moment my fingers brushed the journal, it struck me like lightning.

The dream returned all at once—not in fragments, but in fullness.

The fire.

The light.

Him.

The weight of it slammed into me like a tide, holy and unstoppable. I staggered back, the journal clutched tightly in my hands as my knees buckled beneath me. I sank to the floor, breath shallow, spine trembling.

*I saw Him.*

*I was with Him.*

My hands trembled around the leather binding. I could still feel the fire humming behind my ribs, a warmth not of this world. My skin prickled with the memory of His voice—not sound, but truth.

I bowed my head.

Not because I had to.

Because it was the only thing I could do.

Tears slipped silently down my cheeks. There was no room for fear. No space for doubt. Only awe. My lips moved in prayer, but no sound passed. I couldn't speak. The holiness of the moment had stolen the words from my mouth.

I didn't know how long I stayed there—kneeling on the cool stone floor in the faint gray light of dawn.

But when I stood, the fire had not dimmed.

It pulsed quietly inside me, like it was waiting for my next step.

I was overcome with a kind of joy I hadn't felt in years.

I had to tell someone. I needed to share this good thing—anything to keep the silence from swallowing the joy.

Still barefoot, still trembling, I wrapped a blanket around my shoulders and slipped into the corridor.

The journal remained tucked under my arm like it might dissolve if I let it go.

The temple was quiet.

The wing I stayed in housed the priests, the Blessed, and honored guests—among them Jahiel, Amias, and his men.

Morning hadn't yet fully broken. The air felt thick with sleep.

I padded softly down the corridor, my feet making no sound.

The stone walls were lined with murals of the Guardians, their painted eyes still making me feel like they were following me.

*Who would understand a dream like that?*

The fire in my chest buzzed louder.

I turned a corner too fast—

And collided with something solid.

"Oof—" I gasped, stumbling back.

The journal slipped from under my arm and hit the floor with a heavy thump, echoing into the silence like a gong.

Strong hands caught me.

Warm.

Sure.

Gentle.

His hands.

*Amias.*

He steadied me with practiced ease, his palms bracing my arms like he already knew I'd fall.

My breath hitched as I looked up. His face was close. Too close.

He met my gaze, eyes soft but alert. And then—he lifted one finger to his lips, eyes flicking toward the row of closed doors behind me.

A silent *shh.*

I nodded, still breathless.

His thumbs brushed over my arms before he released me, bending to retrieve the journal. When he rose, he held it out to me carefully, his other hand open—an invitation, not a command.

I hesitated. The journal was still warm in my arms, almost as if it remembered the presence I had encountered. I slipped my hand into his, my chest still rising too quickly, and he led me through the quiet corridor.

I didn't ask questions. We didn't speak. He just walked beside me like he knew the silence was holy.

I wanted to scream. I wanted to tell him *He* had been real.

My dream was not a dream.

But I couldn't speak. Not yet.

The temple opened into a courtyard, and he led me through a glass door to a field beyond it. The sky had begun its slow transformation—soft pink spilling upward from the horizon, washing everything in a quiet, golden hush. The ocean stretched beyond us, waves crashing softly beneath the cliff. The grass was wet with dew, sparkling under the first touches of light.

We stood in silence.

The breeze lifted the hem of my blanket, brushing against my ankles.

I pressed the journal to my chest, my breath catching as the awe I'd buried burst free.

"Amias…" My voice cracked, too full, too heavy. I turned to him, tears already forming again. "I saw Him."

His head snapped toward me, concern flashing instantly in his eyes. "What? Is someone after you—?"

"No." I stepped closer, urgently. "No—not someone. Him. Highest. I saw Him in a dream."

The tension in his frame softened, but his expression stayed cautious, focused entirely on me.

"You saw Highest?" he asked gently.

I nodded, struggling to hold myself still. "Yes. He was…" My eyes filled faster than I could blink the tears away. "He was fire, and wind, and lion, and lamb. He was everything all at once. I got too much and not enough at the same time."

Amias didn't speak. He just listened.

I shook my head. "I can't explain Him. Not really. He was light that pressed against my soul. Like something inside me stretched to meet Him, and now I can't go back to what I was before."

He exhaled softly. "He was… an experience?"

The word caught me off guard. A smile tugged weakly at my lips.

"Yes," I whispered. "Exactly. He was the experience. He told me the fire in me is from Him. That I needed to train it. That I was never truly alone."

The weight of those words made my knees weak.

Relief tore through me—so fast, so consuming I couldn't keep still.

My fingers lifted to swipe at my face, but I was crying too hard now. My shoulders trembled, and my mouth opened in a soft sob. A sound too tender to suppress.

Amias stepped forward without hesitation and pulled me into him.

His arms wrapped around me, firm and sure. I let myself fold into his chest.

There, against his steady heartbeat, I cried harder.

Tears of knowing. Tears of being known.

"I'm glad He met you," Amias whispered, his voice rumbling through his chest into mine. "You were never truly lost, Kae."

I clutched the blanket wrapped around me tightly.

*You were never truly lost.*

I didn't know how long I stood there. Time unraveled in his arms, slow and quiet. The ocean kept speaking. The sky kept bleeding gold.

And slowly—slowly—the ache in my chest eased.

The tears slowed. The fire inside me settled.

And then, like a whisper not made of sound:

*"Tell no one else. Not yet."*

My breath hitched again. I nodded into Amias' chest, wordless.

He said nothing. He didn't ask. He just knew something had passed through me. And that it wasn't meant to be touched by him yet.

I tilted my head to the side, looking past him.

The ocean roared behind him, the sky now alight with

amber and rose.

The sunrise was stunning.

Like a painting made just for me.

"This," I whispered, voice raw, "might be the best morning of my life."

But when I looked up at him, he wasn't watching the sunrise.

He was watching me.

And something in his eyes was… unguarded.

Wonder. Joy. Reverence.

Not for the sun.

For me.

It made me want to turn away.

It made me want to stay forever.

He blinked, as if just realizing I'd caught him, and chuckled softly under his breath.

"You do realize," he said, voice warm again, "you've practically set yourself up for one of my compliments."

I squinted. "What? Were you going to call me the *sunrise*?"

"Actually, no."

His mouth curved as he glanced at the sky.

"I was going to say it's hard to focus on the sunrise—or anything else—when I have the chance to hold you like this.

When I get to hear that you experienced Him.

When I can see the outcome of that encounter in the way you smile, and the joy you radiate.

When I can see that you've been ignited by just a moment with Him."

He paused, eyes softening even further.

"So I guess… you could call it a kind of sunrise too."

I groaned, nudging back from him. "Amias. You ruined

my moment."

He laughed—rich and soft, like melting candlelight.

"You'll forgive me," he murmured as I began backing toward the stairs.

"Will I?" I called over my shoulder, narrowing my eyes.

"Eventually."

He reached out again, catching my hand with such ease it startled me. His fingers guided mine to his shoulder, and before I could protest, he pulled me gently into a loose stance—as if we were about to dance.

"Amias," I said, breath catching, "what are you doing?"

"Shh," he murmured, eyes flicking down to his feet to adjust his stance. "Give me a second."

My hand hovered awkwardly above his chest. His warmth radiated through the fabric. Up close, I noticed the little scar beneath his right eye. The way his smile softened when he wasn't trying to smirk. The faint scruff along his jaw, darker than his deep chestnut skin.

He looked up again, his smile wide now. Entirely unrepentant.

"I'm improvising," he said softly.

"You're impossible," I whispered.

"And yet," he said, stepping gently into rhythm, "you're still here."

My body swayed with his, unsure. Unsteady.

I had just stood in the presence of Highest.

The memory of it still burned in my chest—brighter than any fire I could wield.

Nothing compared. Nothing *could* compare.

But this...

This was something else.

Not sacred.

Not eternal.

But grounding.

Comforting.

Real.

Where Highest had filled me with purpose—Amias reminded me I was still human.

And maybe, just for a moment, I needed both.

Heat curled up my spine.

I was holding hands with a man who didn't tremble in my fire.

Who didn't look away.

"Now I must say…" His voice dropped lower, pulling me from my thoughts. "Once you threw that knife past my head last night and killed that man, there was no turning back for me."

I stiffened. "Amias, what are we doing?"

"Dancing," he said simply, swaying us in place. "You promised, remember?"

I swallowed hard, searching his face. His dark eyes gleamed with amusement, but there was no jest in them— only certainty.

"You were incredible last night," he continued, his voice quieter now. "Your precision, your speed—beautifully executed."

"Amias," I warned. This was ridiculous. We were in the open. Someone could—

"Kae." His grip on my waist firmed just slightly. "What else can you do?"

The curiosity in his tone unsettled me.

"Well," I muttered, looking at the small space between

us. "I've always been good with throwing knives and a bow. Long-range combat. Never close-range, hand-to-hand. My brother was always better at that."

"I could teach you," he murmured.

*Train the fire.*

I did need to be taught.

My gaze snapped to his. His dark gray eyes were steady, sincere.

"Prince Harth."

The voice cut through the air—sharp as a blade.

Amias and I flinched apart as if we'd been caught doing something far more scandalous than swaying on a staircase.

Jon stood at the top of the next set of stairs, arms crossed, eyes narrowed. Annoyance darkened his features—an expression that, I realized, made him look older.

"I send you back to retrieve our weapons, and this is what you return with?" His voice carried an authority that made me take a step back.

"Is that not what I did?" Amias motioned toward me with both hands.

I shoved him lightly, but Jon only exhaled—long and exasperated.

"You told me we were training, Prince. Taking everything seriously. No games."

Amias barely spared him a glance before placing a reassuring hand on my elbow. "Oh, don't worry. I'm still in charge. He's just in *training mode*. That's why I'm letting him yell at me."

"But… aren't we supposed to be celebrating the festival? No work, right?" I asked.

"Highest gave me permission. I petitioned Him—and Him

alone. And now I see why He's allowing us to train this morning…"

His words trailed off as he turned toward his friend.

Jon's glare deepened, but Amias continued. "Train her, Midland."

"What?" Jon and I said at the same time.

"Train our heiress," Amias repeated, descending the stairs. "You're the best fighter I know. The most versatile. Train her."

"The priests select who trains her, Harth." Jon's tone was tight, restrained.

"No, Midland. *She* selects who trains her." Amias turned back, meeting his friend's gaze. "You know you can."

I could hear voices now, just beyond the stone corridor. The sound of men gathering. Preparing.

Amias kept going. "She isn't a blank slate. We already know she has skill. Regular princesses don't hide daggers under their skirts or throw knives with precision. She's got something."

Jon exhaled, stepping closer. "This isn't a small task. This isn't sparring with Ike, Beau, or the twins. This is bigger than us, Amias. This is the fate of our world. *She* is the salvation."

"And she needs to be trained," Amias countered, smooth as ever. A slow smirk tugged at his lips before he patted Jon's shoulder and strode toward the beach.

Jon turned to me. I shrugged.

He sighed, rubbing a hand down his face. "Do you have sparring clothes in the room you're staying in?"

I nodded eagerly.

"Can you change and be back here in fifteen minutes?"

"Yes."

I took a step back toward the house, then hesitated. "Will you train me, Captain Midland?"

Jon sighed again. "Go change. Learn. Watch for today. Then ask me, Princess."

"It's Kae," I corrected. "Just Kae." I tilted my head. "So... is that a yes?"

He leveled me with a look. "You have fourteen minutes, Kae."

I pivoted and ran up the stairs.

I'd already stood in front of Highest.

Facing Jon Midland couldn't be *that* bad.

# Chapter 35

An hour and a half later, I lay sprawled on the side of a hill where the grass met the sand. My chest rose and fell heavily, finally dismissed from the grueling laps up and down the slope.

Amias sat beside me, his arms resting on his knees, his head bowed as he caught his breath. Sweat dripped from the tip of his nose.

Above us, the twins took turns pouring water over their faces before shaking their heads simultaneously. Droplets of sweat and water flung in all directions from their braided hair. I held up my hands in defense.

"Aye, we're down here!" Uriah called up to them. He crouched beside me, breathing hard. I had only met him this morning. Though I'd seen his face—and a few others—over the past few days, this was our first official introduction. His accent was the same as Amias', as well as Jon's and Beau's. But the others—something about the way they spoke and the way they fought stood out to me only now. I could see why they were in Amias' entourage. I only wondered how.

Uriah, Asher, and Ian. Those were the names I learned today.

I turned my head left and right. More than a few sweat-covered chests were bare under the sun. My cheeks warmed—not from exertion, but from me, realizing just how awkward this was. I tore my gaze away and looked toward the sky, watching as the breeze carried plump clouds across the brilliant blue expanse. All of this would take getting used to. These workouts were nothing like the ones back in Floos.

"All right, men," Jon called as he strode up the hillside, still catching his breath. I propped myself up on my elbows. His eyes flicked over me briefly before continuing, "And you. Good work today. If nothing else conflicts, we'll run again at sunset."

Meeting all of Amias' Wolves this morning had been interesting. Jon had initially encouraged me to observe, but after Amias' taunts and a few challenges from the others, I couldn't resist. It reminded me too much of Milo—how he used the same tactics to drag me into sparring with him.

So I joined.

And I regretted it.

Amias stood abruptly, rolling his shoulders, the muscles in his back flexing with the motion. Then he turned toward me and extended a hand. I grasped it with both of mine, pulling myself up far less gracefully than the others. My aching muscles protested, and I let out a long groan.

Amias arched a brow.

"When will we leave here?" Asher asked, looking to Amias. He was younger than the others, his face smooth and unlined. The sides of his head were shaved bare, his glistening skin catching the sunlight. He was about the same height as Jahiel.

"That depends on where Highest is calling us all," Amias answered. "Some may choose to follow the heiress—and that would be fine. Others may choose to return home, and that would be fine as well."

Silence settled over the group. Then, slowly, all the men turned to face me.

"Oh?" I blinked at them. "Follow me? Follow me where?"

"Oh boy," Tye muttered under his breath.

"Relax, she's new here," his twin laughed, throwing a long arm around my shoulders.

The scent of sweat and musk filled my nostrils. I wrinkled my nose and shoved him away. "You stink, Tavin." I pinched my nose for emphasis and turned to walk up the hill.

"Wow," he huffed, throwing his hands out in mock offense. "I have your back, and you throw me down to the ground, aye? No good."

I laughed, using the last of my strength to climb to the top. When I reached the crest, I turned back, looking down at the incline. From here, the half-grass, half-sand hill looked mountainous. And we had run it several times.

The others stopped beside me, following my gaze.

"Contemplating leaving us already?" Ike teased, a sly smile tugging at his lips.

They were all jesters today.

Joy lit up every pair of eyes, their laughter still lingering in the air. As I looked at them—at the strength, the camaraderie, the way they listened—a small ember of pride rose within me.

They gazed at me as if my words held weight. As if I had the power to give them their next breath.

But that wasn't my ability.

*Train the Fire.*

I was learning that it was Highest's.

369

And I had been chosen—and empowered—to do what needed to be done.

I exhaled slowly, straightening my shoulders. "By Highest's power, I'll do what needs to be done," I said, my voice steady. "And if you'll follow and teach me, I believe I can do just that. I'll just need a little patience."

I smiled, and they chuckled in response.

"We'll follow you, of course." Tavin grinned. "You remind me too much of our little sister back home to abandon you now. You both have a ditsy sense about ya."

I scoffed and lifted my hand, moments away from making a rather vulgar gesture—

But Amias caught my wrist, gently folding my fingers into a fist. "Be mindful of your audience, Kae," he murmured, amusement in his voice as he nodded toward The Blessed moving about nearby.

Old Animaian habits still in my flesh.

We had begun walking, following the path from the hill toward the stone stairs of the house. The courtyard was alive with movement—servants harvesting from vines, pruning shrubs, carrying baskets.

Then I noticed something else.

The women.

Their eyes flickered toward us, lingering—then quickly darting away. Some attempted to mask their curiosity behind their work, but the distraction was clear.

*Oh.*

I turned, holding my hands out to stop the procession.

They all looked at me in confusion.

Lowering my voice, I spoke so only they could hear. "Gentlemen, could you please put your shirts back on? I believe the ladies are... distracted from their work."

They exchanged glances, then looked around—finally noticing the stolen glances and averted gazes.

Beau let out a low, teasing whistle. The twins chuckled like boys caught causing mischief. Ian sighed dramatically before pulling a shirt over his head. One by one, the others followed suit.

I turned back to Amias—still shirtless.

His deep brown chest was carved with precision, every muscle defined. But my eyes were drawn to the ink.

A wolf etched over his heart.

It was stunning. The detail—the precision—it must have taken hours. Days, even.

"You know," Amias said, pulling me from my thoughts, "I believe you were right about the ladies being distracted."

His smile was slow, teasing—because he wasn't talking about them.

I realized, too late, that he meant me.

"Amias," I huffed, waving him off as I turned toward the house. I was too hungry to play this game. "I'm too hungry for this."

But before I could walk away, he caught my hand.

Not my wrist. Not my fingers.

Just my smallest two.

The touch was delicate, yet firm.

His deep gray eyes traced the path from my hand to my arm, to my shoulders, my neck—then my lips. When they finally met mine, he exhaled. The weight behind it was heavy—as if something unbearable pressed against him.

"I'll follow you anywhere," he murmured. "Absolutely anywhere. Even back to Anima if that's what you request,

371

you have a nation behind you."

His words landed with a force I wasn't prepared for.

This wasn't teasing. This wasn't lighthearted.

This was a vow.

A promise that belonged to me—and only me.

I swallowed, uncertain how to respond. I didn't want to overpromise or underestimate the weight of what he'd just given me.

So I simply nodded.

He seemed to understand.

Clearing his throat, he released my hand and motioned toward the house. "Let's get you fed," he said, opening the door to the main hall.

# Chapter 36

We entered the hall, greeted by a quick, reverent smile from the Blessed standing by the doors.

"Good morning, honored guests. The rest of your party is waiting for you in the guest dining room. We've prepared a late breakfast." She curtsied before turning. "This way. The priest will meet with you shortly to discuss ramifications from yesterday's... events."

I followed behind her, feeling Amias' gaze on me. I didn't know how I knew, but I felt it—watching, assessing. When I glanced back, his expression seemed distant, far removed from the warmth he had shown just moments ago.

The others walked ahead, leaving Amias and me side by side, though he seemed lost in thought, completely ignoring the chatter around him.

"Amias," I whispered, my brow furrowing. "What's wrong?"

He blinked and turned to me with a small smile, but it didn't reach his eyes. "Nothing," he said. But I knew it was a lie.

His mood had shifted. Was it because of me? Because of my casual nod to his words earlier? I studied his face, narrowing my eyes.

"Don't make that face," he muttered, looking straight ahead.

"What face?" I asked, stepping closer without thinking.

The movement surprised both of us. Amias stepped back, putting space between us.

"That assessing, concerned face. I told you—I'm fine," he said, his tone sharper than before.

I slowed my stride, letting myself drift behind him.

By the time we entered the dining room, the table had already been set for fourteen. In the corner, Jahiel and Maeve stood chatting, glass cups in their hands. I greeted them warmly, deliberately ignoring the empty seat beside Amias and taking the one across from him, beside Jon.

Jon glanced at me, then at Amias, before scoffing and shaking out his napkin in preparation for the meal.

Breakfast was soon brought out—roasted chicken and fish, eggs, pastries, fresh fruit, and juices. The rich aroma filled the air, making my stomach groan in anticipation.

Jon smirked. "Starving, are we?"

I shot him a warning look. "Don't judge me. You nearly killed me out there."

Jon chuckled and held up his hands in surrender. "Fair enough, but you consented."

Jahiel slid into the chair beside me, and Maeve took the seat across from him, beside Amias.

"I woke up and you were gone," Maeve teased. "For a moment, I thought I had failed our world by losing this generation's heiress." She clutched her chest in mock horror. "Then I look out the window and see you running up and down the beach like a madwoman."

I nearly choked on my juice, laughing. "Maeve—"

374

Jahiel patted my back, laughing along with her.

"What?" she said, completely unbothered. " I don't train. I don't run. I don't enjoy being dirty, sticky, or stinky. That's not my calling."

The servants refilled our juice. I reached forward, snatching the serving spoon of eggs before Vance could grab it.

"She learns quickly, boys," Vance commented down the table, drawing a deep rumble of laughter from the others.

Jahiel's eyes flickered between me and them, unreadable, but intrigued. I wasn't sure how he felt about the camaraderie I was building with these men, but he didn't seem entirely opposed to it.

I was adding fruit to my plate when Amias wordlessly stabbed a large piece of sautéed fish and placed it in front of me.

"You need more meat if you're going to keep training," he said.

I raised an eyebrow. "I have eggs."

"You'll need more than that."

His mood was inconsistent—one moment flirting, the next making demands. I parted my lips to protest, then snapped them shut.

I didn't have the *energy* for his shifting mood.

"Since when do you oversee what she eats?" Jahiel cut in from beside me, stabbing a piece of chicken on his own plate. "She's more than capable of managing that herself, no?"

Of course, Jahiel had the energy to bicker. He did no training this morning.

"Since today," Amias said, unfazed.

Then, turning to Ian, he continued, "After we eat, send a raven to Ellarum about our extended stay."

Ian nodded and returned to his meal.

Jahiel, however, didn't let it go. "Don't dismiss me," he hissed.

I sighed aggressively, shoving a spoonful of eggs in my mouth.

Amias met his glare. "Don't question me."

Jahiel set down his fork with deliberate calm. "What authority do you think you hold here?" He gestured between me and Amias.

My eyes widened. He was challenging him—challenging his claim over me—right here, in front of everyone. My gaze darted around the table, but no one met my eye. They were all focused on their food, carefully avoiding the brewing tension.

Maeve, however, arched a brow at me, barely concealing a questioning smirk as she sipped her juice.

Amias laughed—deep, slow, dangerous. It sent a ripple of unease through the table.

"What authority?" He repeated, setting down his cup. "I am the prince of Valdeen, heir to an ancient line of rulers. A country chosen by Highest himself. Authority follows me, its within me." He leaned forward slightly, his tone dropping. "But since we're on the subject, what authority do you have, guest?"

Jahiel's jaw clenched. "You hide behind your title," he snapped. "Like a coward."

The air in the room tightened. The men straightened in their seats, the weight of the insult crashing over them.

I gaped at Jahiel, What is going on?

Amias, however, only smirked. "Come again?" His voice was quiet now, laced with warning.

"Amias," I whispered, my heart pounding. I wasn't sure if I was pleading with him to stop or begging Jahiel to back down.

Amias met my gaze, his storm-gray eyes burning with restrained fury. But as he studied me—my tensed shoulders, my unease—he exhaled and turned away from Jahiel.

"I won't bicker like a child," he said, "not for your sake." He picked up his fork again, but his grip was tight. "But understand this—she needs to eat, she needs to train, and she needs to be skilled enough to do what must be done. I won't let her be unprepared. I'll do whatever is necessary to see that through. Don't question me again."

Jahiel scoffed, shaking his head. "Oh," he said, his voice quieter now, but no less pointed. "So whose authority is she under? Yours?"

I inhaled sharply.

Jahiel met my eyes, then turned away. "I just want an ounce of understanding."

The table sat in stiff silence.

Then the a gasp shattered the air.

The glass of juice in Maeve's hand exploded, shards scattering across the table as she tumbled from her chair. Ike, seated beside her, lunged forward and caught her before she hit the ground.

A servant screamed. Blood streaked down Maeve's hand, tiny splinters of glass embedded in her skin.

"Maeve!" I cried, standing so quickly that my chair crashed to the floor behind me. I rushed around the table, dropping to my knees at her side.

"Blessed!" Amias barked. "Send for another Seer and a healer! Ike, support her neck and shoulders until it passes."

Maeve's eyes had rolled back, her body thrashing violently as if she were drowning in invisible water, her lungs desperate for air.

"Is she breathing?" I gasped, gripping her dress.

Amias knelt beside me, his voice grim. "No."

She continued to thrash for seconds more, but they felt like hours.

My heart slammed against my ribs. "How long will this last?"

His jaw tightened. "Until he is finished showing her what she needs to see."

"What?" My hands trembled as I tried to hold Maeve still, her body jerking so violently that Ike struggled to keep her steady. "Why like this?" Her skin paled before my eyes.

"Amias," I warned, my fear rising. Why wasn't she breathing? How much longer could she last like this? My pulse pounded in my ears. I have to stop this.

"Amias!" I was yelling now.

"I can't do anything, Kae!" His eyes met mine, sharp with frustration—but underneath, I saw it. Fear.

My chest tightened. I sat back on my heels, squeezing Maeve's arm as if that alone could tether her to us.

Then, with a sudden, sharp gasp, she breathed.

The sound cut through the room like a blade. I sucked in a breath, realizing I hadn't been breathing properly either.

"Kae'Dinah," Maeve rasped between shallow pants, her hands frantically reaching for me.

"I'm here," I soothed, brushing damp strands of hair from her face.

But she shook her head violently, her trembling fingers gripping my forearms. Blood—warm and sticky—smeared across my skin.

"No, no, no," she whispered, a single tear slipping from her wide, green eyes.

"Speak, Maeve," Amias urged, his voice steadier than mine.

She gulped in another breath, her entire body shuddering. Then she looked at me, her expression twisted with pure terror.

"They're coming for you," she blurted.

The room fell deathly silent. My heart stilled.

Then—

The doors to the dining hall slammed open.

A breathless servant stumbled inside, clutching a crumpled piece of parchment.

"Your Highness," he gasped, eyes darting between Amias and me. "We received this letter by raven… It's from Floos."

# Chapter 37

"**G**et her some water and a chair," Amias ordered his men as he stepped toward the servant.

Asher appeared with a cup, and with Ike's help, Maeve was guided into an abandoned chair.

Meanwhile, Amias unfolded the parchment, his expression shifting from fear to anger before settling back into the calm, authoritative mask he wore so well. Without a word, he handed the paper to Jon, who read it in silence before passing it to me.

My hands trembled as I took it.

*This is a royal proclamation from the land of Anima, issued by King Santu Milo Ickree, Fourth of His Name.*
*Princess Kae'Dinah Lex Ickree has been taken.*
*Animaian forces have been dispatched to all major cities across Naedorn to find her. We come to your shores in peace. Our only intention is to bring our daughter home.*
*She has brown skin, long black hair, and eyes of gold.*

*She is essential to the growth and prosperity of
our land, and she is dear to all our hearts. We
must find her.*

My vision blurred as I leaned forward, bracing my hands on
my knees. My stomach twisted violently.

Jahiel rushed to my side, but I barely noticed. Wordlessly,
I thrust the letter toward him. He snatched it, eyes scanning
the page before a string of curses hissed from his lips.

I couldn't breathe. Couldn't think.

*Taken?*

No. That was a lie.

My fingers curled into fists, nails biting deep into my palms
as I straightened.

*Taken?*

That word echoed, foul and rotten in my chest.

They weren't coming for me out of love. They didn't care
if I were safe.

They had offered me—like an object. Like a transaction.
Like a seed to be buried so their cursed land could bloom.

There was no love for me in Anima.

Only hunger. Only control.

The proclamation trembled in Jahiel's hand now, and I
ripped it back from him, my eyes scanning the lines again,
each word scorching hotter than the last.

*Dear to all our hearts...*

A bitter laugh tore from my throat as I paced.

Sharp. Cold.

Was it dear, then? To drag me? To bind me in chains and
prepare my body to be offered on the altar?

381

*Essential to their prosperity.*

That was the truth hidden beneath the lie.

Not daughter.

Resource.

And now… now they would dress their betrayal in gold-leafed pleasantries and send armies cloaked in "peace" to drag me back?

My jaw clenched.

"They want me alive now," I said, voice low, shaking as my feet moved me left then right. "Not because they miss me. Not because they love me."

I looked up, fire roaring behind my eyes.

"But because they think I still have value to burn."

I inhaled sharply, then exhaled through clenched teeth.

The room sat in thick, suffocating silence, watching me.

Then Maeve spoke, her voice steady.

"I am your servant, Heiress."

I lifted my gaze to her.

Maeve stood from her chair, the tremors in her limbs gone. Her green eye burned with conviction as she stepped toward me.

"I will go wherever you go. I will do whatever you ask of me. These gifts…" She said holding out her hands, "were meant for you, from Highest himself." Her voice rang clear, unwavering. "I will serve you in your reign of judgment."

I stared at her, my chest tightening, for a new reason now as the fire inside me flared to life. Calmer now.

She knelt before me.

"You are the Heiress of Judgment over the land of Naedorn. You are the one with eyes of fire. You are my leader."

A slow smile curved her lips.

And I felt it.

The fire behind my eyes.

The weight of what she was saying.

Then—

"I am your servant, Heiress," Amias' deep voice boomed.

I turned to find him kneeling before me.

One by one, every Wolf followed suit, their heads bowed.

"All of us, Kae'Dinah," Amias continued, his gaze fierce. "We stand with you, Daughter of Fire. Peace, victory, and success to all who vow to follow you, for Highest himself has imbued you with this power and authority. You have never been alone, and you will never again be alone." He placed a fist over his chest.

My breath hitched.

I looked around the room—at the Wolves, at Amias.

At all of them.

Their eyes burned with loyalty. Determination.

A tear slipped down my cheek and hit the tiled floor—sizzling on impact.

Amias' gaze followed it.

Then, he looked back at me and smiled. Proud.

I exhaled and straightened my spine.

"Okay," I whispered, more to myself than anyone else.

I turned away, walking toward the window, arms wrapping around my core as I bowed my head.

This path was mine.

I would walk in it.

I would lead.

I would learn what else it came with in time.

But for now— the fire had been stocked. I knew this. I knew strategy, studied it well and mastered it. Even better than my brother.

"When was the missive sent?" I asked, my eyes still on the sea.

Jon answered. "Dated two days ago."

I turned to face him. "And it took us about two and a half days to get here, correct?"

He nodded. "Yes, ma'am."

A slow breath left me.

"They could be here any moment."

Silence hung in the air as the weight of those words settled over the room.

I straightened my shoulders. "We cannot confront them here. That would lead to something worse than last night, and I will not spill blood on this land again today." My voice hardened. "I am not going back with them."

"Then we go to Valdeen," Amias declared, standing to his full height.

He turned to Ian.

"Send word to Ellarum's ports that we will be coming home. Notify my father of our plans. And send orders to every border outpost of Valdeen—no Animaian forces are to cross into Valdeen."

Ian nodded, turning to leave.

Asher frowned. "What about those seeking refuge?"

Amias glanced at me, then back at Ian.

"Allow refugees. But only through Cado."

Ian nodded again before sprinting out of the room.

Amias turned to Beau. "How much is in reserve?"

"Enough," Beau answered with a smirk.

"Good." Amias nodded. "Ike, Vance, and Beau—secure a larger ship. Gather rations and water for the trip home.

Enough for thirteen people, planned for fifteen days."

I hesitated. "Will your father accept hiding me in Valdeen?"

Amias' gaze locked onto mine. "My father obeys the will of Highest. No man scares him." Then, more gently, he added, "But this is your decision. We can change course if you wish. You are our leader."

The room stilled, every eye on me.

My heart pounded.

Then—

"*Valdeen.*"

The voice rang in my head alone.

"*Go.*"

That was the only confirmation I needed.

I nodded. "Then Valdeen it is."

Amias squeezed my shoulder—a reassuring pressure.

"Pack only what you need," he commanded. "Can we be at the docks in three hours?"

"Yes," Beau answered. "We'll go now to secure a vessel." He motioned to Vance and Ike before turning to leave.

Jahiel spoke, his tone begrudging. "What's my assignment?"

Amias studied him for a moment, then exhaled.

"Help Maeve and Kae'Dinah prepare. You've traveled and fought. You know what's necessary. Make sure they gather *only* what they need."

Maeve lifted her chin. Eyes suddenly wide with worry. "I need to see the priests."

Amias held her gaze for a moment, then nodded.

She turned and sprinted out of the room.

"Tavin, Tye," Amias continued. "We need weapons. Swords, bows, whips, daggers. Armor. Speak to the priests with Maeve and see Beau if you need funds."

The rest of the Wolves stood at attention, awaiting their orders.

"The rest of you—help where you can. We have three hours."

With that, Amias strode toward the door.

And I clenched my fists.

We had three hours to flee before the past I left behind found me again.

* * *

The Blessed escorted me to my rooms, working swiftly to bathe and dress me within half an hour. They dressed me in fitted black pants tucked into brown boots that laced up my calves. A sleeveless crop top hugged my frame beneath a larger button-up shirt, which they belted at the waist for my weapons. Each blade rested on the table, cleaned and sharpened—even the dagger that was still stained with dried blood from last night.

Seated before a mirror, I watched as one of the Blessed ran a brush through my long, damp hair, preparing to braid it. But the weight of it—the sheer length—felt unbearable. A burden. A burden to manage. A burden in battle.

"Cut it," I snapped.

The woman stilled.

"I'm sorry, Heiress?" the one behind me whispered.

"Cut it," I repeated, firmer this time.

"Are you sure? Your hair is so long and beautiful."

"Cut it. At my shoulders. Quickly—we don't have much time."

They exchanged hesitant glances before one of them rushed forward with scissors. Moments later, thick coils of black hair tumbled to the floor.

By the time they finished, my hair had dried, shrinking into tight curls that barely brushed my shoulders. My scalp felt lighter. Freer. The Blessed handed me a pack nearly the size of my torso, filled with essentials, but I sifted through it, keeping only what I truly needed. I tucked away a brown journal and left behind the red velvet romance novel, *Forbidden Love*, from Aartier.

A knock at the door.

"Who is it?"

"Jahiel and I," Maeve called.

"Come in."

The door clicked open. Jahiel stepped inside, dressed in black pants and boots, his sword strapped across his back, a dagger at his waist. His black hair was pulled into a high bun. Maeve was dressed similarly to me, though her belt held only a single dagger. Their packs were large—too large. Jahiel carried an extra bag.

I eyed it suspiciously. "I thought they said one pack, Jahiel."

"This belongs to her," he said, motioning to Maeve.

"They're books from the priests," she explained, setting it down with a thud. "I'll be teaching you, and these were the only copies they allowed me to take. When we get to Valdeen, we can visit their libraries to see what they have for us to glean from."

"Only?" Jahiel scoffed.

Maeve rolled her eyes, and huffed.

"Are you ready to go to the docks?" Jahiel asked. "They found a ship. Jon says the sooner we leave, the better."

His gaze landed on my hair. His expression hardened.

"You cut it," he stated, displeasure evident.

"Yes," I said, raising a brow. "Do you like it?"

"It's different."

"Yes, well, I'm different."

His eyes narrowed on my curls before flicking back to me. I adjusted the weight of my pack.

"The cut will help me stay cool," I added. "And it won't be a liability in a fight."

"It's gorgeous," Maeve interjected. "The Blessed did well. Your curls frame your face perfectly."

Jahiel sighed. "Yes. They did."

I ignored the dryness in his tone, but my shoulders fell slightly.

"I'll take these things to the foyer," he said, lifting the packs. "The others are waiting. Do you know what you're leaving behind?"

I gestured to the scattered perfumes, jewels, and books left on my bed. His gaze stopped on the red velvet novel.

"Not even that?"

I hesitated. "It brings back too many memories. And…it's banned in Valdeen."

Jahiel gave a slow nod, then turned to Maeve. "Come down once she's finished." With that, he took the bags and disappeared through the door.

Maeve exhaled dramatically. "Highest, help the men you befriend."

I frowned. "What is that supposed to mean?"

"It means only Highest can help you, because you clearly have no idea how to deal with them." She crossed her arms. "They treat you like you're fragile—but care nothing about the decisions you make for yourself. Then they treat you as if you're a prize, then in the next breathe advocating for you to fight your own battles."

She picked up a brush and motioned for me to sit.

"Maeve, we have to leave."

"I know. But I fear that if Amias doesn't like your hair, you'll combust. So I'll put it in a bun."

I turned to face her in the chair. "I am not that weak-minded."

"You're not," she admitted. "But your heart is sensitive. We'll work on that."

She poured a few drops of water from a pitcher over my hair, then poured a few drops of oil from a vial on her fingers, massaging it into my curls before brushing them smooth and gathering them into a tight knot at the nape of my neck.

"Now," she said, satisfied. "We're taking this brush and this oil with us. Men don't care for these things—they think they're unnecessary. But they are, in fact, essential."

I wrapped them in a towel and tucked them into my pack.

Maeve's tone softened. "I've seen you thrive, Kae'Dinah. Not just in authority, but in everything. I dreamt of you before I even knew it was you." She paused. "Do not be discouraged by small beginnings. I'll teach you the ways of Highest. Watch Amias. Pay attention to how he leads. Valdeen isn't powerful just because of its warriors—it's their wisdom that makes them strong. He's a good leader to learn from."

I groaned, covering my face with both hands. "He's also good to look at."

Maeve laughed. "Highest bless that distracted heart of yours. What ever will you do with two men fighting for your attention?"

She pulled my hands from my face and to my feet.

"We need to go," she reminded me. "Hopefully, there's space on this ship for just us."

Grabbing our things, we disappeared from the temple house and made our way to the others.

# Chapter 38

The sea looked endless from the dock—but not free. It churned like it knew something was coming. Like it knew I was coming.

I stood still while the others boarded, the wind catching the ends of my cloak and tangling it around my legs. I didn't untangle it. I just stared at the ship, at the water, at the space between here and Ellarum.

A step creaked beside me.

"You will survive this, Kae. You'll survive it all."

Amias's voice—low, steady. Always offering strength like it cost him nothing.

I didn't look at him. "They're searching for me."

He didn't answer immediately. I could see him tasting his next words. He did that often—considering.

"Then when they find us," he said at last, "we'll give them what they've been searching for."

I turned to him.

Stared into his eyes.

Storms to fire.

He smiled and nodded.

Then he moved ahead, boots thudding softly against the wooden gangplank. He spoke briefly with the captain, then vanished below deck. I exhaled—and followed.

The vessel was massive, at least three times larger than the merchant ship we'd taken to get here. Black wood trimmed its sides, faded navy sails fluttered above, and near the helm was the painted symbol of Valdeen. Below deck, ten rooms lined the narrow corridor. Jon had already divided them, giving Maeve and me the largest—the captain's quarters.

She was already there, unpacking books like we weren't about to be hurled across the sea. Like the floor wasn't already swaying.

"You're quiet," she said, glancing up.

"I'm thinking."

"I see." She smirked and went back to arranging.

Jon poked his head in.

"Priest Aluin sent someone to meet with us," he said, voice even, though something unreadable moved behind his eyes. "Says he's from the Scala archives."

I frowned. "Another scribe?"

"I don't recall any mention of that," Maeve said, standing now. "But of course they wouldn't tell me."

Jon shrugged. "Aluin called it a last-minute decision. Said the man specializes in prophecy and judgment."

Maeve pressed her lips together. Not quite a frown—but close.

"Of course he does."

Her tone wasn't bitter, just... tired. She didn't roll her eyes. She didn't protest.

She'd learned by now that being passed over didn't require explanation—only patience.

I caught her gaze for a second, but she looked away first.

We followed Jon to the upper deck.

The man by the helm was handsome.

That was the first thing I noticed—though it annoyed me to admit it.

He wasn't loud about it. No arrogance. Just composed. Confident.

Olive-toned skin. Well-cut robes in soft, neutral colors. A strong jaw softened by a short, neatly groomed beard. Mid-forties, maybe. His eyes were a striking gray-blue, not tired but knowing.

He carried only a satchel and a rolled parchment.

"I hope I'm not an inconvenience," he said before I could speak. His voice was calm—measured, almost soothing. "High Priest Aluin said you might welcome a recorder. I've studied prophecy. Judgment. Guardians."

His gaze lingered a beat too long on me.

"I've been curious about you."

"Your name?" I asked, wary but civil.

He smiled. "Call me Eshon."

"Is that your name?"

"It is one of them."

Maeve stood just behind me. I felt her go still.

I glanced toward her, but her expression was unreadable.

She didn't speak. And that—more than anything—put me on edge.

I turned back to the sails, shifting uneasily in the wind. One snapped sharply overhead, though the air had stilled.

I didn't like that.

Amias stepped onto the deck just then. He took one look at me and frowned.

"What's your call?" he asked quietly, low enough for only me to hear.

"I'm not sure," I said as he moved off to speak with Jon and Maeve.

"I think he should stay," Amias said when he returned.

"Why?" I asked, still watching Eshon from the corner of my eye.

"Because I want to know what he knows," Amias said. "And I want you to tell me if something feels off. Even the smallest thing. Even a dream."

I didn't know Eshon. I didn't know many from Scala, really.

But I'd come to trust Maeve.

And the fact that she'd gone quiet said more than words could.

Still, everyone else seemed taken by him—Jon had already resumed conversation, and one of the Wolves laughed at something Eshon had said.

Maybe I was being unfair. Maybe Maeve was just territorial. I'd been introduced as the Judge, after all—and she'd spent her life buried in sacred scrolls waiting for someone like me. Now this new scholar had arrived, claiming insight too.

Maybe he was like Jahiel, in a way—devoted to something he didn't fully understand, but too careful to let it show.

Amias waited for my answer. And I knew if I opposed, he'd stand beside me without hesitation.

He had pledged his life—and his kingdom—to my aid.

And I believed him.

I turned back toward the man.

"Very well," I said at last. "You stay, then."

Eshon dipped his head. "Thank you. And Heiress, you need not worry. I won't interfere."

I gave a curt nod and turned to go.

The wind whipped around my neck, tugging at my cloak like fingers. It forced me back a step.

"Should we even be traveling in this weather?" I called to Jon as I retreated below.

"We have no choice. We need to reach Valdeen. If we move with intention, we can steer around the worst of it. The waters will be rough, but the wind will carry us faster."

I thought back to my first voyage— nausea and dizziness.

"Great," I muttered.

Jon chuckled, clapping my shoulders and nudging me toward the door.

"Go rest. Sleep dulls the mayhem."

"Only for a night," I warned.

"You'll get used to it," he said, already heading back topside.

\* \* \*

I had released my hair from the tight bun Maeve had pinned earlier, the tension of it having formed its own headache. Now freed from its restraints, it fell in soft waves, still shaped from drying in the knot.

Maeve had come by earlier to settle into our shared space, allotting us each a corner of the room to keep our things. She was organized and quick, fluttering around like a hummingbird—hastily intentional. I felt awkward when she caught me staring, my legs folded beneath me on my side of the bed.

"What?" she asked, pausing mid-movement.

"What do you make of the scholar?" I asked, genuinely

intrigued by her perception of her own people.

"I think it's just like the priests to send someone behind me to check for loose ends. They never fully trust me. Never fully trust my prophecy."

"Has it all come true?" I asked, unable to hide my curiosity.

Maeve scoffed, offended. "Of course it has. I see more than all of them. In more ways than all of them."

She ran a thumb across the palm of her hand, a nervous habit.

"Then why do they doubt you, if your record is more than enough to prove your capability?"

"Well—maybe because I'm a partially blind seer with no lineage of prophecy in my blood."

We both went quiet, the weight of her words settling between us. Maeve was often overlooked. Underestimated.

"So we're a lot more alike than I originally understood," I said softly.

Maeve smirked, then turned back to her books. But her movements were sharper now—tidy, precise, like she needed order to silence something stirring.

I looked out the window. The boat rocked gently, the sky streaked with orange, pink, and storm-gray.

Scala was almost out of sight.

Everything in Scala had happened so quickly. I hadn't even had time to ask if she would miss any of it. She had left the comforts of her home—the protection of the priests—to serve beside me. To teach me.

She hadn't even hesitated.

"Are you upset about leaving Scala?" I asked quietly.

She scoffed, then chuckled. "Bless no. I was waiting for a summons to leave that place," she said, pulling a journal from the bottom of her bag.

"Scala is beautiful. I never wanted to leave," I admitted.

"Yes, well—you're not a partially blind seer with no friends or family. So you'd say that," she replied dryly. "I've traveled to other temples with High Priestess Edith more times than I can count. Scala's only beautiful if you have nothing else to compare it to. That's why I keep this."

She held up her journal for me to see. "I describe the beauty of the world around me. Mountains. Rolling hills. White sand beaches... so I can revisit them later."

She smiled to herself, like the journal held a secret only she understood.

"So... Ellarum. Is it beautiful?" I asked.

Maeve's expression softened in a way I hadn't seen before—almost reverent.

"I was only there for seven days," she said. "But I wanted to stay forever."

She looked past me, like she was seeing it again.

"It doesn't just sit on the land—it rises from it. Like it was born of the cliffs and light and carved by the hand of Highest Himself. The sky feels closer there. The buildings shimmer like the stone remembers sunlight. Even the wind smells different—like wildflowers and clean air, untouched by sorrow."

She paused. "It's the only place I've ever been that felt like it knew I didn't belong... but still wanted me to stay anyway."

I was quiet. I didn't expect that kind of answer.

Maeve smiled, more to herself than to me.

"Ellarum's not just beautiful," she added. "It's beloved. You'll see."

We both paused. I watched as she turned the pages of her

journal, smiling down at what's written.

"Well," Maeve said, lifting her journal and hugging it to her chest, "I'm going to take this topside and write about our ship. The sway of it, the creaking wood, the smell of salt... might as well capture it while I can."

She paused at the door, her tone softening. "You... get some rest."

"Yes, ma'am," I murmured, my voice weighted with fatigue.

She arched an eyebrow at me, amused. "Didn't think I'd win that easy."

I gave a tired smile, not even pretending to resist.

Maeve nodded, offering one of her rare, gentle smiles before slipping through the door.

The room quieted in her absence. I laid back, the mattress dipping beneath me as my body gave in. The sway of the ship lulled me, exhaustion clawing at my eyes, heavier with each blink.

And then—

Sleep found me.

# Chapter 39

The cabin was too small.

The walls pressed in, tighter with every wave. Even the floor seemed to sway with intent, rolling just enough to leave my stomach in knots. I leaned against the bed frame and breathed slowly through my nose. Salt. Damp wood. Faint traces of Maeve's salve and the metallic scent of the sea. None of it helped.

Her books sat stacked neatly along the wall—orderly, even, precise. But even they swayed.

I needed air. Or company. Or stillness. Something to ground me.

I pulled a shawl around my shoulders and stepped into the corridor, moving slowly toward the mess hall. The ship creaked with each step, and my bare feet chilled against the cool boards. A few candles still flickered in their wall sconces, casting low, golden light on the empty benches.

Someone was already there.

He sat at the end of the table, fingers curled around a cup. Pale robes. Clean-shaven. Striking, not for his features, but the way he carried them—poised and measured, like a painting that had been carefully composed.

"Couldn't sleep?" he asked gently, not turning fully toward

me.

I stiffened, halfway to pretending I hadn't seen him. "No."

"I find sleep evades most who carry more than they can name," he said, then finally looked up. "The sea makes it worse. It shakes things loose."

I didn't respond, but I didn't leave either.

He motioned to the bench opposite him. "You're welcome to sit."

I hesitated, then lowered myself across from him, trying to keep the nausea at bay. "You're Eshon. The scholar?"

He looked up, offering a kind but careful smile. "Among other things, yes. But that title usually gets me invited to tables like this."

I tilted my head. "Is that meant to be reassuring?"

He chuckled, low and warm. "Only if you find scribes less dangerous than swordsmen."

"They cause the same kind of trouble," I said, a shy smirk tugging at my lips.

His smile lingered. "It wasn't meant to be misleading," he said gently. "I imagine you're tired of that—being misled."

His gaze held mine—not bold, not cruel, but measured. The kind of look that made you feel *studied*, not *seen*.

"You've observed a lot in one day?" I asked.

"I observe. I write. It's what I was asked to do." He tilted his head slightly. "I expected someone older. Harsher. You... seem younger than the role."

That made me bristle. "Younger, but not incapable."

His smile widened just enough to suggest amusement. "I didn't say you were."

Before I could respond, footsteps approached from behind. The air shifted—heavier, warmer.

Amias appeared in the doorway, eyes sweeping the room before settling on me.

He didn't speak at first. He crossed to the shelf and pulled down a tin of ginger, his movements quiet, familiar.

"You looked like you could use this," he said, placing it in front of me.

I blinked. "Thank you."

He didn't nod right away. His gaze lingered—on my face, then my hair.

"You cut your hair," he said, more observation than question.

My hand lifted instinctively, brushing the loose waves that framed my face. "Before we left Scala."

He was quiet for a breath. Then, softer than I expected: "You look... lighter. Like you finally got to choose something just for you."

I felt the compliment land—gentle, sincere, without expectation.

My fingers fell to my lap.

I hadn't expected him to like it.

Jahiel hadn't said much—just stared like I'd broken something sacred.

But Amias...

He looked at me like it made sense. Like I made sense.

A breath caught in my throat. I looked down—then up—then smiled before I could stop it.

Small. Flustered. Real.

"Thank you," I murmured, but the words didn't carry nearly as much as the way I felt them.

"What's wrong?" I asked him, watching the faint pull in his features.

His smile faltered, eyes drifting to the far wall like he could see through it.

"Just thinking of home," he said. "I can't wait for you to see it."

There was longing in his voice—a deep, quiet ache that made something twist in my chest.

He turned slightly, his eyes flicking toward Eshon. "Scholar. How's the sea treating you?"

Eshon smiled politely. "Turbulent, but not unkind."

"Good," Amias said, then glanced back at me. His gaze was steady again—guarded, but kind. "Get some rest, Kae."

Then he turned and left, his footsteps retreating down the corridor.

I stared at the tin, fingers curled around its edge. Not because of the nausea—but because of the way his words had settled over me like warmth.

Eshon watched me for a long moment.

"He notices more than he says," he remarked.

I didn't answer.

"He seems to care," he added, quieter now. "That matters."

Still, I said nothing. The tea leaves rustled in the tin as I opened it, inhaling the sharp, grounding scent of ginger.

"I'll let you be," Eshon said, standing with ease. "Rest, if you can. Tomorrow is a new day."

He left without another word.

* * *

Night fell without ceremony. Candles were lit, then blown out. Maeve lay on her side, her breaths deepening.

I drifted between thoughts—of being capture, of Amias, of pages of the journal I hadn't even thought of in so long—when Maeve began to stir.

At first, just a shift. Then a twitch.

Then her whisper—fractured and trembling:

"No—no, not again—burning—*they're screaming—*they're screaming—"

I was on my feet in seconds, reaching for her shoulder.

"Maeve."

She jolted awake, chest heaving, one eye wild with fear. The other, blind and unmoving, stared past me.

"It was the fire again," she gasped. "But closer this time. Too close."

I nodded, offering a damp cloth to her hands. "You're safe. Just a dream."

But I knew better. So did she.

We didn't speak after that. She rolled over, back to me, clutching her journal like a lifeline.

I laid down, the ship creaking under our weight and movement, and pulled the blanket over my shoulders.

The candle had burned low. Maeve's softer breathing steadied behind me, uneven but calm enough to let her rest.

I slid my legs off the bed and moved quietly toward the door, stepping over the creakiest board and easing it open. It was darker in the corridor than I expected—only one flickering lantern swinging with the ship's motion.

That's when I saw Jahiel.

His back leaned against the wall beside my door, one knee bent, arms crossed. Eyes closed. But not asleep.

They opened the moment he sensed me.

"Sorry," I whispered. "Didn't mean to wake you."

"You didn't."

We waited in silence for a moment, the low hum of the sea beneath us. Then, on impulse, I stepped closer.

"I was going to get some warm water for tea," I said softly. "Walk with me?"

His brows lifted, like he hadn't expected the invitation. But he nodded once and fell into step beside me.

We moved slowly through the corridor, our footsteps light on the worn wood. When we reached the galley, I filled the kettle and set it on the small iron stove top. He stayed just behind me, quiet but alert, like he always was.

I turned, leaning lightly on the counter. "Why were you at my door?"

He met my eyes without flinching. "Didn't *feel* right to sleep in my room."

"That's not your job anymore," I said gently. "You're not my guard."

He shrugged. "Doesn't change how I feel."

There was no weight to his words. No pressure. Just truth.

Something in my chest tightened, and I looked away first.

"You don't have to protect me, Jahiel."

"I know," he said simply. "But I want to."

Steam began to rise from the kettle, a soft whistle building in the silence.

"Besides," he added, voice quieter now, "The proclamation from Anima… everything. Felt like someone should be near. Just in case."

I blinked. It was always *just in case* with him.

The kettle whined softly. I extinguished the flame and poured the water over the tea leaves in my tin, letting the scent calm my nerves.

"Thank you," I said at last—unsure what I was thanking him for exactly. The walk. His presence. His silence.

"All right if I keep the spot outside your door?" he asked, tilting his head.

I looked up at him, trying to read the expression behind his easy tone. There was nothing playful about it. Just quiet resolve.

"If you insist."

"I do."

I handed him a second cup without asking if he wanted one.

We stood in silence as the ship rocked gently beneath us, sipping warmth from glass cups, holding our peace.

But the quiet only made the words echo louder.

*Princess Kae'Dinah Lex Ickree has been taken.*

*She is dear to all our hearts.*

They had the audacity to call me their daughter in one breath—and hunt me across the seas in the next.

To dress my execution in softness. To wrap a death sentence in gold.

*Essential to the growth and prosperity of our land.*

I ran my fingers over its edges before flipping it open.

And to my surprise, the pages were full.

A gasp fell from my lips as I rushed to my feet.

From the first to the last page.

"Highest, what?" I exhaled, startled. When had this happened? The last time I touched this book only three entries were written in the front. Now, every single page is full.

I furrowed my brows in confusion as I notice the hand of another, not matching the first or second's penmanship.

Others had written here.

Would I soon have knowledge to share and write after all this is over?

I turned back to the fourth entry, eager for words but hesitant to read them out of order, and began to read the judge's words.

> *I had an encounter with the creator of our world. He spoke to me and told me I have no reason to fear. I heard him, felt his presence and seen his light. I struggle with the theory of being truly fearless. For I know what scurries through the darkest parts of the shadows. Nevertheless, I will shed fear at the door of my heart in battle like a winters coat. For while I am home. I will be surrounded by the warmth of Highest not by stolen skin of a goat. He will be my strength and my confidence. He did not imbue fear in me, but pure power.*
>
> *—3 A.R., Shaunsa of Temoi, son of Syx.*

My mind roamed over the words on the page, my racing mind cataloging the information like a library.

> *I had a dream the other night of stones. Stones that piled themselves up high to create a building. There were dozens of stones being stacked before me. But an unseen force came and knocked them over. Then a voice from the heavens cried out,*

*"Go and rebuild those structures like the others still erected before you. See to it that the others stay protected while you go forth and rebuild."*

*I have this dream often. Some nights it is stone, some nights it is clay or sticks. Either way, I have to rebuild.*

*Highest, ignite what sleeps within me. Burn away all that is false. Lead me, and I will follow—even into the fire*

*—3 A.R., Shaunsa of Temoi, son of Syx.*

My eyes narrowed. Rebuild. Rebuild what? And where? I would have to ask Maeve about this history soon.

I flipped to the next entry—this one much shorter.

*I believe you've surrounded me with everyone that I need to do what you're instructing me to.*

*Highest, ignite what sleeps within me. Burn away all that is false. Lead me, and I will follow—even into the fire*

*—3 A.R., Shaunsa of Temoi, son of Syx.*

The ship rocked gently, the slow sway at odds with the storm churning inside me. The sky outside the cabin had darkened, the sun slipping beyond the waves, leaving behind streaks of gold and indigo. The room was quiet—save for the occasional creak of wood and my own steady breathing.

I sat curled against the headboard, the journal still open in my lap. My fingers traced the inked words of the long-dead

407

judges, my thoughts lost between his prayers and my own questions.

"Rebuild."

What was I meant to rebuild? And how? The journal spoke so much about his mission, and goal. About how Highest sent him away to do what needed to be done. But my mind didn't allow the theory to rest on rebuilding an actual stone building. There was something more to his words that lay unwritten just between the lines. If I could just read a few more pages I'm sure I could find my answers–

The ink blurred slightly as my eyes grew heavier, the soft sway of the ship beginning to lull me, despite the questions circling my mind.

The journal rested open on my lap, its pages whispering promises I didn't yet understand. My fingers slipped from the parchment, falling gently to my side.

I leaned back against the headboard, breath slowing, eyelids growing heavier with each pass of the waves outside.

*"Rebuild..."*

The word pulsed in my mind like a heartbeat, steady and unfinished.

I didn't know what it meant. Not yet.

But for the first time in days, I didn't feel afraid of the unknown.

And I closed my eyes.

# Chapter 40

The sea was silent.

Not calm—dead. A suffocating quiet that pressed against my ears like the world had stopped breathing.

I stood at the ship's edge, peering into the dark. There were no stars, no wind. Just water stretching forever—black and unmoving.

Then I saw it.

A small boat, drifting.

It rocked gently in the water, unanchored, untouched by current. It shouldn't have been there.

But it came.

Empty.

Except for black feathers, scattered like ash, and strips of cloth twisted and torn. In the center—something jagged and burned. A crown of vines made from rope and charred wood, twisted cruelly into shape.

And then came the voices.

Not voices. Mockery.

Laughter, low and layered. Cold breath against the back of my neck. Whispered words coated in venom.

*"Spark of salvation,"* they sneered.

*"Daughter of flame... how noble."*
*"You will burn what you love."*
*"You think you're chosen? You were marked."*
*"You will become the fire that devours them all..."*

I couldn't move.

My hands burned.

I looked down—my palms glowing, skin blistering from within. I stumbled back, choking on air that tasted like ash.

The boat ignited.

My palms stung.

I looked down. My hands glowed red-hot, trembling, flickering like embers—alive with heat. I tried to pull away, to scream, to stop it—

The boat ignited.

Flames erupted with no warning—violent, eager. Black feathers caught first, then the cloth, then the crown. It burned too fast, too bright, lighting up the night like a curse spoken aloud.

I screamed—but no sound came.

The fire roared.

And they laughed.

\* \* \*

I woke with a jolt, my heart racing, and my lungs felt as if they were fighting to breathe. I struggled to understand where I was.

The room was dark—but wrong. It smelled of smoke.

I looked down to where I still felt the burning in my palms. The faint glow of orange receded and black covered my palms.

*Soot.*

My eyes bulged.

On my fingertips. On the sheets.

I rushed to my feet, assessing the bed to see that dozens of my smudged fingerprints had littered it.

"What is this?" I nearly yelled.

Before I could process it, a shout echoed from the corridor. My head whipped towards the sound.

"Fire! There's a fire—below deck!"

Tavin? No—Tye.

"Fire?" I exhaled before I ran barefoot into the hallway.

The smoke hit me first—thin, rising from a low burn near the stairwell. Causing me to cover my nose and cough. The black clouds were rising towards the lower barring ceilings.

Some crates had somehow caught fire.

The flames were small but very, very real. Licking up the wall, seething with life.

The Wolves had already gathered—buckets, cloths, water. Tye and Jon spoke sharp orders, Uriah yelled for help.

I froze at the edge of the scene.

Tavin turned toward me, his eyes wide with concern as he grabbed my shoulders to push me away from the chaos.

When he looked down, he saw my hands.

His face changed from worried to wary.

He dropped his hands instantly, taking a step away from me, "Kae—what is going on—"

"I didn't—" My voice broke. "I woke up like this, from a dream!"

I said, holding up my hand.

He stared at my soot-covered fingers.

Jon yelled, shielding his eyes from the slowly growing

flame. "We need to put this out now!"

From the opposite hallway, Eshon emerged.

"My goodness, how did this happen?" he said, hands braced on the walls around him.

"It's out," Jon spoke, bending over to rest his hands on his legs along with Uriah and Asher.

"It's fortunate we caught it early," Jon said, his voice tight. "Did anyone see what started it?"

Silence.

Tavin shifted. His eyes flicked to me, then back to the group. Without a word, he angled his body to shield me from the others, just enough that their attention slid past.

I furrowed my brow at him.

He shook his head once—subtle. Warning.

A fire had started.

On a ship of guards and warriors, scribes and soldiers.

And only one person on board had soot on their hands.

Me.

I backed away. Slowly at first. Step by step down the corridor until my feet picked up speed and I turned into a run.

Down the hall. Past the rooms. Past the mess. Away from the smell of smoke and the weight of silence.

I didn't stop until the corridor gave way to air—open, salty, thick with sea breeze.

I gripped the railing of the upper deck, chest rising and falling like the tide. The wind slapped my cheeks. My lips. But I barely felt it.

Did I start that fire?

Did I do it while I slept?

Could I have—unleashed something again?

Could I have killed everyone on this boat?

A tremor shot down my spine. I crouched low, curling in on myself, pressing my hands over my ears as if that might still the storm inside me.

No whispers came this time. No visions. Just heat. Lingering. Radiant. Terrifying.

And fear.

So much fear.

A quiet thud of footsteps behind me—then a familiar voice. "Hey."

It was him.

Amias.

That one word settled something inside me. It didn't fix it. But it slowed the spin. The shaking.

I didn't move. Couldn't speak. I stayed curled, eyes fixed on the deck boards beneath me, waiting for the fear to swallow me whole.

Amias crouched beside me, slow and steady. Not reaching yet. Just there.

"You okay?" he asked softly.

I shook my head. Or maybe I didn't. I wasn't sure.

His voice was closer now. "Kae... your hands—are you hurt?"

I peeled my hands from my ears and stared at my palms. Blackened. Trembling.

"They were already like this," I whispered. "When I woke up... I don't know what's happening to me."

His hands found mine—warm and calloused, steady as stone. He brushed a thumb across the soot, clearing my skin, like he could wipe away what I didn't understand.

Like he had before.

He stood, still holding one of my hands, and gently pulled me to my feet. His shadow fell across me, blocking the morning sun. I looked up at him. The sweat on his brow caught the light. His dark skin shimmered, damp from heat and wind. And I couldn't tell where his worry ended and his reverence began.

"Kae," he said again, quieter. "What happened?"

The question cracked something open.

I let go.

I buried my face in his chest, muffling a cry. I let it break free, soundless against his shirt. His arms wrapped around me, one at my back, the other cradling my head.

I cried.

For the fire. For the fear. For the gift I didn't know I wielded.

For the girl threatened in my dream.

"What happened?" He murmured against my hair, "You don't have to hold it all in alone. Not anymore."

I inhaled sharply.

How could he see me so clearly in moments I could barely see myself?

I leaned back slowly, my hands still on his chest. His gaze held mine—dark, solemn, unwavering.

He didn't look afraid of what I was becoming.

He looked ready.

He looked like he believed.

And then—

I turned toward the voice.

Jahiel.

He stood a few feet away, stiff, unreadable. His eyes flicked from Amias's arms around me to my face. Then back again.

Amias let go first—but didn't look away.

Neither did I.

The air thickened. Whatever had been subtle before... was now undeniable.

I stepped back—not from them, but from the chaos inside me.

From the voice in my head whispering that this was my fault.

I looked down at my hands. The soot. The dream. The shouting.

But I hadn't seen flames.

And yet—my presence still felt like a spark.

Not for the fire on the ship.

But the one burning between them.

And I'd just added fuel.

Then I turned and left before either could speak another word.

\* \* \*

My knees buckled, and I slid to the floor. My hands trembled. They looked normal now—clean—but I could still feel the heat, the sting beneath the skin, like something waited to come alive again.

A knock startled me—sharp and quick.

I scrambled to my feet just as the door creaked open.

Maeve stepped in, hair disheveled, arms full of books, her mouth already half open. "You alright?" she asked, not pausing for breath. "I've been looking for you everywhere."

I didn't answer. I backed toward the bed until my legs hit the frame and I sank down.

She studied me—really studied me—and moved closer, sitting beside me without ceremony.

"You look like you saw a ghost," she said.

"I think I saw myself," I whispered. "And I didn't recognize who I was becoming."

Maeve's eyes softened.

"I dreamed again," I said, quieter now. "But when I woke up… they were yelling fire. My hands were—" I held them up. "I don't know what I did."

She shook her head—not in disbelief, but like she was brushing dust off a truth. "You didn't."

I blinked. "How do you know?"

"Because this kind of power doesn't come without design. It doesn't lash out blindly. Not if it's tied to Highest."

She adjusted the stack of books in her lap, then reached over and touched my knee. "You need training. Understanding. You've been chosen, not cursed. And the fire? It's not the enemy. It's the evidence."

I sat straighter, hands braced on my knees, as if her words might tip me over.

"Highest doesn't call you to break you," she added softly. "He calls you to become."

She stood, shifting the weight of her books to one arm. "I'm going to grab something from the mess hall. Do you need anything?"

I shook my head. "No."

She nodded. "Okay. We'll train tomorrow."

I didn't sleep much after Maeve left.

Her words lingered long after the door closed behind her—

*He doesn't call you to break you. He calls you to become.*

I'm tired of reacting weakly to every trouble and dream dressed like an arrow sent to kill me.

I was going to become.

# Chapter 41

The next morning, Jon woke me early for hand-to-hand combat practice at sunrise. We went through a series of drills—some I had learned before, others new—but strength training proved to be the most grueling. By the time we finished, my muscles trembled with exhaustion, my limbs weak and sore.

As soon as I stepped into my room, the scent of dried meat and manneh greeted me. Maeve had laid out breakfast—a simple spread of meat, manneh, an apple, and water. She sat cross-legged on the bed, flipping through a thick tome.

"Eat," she instructed, not looking up.

I obeyed, sinking onto the chair beside her and biting into the apple. "What are you reading?"

"The history of the Judges," she murmured, trailing her finger down a passage. "There have only been three before you. Seers preceded each one with warnings against their corruption. And each Judge was a man."

I stilled.

She continued, her voice thoughtful. "The gods' corruption has spread down from Malcert like a disease for the last two hundred and fifty years. Prophets and missionaries went to reason with their people, but none returned. Many have prayed for a Judge."

I swallowed the bite of apple, feeling its weight settle in my stomach. "Tell me about them—the Judges before me."

Maeve hesitated, her fingers drumming lightly against the pages. "Well... this is the part that might concern you most." She glanced at me. "Maybe we should talk about this above deck?"

I frowned. "Why?"

"Because emotions seem to trigger a Judge's gifts."

"*Gifts*?" I repeated, my grip tightening around the apple. "I thought fire was my gift."

Maeve gave me a pointed look. "Stand up. And bring that tome behind you."

I corked my water, grabbed the heavy book, and followed her out of our room and onto the deck.

The midday sun beat down, hot against my skin. Jahiel, Tavin, Asher, and Uriah sat exchanging stories on the stairs leading to the upper deck. Jahiel looked more at ease with them than usual, laughter flickering in his expression. But that look of ease changed the very moment he saw me.

I caught it. I caught the slip in his mask. I had wounded him.

The men turned at our approach, lifting their hands in greeting. Uriah stood, jogging toward us as the others continued their conversation.

"You look like you're struggling," he teased, grabbing the books from our arms with ease.

Maeve blinked in surprise. "Thank you."

He shrugged. "That's how Valdeenian men treat our women."

Maeve snorted. "Aren't you all Valdeenian men?"

"By loyalty, yes," Uriah said, walking ahead of us. "But not by birth, like me." He smirked

Maeve and I exchanged a glance.

"How's that?" she asked.

Uriah climbed the last step, turning slightly. "Men come from all over Naedorn to train in Valdeen's armies. Some flee their homelands. Others leave their families because Highest calls them. But all have to be refined through training. If you survive it, you become a Valdeenian warrior."

I studied him. "Are they all Wolves?"

He smirked. "No. The Wolves are the only ones chosen by Amias and King Harth themselves. Most of us trained with the Prince, though."

My brows furrowed. "He had to train?" I asked, surprised that the prince had no special privilege.

Uriah let out a low chuckle. "He wanted to train. He wanted to fight. And the King didn't stop him. He once told Amias he had a dream of the wars his son would fight and win." He gave me a pointed look. "Seeing who we're with now... confirms those dreams, don't you think?"

I scoffed. "I suppose."

Uriah shook his head, placing the books down before turning to leave.

Maeve called after him, "Where is everyone from?"

Uriah paused, exhaling. "I'll tell you, but we don't talk about it often. We pledged loyalty to Valdeen, made vows to Highest. Especially those who didn't grow up following Him." His eyes flickered to me.

I straightened, intrigued. Men who had to be taught, like I was now.

Maeve and I nodded, urging him on.

"Jon, Ike, Beau, and I were Valdeen-born. Best of our class. The twins are from Purmee. Vance is from Jouse. Asher is from Aartier. And Ian..." He hesitated. "Ian never told us where he's from."

Maeve's brows shot up. "Asher is from Aartier?"

I frowned. "No one is from Anima?"

Uriah shook his head. "You and Jahiel are. And two of the four men we killed during the attack."

My stomach tightened. "What?"

He nodded. "They were Animaian."

My pulse quickened. That was odd. The only two Animaian men in our ranks had been the ones sent to assassinate me?

"Interesting," Maeve murmured. Then she turned to Uriah, flashing a smile. "Well, thanks for the history lesson, friend. But now I have a lesson to teach our dear Judge, so if you'd kindly leave us—"

"I can't stick around?" he interrupted, grinning.

She paused to think, "Only if you're quiet," Maeve chimed.

Uriah smirked. "Not a sound after this one," he promised, settling onto the deck, his back against the railing overlooking the lower level.

Maeve rolled her eyes and opened her tome, picking up where she had left off.

"The first judge," she said, then hesitated, glancing at me.

"Go on, Maeve," I laughed.

She exhaled. "Just don't burn down the ship," she muttered. "I've seen the fire in your eyes."

"Read, please."

She cleared her throat and continued. "Records state that the first judge's gifts were intense. He could speak plagues

421

upon a land, and they would come to pass. He walked through battles, and his shadow alone could kill anyone it touched."

I stared at her, stunned. Maeve met my gaze briefly before looking back down at the tome.

"The second judge possessed immense strength—never tiring in battle, tearing through enemies, bringing down buildings with his bare hands. The third controlled the sky. He called fire down from the heavens and scorched the land. And forbid rain and it caused a five-year drought."

I swallowed. "How do I know what's in me?"

"We should ask Highest for answers," Maeve suggested, scooting closer.

I reached for my water and gulped it down before realizing too late that I had finished it.

"Those were your rations for today!" she reminded.

I stared at the empty glass before corking it with a sigh. "I got nervous—and it's hot!"

Maeve rolled her eyes. "What have you noticed so far?"

I thought back to the embers at my fingertips, the scalding water I cried.

"That night, when I saw the shadows—"

"You see the shadows? The Caligo spirits?" she interrupted.

"The what?"

"Caligo," Uriah interjected. "Offspring of the Watchers. They possess people, make their eyes go black. You can see them?"

I nodded. "Yes, and smell them. Their shadows split apart, which is how I knew there were four men that night."

Uriah leaned forward. "You smell them?"

Maeve shot him a glare. "You said you wouldn't speak."

"Right," he muttered, leaning back.

I ignored them both. "I smelled evil around my mother. I saw it when I was attacked in Floos by a general. I nearly killed him."

"Are you strong, then? Is that your battle ability?"

I shook my head. "No, I'm not strong. But I've always been... precise." I stood, pulling a dagger from my belt and tossing it lightly in my palm.

"Can precision be a gift?" Maeve mused, flipping to an empty book and scribbling notes.

"What are you doing?" I asked.

"Recording your history—like the ones before us did." Her eyes gleamed with excitement.

I glanced at Uriah. "I'm going to hit the mast with my dagger."

He lifted an eyebrow. "You'd need a lot of force. The wind and the ship's speed—"

"I know," I murmured, exhaling. Heat spread through my core, burning through my limbs. I shrugged off my overshirt, leaving my arms and stomach bare to the warm air. My pulse pounded in my ears. Another breath.

I pulled my second dagger from my belt, focused on the mast, and spun, releasing both blades mid-turn.

It was quick. The blades leaving my hands back-to-back.

I landed in a crouch, but the heat was unbearable. My skin burned, my vision blurred.

"Shoot, man!" Tavin's voice rang out from below.

My vision blurred, and everything pulsed in slow motion.

"Maeve," I croaked, both knees hitting the deck.

"It's on fire!" Maeve yelped. "Put them out! Put them out

now!"

Boots pounded against the deck.

"Fire!" Jahiel's voice roared. A door slammed open beneath me.

"Where is she?" someone shouted.

"Up there!"

More footsteps. More voices.

"Kae!"

I tried to lift my head. My neck was beading with sweat from the rush of heat.

Amias, again.

He crouched in front of me but hesitated before touching me. "You're burning up."

"Thanks," I mumbled, dizzy, my vision nearly black.

He let out a sharp breath. "Aren't you tired of passing out?"

"Tired of you saving me?" I shot back weakly.

Amias chuckled. "You're impossible." He reached for me but flinched at the heat radiating off my skin. "And no."

Then his expression hardened. His hand hovering above my skin. "This isn't good."

I barely had time to process his words before his arms wrapped around me.

"Wait—"

He hissed in pain.

Suddenly, the world tilted.

The ship, the fire, the voices—all vanished as Amias lifted me and jumped.

The rush of wind stole the air from my lungs.

I barely registered the fall, the weightlessness, before the sea swallowed us whole.

# Chapter 42

I gasped for air, coughing up water and spewing it onto the deck beside me. My lungs burned, my body shivering from the shock of the plunge.

"Thank Highest," Amias muttered, leaning over me before shifting to sit on his bottom. Tye and Asher stood beside him, bent over, panting.

Smoke thickened the air around us.

"What the hell was that?" Jon strode over, his expression a mix of fury and disbelief.

I struggled to catch my breath. "I... I don't know." The words stirred another fit of coughing.

Jon scoffed. "What do you mean you don't know? Your blades were on fire, lodged in the mast—you nearly burned the sails!"

"Easy, Jon," Amias growled beside me.

"Easy? We would've been stranded out here—stale in the ocean without sails!" Jon stormed off, kicking over a bucket of water.

"Relax, man!" Tavin called after him.

I pushed myself up onto my elbows, drenched and exhausted. My soaked clothes clung to me, my hair curling in damp waves around my shoulders. The taste of salt burned my throat. I spat onto the deck. "I didn't know they were on fire," I admitted, still breathless. "I don't even know how the actual blades caught."

Jon whirled back, eyes sharp. "Then don't test your powers on my ship!"

"Stand down," Amias barked.

"Amias," I croaked between gasps.

Amias stepped towards Jon. His voice edged with warning. Eyes burned with fury. "It was an accident."

Jon's fists clenched at his sides. "An accident that could've cost us all—"

"I get that," Amias cut him off. "But find someone else to take your frustrations out on—because it won't be her." He stood, shoulders squared as he met Jon's glare.

"Amias!" I yelled.

His eyes landed on me, he placed his balled up fist on the sides of his temple and it was only then I realized he was just as soaking wet as me.

Jon let out a sharp exhale, then took a step back, huffing and turning to leave.

"Ike," Amias called, refusing to open his eyes, "go make sure he doesn't do anything stupid with this tantrum."

The deck had quieted, but my pulse hadn't.

I sat there for a long time—wet, shivering, and stunned—while the others disappeared into the shadows of the ship. No one said much after that. Not even Amias.

Eventually, someone handed me a blanket. I think it was Maeve. Or Tye. I couldn't remember. My body felt like it belonged to someone else.

I peeled myself off the planks and walked without direction, the blanket dragging behind me, salt drying in my throat. I needed to be alone. I needed to feel solid ground, even if it was still made of swaying wood.

So I climbed to the upper deck and folded into myself at the stern, knees to chest, the blanket cocooned around me. The sea had calmed, but my thoughts hadn't.

The gifts. The fires. The dreams.

And now the burning blades.

The way they'd burned.

The night air was cool, brushing over my damp skin, tangling in my curls.

I didn't know how long I sat there, and I didn't care.

\* \* \*

The moon rested high above the ocean before me. I'd changed out of my soaking clothes into something looser, more comfortable, though the salt still clung to my skin. I hadn't dared venture below deck. Not yet.

I was avoiding everyone.

"Hey."

Familiar.

Grounding.

I didn't flinch. I just turned.

Amias stood a few paces away, arms crossed loosely, a cloak thrown over his shoulder. He looked like he hadn't slept. The wool-like hair at the sides of his head had started to grow back, soft curls creeping in. The scruff along his jaw now hinted at a beard.

He walked toward me—not with urgency, but with a steadiness I hadn't known I needed until he was standing beside me.

"I thought you'd be below, resting."

"No," I murmured. "I'm not tired."

I lied. I couldn't bear to sit in the room with Maeve. Not tonight. She'd want to talk—explore what happened. And I just wanted to sit here.

He crouched beside me, resting his forearms on his knees.

"You scared the depths out of me."

I let out a breath. "You and me both."

He looked over at me then, his eyes shaded in moonlight—gray, but softer than they'd been all day.

"I keep playing it back," he said. "How fast it all happened. One second... you're training. The next, your blades are on fire, your skin's boiling hot, and we're jumping—"

He cut himself off, jaw tight.

"I didn't mean to—"

"I know."

"I didn't even feel them ignite."

"I know, Kae."

I looked at him—really looked.

He wasn't angry.

He was afraid.

Not of me. For me.

"I don't know what's happening to me," I said quietly. "I say yes to the call. The role and things get worse again."

He nodded, like he understood more than I'd even spoken. "You will learn. You will get better." He was so patient with me, so much more patient than I was with myself..

The moon poured its light over the deck, turning the sea below into a sheet of silver. The wind had gone gentle. Not even the sails moved much. It felt like the world had paused just to listen.

He exhaled slowly. "I thought about what you said, after you encountered Highest."

He smiled to himself, as if he'd replayed that moment a hundred times.

I stilled.

It felt like ages ago.

Somehow, I'd been so trapped inside my own head, I'd forgotten how whole I'd felt after just one moment spent with Him.

*"He was light that pressed against my soul,"* Amias said. *"Like something inside me stretched to meet Him, and now I can't go back to what I was before."* He looked over. "I'd never heard words describe Him so well. Until *you.*"

A beat of silence stretched between us.

Then he looked at me—and the way his eyes rested on mine made my stomach twist.

I didn't need to guess what he was thinking. I could see it.

Admiration.

Pure and undeniable.

Amias didn't just look at me, He saw me.

*"She* is light that pressed against my soul," he said, repeating my words—but changing them.

*He to she.*

The shift made my chest tighten.

"It was like something from above—or inside me— stretched to find *you,"* he continued, "and now I *won't,* I *can't* go back to what I was before."

A familiar heat touched my eyes, but this time it didn't burn. It simmered.

"Amias—"

"Kae, I met you by no accident," he said, cutting me off. "And I need to tell you something. You can take it how you will, but I have to say it. Because we don't know what tomorrow holds for me."

For him, because we knew I had a calling... I had my tomorrow prophesied and planned by Highest.

He exhaled sharply.

"Can I have another minute of honesty with you?"

A flicker of amusement tugged at my lips. "Are we making a habit of this?"

"Maybe." His gaze softened. "Could be our thing... No judgment. No response. Just—let me say it."

I nodded.

"I want to be the wolf right now—the one on my sigil. A dog of a man with no morals." His voice dropped, raw. "Do what my flesh wants. Say things I shouldn't. Look at you longer than I should."

He dragged a hand down his face. "But I won't. Because I respect you. I admire you. And I want to honor Highest."

His words settled in my chest like an ache I didn't know how to soothe.

I watched him—his tension, his restraint, the way his fingers curled as if holding something back.

"I know you respect me," I whispered. "And Him."

He let out a slow breath, eyes still locked on mine. "Good." Then, softer—rougher:

"But know this—if I'm the wolf..." He turned toward the moon, now full and glowing above us. "Then you're my moon. I look to you for Highest's reflected light in dark places. I look for you. Everywhere. Always."

The world shrank. Quiet. Weightless.

He reached up, brushing a curl from my face.

"Amias," I breathed.

"There are feelings I've acquired for you—ones I don't yet have words for." He paused. "I don't know when they started. But they're there. You move through my mind more than anything else. I pray for you constantly—to feel safe. To feel peace. And I believe Highest meant for us to meet."

His eyes held mine. "Because maybe He's planning something greater... for both of us."

I stared at him, caught in the space between breath and heartbeat.

And I knew—he was right.

He had named the pull between us better than I ever could.

"Can I be honest now?" I asked.

He smiled. "It's only fair."

"I feel it too," I whispered. The confession barely left my lips—but I knew he heard it.

Because his whole body relaxed.

"Like a moth to a flame," I added, my voice barely audible. I pressed my lips together, nervous about what else might come spilling out.

"So I'm a moth and a wolf now?"

He grinned, shaking his head. "That's got to be the strangest combination of loyalty and poor decision-making I've ever heard."

I giggled, nodding slowly.

He sat fully on the ground beside, sliding over as close as possible. Until our legs rested on each other, he'd never been this close, but no part of me felt threatened. No part of me felt like this was wrong.

He was comfort in flesh form.

He reached over, brushing a damp curl from my forehead with the back of his fingers. The touch was featherlight, reverent.

"You're stronger than you think." He said as his large hands cupped my face, just below my cheeks.

"Or more *dangerous* than anyone should be," I said as I wrapped my hand around his wrist as he held me.

His gaze dropped to my mouth, before a mischievous smile spread across his face. Causing my brain to fog and core to melt.

"You are definitely both."

There was something about the way he said it. Like the wolf in him recognized something wild and burning in me. Not a threat—but a match.

The world didn't fall silent—it just softened. The crashing waves, the creak of the ship, even my *own* heartbeat faded beneath the weight of the moment.

I leaned in before I realized what I was doing.

He met me halfway.

I could feel the warmth of him before our lips even touched.

And when they finally did—

It was not rushed.

It was not forced.

It was everything in between.

His mouth met mine like he already knew it. Like he'd carried the shape of this moment inside him for ages. His lips were warm, reverent, like he was thanking Highest with every second they lingered.

My hand gripped the space of his forearm. Not to pull him

closer.

Just to ground myself.

Because kissing Amias felt like being seen fully for the first time. Like he wasn't kissing who I tried to be—but who I was.

His thumb brushed against my jaw, a small motion that undid me completely.

This kiss wasn't a spark.

It was a fire that had waited patiently for kindling.

It was a promise.

And when I finally pulled away—barely, breathless—his forehead pressed to mine, as if letting go of that closeness was too much all at once.

Neither of us spoke.

We didn't need to.

Because some truths were louder in silence.

Amias leaned in again, for another kiss I'm certain would be my unraveling.

But I pulled away.

Not because I didn't want it.

*Because I wanted too much.*

I felt *greedy.* How could I take so much of what Highest has given and still not feel like who I'm called to be.

How could I still not feel like I've accomplished anything for him?

He'd saved me. Restored the family I thought I lost and now... Amias. How could I continue to want more when I've given back nothing of myself?

"I can't be yours and the world's at once. I can't have both," I whispered.

Amias didn't flinch. He didn't argue.

He just looked at me—with a gaze so full of adoration and humility, it made my breath catch.

He leaned closer, cupping my face in both hands. His palms were warm, rough from years of swordwork and sacrifice, and yet his touch was achingly gentle. His calloused thumb traced the curve of my cheek, slowly, like he was memorizing me by touch alone.

"You say you haven't given anything," he murmured, voice thick with emotion. "But you gave everything the moment you said *yes*."

I blinked, the words hitting somewhere deeper than I expected.

"You gave your future. Your family. Your comfort. Your name. You risked it all because *He* called you."

He paused, eyes searching mine. "And if He's good—and I believe He is—then how could He not restore what you lost... and more?"

I didn't realize I was crying until his thumb caught a tear I hadn't meant to shed.

His forehead leaned against mine, breath brushing softly between us.

"And if I'm part of the more... then I'll spend every day making sure it was worth it."

Then he kissed me again.

Not like before. This kiss wasn't cautious.

It was full.

Full of reverence. Full of honor. Full of belief.

And in that kiss, I didn't feel greedy.

I felt chosen.

When we finally parted, our foreheads rested together, our breathing slow, steady, shared.

Neither of us moved to leave.

Instead, he sat back against the railing and gently pulled me closer to him, guiding me to rest my head on his chest. The warmth of him radiated through the thin fabric between us. His arms wrapped around me, not possessive, protective.

Sure.

Steady.

Above us, the moon watched in silence, casting its glow over the waves and the weathered deck, as if blessing what it saw.

I closed my eyes, letting the quiet hold me.

And then, his voice—low, raw, almost reverent—broke through the stillness.

"You burn brighter than even you know, Daughter of Flame."

# Chapter 43

Rain tapped softly against my forehead before I registered it. A few droplets at first—cool and light—then more, faster, heavier. I blinked awake, lashes damp, breath shallow.

Beside me, Amias stirred.

The deck beneath us groaned.

We'd fallen asleep beneath the moon—wrapped in quiet, wrapped in each other.

Now the storm had caught up to us.

Not as a whisper—but a bellow.

Thunder cracked across the sky.

Amias sat up fast, hand going to the hilt at his side before he realized where he was. "Kae."

"I'm up," I said, already pushing off his chest, my body stiff from the night's sleep.

Another flash of lightning lit the sky—this time, close.

Too close.

Then—

BOOM.

The world rocked.

The ship lurched violently as lightning struck something high above. A scream rang out from the crow's nest.

Fire.

Bright and violent, licking the sails and mast—fighting against the rain to consume it all.

"Move!" Jon's voice roared across the deck.

Boots thundered.

Wolves sprinted to douse the flames, but the rain couldn't touch it—it danced with the lightning, wild and untouchable, like it had a will of its own.

I stood frozen.

But inside me, something shifted.

I *felt* it.

Not just the fire—but a pull.

Like the flames were *aware* of me.

Like I could reach them without moving.

Like I could… control them.

Another bolt split the sky.

My hand flew up on instinct.

The flame arched toward me.

And I *stopped* it.

It hovered—alive, searching. It needed somewhere to go, some place to land.

It was too much. Too heavy.

Power surged through me—hot, golden. My skin prickled. My breath caught.

"Kae!"

Amias's voice cracked through the storm. Urgent. Afraid.

My body moved before my mind did—arms raised, palms out—desperate to contain what I had called.

I turned my hand, pointing away.

The energy burst from me like a dam breaking. It shot across the deck—wild, divine, *untrained*.

Then—

A scream.

Uriah.

He'd been too close to the mast. The blast threw him back—his shoulder catching flame as he slammed into the railing. The sound of impact made me sick.

He didn't move.

He *burned*.

"No—" The word tore from my throat. "Uriah—NO!"

I reached for him.

And the flames *recoiled*.

Not in fear.

In recognition.

They knew me.

I clawed at every spark still licking the deck, every flame still clinging to the air.

And they came.

They answered.

A wave of light rushed toward me, pulled into my skin like breath to lungs.

I ran to him.

Didn't think.

Didn't stop.

I *felt*.

I dropped beside his crumpled form, hands trembling above him.

The fire was gone, but smoke still curled from his chest.

His skin blistered beneath damp cloth.

The last embers hovered—long tendrils of gold and orange. Some sputtered out in the storm.

But the rest?

They obeyed me.

My hands glowed gold beneath the storm as the flames rushed into me.

They knew my name.

The fire answered to me.

The rain soaked my clothes, my hair—yet I steamed beneath it.

Heat radiated off me in waves.

The water struck my skin and hissed.

The deck beneath my knees sizzled.

My whole body burned—

Not with pain.

But with power.

I looked up from Uriah's lifeless form—

And every Wolf on deck was frozen.

Staring.

Stunned.

Even Amias had dropped to his knees, awe in his eyes.

I didn't know what to say.

None of them saw the figure in the shadows behind them.

Maeve's voice shouted something, but the storm swallowed it.

It sounded like…

*Eshon.*

He moved quickly. Silently.

Not to Uriah's side—but near it.

He didn't kneel.

Didn't touch.

He only whispered.

Words I didn't recognize.

Not the tongue of the priests.

Not the voice of Highest.

His hands never lifted.

But Uriah's body jerked.

Once.

Then again.

And then he coughed.

The flame died from his skin like it had never touched him.

He lived.

I stared at him, shaking.

"What…" I whispered. "How—"

"You pulled the fire into yourself," someone breathed behind me.

I didn't turn.

I couldn't.

Every pair of eyes was still locked on me.

And none of them saw Eshon disappear quietly into the darkness—robes drenched, mouth curled in something too calm.

Only Maeve saw him.

Her eyes widened. She made her way through the stunned crowd toward me, fingers curling around my wrist.

"Come with me. Now."

I could barely move. Could barely breathe.

Amias stood when I did, reaching gently for me.

"Please," I murmured to him. "Just a moment."

He let me go.

And I followed her.

Behind us, the storm still howled.

And for the briefest second—I caught Jahiel's face through the crowd.

He said nothing.

Didn't meet my eyes directly.

But he didn't look away.

\* \* \*

We didn't speak as Maeve led me below deck.

The lanterns flickered as I passed each flame in the narrow halls of the ship. Water dripped from my clothes in steady beats against the wood. My skin still steamed in the cooler air, the warmth inside me refusing to fade.

She pushed open the nearest door—one of the supply rooms—and pulled me inside. It was dim, cramped, and smelled of herbs and sea salt.

Only then did she let go of my wrist.

She turned toward me, arms crossed tightly over her chest like she could hold in everything weighing on her. I mirrored her posture, trying to smother the flames still pulsing beneath my skin.

She stared at me—her single seeing eye blazing, the blind one somehow even more piercing.

"You didn't see him, did you?" she said quietly.

I blinked. "See who?"

"Eshon."

The name struck something sharp inside me.

Maeve stepped closer, her voice still low but edged with urgency. "Everyone was so consumed with you—the power, the steam, the way the fire bent to your hands. But I saw him."

My breath caught.

"I saw how he stood there," she continued. "Like he was waiting. Like he knew what would happen. He didn't even touch Uriah. He just whispered something—words I've never heard. And then Uriah breathed again."

I shook my head slowly. "No... no, he was just—maybe he was praying—"

"That wasn't prayer," she snapped. "And you know it."

I opened my mouth, but no words came.

Because I did know it.

The unease I'd felt from him wasn't just unfamiliarity. It was the wrongness I hadn't been able to name. That quiet thread of discomfort always lingered when he entered a room.

Then who was he?

What was he?

Was he anything like what we encountered in Scala—or something far worse, hidden among us now?

"Are you scared?" Maeve asked, softer now.

I nodded, my eyes drifting to the wall behind her. I was still listening—I just needed a second to breathe. To process.

"I get it," she said. "I would be too. But don't let your fear blind you or freeze you. We need to act—before he does what he came here to do."

I swallowed hard, throat tight. "What are you saying?"

"I'm saying he's not just hitching a ride to Valdeen. That was shadow magic, Kae. Dark magic. He's here for a reason—and it's not good."

She stepped back, her gaze unwavering.

"He's been watching you. Not observing. Watching. Studying you. Probably Whispering things into the atmosphere about you, your movements, your power. He's taking notes."

The storm outside groaned again—like the ship itself felt the weight of her words.

"He probably has an entire book about you," Maeve said. "What you eat. How you fight. Who you care for…"

Amias.

My thoughts darted back to last night. To his voice. His arms around me. The quiet between us beneath the moon.

What if Eshon had been watching?

"We have to tell Amias," I whispered. "Now."

We found Amias near the helm, barking quiet orders to Jon, Tye and Tavin. His cloak was soaked through, but his voice was steady, focused. He hadn't seen us yet.

Not until I said his name.

"Amias."

He turned, and the moment he saw me, whatever he'd been thinking, whatever storm had settled in his shoulders—it cleared the moment his eyes landed on me.

His entire posture shifted.

The warrior melted into the man.

The tension in his jaw eased. His brows softened. His mouth parted like he'd been waiting to exhale and hadn't realized it until now.

I can see and feel it plainly before me, the effects we had on each other. The ones we always had.

He crossed the deck without a word, quick but not rushed. When he reached me, his hand went straight to the tense space between my neck and shoulder. Grounding me with just that touch.

"What's wrong?" he asked, his voice low and gentle—for me, not the crew. "Are you shaking? Are you cold?"

I shook my head, and squeezed my eyes closed. "I need to

talk to you," I whispered, stepping closer. "Now."

His gaze flicked past me to Maeve, then back again. He didn't question it. Just nodded once and turned, leading us below deck without another word.

Maeve followed behind in silence, her eyes narrowing slightly—not with suspicion, but with understanding.

She saw it.

The shift between us. And even if she knew not of what exactly happened.

She saw the way he looked at me. The way I followed and clung to his hand.

The way I let him ground me.

He led us into a small storage alcove tucked behind the stairwell—quiet and dry. The moment the door closed behind us, I let out a shaky breath I hadn't realized I'd been holding.

Amias turned toward me, his eyes scanning my face.

"What is it?" He said softly, "Talk to me."

I tried, but the words caught in my throat.

He stepped forward, his hands lifting to either side of my face, cupping my cheeks so gently I nearly broke.

"Breathe," he whispered.

And I did.

Because he was there.

Like he always was.

Like some part of him knew how to quiet the chaos in me before I even named it.

Maeve shifted behind me, the creak of wood beneath her boots the only sound. She didn't speak, but I could feel her watching.

I took another breath. Then another. His hand was still

on my face, thumbs gently stroking the space just below my cheekbones.

"She saw something," I finally said. "Something I didn't."

Amias didn't flinch. He just waited—anchored and unshaken, like he knew I'd get the words out if I were given time.

"Eshon," I whispered.

Maeve stepped closer. "He healed Uriah. I'm unsure if that's even what we want to call it."

Amias blinked once, then frowned. "He what?"

"*Healed* him. Without touching him. Without prayer. He said something none of us recognized—and Uriah woke up."

Maeve's voice didn't tremble, but it was sharp. Exact. "He whispered words I've never heard, and they worked. Instantly."

Amias's jaw tensed.

"I didn't see clearly," I said. "Everyone was looking at me. At the fire. I was—" My breath hitched. "I didn't mean to hurt Uriah. I didn't even know I could do any of that. But while they were watching me, he—"

"He's been studying her," Maeve interrupted. "He's been watching her. Tracking her. I don't know what he is, Amias, but he's not what he says."

The quiet that followed was heavy.

Amias pulled back, just enough to look me in the eyes. His hands didn't drop. "Did you see the way he moved? Did he touch Uriah at all?"

"No," I said. "Nothing. Just stood near him, whispering."

Maeve nodded, blurting out anxious words. "It wasn't just strange. It was dark. Whatever that was—it wasn't Highest."

Amias lowered his hands finally, but only to take mine.

445

His eyes moved to the thumb. He rubbed over my knuckles, thinking. Contemplating.

He exhaled, then, the switch I'd seen before—the one I hadn't had words for until now—returned.

He straightened. His expression sharpened. Not cold, not distant—but calculated.

The leader. The warrior. The Prince.

"I'll take care of it," he said. "Quietly. I'll speak with Jon and the others. I want Eshon watched, but I don't want him to know he's being watched."

He turned slightly toward Maeve. "Keep Kae with you unless she's with me. No exceptions."

Maeve raised an eyebrow—not in defiance, but in recognition. She saw it again.

The tether between us.

I blinked.

Amias didn't respond. He didn't have to.

He looked at me like I was flame and light and the world's last breath all at once.

And still—he grounded me.

He winked, then dismissed himself.

Maeve looked at me, then at Amias' retreating form. Something in her face shifted.

She smiled at herself, taking a step closer and dropping her head toward my ear.

"There are old tales in Scala," Maeve said, voice low, "of ones who carry fire in their hands… and the rare few who never flinch when they touch it."

She knocked my shoulder, smirking at me. I looked down at my hands, tracing the path Amias roamed over my knuckles.

446

# Chapter 44

The tables were set unevenly across the deck—makeshift arrangements of crates, barrels, and worn linen. The storm had passed, but the air still carried the electric bite of something unfinished.

Dinner was Amias's idea.

A test disguised as a meal.

He wanted us all together—wanted Eshon close, within reach.

Wanted to watch him.

And see if he watched back.

The Wolves circled the tables, their movements easy, casual, their laughter low and believable—but I caught the flash of their eyes too often.

Toward me.

Toward Eshon.

Then away, just as quickly.

Their hands never strayed far from their belts, their boots shifted quietly under the table.

At a glance, they looked relaxed.

But I could feel the weight of it—the way every conversation, every chuckle, was built on a taut thread pulled too tight.

Some of them didn't trust me.

Not anymore.

Maeve sat at my side, quiet and sharp, her fork untouched. Her whole body drawn tight like a bowstring, ready to snap.

Tavin and Jahiel snickered words back a forth. The thought of the camaraderie was warming. Jahiel had someone, a friend, because I... I had not been.

"If I die, I want it on record this jerky killed me, not the Watchers," Tavin spoke.

Jahiel threw his head back and laughed. His shoulders were loose, his grin easy.

He hadn't seen it. He had no clue why we were all gathered. Not yet.

And Eshon—

He smiled easily as he took his seat, robes dry now, posture serene. As if none of this touched him.

As if he had orchestrated it all himself.

As if he'd invited it.

Amias sat at the head of the table, every inch the prince—even now. Even when the sea air ruffled his cloak and tension gritted through his jaw. He looked at me, his eyebrows furrowing briefly in a question.

*Are you okay?*

I could almost hear him asking about me, I nodded in response. He bowed and turned back to the group, "Thank you all for coming up here, we're halfway home." Amias said, smiling to himself at the thought of home.

We ate in silence for a few moments—at least we pretended to.

Amias rested his hands on the edge of the table, his voice steady but full of something almost tender.

"Ellarum waits for us," he said. "The crown jewel of Valdeen. A city of silver and stone, where the rivers carve through the hills like veins of light. No place in Naedorn shines brighter."

He paused, letting the words settle like a promise.

"It's an honor to serve it. And a greater honor still to serve the one Highest has called to lead us into what's next."

He glanced at me—not as a formality, but something far more profound. "To the Heiress."

He lifted his cup.

Several of the Wolves echoed the motion, a few more stiffly than others.

"To the Heiress."

They all lifted their cups in honor of me. I smiled back at them, waving off their toast.

Eshon lifted his cup and drank slowly, his golden eyes catching the lantern light— and for the briefest second, he smiled straight at me.

We all began to eat together, taking hot porridge, dried fruit, jerky, manneh, and apples we had for rations.

The only *real* sound was the clatter of forks against wood, the murmur of the waves lapping against the hull.

Then—

Eshon set down his cup, folding his hands loosely atop the table.

And he spoke.

"There was once a girl," he began, his voice low and clear, "born with fire in her hands. She was chosen, so she believed. Marked by the heavens to save what others could not."

The Wolves stiffened. Several glanced sideways at me.

Maeve's hand curled into a fist beside her plate.

449

"But the girl judged too soon," Eshon continued, tone almost... sorrowful. "She burned what could've been healed. She destroyed what could've been redeemed. And in the end, she stood among ashes—believing she had fulfilled her destiny, when all she had done... was ruin what was still alive."

The air turned colder somehow.

Maeve pushed back from the table with a sharp scrape of her chair.

"You're not who you say you are," she said, voice trembling—not with fear, but fury.

Eshon turned to her, smiling softly.

A smile that didn't reach his eyes.

"No," he said, standing slowly.

"I am far more."

The world shifted.

Before any of us could move—before swords could clear sheaths—

Eshon's body convulsed.

Black smoke burst from his chest. His limbs twisted, elongated, in ways no human should move. His skin darkened like charred bark, splitting in places where golden light pulsed through like veins of fire.

Curled horns erupted from his skull—jagged and wild.

His eyes burned a molten gold.

And all across his body—ancient, searing symbols flared to life.

Symbols I had seen only once before.

Symbols of the Watchers.

The Wolves scrambled to their feet.

Jon cursed under his breath. Tye backed away, sword

drawn.

But Eshon—no, the creature that had been Eshon—only smiled wider, fangs glinting in the lamplight.

And then—

He turned his burning gaze directly onto me.

The air around us warped, the lantern light flickering like it, too, was afraid.

He lifted a single clawed hand—long, bone-thin fingers curling once, then pointing.

Straight at me.

His mouth moved, but what came out was not a voice.

It was a layered, crackling distortion—like a thousand tongues whispering over each other.

"We are coming, Daughter of Flame. And we will set fire to the world you cling to—until your screams are the last sound it knows."

The force of it slammed into me like a wall.

My vision doubled, then tripled.

The deck tilted sharply beneath my feet.

I stumbled backward, gasping, clutching at my temples as pain lanced through my skull.

The last thing I saw was his twisted form—laughing without sound— dissolving into the black of the night.

Before my world twisted into darkness.

"Kae!" Someone called out.

And I collapsed.

# Chapter 45

I woke to the dawning of a new day outside our bedroom window.

But my body felt heavy—like I was lying beneath something I couldn't name.

What happened?

I sat up too fast, knocking a pile of books off the end of the bed.

"Highest bless!" Maeve huffed, scrambling to catch them before they hit the floor.

"What happened?" I gasped, kicking my legs free from the blanket that pinned me down.

"You've been sleeping for days," she said, the words slicing through my haze.

Days?

My breath caught. "Where is he?"

Maeve paused. "Who?"

"Eshon!" I staggered to my feet, legs unsteady. "The scribe—the one Scala sent with us to record everything. Maeve, we—we talked about it!"

She blinked, confusion clouding her features. "Friend... are you well?"

No.

No, this wasn't happening.

There was no way she didn't remember.

No way.

"Where's Amias?" I rasped. "He'll know. Where is he?"

I lunged for the door, but Maeve blocked me.

"You need a cloak, Kae—what's going on?"

"Call for Amias!" I snapped, shoving the cloak around my shoulders.

Maeve flinched, but turned and called into the hallway.

Moments later, boots pounded down the corridor.

"What is it? Is she awake?"

Amias appeared, eyes wide, breath tight.

And then—he reached for me without hesitation, the same steady warmth he always offered.

I collapsed into him, clutching his cloak like it could anchor me to something real.

He held me up, arms strong around my back. "You're awake."

I nodded against his chest.

"What's wrong?" he murmured into my hair.

I pulled back, desperate. "Do you remember Eshon?"

His brow furrowed. A slow, confused shake of his head.

"What?" My chest tightened. "How could you not—you were the one who welcomed him aboard!"

His arms tightened around me instinctively as my knees buckled again.

"Kae," he said softly, his voice full of something heavier than affection. "No one got on this ship named Eshon."

I gripped his cloak tighter, searching his face for any flicker of memory.

But there was nothing.

453

Just concern.

Just pity.

Behind me, Maeve hovered, hands wringing at her waist.

They shared a glance over my head.

Quick. Quiet. Worried.

Familiar.

It was the same look they all gave me that morning in Anima—

When I said I heard her voice and no one else did.

Milo's hesitation.

My father's quiet disappointment.

Jahiel's doubt.

All of them watching me like I was slipping.

Like the problem wasn't what I heard—but me.

Amias's hand moved to the side of my neck, thumb brushing gently as if to steady something already slipping.

"Maybe…" Maeve's voice was too careful now, too soft. "Maybe it was a dream."

I pulled away from Amias, searching his face.

"Dreams don't last days," I whispered.

He frowned but didn't speak.

Maeve stepped closer. "You've been through so much. Your body… your powers… the weight of what you carry— it's more than anyone should have to bear."

The floor tilted. My head spun.

They think I'm breaking.

They think I imagined it.

They think I'm weak.

But I wasn't.

I saw him.

I *remembered* him.

I shook my head slowly. "No," I said. "You're wrong."

The spinning worsened.

"No," I repeated, louder now. "You're both wrong—"

"Kae—" Amias reached again.

"No!" My voice cracked.

"Get out."

Silence.

They froze in place.

"Both of you—just get out!" I cried, pressing the heels of my palms into my eyes. "I need—I need—"

But the words wouldn't come.

Maeve took a slow step back. She glanced at Amias, then gently pulled his sleeve.

"We're right outside," she said softly.

Then they left.

The door shut with a heavy click.

And I was alone.

I sank to the edge of the bed, chest heaving.

You're losing your mind.

You imagined it.

You're weak.

The thoughts hit like jagged arrows—each one sharper than the last.

I gripped the blanket, squeezing it tight until my knuckles ached.

And somewhere in the middle of the noise—

I remembered.

Anima.

How my mother made our family forget.

Forget her hateful words.

Forget her threat of death.

She made them look at me with concerned eyes.

She made them believe they were whole when they were broken.

And back then, I hadn't felt crazy.

Not when I sensed what was real.

It wasn't until I quieted the fear

—the lies

—the noise—

that I heard it.

That still, steady voice.

The voice of Highest.

Not loud.

Not violent.

But firm.

Sure.

Unshakable.

*"I am still here."*

I shuddered as the warmth of it washed over me—like a candle relit in a dark room.

And for the first time since waking, I let myself believe it wasn't madness.

It wasn't weakness.

It was memory.

It was truth.

It had always been truth.

\* \* \*

I stayed in my room.

Avoidance seemed to be the only solution for the anger I felt toward the Watchers for making them forget.

I'd stayed away. At least until we were on land.

Maeve avoided the room, too.

Probably because she still thought she'd caused something—or was suffocating me.

Asher had offered her his room for the night, while he volunteered for watch duty.

Kind of him.

But not for me.

With the additional time, I read through historical texts and records—words passed down from Judges before me.

I read until the pages blurred, until my stomach protested so loudly that even anger couldn't quiet it.

From the memory of his touch—

Amias and I still happened.

From Maeve's words when she returned—

The fire, the lightning, the chaos on deck—still happened.

But no one remembered Uriah being hurt.

No one remembered Eshon.

No one remembered *anything*.

It was maddening.

How easily he had slipped onto this ship—

And slipped out again.

Unseen.

Unchallenged.

Eventually, hunger won out, and I forced myself to leave.

The small mess hall rocked gently with the ship, the flickering lanterns casting uneven shadows across the low wooden beams. The scent of damp wood, salt, and stale biscuits hung in the air—the rations on the table as unappealing as ever.

Jahiel sat hunched at a table near the wall, idly rolling an almond between his fingers.

457

Across from him, Asher chewed on a piece of hard cheese, boots propped against the bench beside him.

The moment I stepped inside, Jahiel's sharp gaze landed on me like a weight.

Asher's reaction was slower, but he gave a small nod of acknowledgment.

Jahiel had still seen Amias and me.

That memory, at least, hadn't been taken.

"Kae'Dinah," Jahiel called, already pushing a ration toward the empty seat.

"Eat," Jahiel said.

I hesitated—but hunger had already decided for me.

I sat down, picking up the manneh and pressing my thumb into it.

It didn't give.

"These could break teeth," I muttered.

Asher smirked, breaking off a piece of his own and popping it into his mouth. "We're almost home."

Jahiel didn't smile.

"You should be resting," he said, voice flat. "Or something."

I sighed. "Why? I feel fine."

"They say you're imagining a man on board, but sure," he said, shrugging, "you're fine."

Asher shot him a warning look. "Ease up, Jahiel."

Jahiel ignored him, eyes locked on me.

"This—" he gestured between us, the table, the room, "—this conversation is just like the ones we had before in Floos, we're fine."

I broke off a piece of bread with more force than necessary. "And resting will help how?"

"It'll keep you sane," Jahiel said sharply. "And sanity keeps you alive."

I opened my mouth to retort, but Asher cut in first.

"She's awake," Asher said, voice even. "She's speaking. She's breathing. She's well-rested. Let her eat in peace."

Jahiel clenched his jaw but leaned back, crossing his arms.

I exhaled, refocusing on my food, but the tension sat thick between us.

Jahiel cared.

He always had.

He told me he always would.

So I heard him.

But this...

This was why I stayed in my room.

I wasn't ready to speak to him about—any of it.

Then—

A piercing scream tore through the ship.

All three of us snapped our heads toward the creaking hallway.

Asher was on his feet before I could blink, his chair clattering to the floor.

"That's Maeve," he said, already moving.

I stood, heart hammering against my ribs, and followed him into the narrow corridor.

Doors swung open as we raced past—faces groggy, confused, emerging into the dimness.

Asher reached Maeve's door first, shoving it open with a crack of splintering wood.

Maeve's body heaved, her chest pumping like a wild animal fighting for breath.

Her bright hair clung to the pillow, soaked through with sweat.

Her eyes—

White.

Rolled back into her skull, revealing nothing but blank, sightless voids.

"Roll her—get her on her side! Now!" Jahiel barked, vaulting onto the bed.

Asher caught her shoulders, helping him turn her before she could choke.

Her body thrashed violently, limbs jerking with no pattern, no control.

I stood frozen in the doorway for a half-second too long, horror knotting in my throat.

This wasn't a dream.

Something was happening to Maeve.

This was real.

*"Call her name."*

Highest's voice was becoming familiar now, resonating inside me, low and steady.

I exhaled sharply.

"Maeve!"

The room stilled.

Maeve's chest rose and fell, her breath evening—but her face remained vacant, her white eyes unseeing.

Then—

Slowly—

She sat up.

"Familiar darkness awaits you when you arrive abroad," she said, her voice soft. A tan finger rose, pointing straight at my chest. "Do not fear it. Do not flee from it. Incinerate it. It's only light that drives out darkness."

A slow, smile tugged at her lips.

460

"Darkness has to flee light. It has no choice. It won't survive."

Then, her vacant gaze lifted past me, toward the hallway.

"The vision was not what you perceived," she intoned.

"But what will come. Prepare. Do not take your eyes off of it."

And then—

She collapsed.

Asher caught her before she hit the bed, his arms steady around her limp form.

I gasped, pressing a hand to my chest.

"Maeve."

A deep, rattling inhale filled the space.

Maeve coughed violently, shuddering in Asher's grip.

He grabbed a glass bottle, pressing it into her hands, his palm lingering on her back in steady reassurance.

Maeve gulped the water, wiping her mouth with the back of her hand.

Then her green eye flicked up, scanning the room—Asher, Jahiel—

And then behind me.

I turned.

Amias stood in the doorway.

His face was unreadable—

a storm of emotions shifting beneath the surface.

I tore my gaze away from him, a strange weight settling in my chest—

Through the circular window behind his shoulder.

I couldn't breathe.

My body stilled.

The vast city came into view.

My heart dropped.

My voice cracked into the quiet, "Oh no…"

Amias was at my side instantly. "What is it?"

I lifted a single, trembling finger.

"There."

We stared together as fire claimed the skyline.

As Ellarum burned.

# Biblical Parallels in Ignited

This story was born in the quiet moments I spent reading the Old Testament—especially the book of Judges. What began as curiosity turned into a vision of fire, judgment, and redemption. While Ignited is a work of fiction, there are threads of truth and faith woven into every chapter.

## Here are a few intentional parallels that shaped the story:

### The Judge

In the Bible, Judges were not kings. They were chosen by God—often unexpectedly—to deliver His people, call them back to truth, and remind them who they were. Kae'dinah's journey reflects that same weight. She isn't perfect. She doesn't feel qualified. But like Deborah or Gideon, she is called—set apart for a divine task.

*Judges 2:16 – "Then the Lord raised up judges, who saved them out of the hands of these raiders."*

## The Separation

Throughout the story, Kae'dinah feels the ache of not belonging—not to her family, her nation, or even herself. That mirrors the biblical theme of sanctification: being set apart for something holy. It hurts to be different. But difference is often where destiny begins.

*John 15:19 – "If you belonged to the world, it would love you as its own. As it is, you do not belong to the world..."*

## The Watchers

The Watchers in this book are inspired by the fallen spiritual beings described in apocryphal writings like 1 Enoch. These beings were once heavenly but became corrupt—twisting power, truth, and worship. In Ignited, the Watchers represent seductive deception: false gods demanding sacrifice in exchange for control.

*Ephesians 6:12 – "For our struggle is not against flesh and blood, but... against the spiritual forces of evil in the heavenly realms."*

## Fire as Purification

Fire in Ignited is not just destructive—it's transformative. Kae'Dinah's power, though overwhelming, is not meant to consume aimlessly. It's a reflection of divine purification. Fire in scripture is often a symbol of holiness, judgment, and

464

glory.

*Zechariah 13:9 – "I will refine them like silver and test them like gold."*

## Highest

The name "Highest" is intentionally distinct from the gods in the story. He doesn't demand blood to be appeased. He rescues. He sees. He sends dreams and calls people through whispers and visions. He's based on the one true God—ever-present, loving, and sovereign, even when He's misunderstood.

*Psalm 91:1 – "Whoever dwells in the shelter of the Most High will rest in the shadow of the Almighty."*

## The Voice

Kae'dinah begins hearing a voice not her own—gentle, steady, and full of truth. This reflects the way God speaks in scripture: sometimes in fire, sometimes in dreams, sometimes in a whisper. As Kae grows, she learns to recognize that voice as her source of strength and purpose.

*1 Kings 19:12 – "...and after the fire came a gentle whisper."*

## Final Thought

My goal was never to rewrite the Bible into fantasy—but to show how deeply it still speaks. Even in a fictional world of kingdoms, swords, and shadows... His truth remains.

If any part of this story made you feel seen, stirred something in you, or sparked your curiosity about God— follow that flame.

# Acknowledgments

There is beauty in not belonging.

There is beauty in not fitting in with everyone else.

That's because you weren't made to conform.

You were set apart. Chosen. Created for something greater.

It took me a long time to realize that God did the same with me. He set me apart—on purpose. I wasn't made to perform like everyone else. And yes, that was painful for a while. But now I see it: I was never meant to be like everyone else. I was meant to be who He created me to be.

If you're reading this and feeling lost, unloved, or unseen—I want you to know there has never been a moment where God did not see you. Not one. He sees you now. He loves you now. He will find you wherever you are. He sent Jesus to save and lead us. Just call on His name—He will come.

\* \* \*

First, I want to thank **God**.

This book came from a vision He gave me while I was reading *Judges* in the Old Testament. Studying biblical history stirred something in me—I could see the journeys, the tension, the purpose in every step. That vision inspired the fictional world of Naedorn. A world shaped by conflict, truth, and the pursuit of hope through trials. Thank you, God, for entrusting me with this story.

To my **family**—thank you.

To my **sisters**: thank you for enduring the read-alouds in the kitchen, the car ride storytelling, and the constant graphics I asked you to review. To my eldest sister: thank you for downloading the book, sharing it, and hyping me up when I needed it most. For the late-night pep talks and the reminders to stick to my deadlines—I'm so grateful.

**Mom and Dad**—thank you for more than I can ever put into words. For giving me space to write when I needed it, for asking if I had what I needed, and for stepping in to help when I didn't. You even helped finance the dream of this book when it was still just a dream. This story exists because of your love, your sacrifices, and your steady belief in me. I am forever grateful. (And Dad, I owe this, and so much more.)

To my **friends**—you know who you are.

Thank you for reading the printed drafts, maps, and notes—even when I gave you rubrics like it was homework. Thank you for letting me pause conversations so I could record your feedback. For the living room chats, the coffee shop meetups, the FaceTime calls, and the prayers. You helped carry this story with me.

And lastly, **thank you**—the reader.

Thank you for purchasing this book. Thank you for exploring Naedorn, the world that once lived only in my head. It's not easy to let others into the sacred spaces of your imagination—but I'm glad I let you in. I hope you found something here that stays with you. I pray you'll return for the next part of the journey.

Thank you, truly.

# About the Author

Michaella Neal is a storyteller from a small town just outside of Charlotte, North Carolina, where she first discovered her love for writing in a high school creative writing class—and never stopped. She studied journalism because she's always believed that every story, whether real or imagined, deserves to be told well. These days, she writes fiction full of adventure, high stakes, and heart-pounding romance, all while teaching elementary school students how to use their imaginations too. Michaella is a proud book "collector," a devoted dog mom to her border collie-pointer mix, Myka, and a self-declared iced latte connoisseur with a homemade coffee bar that might rival your favorite café.

**You can connect with me on:**

🌐 https://www.michaellaneal.com

🔗 https://www.instagram.com/authormichaella

www.ingramcontent.com/pod-product-compliance
Lightning Source LLC
Chambersburg PA
CBHW052347110726
47901CB00005B/1389